Praise for *The Girl ...*

'A funny, touching tale . . . Let the escapism begin' *Cleo*

'Her hilarious novel is authentic in every detail. More than an enjoyable comedy, it's a blinkers-off expose of a workforce employed to extend to an industrial wharf: five women and 350 men. These males aren't lovable larrikins; they need help. My tip for the next Miles Franklin Award' *Country Style*

'An A-plus debut novel' *Grazia*

'Drama, humour and romance – Hill provides it all in this insightful glimpse into the life of an engineer in the Pilbara' *Sunday Herald Sun*

'A fun story of friendship, overcoming preconceptions, and unexpected love. The ideal summer read' *West Australian*

'Well written, funny and fascinating, The Girl in Steel-Capped Boots is a wonderfully entertaining novel' *Book'd Out*

'A charming down-to-earth love story' *Take 5*

'Romantic and entertaining reading for the girls' *Weekend Gold Coast Bulletin*

'Laugh-out-loud fiction delivered with relish' *Write Note Reviews*

About the Author

Loretta Hill was born in Perth, the eldest of four girls. She enjoyed writing from a very early age and was just eleven years old when she had her first short story published in the *West Australian* newspaper.

Having graduated with a degree in Civil Engineering and another in Commerce, she was hired by a major West Australian Engineering Company, and worked for a number of years on many outback projects.

But through all this she continued to write, and her first novel, a short romantic comedy called *Kiss and Tell*, was published in America in 2009 under the name Loretta Brabant.

The Girl in Steel-Capped Boots, her debut in mainstream women's fiction, was an acclaimed bestseller. Its eagerly awaited sequel, *The Girl in the Hard Hat*, publishes in early 2013.

She lives in Perth with her husband and three children.

The Girl in Steel-Capped Boots

LORETTA HILL

BANTAM

SYDNEY • AUCKLAND • TORONTO • NEW YORK • LONDON

A Bantam book
Published by Random House Australia Pty Ltd
Level 3, 100 Pacific Highway, North Sydney NSW 2060
www.randomhouse.com.au

First published by Bantam in 2012
This edition published in 2012

Addresses for companies within the Random House Group can be
found at www.randomhouse.com.au/offices

National Library of Australia
Cataloguing-in-Publication entry

Hill, Loretta.
The girl in steel-capped boots / Loretta Hill.

ISBN 978 1 74275 805 3 (pbk.)

A823.4

Cover photograph (girl) © WestEnd61/Getty Images; (men and
landscape) © iStockphoto; (back cover photograph) © Loretta Hill
Cover design by Christabella Designs
Internal design by Midland Typesetters, Australia
Typeset in Sabon by Midland Typesetters, Australia
Printed in Australia by Griffin Press, an accredited ISO AS/NZS
14001:2004 Environmental Management System printer

Random House Australia uses papers that are natural, renewable and
recyclable products and made from wood grown in sustainable forests.
The logging and manufacturing processes are expected to conform to
the environmental regulations of the country of origin.

For the real Lena,
My beautiful sister and successful engineer.
When we were younger, I wrote stories to make you laugh.
Nothing much has changed.

Chapter 1

'We'd like you to go to the Pilbara.'

Oh no. 'Er . . . the Pilbara?' Wasn't that a wasteland of bush, red dirt and hot weather? Lena clutched her hands together in her lap, noticing even in her dazed state that she had chipped her nail polish.

Damn.

'Yes, Cape Lambert to be precise,' her boss, Ivan, continued.

Focus.

'Oh right.' She smoothed her cream skirt across her thighs and regarded him with what she hoped was an expression of intelligent interest. 'I've heard about the project we've got going on out there. Sounds big.'

It was. It was one of the biggest projects Barnes Inc had taken on that year. Theoretically, Lena should have felt honoured that she had been chosen to go, but she didn't.

Not even slightly.

The outback was something to be celebrated on Australia Day, or perhaps on a stroll through Perth Museum. But as far as Lena was concerned, one should never *live* there. Lena liked the city. She liked the nightclubs. And she loved shopping.

Couldn't she use her skills here?

Ivan pushed the papers on his desk together into a neat pile. 'We believe as a graduate engineer this experience will enhance your site skills. This is a vital requirement for a good engineer. Would you be interested in taking this position?'

Lena's skin prickled as she registered the importance of the question.

It was a test. He was asking her if she was serious about her career.

'Yes, yes, I would.'

For goodness sake, sound convincing.

She cleared her throat and tossed her dark blonde mane. 'It's very important to me to do well here, Ivan.'

'Glad to hear it.'

Oh good. The Tone. It wasn't the first time Lena had heard that particular blend of condescension and sarcasm in someone's voice. In fact, she got it a lot. Heard it on her first day of work when she'd arrived wearing her lucky red suit. Heard it at her first meeting when she'd laid her turquoise smartphone on the table next to her notebook. What was it with engineers and fashion? Was there some rule against bright colours and quality accessories that she hadn't read about at university?

An internal groan echoed in her head. There was a lot she hadn't picked up on over her four years at university. She hadn't even worked out that she was there to study not party until her third year. It was her parents' fault really, sending her to a strict private school for girls. It was no wonder that when she broke out, all she wanted to do was let her hair down. She licked her lips. 'So . . . er . . . how long do you need me there for?'

'About three months for starters.'

For starters!

Lena swallowed. She had been told about others who had been transferred there. They never came back. The outback was like the Bermuda Triangle. It sucked you in and pretty soon the people in the city didn't know where you were or what had become of you. She'd be leaving all her friends behind. She pictured the parties booming without her. No one glancing up from their cocktails to ask where she was. No one looking at the door to see if she had arrived. The scene cut unhappily to her sitting under a gum tree in dirty clothes, fanning herself against tropical heat. Her hair, unrecognisable – fuzzy and teased to an enormous height by the weather. Unconsciously, her fingers reached behind her ear to pull at strands.

'Are you all right?'

'Fine. Fine.' But her throat had constricted painfully as Ivan's face came back into focus. She knew she couldn't say no. This was the point where she was expected to fail, give up the ghost, show herself to be unfit for the profession she had chosen.

But I can do this. She sat up straighter, determination thickening her spine. She had too much to prove – more than the other engineers who didn't wear skirts and clips in their hair. She could be as good as any of them; and here was her chance to show it. So she stretched her lips into a gorgeous cherry-gloss smile.

'When do I start?'

'Immediately. Have Megan book a flight for you.' His heartless and dismissive assent had Lena biting her lip, desperate to buy back time.

'Could I have a few days to organise myself?' The Myer Stocktake Sale hadn't finished yet and she wanted to catch up with all her friends before she left – perhaps even throw one of her famous parties at her favourite club.

Ivan raised his eyebrows. 'Okay, Monday then.'

Lena knew by the tightness around his mouth that she couldn't push her luck any further. 'Perfect.'

She headed back to her cubicle on wobbly legs and had to clutch her desk as she lowered herself into her chair.

What have I done?

She grabbed her mouse and as she moved it the Barnes Inc screensaver on her monitor disappeared and her email flashed up on the screen. There was a new message from Robyn.

RE: Dinner at il Ciao tonight?

Lena clutched her mobile and tapped her best friend's name in her favourites.

'Hey. Did you get my email?'

'Sure, yeah. Dinner's fine,' Lena rattled off, her head darting from left to right to see if any of her colleagues were within earshot. They weren't but she lowered her voice further anyway.

'Something terrible has happened.'

Robyn gasped. 'You've ruined your red velvet coat.'

Lena rolled her eyes. 'Not that bad.'

There was a pause and then another deep breath. 'OMG. *They found out.*'

'Close.' Lena gritted her teeth against a wave of panic. 'They're *going* to find out.'

'How? When? Did you stuff up?'

'No.' Lena shut her eyes. 'If anything, I think they're impressed with me. I mean, they've got to be. They've just decided to send me to the Pilbara.'

Robyn snorted. 'Then what the hell are you worried about?'

'Have you not been listening? They're going to send me to the *Pilbara*, Robyn – as in the outback, as in the rear end of nowhere!'

The gravity of the situation had finally dawned on Robyn: her reply came back breathless. 'OMG. You're right. You'll die out there. Tell them you won't go.'

'I can't do that.' Lena bobbed her head over the wall of her cubicle again, on the lookout for eavesdroppers. 'It's all part of my initiation. They're trying to find my limits. I have to prove that I can do this. I have to show them I'm a good engineer.'

'Puh-lease. *We* know you're a good engineer.'

'No, we don't.' Lena moved the phone closer to her mouth so that her lips brushed the receiver. 'Don't you see, Robyn? Maybe this is exactly what I need.'

'No life and a tropical cyclone?' Robyn's voice was firm. 'I don't think so.'

'It's not quite cyclone season there yet.'

'Who cares? Whatever. Just don't go.'

'I have to do this.'

'Lena, you *don't*,' Robyn said. 'Nobody knows about what happened in uni except for you, me and Intellectually Impaired. And let's face it, he's not going to tell anyone.'

'That doesn't make it right.' She shook her head. 'This might.'

Robyn's sigh was long and exasperated. 'Well, if you're going to the Pilbara, for goodness sake don't take your red velvet coat.'

The flight to Karratha was relatively short and Lena whiled away the time reading a magazine. Immersing herself in articles such as 'Ten Ways to Liven Up Your Wardrobe This Summer' and 'Is He Cheating on You and How to Find Out . . .'. Anything to distract herself from the fact that she was off to live on a construction site for three or more months, just to prove that Intellectually Impaired didn't have a point: 'You're a beautiful girl, Lena . . . the real world won't fall for you as easily as I have.'

She could still see the fury on his face when he'd said that to her. That wrinkled brow she used to love kissing smooth – in the beginning, when she'd idolised him.

He'd come into her life at just the right time. He was so smart and dedicated and so good at everything she wanted to be good at. He'd helped her too, helped her a lot. She never questioned that part and would probably always be grateful for it. But people change. People grow up. She certainly had.

Wheels colliding with the tarmac jolted her from her thoughts and she shot a glance out her oval window. There wasn't much to see. Karratha Airport was small compared to the Perth one: just a single-storey country terminal, surrounded by low scrub. She grimaced. This town was considered the big smoke. Her boss said she'd be taken from here to live on the outskirts of a much smaller place called Wickham.

The man waiting to pick her up was similarly disappointing: short, bald, tubby and decidedly cranky-looking. He was clearly a Barnes Inc employee because the blue shirt he was wearing had the company logo embroidered over the breast pocket. His legs were covered by navy army surplus pants. Lena's mood slipped another notch. *That uniform better be optional.*

Taking a deep breath, she strolled forwards, her hand held out before her in what she hoped was a friendly and enthusiastic manner. First impressions always paid and she needed to make a good one.

'You must be looking for me. I'm Lena Todd.'

She stood there frozen in greeting for a good three seconds, while he simply stared at her like she had sauce on her face. Sweat dampened the back of her neck as she began to wonder whether she actually did. Withdrawing her hand, she lifted it upwards towards her nose.

It was only then that he spoke. 'I'm Mike Hopkins.'

'Pleased to meet you.' She stuck her hand out again.

This time, however, he simply turned away and started walking towards the carousel. She hurried after him, realising that it wasn't her imagination – he *was* being deliberately rude.

Great. What's wrong with me now?

She squared her shoulders and turned on the charm. 'It's rather hot here, isn't it? I mean, considering we're just coming into winter.' She fell into step beside him, passing a French-manicured hand across her forehead and flashing him her most winning smile.

Mike snorted. 'This is nothing. And you'll get nowhere if you're complaining already.' He stopped walking abruptly as they reached the carousel.

'Oh, I wasn't complaining,' she assured him. 'I love warm weather! Don't you?'

He ignored her comment. 'What does your bag look like?'

'Bags,' she told him. 'I have three.'

'Three!'

'Three red ones.' She nodded. Red was her lucky colour. Most of her things were red.

'You can't be serious.'

The smile dropped off her face. If he was going to insist on being rude, there was no point in wasting her perfectly good charm on him. 'Why not?' She put her hands on her hips.

'That you have to ask only reinforces my point,' he replied.

Unbidden, Kevin's voice echoed in her head: 'I told you, you weren't built for this profession. But you wouldn't have it.' She shook it off. Sexist rubbish. She was wise to Mike: he was a dinosaur. The subject of her observation took the opportunity to turn back to the carousel and seize a red bag that was passing them.

'Is this yours?'

She lifted her chin. 'Yes.'

A few seconds later, he had piled her vanity onto the rolling case and had the carry-on in his hand. She moved forwards to take it, but he pulled it out of her reach. Fuming, she caught up with him as he marched off and firmly tugged at the carry-on. She was perfectly capable of carrying her own gear. She had a lot of clothes, but she wasn't a princess. He returned her glare but let her bag go.

'What's in these things anyway?' he demanded as he neared the airport main entrance. 'Have you packed your boyfriend as well?' As she opened her mouth to tell him, he stopped her with a hand held palm out. Then came The Tone. 'No, don't tell me. I already know.'

Lena knew she had been optimistic to believe The Tone wouldn't follow her to Karratha, but she was aghast to hear it so soon. She had foolishly hoped that at least the first person she met might give her the benefit of the doubt. It was her disappointment which made her snap. 'You know, you're pretty rude.'

Having drawn her sword, Lena waited with bated breath for Mike to pull out his own. But he didn't, merely throwing her a contemptuous look – half smirk, half smile – and exiting the airport.

Her temper spiked. She caught hold of it and breathed deeply until her heart rate dropped to below Livid (if just above Cross). Mike was unquestionably and deliberately spiteful for no reason. After all, they'd only just met: how could she have offended him?

The vehicle Mike led her to was a two-seater ute covered in red dust. It was only just possible to see that its original colour had been white.

'Are all the cars out here this dirty?' she asked.

Mike's expression was scornful. 'You haven't seen dirty yet.' He paused. 'We'll go to the camp first to drop off your stuff. And then I'll take you to site.'

She swallowed. 'Er . . . camp? You don't mean tents, do you?'

His smile was positively evil. 'No.'

'Oh good. I was led to believe I would be given my own place.'

His smile broadened. 'You'll be given your own place.'

She studied him with narrowed eyes but he said no more, confining his attention to starting the ute. It made a gurgling, choking sound before roaring to life, almost as if it were coughing out the red dust first. Soon they were turning onto the main road. Mike adjusted the music volume just loud enough so they didn't have to talk. She was quite happy with that and focused on the view out the window.

It was the outback.

Harsh, unforgiving and seemingly barren.

Lena was too much of a city dweller to find the stark flat redness inspiring. It was shrubs not trees that dotted the landscape beside the road. And the greenery was not lush. It was a dry green that looked parched – the colour of army personnel uniforms. The soil beside the road was red and pebbled. The only thing that was nice was the sunshine: bright and unfettered by a single grey cloud.

She was disappointed that the main road that led out of the airport took them past Karratha without entering it. Wickham was supposed to be a lot smaller and it would've been nice to have a benchmark.

Her first glimpse of the 'camp' was a bit of a shock, though Mike's unmistakable enjoyment of her horror kept her from mentioning it.

She decided that she didn't like Mike Hopkins, and set her face. He wasn't going to have the satisfaction of disconcerting her.

I am perfectly okay with this.

'This' was a grid of identical white boxes sitting on weed-ridden rock and soil. There were hundreds of them in neat rows making up a giant rectangle. Lena had seen these types of buildings before – at outdoor concerts. Her skin crawled. In her experience, they functioned as toilets or first aid offices, not bedrooms. Mike parked the ute, grunted and got out. He walked around to the rear of the vehicle so he could retrieve her bags from the open loading tray, but she jumped out after him and grabbed two bags before he could get to them. He simply shrugged, took the last bag and told her to follow him.

They entered the maze of boxes, gravel crunching underfoot. Lena looked around in vain for any sign of life, but empty, grimy cabins stretched as far as she could see. When they reached a T-junction, Mike pulled a key out of his pocket and examined the tag attached to it.

'You're number E32,' he said and handed it to her. Turning away, he went left down one of the roughly hewn paths that cut through the maze. She followed him, trying to remember each turn they took.

He stopped. 'This is it: your donga.'

Donga?

She looked over at what appeared to be no more than a garden shed on stumps and decided it was an apt name. Under Mike's smug grin she climbed the two concrete blocks that led up to her front door. Unlocking it, she pushed it open. A gust of dry heat whooshed out and fried her. Bracing herself, she stepped in.

The box was smaller than an average bedroom for one and filled to capacity with mismatched furniture. She turned on the air-conditioner that was clumsily fitted into the window and then took a step back to take stock as it rattled into noisy life.

The plasterboard walls were covered in an ugly paper that she wouldn't line a drawer with let alone a whole room. The glass window above the air-conditioner was barred by security mesh which made her feel like she was in a cell. There was a single bed against one wall, a tall thin wardrobe at the foot of the bed and a small desk and plastic chair against the other wall. In the corner beside the front door was a bar fridge. The thin strip of space she was supposed to move about in was only half a metre wide. Unfortunately this small area was completely covered once she unhooked her bags from her shoulders and lowered them to the floor. She knew one thing for certain: the wardrobe was not big enough to contain her clothes.

A snigger sounded behind her. 'Do you want this one as well, or should I just leave it outside?'

She spun around and held out her hands. 'I'll take it.'

'You better hurry up,' Mike informed her as he dumped the bag at her feet. 'There's still a lot to do this afternoon.'

Lena stashed it in the wardrobe and then stepped outside, closing the door behind her. Again, she followed Mike through the maze, struggling to remember the way as they weaved between the dongas.

'How many people live here?' she finally asked.

'About three hundred and fifty, give or take.' He paused. 'Your amenities are directly in front of E block. There's only one toilet and bathroom block for the ladies.'

'Why?'

'There are only four ladies,' Mike said. 'You'll make a fifth.'

Lena's mouth dropped open. She was used to being in a workplace minority. But five out of three hundred and fifty? For every female on the job, there were seventy guys! She chewed her lower lip. The gap was much narrower at head office – *and* she could easily escape the odds after work by stepping out into the street. She *lived* in this camp now.

There was no escape.

Oh crap.

Mike seemed oblivious to her alarm. 'I'll take you to meet Ethel,' he said without stopping. 'She's in charge of the camp. She was the first female we ever had living on site.'

The endless dirt track widened to reveal a larger dark brown brick building on the edge of the plain of dongas – the only permanent building on the entire site. They entered a small room with a long white counter against one wall. The place was clearly an office but it reminded Lena of a hospital. The decor was all white and plastic. A woman seated behind the counter looked up when they entered but continued to talk on her phone. She had bad hair, bad make-up and horrendously yellow teeth.

'I'm sorry but it's not our policy to try and position brothers next to each other,' the woman was saying. 'Yes, I realise the donga next to yours is empty but it's not our policy to reserve them, especially not for two weeks. This is not a motel.'

Clearly, the woman was neither tolerant nor flexible. Ethel's half-veiled eyes remained fixed upon Lena the whole time she was talking. It was a move, Lena realised, that was deliberately made to intimidate her. So she pulled back her shoulders and stood taller, not keen to be bested at this game.

Ethel hung up the phone without a goodbye and raised a pair of impatient and poorly pencilled eyebrows by way of greeting. Unabashed, Lena came forwards.

'Hi, I'm Lena Todd. I just arrived –'

'I know who you are,' Ethel returned without warmth. 'You look far worse than I expected.'

Riled and still sore from Mike's insults, Lena couldn't stop herself saying, 'So do you.' This impulsive rejoinder seemed to amuse Ethel. Lena was privileged with the first glimpse of what could've been a smile but was more like a cross between gas and a sneer.

Mike interrupted and for once Lena didn't care. 'I've just finished showing her her donga,' he said.

'I see.' Ethel swivelled in her chair to the shelving behind her, grabbing forms out of pigeon holes. 'Breakfast is from five am to seven am. Dinner is from six-thirty pm to eight pm. Do not come outside those times because the mess hall will be locked and you will not be fed. A packed lunch will be provided for you to take to work at breakfast time. The door on your right leads to the mess hall, the door on the left leads to the games room. There is a gym next to the car park.' She slapped the forms on the counter. 'On these, fill out your details and who we are to contact in case of emergency. These others are a map of town, a map of the camp and a form for television hire.'

Lena nodded and Ethel slapped a pen on the counter, sat back and began to file her nails.

Lena glanced at the television form. 'Surely the dongas aren't big enough for a television as well.'

The file stopped moving and Ethel's eyes flicked upwards, though her chin didn't follow. 'Do you have a problem with the accommodation?'

Lena decided to be honest. 'It's just a little smaller than I was expecting.'

Ethel snorted. 'And no sweet-smelling soaps or chocolates on the pillow either. Welcome to the real world, honey.'

Lena stopped arguing and started on the personnel form – she didn't imagine she'd want to watch the limited television channels the outback offered anyway. In any case, she was in a rush: she needed to get straight to the office so she could reassure herself that she hadn't left Perth in vain – that there really was an opportunity to prove herself in this godforsaken place. That the Pilbara, for all its warts, would teach her something about being a good engineer. An engineer who was *built* for this sort of work. No pun intended.

She checked her watch. It was four-thirty. If she went to the office immediately, she'd catch the staff before they clocked off. She turned back to Mike. 'Shall we go to site?'

He looked her over. 'Do you want to get changed?'

For half an hour, she couldn't be bothered. Her khaki shorts and collared shirt were casual, but neat. 'No, I'll be fine.'

Ethel and Mike exchanged a look. A look Lena didn't trust, but didn't have time to worry about. She was desperate for good news before the day was over. She had to get to the office before she lost control and begged to be taken back to the airport for the next flight home.

The Cape Lambert work offices were located about two kilometres off the main highway, at the end of a lonely gravelly track that stopped right on the beach. The first thing that struck Lena when the sea came into view was that it didn't look right. She had never seen a beach where the sand was red almost right up to the water's edge. Here, just where the water lapped, it changed to a light yellow colour. There were black jagged rocks everywhere. It wasn't the kind of shore she'd want to wander along in bare feet. Opposite the coastline were three giant office dongas. One was labelled with a dusty sign: *Barnes Inc.* In the background she could see the giant stockpiles of iron ore, plant and other port facilities. Mike pulled the ute to a halt next to some others parked outside one of the office dongas. They both alighted and Lena held a breath as she made the last few steps to meet her fate.

There was no way she had intended to make an entrance, but the second she strode into the donga everyone stopped what they were doing and stared at her. Gooseflesh broke out on the back of her neck as she stood there, rooted to the spot, uncertain what to do. Everyone in the room was male except for two women operating a photocopier. They were also dressed in the same uniform as Mike.

Suddenly her perfectly respectable shorts felt inappropriately short and her smart business shirt much too fitted and much too pink. Many pairs of eyes raked her from head to foot more thoroughly than an MRI scans for cancer.

'Well, blow me away and send me to the crazies,' said a bald gentleman sitting closest to her. He stood up and held out his hand. 'I'm John Lewis. Who might you be?'

Relieved, Lena smiled warmly at him and shook his hand. 'Lena. Lena Todd. I'm the new engineer.'

'The new *engineer*.' The Tone was unmistakable. Once again she cursed her outfit.

'I better take you to see Carl,' Mike said, clearly enjoying the situation. 'Come on.'

Lena smiled tightly at John Lewis and followed Mike past the clutter. The office donga looked roomy from the outside but wasn't on the inside. It was broken up into cubicles and filled to capacity with cheap furniture and computers, all of which were covered in a film of red dust. The Barnes Inc staff continued to watch her.

There was a kitchen tucked away in a corner. It was filthy, as though it hadn't been cleaned in months. Both the bin and sink were overflowing and the counter was red and black at the same time with a zillion handprints all over its surface. Just as the 'why me?' questions started bubbling up, Mike gestured

Lena towards an office. It was the only one in the building with proper dividing walls and a door that opened and shut. Lena was eager to make the project manager's acquaintance. Maybe someone as senior as Carl Curtis would bring some sanity to her arrival. She stuck her head tentatively through the doorway.

'What the fuck do you want?'

At first she thought he was talking to her and almost jumped back. But then he waved grumpily at her to come in and she realised he was talking on the phone.

'No I don't have a fuckin' spare crane driver.' He pointed at the chair in front of the desk. 'Greg, you've got twelve fuckin' blokes out there, for fuck's sake. What the fuck are they doing?'

Lena swallowed as she sat down and looked around at his messy desk, over-filled bookshelves and squeaking desk fan. The man behind the desk looked to be in his early forties and was in dire need of a shave.

'I don't fuckin' care, Greg. Surely one of the fuckin' bastards can drive a fuckin' crane!' He paused. 'No worries, Greg. I'll just pull a fuckin' crane driver out of my fuckin' arse.' SLAM.

He ran two giant paws through his dark brown hair and rolled a burly set of shoulders. 'What can I do you for?'

Lena smiled and tried for a cheery note. 'I'm your new engineer.'

His eyes flickered over her. 'Fuck.'

'I beg your pardon?'

'Don't,' he warned, ''cause I sure as hell ain't begging yours. And you may get offended by what I say next.'

She didn't doubt it but raised an eyebrow with what she hoped was haughty discouragement. He merely grinned. 'You think that expression makes you look highly superior, don't you, little lady? But let me burst your city bubble for you. The blokes out there, they don't care. They don't care about you.

15

They don't care about me. And they don't care about this job. This is the Pilbara. And it's the Pilbara that makes the rules.'

Lena folded her arms and sighed. 'It seems to me,' she noted, 'that all the Pilbara seems to make is rude people.'

He gave a short sharp laugh. 'Been treating you to a bit of home brew, eh?'

She nodded. Carl was offensive on so many levels but for some illogical reason she liked his abrupt manner far more than Mike's underhanded comments.

'How old are you?' he asked.

'Twenty-three.'

'Almost fresh out of university,' he mused.

What's that supposed to mean? Her nerves shot through the roof. 'I've been working six months now and there hasn't been one complaint, thank you very much.' Too late she realised she had protested too much.

'Don't get your knickers in a knot,' Carl shot back. 'That's not what I was getting at. Just because you're smart, doesn't mean you won't get stepped on.'

Her brain latched onto the first part of his last sentence. He thought she was smart. Her heart jumped with hope. Had somebody said something? Had she come with a recommendation?

'Perth said you were as green as a cucumber.' He rubbed his forehead. 'So don't do anything without consulting me first. I have no time to make sure you don't fuck up.'

'I have no intention of f– . . . stuffing up.' She straightened her back. 'You have no right to judge me. I haven't done any work for you yet. You –'

He held up a hand for silence, nodding impatiently. 'Yes, yes, yes. I fully realise your feelings, etc., etc. But fuck, why are you here if you expect to sit in an ivory tower and be admired?'

'I'm here,' she gritted her teeth, 'to get some good experience as an engineer. Experience I couldn't get if I remained in the city.'

I'm here to prove I deserve my degree.

He scratched his head. 'Well, if that's what you're after then I'll be damned if the Pilbara won't give it to you. But do us all a favour. Get yourself a uniform and boots – steel-capped. Tie up your hair and –' he waved a hand at her in helpless frustration, 'I don't suppose there's anything you can do about the rest of it.'

The news that fashion was frowned upon on the Pilbara was depressing but she was reasonable enough to note that perhaps there was just cause for the concentration camp outfit. She couldn't take everyone staring at her all the time. She wanted to blend in. Besides, from the look of the place, the uniform was the only clothing hardy enough to take the punishment. 'I will see what I can do,' she replied gruffly.

Carl opened his desk drawer, pulled out a manila folder and pushed it across to her. 'Here's something you can get on with.'

'What is it?' Lena flipped open the file.

'We're compiling a spreadsheet of all steel piece marks on the drawings. The drawing files are in the cabinet next to the office entrance.'

'You want me to do data entry? Can't you get a secretary to do that?'

'For now we need you to do it.' His phone rang and his hand was on the receiver before she could utter another word. He spun his chair around so that his back was to her and started talking.

'Don't fuck with me. Those parts were supposed to arrive two days ago. I'm not fucking around because some fucker –'

Lena didn't wait to hear what the 'fucker' had done. She stood up, sucking a breath in between her teeth. Frankly, she was very disappointed with Carl Curtis and his language difficulties. Everything was unfolding just as she had feared. Even without knowing the whole truth about her, the Pilbara Barnes Inc crew thought she was useless. If she wanted this posting to change things for her, she was going to have to fight for every opportunity. And fight hard.

She could almost feel Kevin's eyes burning a hole in the back of her head. Chills feathered down her spine as she fought to suppress the memories. 'How can I believe in someone who spent more energy on her wardrobe than on a subject at the heart of her degree?' *No one's asking* you *to believe any more, Kevin.*

She stepped out of the office and found that Mike hadn't bothered to wait for her.

'Great,' she muttered under her breath. 'Where am I supposed to go now?'

Someone standing behind the kitchen counter was watching her – a tall gentleman, broad shouldered, slim hipped and chisel jawed. He was dressed in the usual site shirt, blue jeans, an orange and yellow reflector vest and a pair of worse-for-wear steel-capped boots. This was complemented by a coat of dust and sweat. Nonetheless, there was something appealing about him. Cowboys. Smelly and dirty, they still managed to be attractive.

'Good afternoon,' she said.

'Hey.' He inclined his head, crow's feet crinkling his laughing eyes.

Buoyed by his friendly expression, Lena approached the counter. 'I've just started here and I don't know where I'm supposed to go next. Mike, the guy who was showing me around, seems to have disappeared.'

He grinned and Lena's confidence rose to the next level. He had perfect white teeth and beautifully shaped lips. She smiled back with unreserved enthusiasm.

'Mike has a tendency to get distracted.' He held out a hand. 'I'm Gavin, the piling engineer. They told us you were starting.'

'Really?'

'Yeah. Believe me,' he glanced around, 'this place could do with someone like you.'

'Thanks,' Lena crooned somewhere between incredulity and relief. 'I plan to do the very best I can. I really want to make a difference here. And I'm just so glad that not everyone is so unwilling to give me a proper chance.'

'Are you kidding?' Gavin shook his head. 'You're a godsend. Look, if Mike isn't around, I could probably give you a few pointers.' He looked at her shorts. 'But have you got anything to get changed into?'

Lena groaned. 'Don't worry. I've already spoken to Carl about getting a uniform . . . well, sort of.'

'Oh okay,' he nodded. 'Well, when you've changed, you should probably start in the kitchen. As you can see,' he gestured at the full sink, 'it by far needs the most work. We haven't had a proper cleaner since the project started. This dirt is months old. I think there are some mops and cleaning products in the steel container out back.'

This statement took less than a second to suck all the joy out of Lena's smile.

'What did you say?'

'I have no idea if we have a vacuum,' Gavin continued, unperturbed. 'But I'm pretty sure there's a few brooms out there too. Geez, it would be so good to have this place clean.' He winked at Lena. 'Like I said before. You're a godsend.'

Chapter 2

After that disaster of a first day, all Lena wanted was a cup of tea and a quiet evening alone. She needed a chance to regroup, maybe call Robyn, have a whinge. Of course, that wasn't going to happen. Firstly, there was no mobile reception in the camp. And secondly, she had a dinner date with three hundred and fifty men who hadn't seen a new female on site in months. It was going to be hard to keep a low profile. Being a female on site was almost like being a celebrity. Everybody knew her even though she didn't know them. She'd been there just over two hours but word had spread like a cold on an aeroplane. By the time she walked into the mess, there were guys greeting her by name.

The mess reminded her of school camps. Trestle tables and plastic chairs were set up in neat rows across most of the room. The food was served buffet style, presided over by two male chefs.

As soon as she spotted Gavin, she made a beeline for him. Despite their earlier misunderstanding, he was the only person in the room she recognised. The sleazy grins being thrown at her from other tables were making her nervous. Better the devil she knew.

'I have to admit,' Gavin said as she sat down beside him, 'after my mistake this afternoon, I thought I'd be the last person you'd want to sit next to.'

Some of the tension eased out of her body under his apologetic smile. He was, after all, still both good-looking and friendly.

'That's all right,' she sighed.

'Can we start over?' He held out his hand.

'Sure.' Lena nodded, taking it. She needed a friend on site and if he was offering, she wasn't about to turn him down. She really missed Robyn and it hadn't even been twenty-four hours yet.

'Hey, Gav,' one of the other boys at their table interrupted, 'you going to hog her or what?' He – in fact most of them – winked at her.

Gavin grinned at the expectant faces. 'Guys, this is Lena. Lena, these are the barge boys.'

The barge boys were friendly, abrasive and completely sexist. If Lena had been at a party in the city, she might have enjoyed the attention. But she had to work with these people and spent the next couple of hours constantly drawing the line. If only they didn't keep stepping over it.

The experience certainly played a part in Lena's decision to dress down the next day. She didn't want to be constantly playing second fiddle to her sex. She wanted to be taken seriously as an engineer – gender irrelevant. The uniform shirt Mike gave her was a size small but hung loosely from her and she bunched it up so as not to over-accentuate her waist. Not that much waist was afforded by her oldest, droopiest pair of cargos. They'd do her until she could get some unflattering army pants of her own. She tied her hair back in an extra boring ponytail – too low to be bouncy, too high to be sophisticated. Then she doubled it over so her curls were hidden.

She refrained from make-up, which cost her a pang. But serious times called for a serious face, so she confined herself to lip balm and a SPF 15+ moisturiser. When she was done, she stood back from her mirror and smiled: plain, frumpy and utterly unworthy of a second glance.

Lena was so caught up in her drastic physical transformation that she missed her ride with the management team to site. Gavin told her they left every morning in a ute convoy at quarter to six. She'd have to catch one of the bus runs with the labourers – they started at six-fifteen and nearly everyone would be out by half past.

She regretted her slowness the second she saw the bus.

It was like high school all over again. They were hanging out the windows yelling expletives at each other, sitting by the wheels eating their breakfast or leaning on the back door having their last cigarette before the day began. When they saw her approaching the vehicle, their focus turned.

'Oh·ho ho, Lena is coming with *us*.'

The men leaning on the bus straightened, the smokers dropped their cigarettes and stomped them out. Then they all scrambled to get on the bus before she did.

Her heart sank. Plain Jane hadn't worked. As she got closer, she wondered if it had made any difference at all. They were all speaking about her like she wasn't even there.

'She's not gunna sit next to you. You smell like a pig's arse.'

'You think you're any better, mate? They can smell your pits in the back row.'

Lena cringed as she put her foot on the step at the front of the vehicle. The driver grinned down at her.

'G'day, g'day, g'day. Haven't we got a special guest this morning?'

'Hi,' she said quietly. 'Have you got room?'

'Have we got room, boys?'

There was a chorus of 'Bloody oath. Yes!' and she heard the chaotic shuffling of bodies, pushing and shoving, and groans, followed by more expletives.

'Don't just stand there,' the driver said. 'Get on.'

Lena hauled herself up the step and stood at the top of the bus aisle.

Just remember, you're doing this for your career.

She surveyed the situation. Technically, the bus was full. The seats that were available had been squeezed vacant by men who had pushed their mates onto the floor or up against the windows.

A man with a thick Scottish accent was yelling at the guy beside him. 'Get up. Can't you see the lass needs a seat? Over here, me darlin'. Plenty of room.'

Lena desperately wanted to crawl into herself. She took two steps forwards and sank quietly into the nearest seat, avoiding eye contact with the leering guy beside her. The driver started the engine just as a latecomer hopped onto the bus. Once more the bus fell into pandemonium. The men started stamping their feet and yelling abuse at him.

'Fuck off, yer bastard! Can't you see there's no room! Get off!'

Immediately the seats that had been created for Lena filled as squashed bodies expanded.

'Fuck yers!' the latecomer cried out, giving everyone the finger before turning away and jumping off the bus to wait for the next run. The men all laughed at him and the guy sitting next to Lena nudged her in the ribs.

'Don't worry, love, I'll look after ya.'

She smiled weakly and he grinned till she thought his teeth might pop out and smack her in the face.

Lena swore on her favourite handbag she'd never be late for the management ute convoy again.

On her sixth day on site, Lena realised her life had finally come down to two options:

1. Take it.
2. Leave it.

'What's wrong this time?' Robyn demanded, when she made yet another emergency call to Perth from her dusty cubicle.

'No one here will listen to me. My opinion is worth less than the new cleaner's – and she just pushes red sand from one side of the office to the other.'

'Maybe she should be using a vacuum instead of a broom.'

'Robyn, *focus*.'

'*Okay*.' Her best friend's voice was sulky. 'But I really don't know what you expect me to say that I haven't said already.'

Lena sighed. She couldn't exactly blame Robyn for being irritable. It was her third phone call to her in as many hours – only one down from her daily average. She knew she was being annoying but couldn't seem to stop herself. Every time she heard Robyn's voice, it was like getting a little slice of Perth back. It was balm to a battered soul.

She was just so homesick.

Homesick and angry.

Carl's data entry job was anaesthetising her brain – which wasn't the only thing that needed a work-out. Her legs and arms ached from sitting in the same creaky chair for twelve hours straight, day in, day out. Robyn had told her to complain but who would listen? Carl was always out. Gavin was unreliable. And The Tone was everywhere.

Lena knew she was considered the dud they had all been lumped with. Foremen, painters, welders, boilermakers, scaffolders. It didn't matter who they were. They didn't trust her. She was like the child no one wanted to babysit.

A nuisance.

The two women in the office, whom she thought she could befriend, were polite but uninterested. They were both hired locally, didn't live in the camp and already had their family and friendship networks firmly established.

Talking to Robyn was like coming up for air.

'Robyn, I need you.'

'You don't need me,' Robyn said. 'You need to make a decision. Either take the punishment or come home.'

'You know I can't come home.'

'Why the hell not? It'll be much easier –'

'I don't want to take the easy road this time,' Lena snapped. She gripped the phone cord tightly as she saw Kevin sitting across from her, his black brows drawn together in confusion. 'But I thought this was what you wanted me to do.'

'Lena? Lena? Are you still there?'

Lena blinked. 'Sorry, Robyn.'

'No, I'm sorry. I didn't mean to suggest anything. I only meant –'

Lena bit her lip. 'I know what you meant. But I can't come home because if I fail on the Pilbara it will mean Kevin was right.'

'You can't fail if you haven't had a chance to do anything.' Her friend breathed in sharply then added, 'Listen, if you're going to be stubborn about it then you might as well go all the way.'

Lena sat up hopefully. 'All the way. What do you mean?'

'I mean, rebel.'

Lena frowned. 'What?'

'*Rebel*,' Robyn repeated. 'Or come home. One or the other: just don't ring me again until you've made a choice.'

'But –'

There was some rustling of paper. 'I've gotta go, honey. The boss wants me and she doesn't look happy.'

Lena listened to the dial tone for a full ten beeps before slowly replacing the receiver.

Rebel.

How did she do that? Go on strike? Take a long lunch break? She snorted. That would probably be more torturous for her than anyone else. She generally ate lunch at her desk – there was no cafe just down the street or lunch bar across the road. The benches outside weren't inviting either. The most comfortable option was to stay inside where the air was cool and the dust and flies didn't blow into her food.

If she stole a ute and drove off down the beach, that might create a bit more of a stir. Not because she was missing, but because the car was. Carl and Gavin were always dashing off after some crisis – having a vehicle at the ready was essential to their daily routine.

But not her.

Why did they even bother to hire me?

Her hands curled into fists. It didn't matter what their reasons were: it was her own agenda that counted. She had come to the Pilbara to see some real work and so far all she'd got was the four walls of a dirty office and hourly doses of sexual harassment.

She wanted to see the project. The real project.

The jetty.

She had heard some of the men calling it the wharf because it was so big – stretching over two and a half kilometres out to sea. It supported a conveyor belt that carried iron ore from land to the gigantic ships that were docked at the end of it. Barnes Inc was there both to extend and widen the wharf.

Her fingers drummed restlessly on the desktop, her mouth twisting as she chewed her dilemma. *Maybe I'll just go out by myself. Who's going to stop me?*

Before she could change her mind she stood up, walked to the kitchen and slipped out the back door when she was sure no one was looking. She grabbed a hard hat, reflector vest and safety glasses from an open steel container doubling as a supply room behind the office donga and then looked for transport. She knew there would be a bus waiting outside because she saw it there all the time. Every hour it left the site office to run errands and men down to the end of the jetty. She walked over to the stationary vehicle, determined to catch a ride.

She was prepared to meet with some resistance and was surprised to see a female driver with an inviting smile seated behind the wheel.

'Well, hello there.'

Lena's mouth dropped open. 'Er . . . hi.'

The woman had short red hair and looked to be about thirty years old. Her eyes danced as though she knew in part what Lena might be thinking.

'What?' Her lips quirked. 'You got a problem with a female driver?'

Lena put her foot on the step and her hands on the railing. 'Not if you don't have a problem with a female engineer.'

The bus driver jerked her head up with a grin. 'All right, get on.'

Lena could tell already they were going to be great friends. 'My name's Lena,' she offered as she boarded the bus.

'I know. I've heard about you. Word travels fast.'

Lena rolled her eyes. 'Tell me about it.'

The woman held out her hand. 'I'm Sharon. I'm the sanest person you're going to meet today. Are you ready for this?'

Lena took her hand and grinned. 'I've been ready for six days. Let me have it.'

'The Engineer has spoken.' Sharon gave her a cocky salute as Lena found a seat behind her on the otherwise empty bus.

'Not many people going out at the moment,' Lena commented.

'They're already there,' Sharon said over her shoulder. 'Big day today: the first pile is going in. Just watch yourself. Everyone's a little overexcited.'

'Thanks for the tip.' They fell into silence as they drove until Lena caught her first glimpse of the wharf.

'Oh my,' she breathed.

It was, in a word, magnificent. Lena knew how long it was, but nothing prepared her for the awesome power of it. She felt like a pharaoh looking at the pyramids. A rush rippled through her body.

From the shore, she couldn't see the end of it. It just went on and on and on until it faded into the horizon. Due to the fact that it was standing at least five storeys above the ground, they had to drive up a steep embankment to get to the start of it. The deck sat on huge white cylindrical piles, set in diagonal pairs roughly every thirty metres.

The crisscrosses of the piles grew smaller and smaller to her eyes as the jetty weaved out like a giant centipede. She heard the hum of the conveyor before she saw it. It was moving almost as fast as the bus, pile after pile of iron ore, red and moist, on its black weathered length. Everything else – the road, the steel frames supporting the conveyor – was stained red. Iron ore had got into every nook and cranny.

This is why I became an engineer.

For this feeling.

The thrill reminded her of her first days at university, the newness of the material, the joy of first discovery, that itching to know more. It was a sensation that predated the mess that Kevin had made of her career and her confidence.

I want to get back to this.

Just this.

Lena heard Sharon laugh. It was only then that she realised she had her nose pressed up against the glass.

'Would you like a tissue for your drool?' Sharon asked.

Lena blushed and wiped her smudge off the window with her overlong sleeve. 'I've just never seen anything like it. At least not up this close.'

'Don't worry, it gets me almost every day too.'

It took them at least ten minutes to get to the end of the wharf. Enough time for Lena to take in the sights, smells and sounds. The road on which the bus travelled was narrow. On their left there was about half a metre between them and a sheer drop straight into the ocean. On the right-hand side was the same gap between them and the moving conveyor. There were no guardrails, so Sharon definitely needed to focus. Lena panicked when she saw a car heading off the wharf, coming straight for them, until the redhead pulled them over into a turning bay. These were little areas where the jetty widened momentarily so that two cars could park on the side of the road while another passed.

'People going off have right of way,' Sharon explained, 'though generally whoever is nearest to the bay parks and lets the other pass.'

Chaos reigned at the end of the wharf. Every available space was packed with men, equipment or amenities. There was barely enough room for five cars to park. The bus turned into the last remaining space.

'I wait here for fifteen minutes,' Sharon said. 'After that, you won't see me for a ride back till next hour.'

'Okay.' Lena nodded. 'I think it'll take me till then anyway.'

She knew fifteen minutes wouldn't be long enough to explore. Small as it was, there was too much going on at the end of the jetty.

A temporary office had been set up next to the cars – another crusty white donga that looked like it had been just dropped there on the roadway. Next to it was a similarly temporary toilet block. Beyond that, the wharf ended. Someone had erected a guardrail along the very end – *about time*, thought Lena – and there were a bunch of guys standing there looking out over the water at some pretty impressive business.

Out on the ocean sat a barge about the size of a suburban house block. Only it wasn't floating on the water. This thing had put down three large steel legs and was currently standing elevated over the waves like something out of *War of the Worlds*.

There was a control room on one side of the barge. On the other side, it had a giant clamp which held a long cylindrical pile, so that one end just dipped into the water. A crane situated on the barge deck was placing another cylinder over the pile like an enormous sleeve. Lena saw that this sleeve was supposed to somehow drive the pile into the ocean bed.

The challenge the crane driver faced now though was getting the sleeve on the pile – it wasn't a straight lift and drop because the pile was on an angle.

The men at the end of the jetty were signalling the men on the three-legged barge with hand signs and radios. Lena was suddenly very conscious of the fact that she had no reason to be there. She hung back trying to remain unnoticed. But this was hard to do considering she was the only woman within a five-kilometre radius.

'Hey there, missy – you lost?'

She turned her head to a mischievous-looking man standing on her right. He was short, blond and well burnt by the sun. He tipped his hard hat. 'How'd a nice girl like you end up in a dump like this?'

She laughed. 'Same reason you're here.'

'Ah,' he sighed. 'The money is like a drug. The more you get the more you want.' He stuck out his hand. It was as red as the clothes he wore so she grasped it only briefly.

'The name's Leg.'

'Leg?' Lena repeated. 'As opposed to arm?'

'That's right.'

'How'd you get a name like that?'

'My name's Bob Legg, you see. So the boys just call me Leg.'

'Oh.'

A second man joined them. He looked like a monkey with skin as brown as his hair, big cocoa eyes and an agitated swagger. She noticed the harness he was wearing and realised that he was a rigger . . . swagger thus explained. 'People call this guy Radar.' Leg indicated his friend with his thumb.

'G'day, mate,' said Radar.

'So is your last name Radar then?' Lena asked the monkey as he shook her hand with gusto.

'Nah.'

Leg grinned. 'Radar got his name from being the site gossip. There isn't anything this guy doesn't know. Picks it up on his radar, so to speak.'

Immediately Radar fired his first questions. 'So you single then? Boyfriend? Married?'

Leg nudged him disapprovingly and Lena laughed. 'Doesn't waste any time, does he?' Leg groaned.

'No,' she agreed.

'So you didn't answer my questions then.' Radar was nothing if not persistent.

'I'm not available,' Lena returned in a tone that she hoped sounded like irrefutable fact. She was now glad that she'd run into the Cape Lambert gossip. Best the men knew exactly where she stood right from the start. 'I'm here to get some good experience in the field, nothing more.'

'And I'm sure you will.' Radar winked at her in a way that made her certain they weren't talking about the same sort of experience.

Leg clocked him on the back of the head. 'Be nice. Can't you see she's a lady? Sorry, mate: Radar will have it all over camp that you're single by nightfall and not in the way you're hoping.'

Lena sighed. 'Maybe I better go then, before he gets anything else out of me.'

'Go where?' He pounced as she turned away.

Lena turned back slowly. 'I'm just taking a look around. I'm the new site engineer, you know.'

Leg stepped back in hammed-up reverence. 'Ooooh, an engineer. I make my humble apologies. I didn't mean to question your divine mightiness.'

Despite herself, Lena chuckled.

'Madame Engineer.' Radar sketched her a mock bow. 'And what do you know about jetties?'

The truth was nothing, of course. Even if she didn't question the legitimacy of her own degree, she would still be a graduate engineer. And that generally meant two things. Zero experience and a lot to learn.

She knew that.

They knew that.

But she sure as hell wasn't going to admit it point blank and walk right into the trap they had obviously set for her. So she said with perhaps more confidence than she felt, 'Enough to be here. I've actually just come out for a look, to see what you guys were up to –'

'And perhaps give us a few pointers.' Leg raised his eyebrows mockingly then looked at Radar, who was chuckling and tapping his nose. Lena was hard pressed not to bang their cheeky heads together. But she held her ground.

'I can hardly give you any pointers until I've seen what you're up to.'

Fortunately, they relented and led Lena to the temporary-looking guardrail at the very end of the existing jetty.

'Today,' Leg explained, 'once we get the hammer on, we're going to drive a pile.'

Ah. The sleeve had to be the hammer, as Lena had thought. Excitement curled in her belly as she realised she was going to see it in action. She had made the right decision. The Pilbara could give her back all that she had lost.

Energy.

Confidence. Innocence.

She heard footsteps behind her as a new masculine voice joined them at the rail.

'So what's the update?'

Leg and Radar glanced over her shoulder at the newcomer and she saw their grins fade. Curious, she spun around.

The first thing she noticed about the new guy was that he wasn't wearing a Barnes Inc uniform. The second was that he was drop-dead gorgeous, tall and broad shouldered. His features looked like someone talented had taken a hammer and chisel and carved them out of his face. As he turned his dark head and met her eyes she realised that, three hundred and fifty workers or not, he knew she was brand spanking new.

And for reasons past understanding, he wasn't pleased about it.

'Who are you?' His magnetic gaze cut through the air between them, making her insides fizz like Coca-Cola.

'I'm . . . I'm Lena.'

His impassive expression swept her body from head to foot before turning to Leg and Radar who were shuffling on their feet behind her. They stopped moving the second his gaze touched them.

'What is she doing on the wharf?'

Lena's euphoric mood faltered. 'Er . . . excuse me,' she said. 'I can speak for myself.'

But he continued to talk to Leg, who was being anything but helpful. 'You can't just bring your admin staff out here for a stickybeak; it's too dangerous if they haven't had the safety induction. Besides,' he added with a glare at Lena, 'it's not a damned tourist spot.'

All her joy disappeared. 'How dare you make assumptions about me?'

He raised one black brow. 'Have you had a safety induction?'

She blushed. 'No, but –'

'Then I suggest you go wait for the bus. You shouldn't be here.'

'But I –' Lena began, but was cut off by the loudest *BANG!* she'd ever heard in her life. The wharf trembled slightly under her feet and she heard the crash of a wave hitting the piles beneath the deck. As she swayed unsteadily the stranger reached out and caught her by the shoulders. Another loud *BANG* erupted from the piling barge. She put her hands over her ears.

'Geez,' she muttered.

'You silly girl.' He released her shoulders and retrieved a small plastic packet from his pocket. He held it in front of her face and Lena realised they were foam earplugs. As she removed her hands from her ears to take them, another *BANG* crashed over her head. Hastily, she ripped open the packet and shoved the plugs into her ears. She looked around and noticed for the first time that everyone had them in.

BANG!

Lena could still hear the hammer loud and clear. The earplugs just took the edge off.

Now that her comfort had been somewhat improved, curiosity took over. She stared up at the hammer. It was obvious how it worked: a heavy weight moved up and down inside the sleeve. As she looked over the railing at the base of the pile, she could see fish rising out of the water. They were floating on their bellies around the pile base, stunned by the vibration.

Her fascination was no camouflage, however. She felt a tap on her shoulder and turned to find Mr Tall, Dark and Obnoxious still glaring at her. And someone else had joined him.

It was Carl Curtis. Her boss had picked this of all moments to finally make himself available. Shame impaled her as Carl crooked his finger. He walked her back to the bus; Sharon was about to leave. Blood pulsed behind her eyes.

So much for her rebellion.

So much for earning respect.

All she had done was show Leg, Radar and the smart aleck with the earplugs how to be humiliated in public.

'I'll see you back at the office.' Carl dismissed her and then left. Lena's fingers curled into fists as she stood there watching his retreating back, cursing him and the stranger who had led him to her. But she obeyed. After all, it was one thing to talk back to some random, but she couldn't very well tell her boss to go to hell. No matter how much she wanted to.

'That was quick,' Sharon commented as she got on the bus. 'I thought you were going to stay the full hour.'

'So did I.' Lena grimaced. 'Something came up.' Like it always did just when she thought she was getting ahead. It took all her willpower not to just scream. She quickly turned away to contemplate the view out the window.

'Hey,' she heard Sharon say, 'if they're giving you a hard time –'

'No, no.' She deliberately kept her voice even and expressionless. 'I'm okay, Sharon, really.'

Convincing herself of that took the rest of the drive back to the office. Not that she achieved much work when she got there. She was too busy counting the minutes till Carl returned to yell at her.

She knew the second he walked in the door because she felt a gust of hot wind on the back of her neck, shortly followed by a loud door slam and the stomping of boots.

'Todd, my office. Now!'

Everyone in the room heard. All eyes followed her progress to his door. Of course they pretended not to notice, shuffling their papers loudly as she passed their desks, feigning absorption in whatever task they were doing.

Yeah right. They were enjoying her humiliation – had probably been waiting for it.

Once standing in front of Carl's desk, she was transported back in time to her high school principal's office. Only, instead of detention, she was facing outright expulsion. Rationally it shouldn't have been a bad thing. She should be happy that she was about to be ejected from the place she thought represented hell on earth. But going home would be failing. And if there was one thing she couldn't do, it was fail.

Carl's first words startled her back to the present. 'What the fuck were you doing out there?' He was standing behind his desk with his hands on his hips.

She racked her brain for an excuse and decided she might as well give him the truth. After all, what privileges did she have to lose? 'I needed a breather.'

'What the fuck?'

He took off his helmet and flung it on his desk. There was a giant band mark across his sweaty forehead from the plastic strap inside the hard hat. The comical crease distracted her for a second and she found herself biting back a laugh.

'You think this is funny?' he demanded.

Lena sucked in her cheeks. 'No.'

'Don't you know you're not allowed out on the wharf without a fuckin' safety induction?'

Something broke in Lena's brain. He'd left her sitting in his *fuckin'* office for six days straight doing a job a monkey could probably do *blindfolded*. She crossed her arms. 'No, Carl, I didn't know that. Why should I? You never bothered to tell me. No one has.'

'Don't try and pin this shit on me.' He pointed a finger at her. 'You shouldn't have been out there and you fuckin' know it.'

She gaped at him, her indignation growing like a hot air balloon being filled. 'With all *due* respect, Carl,' she said, 'yes, I should. I was sent here from Perth to be a site engineer. And instead I've been nothing but a prisoner in this office for the last six days. If I needed an induction, you should have given me one on my first day. So yes, I blame you.'

'Prisoner, *my arse*.' Carl rolled his eyes. 'There's no need to be so fuckin' melodramatic.' He pulled back his chair and threw himself down on it. The action caused a number of loose papers to fly up and then settle again.

Lena put her hands on the edge of his desk and leaned forwards. 'I can't do this any more, Carl. I can't stay in here, day in, day out and play with your database. It's a waste of my . . .' she faltered, 'degree.'

Carl didn't appear to notice the strange inflection in her voice. His eyes flicked to hers. 'No shit. So why didn't you tell me this before you went fuckin' walkabout?'

'I've been trying to get hold of you for days; you're never here.' She threw up her hands as her courage returned. 'Besides, it's common sense. What does an engineer from Perth come here to do?'

He snorted. 'You forget that you're also young, female and fuckin' inexperienced.'

'Believe me,' she said through her teeth, 'I'm never allowed to forget it.'

At that point she spun on her heel and headed for the door. There was no way she was having an emotional breakdown right in front of him. Clearly she was going to get nowhere with him anyway. She might as well go back to her donga and pack instead of wasting more time. If she was going to be sent back to Perth, she'd much prefer just to get on with it.

'Hold it, Todd.' Carl's voice rang out sharply from behind her. 'We're not finished yet.'

Lena stopped walking but didn't turn around.

'You want me to admit I fucked up. Fine. I fucked up. I should have sent you for a safety induction.'

She turned back slowly. His surrender was so unexpected that she didn't trust it and scanned his eyes for mockery.

'Sit down and we'll figure out what to do with you.'

Lena still didn't believe it and continued to stand there speechless. Men *never* admitted they were wrong – at least not in her experience. Things couldn't be *that* different on the Pilbara, surely.

Carl grinned. 'For fuck's sake, Todd, sit down. You're giving me a crick in my neck.'

A little devil prompted her to test the limits of his benevolence. 'Do you always swear so much?'

'What the fuck are you talking about? I never swear.' Carl looked down and became absorbed in his right thumbnail.

She laughed, partly in amusement but mostly in relief, and ventured back to his desk.

His eyes snapped up from his hands to her. 'If you were hoping for some bullshit apology about my French, you're barking up the wrong tree. A man doesn't change, and especially not for some female with an identity crisis.'

'I beg your pardon?'

'Pardon granted,' he grunted. 'Now, for fuck's sake, *sit down*.'

Grinning, Lena plonked herself in the chair opposite his. 'Okay, I'm listening.'

'Did you see much out there today?'

'Not really,' she began. 'I saw them banging the first pile in but you told me to go away before they'd finished.'

'We *drive* piles, Todd, we don't bang them in.'

Heat scorched her skin. 'Right. Yeah. Of course.'

His lip twitched suspiciously before he continued. 'At this stage, we've got the piling sorted. Gavin's looking after that and that's not where I need an engineer.'

He folded his arms on the desktop. 'I need you to widen the jetty for the second conveyor.'

'*What?*' Her mouth dried. Lena had been expecting responsibility but not this much.

'Not running scared, are you, Todd?'

'No.' She shook her head immediately, though her palms had begun to sweat.

He spun on his chair and stabbed a finger at October on the calendar behind him. 'You have five months. Don't disappoint me.'

She felt adrenaline pump from her heart to her temple. Had she just dug her own grave and jumped into it?

'However,' Carl added severely, 'you will not be setting foot on the wharf again until you've had a fuckin' safety induction. The amount of fuckin' excuses I had to pull out of my arse this morning because that dickhead saw you fuckin' around was un-befuckin-lievable.'

Lena was momentarily diverted. 'Excuses?' she retorted. 'To who? Not that jerk I met on the wharf. He wasn't even in uniform.'

'That's because,' Carl told her with awful patience, 'he's the bloody client.'

Chapter 3

'I'm not a gynaecologist, but if you have a need, I can take a look at it for you.' The guy who had spoken raised his stubby in a silent toast. His friend leaned forwards with a slow cringe-worthy wink.

'That goes double for me.'

Lena shuddered, turned away and kept walking. Raucous laughter followed her down the gravelled path.

The worst part about camp, she decided, was evening drinks. Six o'clock, when everyone went back to their dongas to chew the fat and drink a carton. They congregated in groups of five or six, sitting on the concrete steps in front of their tin rooms-for-one. Usually boots and pants were substituted for shorts and thongs. Lena could have joined any number of these groups if she wanted to. Invitations flew out across the yard, loudly and daily. But she didn't like the way some of the guys got when they were drunk. Brave was one way to describe it. Sleazy was probably more accurate. Besides, Lena wasn't big on beer. She thought there was a reason they called it piss. In her opinion it tasted worse than awful. Even when Party-Girl had been her middle name, she hadn't managed to acquire the taste. Kevin had come along in her third year and also had a preference for wine. She'd thought it was another great thing they had in common. Looking back now, she realised how desperate she'd been to justify their relationship. It was a beverage, for goodness sake, not a sign of compatibility.

She quickened her step. There was one advantage to happy hour. While the guys were busy with their beer, the gym was usually empty and she wanted to make the most of the time. It was Ethel who had tipped her off about that. The rude camp receptionist was slowly changing her tune. Ever since she'd seen Lena's efforts with her site uniform, as ineffective as they had been, she had started giving Lena some modicum of respect. In fact, every time Lena ran into her, she seemed to drop a new hint.

'They're making steak tonight so get to the mess early.' Or 'The washing machines in C block are brand new.' Or 'There's mobile reception in the car park.' These tips were always pronounced in a gruff voice as if torn from her against her will. She never waited for a reply, just kept walking as if she was worried someone would see them together. Lena regarded the gym membership as a lifesaver. Having nothing but work in her life had been taking its toll. The gym gave her some personal time that wasn't spent confined to the four walls of her donga.

The equipment was old and the room was small but she had it all to herself. It was finally an environment where she had control. For the last three days she'd been there every night, working off the stress of her new-found responsibility.

The pride and bane of her life.

She wished she was ready for it.

Carl had been right. Lena was as green as a golf course – and getting greener by the minute. She had spent the last couple of days researching her position, going through files and reading correspondence. All she'd found out was how much she didn't know. She had so many questions and no one to answer them.

Not that she wanted to be spoonfed. She knew the dangers of that better than anyone. But just a hint or two would be nice. Carl never had time for her. He was always too busy putting out fires. It was going to be a teach-yourself job and doubts assailed her.

Can I do this? Can I really do this?

How will I know if I'm doing it right? Do I have to wait till some piece of the jetty falls off to find out?

Sometimes the fear almost paralysed her; other times it kept her moving like day-old meat does a hyena. All she could do was keep trying – and hope and pray that she was making the right calls.

Another anxiety which constantly plagued her was stuffing up again in front of Dan Hullog. The client. Every time Lena thought about their first meeting, she cringed. Had she *intended* to give him a complete lack of confidence in her, she couldn't have done a better job of it.

'Don't worry about it,' Sharon had tried to reassure her. 'He's not worth impressing.'

But Sharon didn't understand. Sharon didn't know what was at stake. Sharon, as far as Lena was concerned, had the mentality of everyone else in Barnes Inc. It was like a religion with them, a fanatical belief that all the Barnes Inc personnel followed. The project was divided into two teams. *Us and Them.*

Dan Hullog was the leader of the foe, the nemesis of the Barnes Inc project. If Lena had any sense of loyalty to her people, she would hate him on principle.

There was no love lost between Barnes Inc and TCN, whose staff worked in a smaller set of office dongas on the other side of site near the start of the jetty. They watched Barnes Inc's every move like white-bellied sea eagles.

'Nitpicking bastards,' Leg ruthlessly labelled the lot of them. 'Don't know a nut from a bolt and they want to tell us how to do our jobs.'

Sharon often delivered the mail between the two offices during her bus runs and was one of the few Barnes Inc personnel to have actually been behind enemy lines. 'They're a lot tidier than we are,' she told Lena, as though it was proof that they were hiding something. 'You wouldn't think it was a site office with Bulldog's floors so clean.'

That's what Barnes Inc staff called Dan Hullog – Bulldog. Apparently, once he got it between his teeth, he didn't let go – a perfectionist with impossible standards. Apparently, he had an overly critical eye and a penchant for finding the tiniest flaw in anything.

Like that was supposed to make Lena feel better.

She was surprised to learn that he lived in the camp. Carl chose to live in a proper house in Wickham, so Lena would never run into him on the way to the shower. She was grateful for that. It was good to have a bit of distance from her boss after knock-off and at least Carl had the common decency to give it to his staff.

Not Bulldog.

He lived right in among Carl's staff and his own. The Barnes Inc boys said it was to keep his nose to the ground – sniff out any insurrection or laziness. He wanted them on their toes day and night.

'Does his laundry every Monday at six-thirty pm in laundry donga seven,' Radar tipped her off one day. 'All the guys know it's the place to avoid at that time, if you know what I mean.'

Despite the instructions on how to evade him, Lena saw Dan at breakfast the day after their run-in on the wharf and then at dinner that night. He didn't acknowledge her and she made sure to ignore him, but it didn't stop her knowing more about him than she cared to. At camp, titbits about the personal life of Dan and his staff were not only available, they were sought after. Gossip was the most common form of entertainment. After all, there wasn't anything else to do. People couldn't go down to the local cinema and catch a movie. Project workers got their soap operas and dramas at work.

Word on the street was that Bulldog had a secret.

It made Lena roll her eyes. *A secret? What did that mean and why was it a crime?*

Hell, she couldn't point fingers. If Barnes Inc knew her history, she'd be fired on the spot: no notice, no questions asked. So how could she judge a man who kept his cards close to his chest? She couldn't. That being said, it didn't stop her from being curious with the rest of them or speculating at his expense. She listened in when his name came up at the dinner table and followed the stories about his eccentric behaviour with an interest that she couldn't resist.

Generally, if she didn't see Sharon, Lena would sit with Radar and Leg for dinner. They were the only two guys who had taken an interest in her that wasn't sexual and even then she couldn't be certain. Leg was an outrageous flirt. However, she found out over the course of several dinners that he was married with a five-month-old daughter. So it seemed unlikely that he was really in the market.

'Don't you find that hard?' she asked one time. 'That you only see your family ten weeks of the year?'

But he'd just grinned. 'Makes them appreciate me more, doesn't it?'

Leg was right about Radar. The man always had something to report back at the end of the day. Sometimes it was about one of the riggers or a barge boy, but more often than not, it was about Bulldog.

'Heard he's not taking his R and R,' he told them towards the end of the week.

'Not taking his R and R,' Sharon scoffed. 'The man will go nuts.'

Lena nodded. 'The only thing that's keeping me going is the light at the end of the tunnel. If I didn't know there was a week off after five, I'd go mad.'

'So would most guys,' Radar agreed. 'Bulldog's a worka-holic, or maybe there's nothing at home to go back to.'

'Hasn't he got a family?' Lena enquired, unable to picture them even as she asked it. A wife and kids, brothers and sisters, Christmas at home and Mother's shepherd's pie just didn't seem to fit with Bulldog's hard-nosed persona.

Radar lowered his voice as though imparting something he normally wouldn't give away. 'He ain't married. But I think there's a woman in his life.'

Despite herself, Lena's curiosity jack-knifed. 'He's dating someone?'

Radar shrugged. 'Maybe. He's always on the phone to someone back in Perth or at least that's what my sources tell me.'

Sharon rolled her eyes. 'Geez, can you imagine it? Dating him, I mean. "I'll pick you up at eight, dinner's at nine, sex is at ten. I will review everything in the morning and get back to you about the possibility of a repeat."'

Leg sniggered. '"But if you're successful, you'll get a list of improvement requirements with the go-ahead."'

Radar laughed. 'Ain't that the truth.'

'Speaking of having a personal life,' Lena said. 'What are you guys doing Sunday?'

Every two weeks Barnes Inc had a Sunday off. Lena's first experience of this was in three days and she was counting the minutes.

Leg and Radar shrugged. 'Nothing.'

'Come on, guys.' She scanned their faces for a hint of enthu-siasm. 'What do people do here for fun?'

'Fun?' Sharon joked. 'What's that?'

Lena persisted. 'Seriously. Don't you guys have plans?'

'What do you think this is?' Leg said. 'New York City?'

'I have a plan,' Radar said. 'Pick me up a carton, a few girlie mags and the newspaper, then sit in the shade under the gum behind the mess for a few hours.'

'More drinking.' Lena frowned. 'Aren't you an alcoholic by now?'

Radar grunted with greater satisfaction than contrition. 'I'm working on it.'

Lena closed her eyes, conjuring her perfect day off – a half-price sale at Georgette's, followed by a Caesar salad and a skim latte at Dome with Robyn. But she had to work with what she had. Opening her eyes, she looked at Sharon. 'What do you normally do?'

Sharon shrugged. 'Read . . . sleep.'

'You've got to be kidding me.' Lena sat back in her plastic dining chair, arms folded across her chest. Her stubborn streak was digging in its heels again. 'I refuse to stay in this camp. I've got to get out of here. Come on, guys,' she protested. 'There's got to be something we can do to get us away from these bloody dongas. What do the locals get up to?'

'Well,' Radar said slowly, 'there's always fishing. Pilbara's bloody ripe for it.'

'Hmmm.' Lena thought it over. Fishing was only a slight step up from drinking. Generally she wasn't into playing with her food besides being strictly a deadatarian. As in, she only ate stuff that was already dead the first time she saw it. The thought of pulling a slimy wriggling fish from a hook and chopping its head off so that she could cook it gave her the heebie-jeebies.

'Anything else?' She scanned Radar's face with faint hope.

'Nup, that's it.'

Lena sighed and glanced at Sharon.

'Hey, I'm willing if you can muster up a vehicle.'

She had no choice. It was this or nothing. 'Fine.' Lena blew at her fringe. 'Let's go fishing.'

The safety induction Carl had booked for Lena took most of the following day and bored her senseless. She was further disappointed by the fact that it took place in a small community hall in Wickham instead of in the client's site office – she'd hoped for a chance to check out the forbidden building. The unnatural need made her realise that the Pilbara was starting to get to her. Even so, her brain had not yet hit madness, like Gavin's. His return to the office coincided with hers.

She saw him jump off the bus from the wharf, his face red with sweat and annoyance.

'You'll never believe what they've done now.'

'Who?'

'Who do you think?'

The client. 'What have they done?'

'They've erected a bloody flag on their front donga.'

'A flag?'

'Big blue thing with their emblem on it.' Gavin wiped the sweat off his brow. 'It's giving my men the shits.'

She laughed. 'It's just a flag.'

'It's a bloody offence is what it is,' Gavin said. 'The boys reckon we should wait till nightfall, steal it and erect a Barnes Inc one in its place.'

Lena raised her eyebrows. 'You're kidding, right?'

He was silent.

'Gavin,' she began slowly. 'You can't do that.'

He hesitated. 'You're right. It's not enough. We need a bigger flag if we're going to make a statement.'

'You're not serious.'

'I'll need a 200 CHS for the pole at the very least.' Gavin was already striding past her. 'I'll go see Tony.' Tony was one of the yard foremen. He was in charge of all the fabricated steel that arrived on site, storing it and distributing it to the correct area of the job.

Lena watched Gavin head for the donga that housed Tony's office and could tell he had already forgotten her presence. Shaking her head, she entered the main donga in search of Carl. She had to ask him about getting a ute for Sunday among a score of other things.

'Good afternoon, Carl.'

He looked up from his computer screen as she walked into his office. 'Since when?'

Lena smiled. 'Bad day?'

'The fuckin' worst. How was your induction?'

'Boring.'

Carl shrugged. 'Bulldog likes 'em very thorough. What can I do for you?'

'I've done my research. I just want to know where we're at in terms of progress and how I take it from here.'

'Best to talk to Mike about that.'

Lena's heart sank. 'Mike Hopkins?'

'He's in charge of the skid frame. He'll be your site supervisor.'

Lena's heart plummeted even further.

It couldn't have been more unwelcome news. The first image that popped into her head was Mike's contemptuous smirk as he handled her luggage at the airport.

The last thing she wanted was a subordinate who had zero faith in her. She needed an ally. Someone who was willing to work with her and respect her suggestions. Mike Hopkins wasn't going to do that. If anything, he was going to make things as difficult for her as he could.

'Listen, Carl,' Lena began, but the phone rang and he picked it up instead.

'What? Fuck! No! Who told you to let fuckin' Eric drive the crane? You know he's fuckin' incompetent. Me? Get fucked. I didn't tell you *shit*!'

He shook his head at Lena, waving his hand in dismissal. It was clear her questions weren't a priority. She bit her lip and exited his office. The only thing left to do was meet trouble head on.

She looked at her watch. There was one last bus run for the day. Just enough time to get out to the skid and talk to Mike. Who knew? He *might* be reasonable.

So she donned her hard hat, safety glasses and reflector vest and caught the bus out to the wharf to find him. The skid frame was about five hundred metres down the jetty. Lena got a glimpse of it as soon as the bus left the land. It was a giant steel table-like structure that straddled the existing conveyor belt. She could see the men working on top of it while the conveyor operated normally beneath. They had a little five-tonne crane bolted to the deck and were lifting a beam over the side to attach to the main girders below the jetty deck. This was one of many that would be used in the first step towards broadening the wharf.

She wasn't sure why they called it a skid frame until she got close enough to see that the legs of the table were attached to long steel beams that could act like skis. 'Oh I see.' She nodded. 'It skids along.'

'Yeah,' said Sharon. 'It's pulled by winch along the deck.'

Sharon dropped her off at the base with a smile and a wave. Lena straightened her hard hat, pulled her vest into place and walked over to the ladder on the side of the skid. Seconds later, she was standing on the checker plate.

'Here's trouble.' A rat-faced little man tipped his hat at her.

'Hi,' she greeted him.

'Mike,' he called out over his shoulder. 'Seems we have an engineer on board: a *madame* engineer.'

Mike turned around and squinted at Lena. He made a noise between a snort and a grunt and then returned his gaze to the ocean.

'Lena!'

She saw a head pop up over the other side of the skid. 'Radar.' Lena smiled. 'You never told me you got transferred to the skid team.'

He shot a mischievous glance in Mike's direction. 'And spoil the surprise? Not on your life.' He hauled himself up onto the skid.

'Word about town,' he told her rat-faced companion, 'is that Lena here is our new leader.' Again he glanced over his shoulder with a grin. 'Mike's *new boss*. Isn't that right, Mike?'

Lena ground her teeth. Trust Radar to stick his spoon in the pot first. She glared at him, mouthing, 'Cut it out,' as Mike continued his silent vigil.

Mike didn't turn around so she joined him by the hand-railing at the edge of the skid.

'Mike,' she began, 'has Carl spoken to you about my new appointment as the engineer for the skid? I just thought we should touch base and –'

'There's nothing to talk about,' Mike said roughly, without looking at her. 'As you can see, I have everything under control here.'

'I don't think Carl would have appointed me if he felt there was nothing for me to do,' Lena said firmly, suppressing her anger as it attempted to flare. The trick was to stay calm. Calm and rational.

'Maybe he just wanted to get you out of his hair for a while by palming you off on me.'

She gaped at him. 'You've got some attitude, Mike. And what I can't figure out is what I've done to deserve it.'

'Do you know how many years I've been in this industry?'

'Er . . . I don't know.' Lena winced. 'Ten?'

'Fifteen,' he snapped. 'The very last thing I need is you.'

He looked away. Clearly, her sex wasn't his only problem. How was she supposed to get the experience she needed if she got this at every turn?

'Listen, Mike,' Lena began, but he wouldn't look at her. 'Mike,' she tried again in vain.

Lena followed his gaze out across the water, her fury gathering steam. Then instantaneously it fizzled. 'Whoa.'

Whales, two of them, were frolicking about half a kilometre away from the wharf. Their huge black bodies slid in and out of the water like islands, appearing and then disappearing. Every now and then a huge tail would emerge, flip upwards and then smash the ocean surface with as much strength as the pile hammer. One of them sprayed a fountain from its blowhole before its black body curved into the waves. She had never seen anything more humbling.

Radar came up and stood beside them. 'Been keeping us company all morning,' he told her. 'I think they know we're up to something.'

'Pity they're wrong,' Mike snapped. 'We haven't welded that headstock on yet and won't do so if you continue to stand there gaping like a frog catching flies. Get over the side.'

Reluctantly, Lena tore her gaze from the whales. 'Mike –' but he wouldn't let her finish.

'If you'll excuse me, I have two headstocks to get in today and unless you've got any tips on how to do that more efficiently, back off.' He moved away from her to walk over to the other side of the skid. She watched his back in frustration as he leaned over the railing, yelling more orders to the guys below.

She'd been dismissed. Fully and utterly dismissed.

And she had no way to regain ground. Lena didn't have any tips to make him more efficient. She was hoping they'd be able to come up with something together. But there was no way she was going to beg for an alliance. That would be tantamount to admitting everything he thought about her was true.

You're going to prove him wrong if it kills you.

All she needed was some time to regroup.

That evening, Lena was dying to get to the gym to do just that. Maybe sweating out her anger would make room for ideas. She needed a plan or a miracle to make Mike cooperate. As the former was more accessible than the latter, she knew she'd better get on the treadmill and hope that something came to her. It was unfortunate that when she finally entered her sanctuary, it was contaminated.

Dan Hullog was on the treadmill.

She stopped just short of the door, the hairs on the back of her neck rising like porcupine spikes.

Perfect.

She toyed briefly with the idea of leaving and then his gaze flicked upwards and their eyes met in the mirror on the wall in front of him. His were cool and knowing. Dignity now dictated that she stayed.

She walked over to the bicep-building machine and perched on its worn vinyl seat. Dan went back to ignoring her. Despite her resolve to do the same, her eyes were continually drawn to his solid male back. Perhaps it was because he didn't look like a client in gym shorts and a sweat-soaked tank top.

Muscled shoulders. Generous biceps. Powerful calves.

She swallowed with difficulty as his masculinity hit her like a smack in the face.

Now more than ever, Bulldog seemed an apt name for him.

Suddenly the treadmill beeped and slowed. She tore her eyes away, pumping her weights unnaturally fast till a spasm in her right arm told her to stop. Lena released the weights as heat that wasn't from the work-out crept into her face. Had he seen her checking him out? She gave herself a mental slap.

You'd think after everything that had happened at university she'd have a mental circuit-breaker that got thrown whenever she was attracted to the wrong kind of man. Apparently not. She steeled herself. Crushing on the client was not an option.

She confined her gaze to the floor as she tried to slow her racing heart.

A pair of old white sneakers entered her field of vision.

Oh crap.

Was he going to say something about it? Her fingers trembled. She raised her eyes to his and took in their colour for the first time – a deep ocean blue.

'Carl told me he put you on the skid frame.'

Lena breathed again. 'Yes, that's right.' She nodded, searching his face and finding it unreadable. So now he knew she was an engineer. Maybe he had approached her to apologise for his behaviour on the wharf. Her heart buoyed. That would be it.

'You need to go faster.'

Maybe not.

'I beg your pardon?'

'You're too slow.'

Lena was confused. 'On the bicep curl?'

'No,' he said impatiently, flipping a white towel across one broad shoulder. 'On the skid frame.'

'Oh.' She couldn't believe it. He was telling her off again. She shouldn't have expected any differently. Although at this rate, she'd rather he'd caught her checking him out.

'You're ten per cent behind schedule.'

'I see.' Her mind did backflips as she tried to recall whether Carl had said anything about how much she was supposed to get done per day. Her mental database came up blank.

'At the pace you're going,' Bulldog continued, 'we'll be here till next Christmas.'

She bit her lip. Bloody Mike: she'd bet her left arm he'd known this. He'd be loving her humiliation now if he could see it.

'Did you hear what I said?' The Tone was blaring in his voice: Lena couldn't help but snap back at him.

'Of course I heard you, damn it. But I am off duty, you know. I didn't expect to be accosted in the gym.'

He seemed to be slightly taken aback by her tone because for a moment he said nothing. Immediately, she got the uncomfortable feeling that no one else had spoken to him like this before. Not even Carl. She silently cursed her temper. Wasn't the first rule of thumb, the client is always right?

Damn.

'Sorry,' she apologised gruffly. 'Bad day.'

'Would you rather I had called you in formally for a meeting?'

Lena couldn't seem to help herself. She shot him a look of disdain. 'You mean for a dressing-down.'

'Oh, you're dressed down enough already, don't you think?' While she was trying to figure out what he meant, his gaze roved over her fitted gym shirt, short bike pants and bare legs. Then it all became clear. Her relatively understated gym clothes had suddenly become indecent. Her chest tightened as his slow perusal seemed to go on forever.

This is not happening.

Not again. She had to stop it.

'Do you mind?' she finally breathed.

His lips twitched. 'What's good for the goose.'

Lena felt ice slide down her spine.

Crap.

He *had* seen her checking him out. In a second, she went from cold to hot as her skin pinkened like watermelon. She couldn't meet his eyes.

'If you think you're not cut out for this job, you should just ask Carl to send you home. No one will hold it against you.'

Lena stiffened. An unnatural rage seized her and she stood up too fast, hands on her hips, eyes on fire. 'Don't worry about the skid,' she bit out. 'I'll get it moving faster for you. Now if you'll excuse me.'

He stepped into her path and she was pulled up short. She turned her head to meet his eyes but had to look up, and so braced herself against being intimidated by his height.

'You know, you shouldn't walk around so scantily dressed. You're not in Kansas any more.'

Lena's anger pounded through her body. 'I don't think what I wear is any of your business.'

He backed off and his face closed. 'Just concerned for your safety.'

'You seem to have a thing for that, don't you?'

Was it her imagination or did he just flinch? She couldn't be sure of anything with Bulldog. He was about as decipherable as a menu in a Japanese restaurant. 'Well, for your information,' she added to soften the blow, if that's what it had been, 'usually there's no one in here at beer o'clock. So I feel safe to wear whatever I want without being harassed.'

'They'll find out.' He shrugged, pushing his dark damp hair off his forehead. 'It's only a matter of time.' On these cryptic words, he turned and walked out, leaving Lena simmering like a nearly done curry.

He was insufferable, domineering and completely arrogant. And yet, pleasing him was now her number one priority. A sure way to prove her worth was to meet Bulldog's impossible standards. She returned to the machine and began pumping iron again, barely even noticing the rise and fall of the bar as she made the decision to nail Carl to the floor first thing in the morning. She had to sort this progress thing out. Make sure she knew what slack she needed to make up. Bulldog was going to get his extra ten per cent if it killed her.

Just keep it professional.

She bit her lip, tasting blood and sweat. But she kept pumping: it helped her focus on her feelings. She was under no illusions. For some insane reason, she was attracted to the idiot. She had to pack that away and never look at it again. With a heavy breath, she released the weight, stood up and wiped the sweat from her brow. At least this time she knew what trap she could be walking into.

At university she'd had no idea. It was her third year. End of semester exams were three weeks away and she was struggling. No – understatement. She was desperate. One more failed unit and she was going to have to repeat a whole year. Her enjoyable lifestyle had led to too many missed tutorials, hungover presentations and very very late assignments. She was stressed and anxious. She'd tried talking to some of the other students in her class about it but it hadn't really helped. She had too much to catch up on. Her schedule was insane and she finally threw herself at the mercy of her teachers. They were mostly unsympathetic, showed her where to watch podcasts of their lectures, reminded her which textbook chapters to focus on, but in general just wished her luck. It was her Structural Analysis professor, Whiteman, who really helped.

He'd been easy enough to approach as he packed up his laptop and turned off the projector. He smiled at her in a way that made her feel at ease, comfortable. When she asked him stilted questions he was patient and kind.

'Don't worry, you'll get it,' he said. 'We'll make sure you get it.' He zipped up his computer bag and rested his forearms either side of the handle, an indulgent expression crinkling the corners of his eyes. 'Tell you what, why don't you stop by my office tomorrow evening? I've got some time. We can go over it again . . . slower.'

She'd been so grateful. So relieved. 'That's great, Professor Whiteman. I'd really appreciate that.'

'Not a problem. See you then. And please, call me Kevin.'

Chapter 4

When Lena arrived at work the following morning, someone had erected a flag beside the driveway leading up to the office dongas. She didn't know how Gavin's crew had managed to get a Barnes Inc flag on such short notice but it was definitely the genuine article. Of course, the pole wasn't a cylindrical section but a length of angle which had obviously been spare. The flag itself was bolted on instead of strung so it couldn't be raised up or down. It was a permanent flying fixture, no doubt a pro rather than a con. Lena shook her head as she walked past the monstrosity, certain it was twice the size of its counterpart at TCN.

Gavin pounced on her when she walked in, his expression hopeful, like a dog waiting to be thrown a bone.

'So,' he demanded, 'what do you think?'

'Of what?' She feigned ignorance.

'*The flag.*'

'What flag?' she countered. 'Didn't see it.'

'What!'

'Gavin, I'm kidding.' She rolled her eyes. 'You'd have to be half blind not to see that thing. It's huge.'

'You better bloody believe it.' He shook his pen at her and returned to his work station.

With a sigh, Lena dumped her backpack on her own desk and went to find Carl. He was on the phone as usual.

'Fuck that! Do something about it! I've got a fuckin' flagpole out my window that's straighter than your fuckin' pile caps.' He slammed down the receiver and glared at her. 'What do you want?'

'Sorry to interrupt you,' Lena began. 'I just wanted to know what my schedule is.'

'You *what*?'

Uh-oh. Hit a nerve.

He stood up and crooked his finger. 'Come with me.'

Lena swallowed, chewing on her lower lip as she followed him. He took her to meet Harry, a thin guy with greasy hair and a tendency towards acne. She'd seen him around but hadn't yet had a chance to talk to him. He was the quiet sort and kept to himself.

'Harry does all the scheduling here,' Carl informed her. 'Every fuckin' task has a date on it. Doesn't it, Harry?'

Harry nodded shyly and Lena was moved to give him a reassuring smile.

Carl continued, unaffected. 'How far behind are we on piling, Harry?'

'Five per cent.'

'Steel girder fabrication?'

'Three per cent.'

'Truss fabrication?'

'Five per cent.'

'NDT testing?'

'Ten per cent.'

'Headstock installation?'

'Ten per cent.'

'Okay, okay!' Lena held up her hands. 'I get the point, we're running late.'

'Running late!' Carl practically snarled. 'If we were a football team, we'd be the fuckin' Dockers.'

Out of the corner of her eye, Lena saw Harry quickly scoop a coaster that had the Fremantle team's emblem and colours on it into a drawer at his elbow.

She bit her lip to keep from laughing. Carl remained oblivious. His attention was still on her.

'Your schedule is asap. Your due date is yesterday and your pace should be the speed of light. Don't fuckin' get me to explain fuckin' common sense concepts. Just fuckin' hurry up.'

'Carl,' one of the secretaries called out from across the office, 'phone for you.'

'Fuck!'

Lena watched with relief as he disappeared back into his office. 'Close call,' she said to Harry.

'T-tell me about it,' he stuttered.

'Well, thanks.' She turned to go back to her desk, dragging her feet on the dirty vinyl floors.

What am I supposed to do now? Carl wasn't any help at all.

'If . . . if I may.' Harry tentatively solicited her attention.

At this point, Lena was desperate for help of any kind. She turned back without hesitation. 'You may.'

Harry opened a large black file and ran a nimble finger over several coloured dividers before finally resting on the tab of his choice. He flicked open this section and turned the file around so that it was facing her. 'This was the original plan for headstock installation.'

In front of her was a bar chart, with dates running along the horizontal axis and milestones running along the vertical axis.

Lena gasped. 'According to this we're supposed to be putting in four headstocks a day.'

'How many are you putting in now?' Harry enquired.

'Two.'

'I'd say you've got room for improvement.'

'But how?' Lena said, more to herself than to him. 'Mike's just . . . *Urgh!*'

Even if she did come up with a solution, it was highly unlikely that Mike would cooperate with it.

'I . . . I know.'

Lena's eyes flicked back to Harry. His hands fidgeted on the desktop like he wanted to say something but was too afraid to.

What does he know that I don't?

'Don't go quiet on me now, Harry,' she warned. 'Spit it out. I won't bite.'

His Adam's apple bobbled in his throat. 'Sometimes I hear the guys bitching about Mike after work.' He lowered his voice. 'They say he's got tunnel vision and doesn't listen to any of their suggestions. Maybe –'

A flash of light! 'It's all right, Harry. I know exactly what you're telling me. In fact,' Lena's grin stretched from ear to ear, 'I don't know why I didn't think of this before.'

She headed back to her own desk, eagerly rubbing her palms together. Mike was an obstacle and the only way to deal with obstacles was to walk around them. After all, what did she do when the shoes she owned didn't match her new outfit?

She bought new shoes, of course. True, she probably had too many pairs. But that wasn't the point. The point was, Mike was a pair of shoes that didn't go with anything. She had to stop trying to fit him into her plans, when she could do much better without him.

Excitement made her move faster. She rolled up a couple of drawings to take with her and went outside to catch the bus. Sharon was leaning against it, munching an apple and waiting for the hour to tick round. She threw the core in a nearby bin when she saw Lena and boarded the bus. 'I suppose you're coming with me.'

'You bet.'

Sharon started the engine as Lena got on. Once again, there was no one else making the trip out to the wharf. She took the seat directly behind Sharon and the redhead drove the bus out onto the dusty site track.

'So,' Sharon looked at her in the rear-view mirror, 'I've been hearing some interesting rumours about you.'

'You have?' Lena tried to look innocent as images of Bulldog's incredible calf muscles flashed across her mind. She veiled her eyes. Sharon couldn't possibly have heard about her run-in with Dan at the gym, could she? Nobody knew about that.

Not even Radar.

Of course, Sharon wasn't exactly out of the loop when it came to gossip. Being the bus driver put her front row and centre to most site dramas. The boys seemed to forget her presence when they rode up and back from the wharf. She heard many a private conversation without even trying, much to Radar's professional disgust.

'Geez, you look guilty.'

Sharon's voice jolted her back to the present and Lena felt her cheeks heat. 'Do I?' Her voice sounded squeaky even to her own ears. Lena cursed silently and tried to swallow her nerves, without much success.

'I wouldn't show that face around town,' Sharon continued. 'You'll have the boys talking more than they already are.'

Lena licked her lips. 'They can't really be that interested in the comings and goings of my boring life.'

'Are you kidding?' Sharon snorted. 'Next to Bulldog you're the most talked-about person on the project.'

Embarrassment forgotten, Lena started. 'I am?'

'Hell yes. But you must know that.'

'Well, not really,' Lena replied, just a little stunned. 'I mean, I know being female makes me a bit of a novelty, but surely they must have got over that by now.'

'Not so much. You've got quite a few admirers, you know.'

'Well, so do you.' Lena shrugged. 'The odds are in our favour, aren't they?'

'Uh-huh,' Sharon returned cryptically.

'So what's the rumour?' Lena prompted, fingers tapping on her knee. 'You can't lay it on the table and not tell me.'

Sharon grinned. 'Well, let's just say some of your admirers are pretty pissed off because you haven't shown an interest in any of them.'

'They're not my type.' *Yeah, only people who are strictly off limits make it into that category.*

'Well, the boys are beginning to figure that out.' Sharon was still talking. Lena looked up and caught the mischievous twinkle in her friend's eyes via the rear-view mirror and knew Sharon was holding something back.

'What are they saying?' Her voice was low with resignation.

'Well, they're not all saying it. But a group of guys in Tony's yard have a theory.'

'What sort of theory?'

'They're laying bets that you're batting for the other team.'

'I'm batting for the –?' And then realisation dawned. '*Really?*'

'Well, some of the guys seem to think that you and Ethel have a . . . *thing.*'

'Me and Ethel?' Lena gasped.

'You do know she's gay, right?'

Lena's mouth fell open. 'No way.' She thought back over the past week and groaned. 'It's the tip-offs, isn't it? They think we're an item because she keeps being nice to me.'

'Well, let's face it,' Sharon said, 'Ethel isn't nice to anyone. I've got to admit that even I've been a little suspicious.'

'You have *not*,' Lena protested.

'Okay,' Sharon smiled. 'Maybe I haven't. But seriously, if not Ethel, there's gotta be somebody you've got your eye on, what with the smorgasbord of choices and all.'

To Lena's great annoyance, Bulldog's enigmatic countenance once more floated before her eyes and she said just a little too thickly, 'Nup, no one.'

'Okay, dish.'

'Dish what?'

'Lena,' Sharon retorted, with the patience of one who had the wisdom of the world sitting on her shoulders. 'I saw that guilty look earlier and now it's back. You can't pull the wool over my eyes forever.'

'What wool?' Lena prevaricated. 'There's no wool.'

All the same she kept her eyes downcast. Truth be told, she was an expert on wool. In university she'd practically had her own flock of sheep. It was shameful, really.

After a few seconds, Sharon turned her attention back to the mountains of iron ore stacked around them and Lena thought with relief that she wasn't going to question her further. She was wrong.

'What about Gavin?' Sharon's tone was just a little too casual.

'Gavin?' Lena screwed up her nose.

'What?' Sharon protested, her eyes flicking to Lena's again. 'He's good-looking, sweet, intelligent and –'

'He's Gavin.'

'He's a great engineer. All the guys really admire him and he's –'

'About as mature as a ten-year-old,' Lena finished for her. 'Have you seen the flag he's had erected?'

'Yeah,' Sharon chuckled softly. 'I think it's kinda cute.'

'Kinda cute?' Lena covered her mouth as realisation struck her. '*You* like him.'

'I do not.'

'You do too.'

Sharon blushed. 'Okay, you got me.'

Lena sat up eagerly, a silly grin stretching across her face. 'Are you going to ask him out?'

Sharon choked. 'And have the whole of camp follow our romance like *The Bold and the Beautiful*? I don't think so.'

Lena laughed. 'Well then, stop bothering me about my love-life.'

'Hey.' Sharon lifted her hands briefly before returning them to the wheel. 'What's between you and Ethel is none of my business.'

Lena whacked her on the back of the head with her rolled-up drawings.

The bus rounded the corner and the TCN site offices came into view. Lena saw Bulldog standing outside talking on his mobile and her nerve endings tightened. She wondered who he was talking to. Was it that girlfriend Radar had alluded to? Certainly a private conversation as he was taking it outside.

It's none of your business. Stop thinking about him that way.

She tore her gaze from Bulldog and focused instead on the buildings behind him. That's when she noticed someone had erected two smaller flags at each corner of the roof of one of the TCN dongas.

Oh brother! How old are they? Five? There's going to be trouble in Wickham tonight.

The bus rolled out onto the wharf and the salty sea air hit her as the land fell away. Lena breathed deep, her excitement building with the inflation of her lungs. Two minutes later, Sharon pulled up right beside the skid and waved good luck.

Climbing the ladder to the deck of the skid, Lena took stock of her surroundings. It was a great morning. The sun was out but not full force. A gentle breeze tickled her neck and the sound of languid waves soothed her tension. If there was a pro to working on site, that was it.

The one and only.

She hadn't expected Mike to greet her, and he didn't, turning his back instead and looking out beyond the handrail while the men worked below. This time, however, there were no whales. No distractions. No excuses.

'Mike,' Lena said firmly. 'We need to talk.'

Predictably, he grunted.

'I'm serious,' Lena said. 'I had a chat with Dan Hullog the other day –'

That got his attention. 'You saw Bulldog without me?' he demanded, finally looking at her.

Okay, maybe not perfect but at least he's talking to me. 'It wasn't a meeting,' Lena told him. 'We spoke about the head-stocks in the gym.'

'In the gym?' Mike's voice clearly denoted his contempt. 'That'd be right, wouldn't it?'

'The gym?' A head popped up over the side. It was the rat-faced little man Lena had spoken to the last time she was there. She'd found out later from Radar his nickname was Fieldmouse.

'What's that?' He was up and over the handrailing in a flash, winding a rope around his arm as he came. 'You go to the gym?'

'Sometimes,' Lena answered distractedly.

'When?'

'Does it matter?' she returned in exasperation. She turned back to Mike. 'The fact is, Mike, we're running ten per cent behind and we need to pick up the pace a bit.'

'Like that's news,' Mike smirked.

Lena squared her shoulders and tried to infuse authority into her voice. 'Mike, I didn't come out here to argue with you. I came to warn you.'

'Really.'

'If you don't cooperate with me, I'll fix this without you.' She held her breath.

Mike threw back his head and laughed. Lena just stood there watching him. She was, in fact, glad to have confirmation that he was abandoning her. She would never be able to prove her ability with Mike constantly acting as a roadblock.

When he finished laughing and she remained silent, he left her and climbed down the ladder to stand on the walkway, sea side of the skid.

Good riddance.

Fieldmouse finished winding up his rope and looked at her with some sympathy.

'Don't worry.' Lena smiled. 'I've got a plan.'

He grinned back. 'Mike is old school, Madame E. He doesn't like taking orders from females.'

'And I don't like putting up with rude men,' she retorted. 'Tell me how things have been going out here.'

'Slow.' Fieldmouse nodded.

'How long does it take you to get the headstock in?'

'Five hours.'

'That is slow.' Lena rubbed her chin. 'What part of the installation takes the longest?'

'Moving,' Fieldmouse told her without hesitation.

'Moving? You mean skidding.'

'Sort of.' Fieldmouse squinted at the sky as he considered the question. 'It's the access platform that takes the longest to move.'

'You mean the access platform under the girders,' Lena said.

'That's the one.'

Lena couldn't see this platform because it was under the jetty. But she knew it was clamped to the main girders via some hanging struts. The men needed it to stand on when they welded the extension beams, called headstocks, to the main jetty girders. Except for this, there was nothing under the deck but piles and a fifteen-metre drop to the ocean.

'Okay, start at the beginning,' Lena said. 'Let's go through the current method of installing headstocks.'

'First we wait for the truck to bring one from the yard,' Fieldmouse explained. 'The truck parks next to the skid and

Radar and I work the crane. We pick the headstock off the back of the truck, lift it over the skid and lower it into position.'

'Then the boys on the access platform weld it in place,' Lena finished for him.

'Yup. That takes an hour, give or take.'

An hour? *That's* it? Out loud she said, 'At which point you're ready to move on to the next position. The skid is winched to the next bent. How do you move the access platform?'

Fieldmouse grimaced. 'We have to unclamp it and lift it onto the deck of the skid with the crane. It stays on the skid during the move. Then we have to reinstall it with the crane at the next bent. That takes time 'cause it's fiddly.'

Irritating and dangerous as well, Lena was prepared to bet. Well, that was the crux of it. How could she speed up moving the access platform, apart from telling the boys to get their skates on – which would just cause unnecessary stress and workplace accidents?

'Listen, Fieldmouse,' Lena said, 'can you pass a message to the rest of the skid boys?'

'Sure,' he agreed.

'Tell them,' she said, 'that I want to see all of them today.'

'All together?' Fieldmouse looked a little dubious.

'One at a time,' she corrected him. 'Just tell them that sometime today when they're not so busy they have to come see me in my office and if Mike chucks a sad about it, just tell him it's my instructions.'

Lena walked over to the railing and looked down at the man in question, wondering whether she should tell him herself. But he was shouting an order at the men on the access platform and she figured he'd probably tell her to get lost anyway.

She turned back to Fieldmouse. 'While he's distracted, do you mind talking to me for a little longer? I'd really like to hear your opinion on our current use of the winch for moving the skid.'

'No worries,' Fieldmouse replied, clearly chuffed even to be asked. He proceeded to tell her this and a whole host of other things. Lena furiously scribbled notes until she saw Sharon approaching with the bus from the land. She looked at her watch. She'd been on the skid a whole hour and Sharon was doing her next run. As the bus could only travel in one direction, Lena knew it meant she'd have to go to the end of the jetty before she could go back to the office. She didn't really mind. They'd driven three more piles since her last visit, which would be interesting to see. So she waved Sharon down.

As they approached the end of the wharf, Sharon, Lena and the rest of the guys on the bus noticed that there was some sort of commotion going on near the portable loos. A bit of a crowd was gathering around one of the large blue plastic demountables, which had its door flung wide. Due to the number of men pointing and jeering, Lena couldn't quite see what was going on inside it. Sharon parked the bus in its usual bay and they all got out and pushed to the front of the crowd.

Lena could not believe her eyes.

There was Leg, kneeling on the floor of the toilet cubicle, his sleeves rolled up and his right arm elbow-deep in the bowl. His head wasn't too far behind either.

Lena choked back a gag. 'Leg, what the hell are you doing?'

But he didn't hear her.

Sharon nudged one of the amused spectators next to them. 'What's going on?'

'He dropped his wedding ring in the dunny.'

'Oh no,' Lena exclaimed. She knew that Leg wore his wedding ring around his neck on a piece of black string. It was quite beautiful: two toned, with white- and yellow-gold segments. He had his wife's name engraved on the inside of it. He'd told Lena that his hands got so grubby during the day, he was reluctant to wear it in the traditional spot, which she thought was a fair enough call.

'How on earth did he drop it?' Lena wondered out loud.

The man beside her sniggered. 'The string came undone while he was working but he didn't know. Anyway, so he goes into the loo, pulls out his shirt and the ring flicks out, straight into the dunny.'

'Leg, don't.' Lena stepped forwards, covering her nose with her hand. 'Your wife will forgive you.'

This time he heard her, looked up and grinned. 'Don't worry, Madame E, I've put my hands in worse.'

As he finished speaking, Gavin jumped out of the office donga a few metres away with a pair of large pink rubber gloves. He came running towards the group but was seconds too late.

'Found it!' Leg cried out and withdrew his large rather brown-looking hand from the bowl.

Everyone, Lena included, took a giant step back as he held up his prize. You could barely make it out – it looked like he was holding up a piece of mud.

'Shit, Leg!' Gavin swore, putting one hand over his nose.

A laugh rippled through the crowd at Gavin's unfortunate pun. He waved the gloves at his unrepentant subordinate. 'You could have waited.'

Leg lowered his hand and turned passionately towards him. 'And disrespect my wife? Nothing on earth would allow me to leave this ring in there for a second longer than necessary.'

While his actions inspired horror, Lena couldn't help but sigh over the sentiments behind them. Would she ever meet a man who would do anything for her? *Anything*. It seemed like an impossible dream.

She bent her head towards Sharon's and said softly, 'How romantic.'

Unaware that she'd spoken loud enough to be heard by anyone else, she was surprised when Gavin's gaze snapped from Leg to her. 'The guy just shoved his hand in a pile of shit and you reckon it's romantic?'

'Well, in a way . . .'

'Women,' the man beside her groaned. 'No wonder we can never please them.'

'I don't know.' Gavin jokingly rolled up his sleeve and made as if to join Leg by the violated toilet. 'Whatever it takes.'

A jovial cheer rose from the men. 'Go, Gav, go! Go, Gav, go!'

Lena grabbed his arm and pulled him back. 'Don't you dare!'

He looked back at her with a twinkle in his eye and sighed, 'You say that now.'

She let go of his arm immediately and shoved him. 'You deserve a fistful of shit.'

There were guffaws and knee-slapping. 'Whoa ho ho! Kitty's got claws.'

Gavin laughed but turned back to his men. 'Okay, guys, show's over, back to work!'

Reluctantly, they dispersed.

Lena sighed with relief and turned around to find Sharon studying her.

'What?' she demanded.

Sharon's eyes narrowed slightly. 'He was flirting with you.'

Lena frowned. It seemed to her that Gavin was being more of an idiot than anything else. She placed a reassuring hand on Sharon's shoulder. 'No he wasn't. He was just joking around. Gavin being Gavin.'

'Are you sure?'

'Of course.'

'I don't know.'

'Come on: it was toilet humour, literally.' Lena removed her hand. 'Besides you know I have no interest in him. Like I said, maturity of a ten-year-old.'

Sharon's clouded countenance lifted slightly. 'Hey,' she protested, 'some girls like a boyish charm.'

Fifteen minutes later the bus was repacked with men wanting to return to land, including Leg, who was being sent home to shower. No one sat next to him.

When they arrived back at the land office, Lena headed for her desk and waited for the instructions she'd left on the skid to be carried out.

Radar was the first to respond and he seemed pleased as punch to do it. She was beginning to notice that she wasn't the only one Mike bullied. His men were dying for an opportunity to overstep his power. They wanted their say as much as she did.

Radar and Lena spoke for a good hour. Some of it was whining but the rest was quite useful. She took notes, lots of notes. When another skid boy came along to see her, she did the same thing with him. By the end of the day she had a notebook full of ideas and suggestions, some of which were her own after examination of the facts. Her confidence was building: for the first time she'd fixed a problem by herself. No boss to guide her; no Kevin to bail her out. This one was a hundred per cent Lena Todd, and boy did it feel good.

The following day was Sunday – the big day off. After two weeks of solid slogging most of the staff of Barnes Inc were going to get the rest they'd all been craving. Lena cursed the fact that she wasn't one of them. She and her fishing party of twelve were leaving at the crack of dawn instead.

What was I thinking?

She should have known how exhausted she'd be. But no, she had to be out there proving that there was more to life than work.

The closest she'd ever come to fishing in the past was going out for dinner on Fremantle Esplanade and watching the hard-cores sitting on the edge of a five-metre-long jetty with a bucket and rod. She'd never envied them. Never thought, *Geez, what fun; wish I could do that someday.*

But there she was in Wickham, living in a box, constantly covered in red dust, treated like a sex object and scorned by her subordinates.

What's a slimy fish in the grand scheme of things? If anything, it's a step up.

Of course, the initial fishing trip plan she'd conjured up with Radar, Leg and Sharon had kind of escalated. The trouble started when she'd asked Carl for a ute.

'What the fuck?' He looked at her incredulously. 'You think I'm running a free shuttle service?'

His loud protest brought a couple of other interested faces into his office. Gavin's was one of them. 'What's this I hear about a fishing trip?'

'Now look what you've done!' Carl pointed an accusing finger at her. 'Next you'll be wanting a fuckin' barbecue lunch to take with you.'

'Hey, you know what?' Lena's face lit up. 'I never thought of that.'

She felt Gavin's hand on her shoulder. 'I wouldn't,' he warned as Carl's expression progressively blackened.

Lena swallowed. 'Maybe not.'

'Besides,' Gavin added, 'we can have fish for lunch.'

'Yeah,' said a draftsman who had come in behind him.

'We should ask Harry too,' said Lena. 'He's so quiet, he'd never say so, but I know he'd love to come.'

'Fuck!' Carl exclaimed, making her start and look quickly at him. 'Whose fuckin' office is this?'

Lena winced. 'Sorry, Carl, I –'

'Fuck it.' He waved a hand in dismissal. 'Just take the bus. Looks like you're going to need it.'

Her spirits lifted. 'Did you want to come too?'

Carl's eyes narrowed on her. 'Are you deliberately trying to piss me off?'

'No, I –'

'Bulldog's gone up a fuckin' tree. I'll be working tomorrow, thank you very fuckin' much. Now piss off, the lot of you, and give a man some fuckin' peace.'

They pissed off.

So in the end there were about twelve of them going, including Harry, who was indeed very pleased to be invited. Lena had left it up to the experts to choose their destination and in the end one of the cluey draftsmen had nominated Cleaverville. It was about half an hour's drive from camp and supposedly a prime fishing spot.

'Geez, there are so many of us,' Lena told Sharon. 'Do you think there'll be enough fish in the water?'

'Where we're going, for sure,' Gavin said on his way past them to board the bus.

Apparently, Gavin was a bit of a fishing pro. Or so he informed everyone on the drive to the coast, boasting about his past conquests. Sharon listened raptly but Lena only gave him half an ear. She couldn't have cared less how many kilos his last catch had weighed but she mumbled exclamations here and there for Sharon's benefit.

'You must really love fishing,' Lena said at last, as he wound up another story.

'Why do you think I took this job,' he smiled, 'if not for the perks?'

'The perks?' she repeated faintly. '*Right.*'

Lena waited until he turned away. 'Are you sure about this guy?'

'Ssssh,' Sharon hissed. Her face had turned pink.

Lena sighed.

Gavin hadn't heard: she'd made sure her voice was low enough. It was so weird, seeing assertive Sharon all quiet and bashful. Frankly, Lena was beginning to find it just a little frustrating. She was glad when the bus ride was finally over.

Cleaverville was beautiful.

Lena hadn't been prepared to be impressed. But as they

approached the beach, the red sand got lighter and browner and much more rocky. The water's edge was like an embankment of hazelnut praline riddled with dark chocolate chips. The rocks varied in size from loaf of bread to mini Milky Bar. Further out in the crystal-clear water, the sharp edges became polished and smooth.

A few metres beyond the point where gentle waves could lap at her feet, short water trees known as mangroves clumped in groups around the coastline. It was strange that the land was so infertile and yet the water was flourishing with plants. For a while she just stood there transfixed, taking in the contrast with awe.

Others were putting their gear down behind her, unpacking their bait and preparing their fishing rods. Sharon and Lena had no gear and were hoping to borrow something from Gavin or Leg.

Lena turned around and saw Leg with a pair of snorkels.

'I hope you've taken your wedding ring off,' she teased him. 'You wouldn't want to lose it again.'

He grinned at her but said nothing. As he disappeared down the beach, Lena turned to Sharon and whispered, 'Now's your chance.'

'Now's my chance to what?'

'Make your move on Gavin.'

'*Lena.*'

'Ask him if we can borrow a fishing rod or something.' She prodded her friend from behind. 'Go on.'

Sharon licked her lips, squared her shoulders and walked over to where Gavin had parked himself on a rock, his gear scattered by his feet.

'Er . . . Hey, Gavin.'

'Hi, Sharon.'

'So . . . nice day for it.'

'Yeah.'

'Um.'

'What can I do for you?'

'Er.'

Oh, for crying out loud.

Lena walked over.

'Have you got a rod we can borrow?'

Gavin looked up and grinned. 'Not a rod. But I've got a couple of hand reels I can spare.' He reached into his bag and withdrew two red plastic reels with fishing line wound around them.

'Thanks,' Lena said, turning hers over. She figured out how to use it when she saw the little hook tied to the end of the line.

'Here.' He took it back. 'I'll help you bait it.'

He opened his bag again and Sharon and Lena watched as he withdrew a large plastic container.

'Worms?' Lena made a face.

He chuckled. 'No, shrimp.' He opened the box and Lena caught the gentle waft of freshly chopped bait.

Pong. She held her breath as he picked up a little shrimp and squished it onto the end of her hook.

'Why don't you do Sharon's too?' she suggested as he handed it back to her. 'I'm going to head into the water.'

'You have to wade out – at least to your knees,' Gavin said. 'Then throw out your line.'

She nodded, itching to get off the land, literally. The sand-flies were buzzing round her legs, nipping at her calves. She wished for the third time she had some repellent.

Lena glanced over her shoulder at Sharon, who was shyly handing Gavin her reel. She hoped she stayed with him a little longer. They did look good together.

Helping Sharon find happiness was a distraction she was willing to indulge. In fact, Sharon deserved it. The bus driver was the one person who had made camp life bearable. If Lena could return the favour in any way, she would. Satisfied that she had done the right thing leaving the two of them alone,

Lena bit the bullet and cast her line. After all, if she was there, she might as well make a go of it.

However, half an hour and no luck later, it was getting more and more difficult to persuade herself she was having a good time. She could feel the sun burning the back of her neck and knew she was going to be sore that night.

Is fishing supposed to be this hot and boring?

'I've caught something! I've caught something!' Sharon called out and Lena turned to watch triumphantly as Gavin immediately rushed to Sharon's side. At least the day wasn't a total waste. She watched them laugh as they both tried to grab the writhing fish thrashing about on the end of Sharon's line.

Suddenly, Lena felt a slight pull on her own line. It didn't feel like a rock this time, so her excitement rose a little. Perhaps all that waiting had just cashed in. She eagerly started to wind up her reel. And then she shrieked.

'What's going on?' She heard splashing in the water as Sharon and Gavin hurried over to her.

Lena pointed into the water at the white jellyfish floating at the end of her line. Its translucent body contracted and expanded in the gentle waves. She shuddered, unable to take her eyes off it in case it moved any closer.

Gavin chuckled. 'For a second I thought you'd seen a sea snake.'

Lena's gaze snapped to him. 'What?!'

He waded over and slung a friendly arm across her shoulders. 'Don't worry,' he said softly. 'I'll protect you.'

'Yeah right.' She shrugged off his arm and turned to Sharon. 'I don't really feel like fishing any more. I'm going back in.'

As she turned, she heard Sharon's voice behind her. 'You'll get eaten by sandflies.'

Lena glanced back at Gavin. 'Do you have a towel I can sit on or wrap around my legs?'

He reddened slightly, lifting a hand up over his head and scratching behind his ear. 'Not a towel exactly.'

'What do you mean?'

'You'll see. Go look in my backpack.'

Sharon and Gavin followed her up the shore. Lena opened Gavin's bag and withdrew a large folded piece of material that felt like a cotton tablecloth until she pulled it out into the sunshine. She gasped.

'Gavin, this is a TCN flag.'

'Yeah.'

'What do you mean, yeah?' Lena replied in exasperation. '*Gavin*, how could you?'

'I didn't,' he said hastily. 'My boys did it last night and gave it to me as a present this morning.'

'And you shoved it in with your fishing gear?'

'I was on my way to the bus when they gave it to me.'

Lena shook her head. 'Carl is going to kill you.'

'Not if he doesn't find out.' Gavin squared his chin.

'We won't tell him.' Sharon looked at Lena pointedly.

'Oh fine,' Lena grumbled. 'But what am I going to use to protect my legs?'

Gavin shrugged apologetically. 'I haven't got a towel: it's that or nothing.'

After re-baiting their hooks, he and Sharon went back into the water. Lena was left standing there in indecision. It went against the grain, but after fifteen minutes she was desperate. She took the flag, wrapped it round her legs and sat on a rock. Unfortunately, it didn't help much. The sandflies nipped at her ankles and picnicked on her feet. In the end, she decided to go for a walk. Maybe if she kept moving they would stop treating her like free food.

She shaded her eyes and studied the others. By the looks of it, Gavin had caught something big. The top of his rod was starting to curve and Sharon was racing over to aid him. Other members of the group were scattered along the beach. They were all pretty much absorbed in what they were doing. Nobody would miss her. Wearing the flag like a sarong over her shorts, she headed down the beach.

By now, her legs were itching something crazy and sweat was running down her back, making her feel sticky and short-tempered.

Bloody fishing. Never again.

Lena meandered over the rocks, cutting her feet and cursing some more. Before long she had put a lot of ground between herself and the rest of the party but still found no relief from the sun or the flies. Her gaze drifted over the water beside her. It was very shallow there: clear and sparkling in the sunshine.

What would I do for a soak?

Lena cast her gaze down the coast. The others were now dots in the distance.

Who would notice, or even care, if she stripped down to her underwear and had a dip under the cover of these mangroves? She could use the flag to dry off. She knew it was risky. But at that point she would have shed her own skin to get away from the itchiness and the heat.

Darting one more look around her to make sure it was safe, she slipped off her shorts and T-shirt. Her underwear wasn't actually too bad: she owned a bikini that was more revealing. It was the lace that was the problem. If anyone saw her, they would know straight away she wasn't wearing bathers. She laid her clothes on a rock and hurried into the water with the flag. Lena hung this on one of the mangrove branches for easy access. Then, with blissful slowness, she submerged her body to the neck, so that she was sitting on the polished stone bed.

It was ecstasy.

Her skin sizzled as it cooled. The water lapped over it like balm – even the itches subsided. She dunked her head under briefly, wet her hair and immediately felt energised. For a long time, she just sat there, the tension in her muscles easing as the water enveloped her.

She sighed. *Peace.*

At least half an hour went by before she contemplated going back to the others, though the last thing she wanted was for them to start looking for her. Lena stood up and grabbed the flag, wrapped it around her body and knotted it above her breasts. Picking up the hem to keep it above the water, she started to head back to the shore for her clothes.

'Hold it there, Lena.'

She froze. Couldn't be.

She squeezed her eyes shut, sending up a silent prayer. *God, please don't let it be.* The eerie quiet behind her seemed to indicate that her prayers had been answered.

Unhurriedly, she turned around.

The scene unfolded in slow motion as a man emerged from the cover of the mangroves. He was wearing snorkels but the deep velvet voice was enough to identify him, not to mention the expanse of familiar male torso glistening sinfully in the sun.

Bulldog pushed the goggles off his face and she sucked in a haggard breath as his piercing blue eyes were revealed. He raised his eyebrows, stripping away the last vestiges of her courage.

'I believe that flag is mine.'

Chapter 5

'What are you doing here?' Lena hissed, convulsively clasping the knot between her breasts.

'Snorkelling.' Lena looked in the opposite direction to the Barnes Inc party and saw a TCN ute parked a couple of hundred metres back from the shore.

'That would be right, wouldn't it?' she muttered.

The coincidence was so unlucky, you'd think he'd planned it.

Lena looked up to see if God was interested in helping her. But the deep voice that boomed back did not come from heaven.

'So are you going to tell me why you're wearing my flag or am I going to have to ask?'

Lena groaned inwardly and returned his gaze. Nerves tightened her throat. *Damn Gavin and his bloody adolescent behaviour.* She didn't want to get him in trouble but she couldn't stall Bulldog forever.

'Well?' he prompted her again.

'I needed a towel and it was handy.'

His laugh was a short bark. 'You're really something else, you know that?' He shook his head. 'You're wearing stolen property. Its theft will cause a great deal of outrage and dissension among my men when they discover it.'

'I'm sorry.'

'Don't give me that,' he retorted. 'You'll be lucky if I don't get you fired for this.'

As white-hot panic sliced through her brain, she lost her vision for a split second.

Not yet. Please not yet.

She hoped her voice didn't sound too desperate when she blurted, 'Look, I realise how it looks, but I didn't steal your flag.'

'Then who did?'

'I . . . I don't know,' she ended lamely.

'You expect me to believe that?'

'It's the truth,' she insisted. Technically, it was. She didn't know exactly which of Gavin's men had stolen the flag, did she?

'Who are you protecting?' He waded closer, droplets of sun-kissed water leaving trails as they scattered down his chest. Lena shivered despite the heat.

'No one.'

'Who are you here with?' He scanned the area around them as though expecting to see someone else hiding in the mangroves.

'No one,' she insisted again and then foolishly decided to rephrase her answer. 'Well, actually I'm here with a group of people from Barnes Inc. We're on a fishing trip.'

'*Right.*' His voice flayed her with its sarcasm. He pushed his thick wet hair off his forehead. Water glittered as it slid down the side of his neck. Awareness tickled her spine. *Why is it that the good-looking ones are always such jerks?* Lena passed a tongue over her dry lips. 'Honestly, my friends are here. They're further up the beach. I just went for a walk.'

'And a quick swim.' His expression was unreadable. Was he mocking her again?

Lena watched him silently for a moment, trying not to become mesmerised by the gentle rise and fall of his chest. Since when had breathing become such a turn-on? She had never felt a pull this earthy or this irresistible before. Not even with Kevin. She shook off the dangerous thought and lifted her chin. 'Well, yeah. I needed a swim. It was hot and I didn't have any repellent. The sandflies were eating me alive. I had to –' She broke off.

Why the hell am I explaining myself to him? 'Look,' she changed tack. 'I'm not trying to cause trouble –'

'Then you'll need to return that flag to my offices immediately,' he interrupted, switching straight into lecture mode. 'If you're lucky, its quick return might not taunt the men into a counteraction which I refuse to be held responsible for. The sheer audacity of Barnes Inc personnel in this instance boggles me. I cannot believe . . .'

Lena didn't really hear the rest. It was no doubt a tirade of abuse against her company, her coworkers and her own lack of professionalism. And yes, maybe in this instance she was slightly . . . a little –

Okay, she was being *very* unprofessional, but he was going to have her fired anyway so why listen to a lecture about it? She'd definitely had enough of those. Enough lectures that week from Carl, enough abuse from Mike and certainly enough of her personal life being bandied about like it was the score for last month's Derby.

She'd had it, and then some.

'You want this flag back?' she demanded, striding towards him, anger arcing through her body. 'Fine. I'll give you your damn flag back. Is this *immediate* enough for you?'

She whipped the flag off her body and threw it at him. He dropped his snorkel in the water as he lifted both hands to catch it. She didn't stop to watch him do so. Instead, she turned around and walked with as much dignity as a girl in sopping wet underwear could back to shore, praying to God her bum wasn't too visible through the clingy fabric.

In any event, she had managed to shut him up. Lena heard nothing but the sound of birds and soft waves. Her feet hit dry rocks and she made her way swiftly up the bank. Bending over, Lena picked up her T-shirt and put it on, and then her shorts. She lifted her wet hair off her neck and twisted it into a knot. He was so quiet, she wasn't even certain he was still there.

Finally, she spun around, her heart fluttering like a deck of cards in a casino. This wasn't a hand she was used to dealing.

He was still there all right. Standing as though frozen, the water lapping gently at his kneecaps, the flag still in the position in which he had caught it. The only thing about him that gave any sign of life was his eyes. Big blue sizzling orbs that fried her senses, making her feel like she was still naked despite now being fully dressed. Lena had meant to lift her chin, but it kind of wavered and stopped halfway to Confident. 'Happy?' she asked.

A muscle worked in his jaw as he rolled the flag up and looped it round his neck. He picked up his snorkels with an expression that was more hostile than appeased. Then, without a single word, he turned and disappeared into the mangroves.

Lena sucked in a huge breath of air, panting as her heart attempted to slow down.

Thank goodness.

With wobbly steps, she took off down the bank, hobbling over the stones as fast as she could.

'You look like you've seen another jellyfish,' Sharon said, laughing as she rejoined them. 'Or maybe it was a sea snake this time.'

'Worse,' Lena choked, out of breath. 'Bulldog's up the beach. He saw me with the flag.'

Gavin dropped his fishing rod. 'Aw, shit.'

'That's not the half of it.' Lena put a hand to her forehead. 'I'll be lucky if I have a job in the morning. He was talking about getting me fired.'

Now that the confrontation was over, the gravity of her situation was beginning to sink in. She was going to lose her job. She had come to the Pilbara and failed. It was all over already.

Some of her panic must have showed in her face because Gavin came over and briefly hugged her non-responsive body. 'Nah – I'll come forward and take the fall, if it comes to that.' He shook his head. 'Like I would let you take the blame for this.'

'Where's the flag now?' Sharon asked.

Even though her career was in the toilet and she had more important things to dwell on, a blush still managed to infuse Lena's cheeks. 'I gave it back.'

Sharon eyed her suspiciously. 'I see.'

Lena deliberately looked away. In her haste to avoid her friend's gaze, she noticed the others congregating back from the shore around a couple of portable barbecues. Gavin left her side to pick up his bucket and rod. 'Come on,' he said briskly. 'There's nothing we can do about it now. We might as well join the others.'

So they made their way over to the barbecues where all up there were thirteen fish to cook. Lunch was absolutely delicious. It was unfortunate that Lena was so pre-occupied with what Bulldog might do to her the next day.

That evening at dinner, before Radar and Leg arrived, Sharon demanded to be told exactly what had happened to Lena on her walk up the Cleaverville coastline. She hadn't believed for a second that Lena had told them the full story on the beach.

'For starters,' Sharon pointed out, 'you were all wet when you got back.' Her eyes narrowed. 'Did you go skinny-dipping?'

'*No*.' Lena's fork clattered to her plate.

'Then what?'

With a groan of resignation, Lena confessed everything and Sharon whistled low and soft. 'What colour underwear?'

'That's your first question?' Lena's jaw dropped in disbelief.

'Come on.' Sharon wiggled in her chair. 'Just tell me what colour?'

'Red.'

She let out a whoop and hit Lena on the shoulder. 'You naughty girl.'

'Keep your voice down.' Lena glanced around as several heads bobbed up.

Sharon giggled. 'I'm sorry but, honey, what were you thinking?'

'Clearly, I wasn't,' Lena retorted grouchily, knowing that she wasn't going to sleep very well that night.

And she didn't – waking every couple of hours with bad dreams involving being fired in her underwear. Red underwear. Maybe it wasn't her lucky colour any more. In any event she wasn't in the least bit refreshed the next morning. Sunday's holiday spirit was by now a distant memory. As soon as she walked into the site office at six am she felt the stress of the day ahead settle firmly on her shoulders.

Today is the day I will be fired.

But seven am came and went. Eight am followed uneventfully.

Carl did not storm into her cubicle demanding why she had stolen the TCN flag. He was too busy welcoming the new deck engineer, called Lance. Apparently, the two were old friends and the second he arrived Carl took him off to show him the wharf.

Sharon had met Lance on his way in and was singularly unimpressed. 'He's fishy,' she reported to Lena at the first opportunity.

'As in suspicious?'

'No.' She shook her head. 'As in fishy. The first thing he asked me when I picked him up from the airport this morning was, "So where do you dip your rod for a bite?"'

Lena grinned. 'What did you say?'

Sharon shrugged. 'I told him the truth. I don't. At which point I think I sank very low in his estimation.'

Lena absorbed the information, but didn't spend too much time worrying about it. After all, she wasn't going to have much to do with Lance. Gavin would have to interact with him more because the deck went on top of his piles.

In any case, the possibility she might not have this job for much longer and the question of how she was going to get a new one were more pressing concerns. Which engineering firm would ignore the black marks Bulldog was going to apply to her name?

Lena Todd.

Structural Engineer.

Notorious stealer of client flags.

Inappropriate displayer of red underwear.

Incredibly slow installer of headstocks.

By the time nine am came around, Lena was so highly strung that she jumped a mile when Gavin stuck his head over her computer and said, 'Any word about the flag?'

Lena pressed a hand to her chest. 'You scared me.'

'Sorry I –'

He broke off as they both heard heavy footsteps behind him.

'Which one of you pissed the shit through Bulldog?' Carl demanded.

Gavin and Lena looked at each other. This was it.

Gavin spoke first. 'Er . . . Why do you ask, Carl?'

'Bloody dickhead's suddenly full of orders, crapping on like an arsehole after fuckin' chilli con carne.'

Lena's eyes smarted at this analogy and her speechless state continued. Fortunately, Gavin wasn't so incapacitated. 'What's it about this time?'

'Well, for starters he's cracking down on fuckin' PPE. Reckons we're too complacent.' Carl grunted indignantly. 'Like fuck.'

Gavin and Lena looked at each other again. PPE was Protective Personnel Equipment. It was the stuff they were supposed to wear on site – hard hats, reflector vests, steel-capped boots and safety glasses. It had nothing to do with Bulldog's flag. Could it be that he wasn't going to raise it? No pun intended.

'Okay,' Carl demanded. 'What have you two fucked up?'

'Nothing,' Lena started.

Carl wagged his finger at her. 'Don't you fuck with me, Todd. You're not hiding some fuckin' workplace accident, are you?' He looked at Gavin. 'Have you been safe?'

'Safe as houses, Carl,' Gavin told him cheerfully and Lena was beginning to think his nerves were made of steel.

'That's what I fuckin' thought.' Carl nodded with renewed contempt for his interfering client. 'Anyway, from now on there'll be fuckin' checks before you're allowed on the wharf. Make sure you've got your fuckin' gear on.'

Before Lena could breathe a sigh of relief at this seemingly harmless order, Carl added something else for good measure. 'Oh and he wants us to change our fuckin' suncream to this new stuff. It's got insect repellent in it. The shit arrives next week. You'll each be getting a bottle.'

'Right.' Gavin's face was nonchalant.

Lena looked down, sticking her wrist under the desk, sure that her pulse was hammering visibly beneath her skin. She repeated the same phrase over and over. *This has nothing to do with you. This has nothing to do with you. This has nothing to do with you.*

'Todd.'

'Yes?' she squeaked.

'Make sure it happens.'

Lena nodded with perhaps too much enthusiasm. 'Sure.'

It was fortunate that Carl didn't seem to notice. 'All right then,' he finished with a stamp of his boots. 'I'm off to do a fuckin' yard inspection. I'll be on the two-way.' He fingered the radio receiver he had hanging over his shoulder. 'So if anyone needs me, don't hesitate to fuckin' kill 'em.' On this jovial order, he left.

Gavin rubbed his hands together, like the thief who has just got away with the necklace. 'Looks like Bulldog's keeping mum for once.'

Lena nodded. 'I guess so.'

'I wonder why.'

Lena clasped her hands tightly together under the desk. She didn't want to think about it, didn't want to question too deeply the reprieve that had so amazingly and so wonderfully come her way. One day, she was going to run out of second chances. She had to take the good times while she had them.

'Who knows?' she responded as airily as she could. 'Who knows why Bulldog does anything?'

Gavin grunted. 'Amen to that.'

Galvanised into action by the near miss, Lena worked vigorously for the rest of the morning. By the time afternoon arrived she was ready to take back control of the skid.

'Geez, you look very pleased with yourself,' Sharon noted when Lena hopped on the bus. Lena glanced down the aisle and noticed only a few men on board. They were seated right up the back, which was good because she didn't want her conversation with Sharon overheard.

'Bulldog hasn't mentioned the flag,' she said in a low but gleeful voice. '*And* I've come up with a great idea for the skid.'

'Really, Bulldog said nothing?' Sharon raised an eyebrow. 'Anything to do with the eyeful he got yesterday?'

Lena moved swiftly onto the seat directly behind her. 'I don't know and I don't care. It's back to business and that suits me perfectly.' The opportunity to prove herself had almost slipped through her fingers. This second chance was not going to go unused. She changed the subject to a far more agreeable topic.

'So how about you and Gavin?' she whispered. 'Did anything happen when I left the two of you fishing together yesterday?'

Sharon blushed and started the engine. 'We just talked.'

'Talked is good.' Lena scanned her face. 'Still like him?'

Sharon looked wistful. 'More than ever.'

Lena smiled. 'We need to formulate a plan to get you two together.' She tapped a finger against her chin. 'Leave it with me.'

'What about you?' Sharon threw over her shoulder. 'When do I get to help you snag the man I know you're hiding in that head of yours?'

'Just drop it, Sharon.' Lena grimaced and looked away. 'I'm not on the market.'

'I didn't mean to upset you.' She could feel Sharon's eyes studying her face via the rear-view mirror and after a few seconds her friend added, 'Someone hurt you real bad, didn't they?'

Lena started but decided not to deny it. After all, this was Sharon she was talking to. Not Radar. 'Well, I'm definitely not keen to get back into the dating game, that's for sure.'

'That bad, huh?'

'Let's just say there was an unwanted parting gift involved.'

Sharon's nose wrinkled. 'Herpes?'

'No, *gross!*' Lena gasped, torn between horror and amusement.

'Sorry.' Sharon shrugged. 'I've been living in the camp too long. But seriously, surely one bad break-up can't have turned you off men for good.'

'Not all men,' Lena agreed. 'Just the ones I work with.'

'Oh right. Gotcha.' Sharon's tone seemed to indicate that she did but Lena doubted it very much. She wondered what Sharon would say if she told her she was still dealing with the aftermath of her last relationship. There was no way she was making herself vulnerable to someone like that ever again.

The bus reached the boom gates at the entrance to the wharf and Lena was able to turn her thoughts to other matters. Normally the booms were always up and the bus simply drove through. Today, however, they blocked the way and she guessed that they were about to experience firsthand Bulldog's new laws. A TCN gatekeeper boarded.

'PPE check,' he announced.

Sharon rolled her eyes but indicated with her hand that he should continue. With a haughty tilt to his head, he made sure everyone had their equipment on before jumping off again. He lifted the gates and Sharon drove through. She dropped Lena off at the skid as usual and Lena climbed the ladder to the deck. When she saw Mike glaring grumpily back at her, she approached him.

'Hi, Mike.'

'You're interrupting my work,' he said without preamble.

'I just came to tell you about the new access platform.'

'What? Since when –?'

'Since I decided to come up with it,' she told him. 'It will definitely speed up this operation. I have spoken with all members of the team –'

'Except me,' he said hotly.

'You didn't want to talk to me,' Lena countered. 'So, as I warned, I've pushed ahead without you. It came to my attention that the slowness of the process is due to moving the current access platform at each bent. So I've designed a new access platform that can move without the crane.'

'I beg your pardon?'

Lena opened up her file and withdrew a sketch. Holding up the sketch she pointed to the relevant areas. 'This access platform has wheels that hook over the lower flange of the main girder. The men will be able to pull it along into the next position.'

Lena shut the file before he could look at the drawing more closely. 'I'll be writing you a detailed document on how to use and install this platform and also presenting it to the client tomorrow.'

'But –'

'If the client agrees, which in all likelihood he will considering his complaints were about speed, I'll expect you to give up a couple of the guys to help fabricate it. But until the new platform is ready, you'll continue as before.'

'Don't I get a say in the design of the new platform?'

Lena frowned. 'I gave you a say last week. You told me to stop interrupting you. Not much has changed since then.'

'That was before I knew that this was what you intended. You never said anything about running rough-shod over me and my men.'

'You'll find, Mike,' Lena told him indignantly, 'that your men are very keen for the new access platform to be built. But please, if there are any complaints from the team, refer them to me.'

'Fieldmouse,' Mike barked across the deck. 'Do you know anything about this new platform?'

'Yes, sir.' Fieldmouse snapped to attention. 'Madame E discussed it with all of us last week. We all thought it would make things a lot easier because –'

'Oh, enough,' Mike waved his hand. 'You,' he pointed a finger at Lena, 'may not be so lucky getting Bulldog to agree to this idea. Is it safe?'

'Of course it's safe,' Lena said.

His expression was an ugly smirk. 'You designed it yourself, right?'

'Yes.'

He tossed his head as if her admission spoke volumes and moved away to the railing. The silence below deck was deafening. Lena knew the boys down there had been listening to their conversation as well. Suddenly she felt uncomfortable. Had she gone overboard punishing Mike? Was she overconfident about her design? A design that no one had checked . . . Unbidden, Kevin's contemptuous voice rang in her ears.

'Face it, Lena. Without my help, you never would have made it through.'

'Look,' she addressed Mike again in a slightly milder tone. 'I need to take a couple of photos of the underside of the jetty. I haven't finalised the connection design for the platform yet. If you have any suggestions, I could certainly use some –'

'Just take your bloody photos.' Mike dismissed her peace offering, confining his gaze to the ocean.

She let it go. He was a lost cause. The whales were back, she noticed. Perhaps he found solace in their gentle might. Whatever the case, he couldn't say she hadn't tried to give him another chance.

Lena climbed down the ladder on the other side of the skid so that she was on the walkway, sea side of the conveyor. As she looked under the wharf, three monkeys on the current access platform greeted her with the thumbs-up sign. There was no room for her with the three of them packing out the access platform. She laughed. 'All right, you're going to have to come up,' she called. 'I need to get down there to take some photos.' She showed them the camera hanging round her neck and they climbed up onto the walkway.

'Aw, we thought this was a social call, Madame E, to thank us for all our input.'

Lena could see that they were in a teasing mood so she tried to inject firm professionalism into her voice, hoping it would put them off. 'I did appreciate all your suggestions and, as you probably heard, they're going to be put to good use.'

'That's it?' the tall, skinny one complained. 'You never talk to us.' His nickname was Biro – his real name was Jack Penn. His body shape didn't help his cause either.

His coworker winked at Lena, tipping his hard hat with one grubby hand. 'Heard you went on a fishing trip, Sunday. Why didn't you invite us?'

'I didn't know you'd be interested in coming.' She tried to gently brush him off. 'Now if you'll just –'

But of course, they weren't done with their goading. Lena wondered if Mike was listening upstairs, enjoying every second of her frustration.

Geez, just when I thought these men were finally getting used to me as the engineer and not as the community toy.

''Course we'd be interested,' Biro protested. 'Wouldn't we, boys?'

The other two nodded their enthusiasm and Lena sighed. 'Come on, guys, I need to get these photos. I've got a lot to do today.' The walkway was too narrow for her to brush past them without physical contact. She knew that was the idea.

'Shoot away,' they grinned. 'We don't mind.'

That's when the posing started, first with the flexing biceps and then puffing out their chests to display non-existent pecks.

Oh brother.

They weren't going to let her pass. If she was going to do this, she had to get creative. 'You know what?' Lena lifted her camera. 'I should really get a group photo of the skid boys. Why don't you guys hop up on the deck and I'll take a shot of the lot of you?'

The three of them beamed with surprised pleasure.

'Really?'

'Yeah. Why not?'

It was like she'd just handed them a hundred dollars each. They grunted with pride and scrambled up the ladder. Lena followed, trying not to laugh.

Fieldmouse and Radar, who had been operating the crane, joined in, delighted at the opportunity to strut their stuff. Mike stared at the group in horror. 'You're turning this operation into a bloody freak show,' he accused.

Having by now warmed to her idea, Lena frowned at him. 'It might be nice to have a memento. After all, you're devoting at least a year of your life to the skid.'

Mike choked. 'Are you insane? This is not some tea party with your girlfriends, you know.'

What a spoilsport.

Lena ignored him as the men lined up, laughing at each other as they struck poses. They crowded around the crane, using it as a prop, perhaps because they thought it emphasised their masculinity. Lena began to enjoy herself as she snapped a few photos.

Mike made a strangling sound deep within his throat. 'This behaviour belittles the project.'

Lena ignored him, too busy taking requests from the boys to capture different parts of the skid and the jetty. This *wasn't* belittling their job. The men were proud of their work, proud of their part in the project and they wanted it to be recorded, so that they could show it off.

They were asking for the pictures. She gave them her drawings so that they could scribble their emails on the back of it. She assured them she would forward the pictures on.

'Thanks.' Biro shuffled in his boots. 'It would be good to send home. You know, for the wife and kids. Sometimes it's hard to explain what we do here.'

'Sure,' she said, smiling, pleased that the guys were finally putting away their bullshit and getting real. 'All right then. If you don't mind, I think I'll go down to the access platform and get what I really came for.'

This time they let her pass.

Lena walked into the gym that night for her hour of solitude to find twenty guys working out. This was some feat given the room only sported nine machines and a couple of mats. Half of the exercisers were simply standing around pumping hand weights.

Their eyes moved to her in unison as the door swung shut behind her, tracing the outline of her T-shirt and then her bike pants. Gritting her teeth, she looped her towel around her neck and waited for the nearest machine to become available.

When its user realised what she was doing, he immediately jumped off, grabbed his towel and wiped it down with so much flourish, it might have been a show pony.

'Need some help with the settings, darling?' he asked.

'No thanks.' She moved the hook from thirty kilos to ten and got on the machine, making sure not to meet his eyes for fear he might interpret it as an invitation to stay. He stayed anyway and proceeded to chat to her about the size of his biceps and how much they had benefited from use of said machine.

It was in this moment that she realised it was official. Her quiet evenings at the gym were over. Her hour of solitude . . . gone. *But how did they find out about my routine?* She had been so careful. No one knew of her trips to the gym except Bulldog and Ethel. Had Bulldog let the cat out of the bag to punish her for the flag incident? It seemed too churlish even for him. Twenty minutes later, Lena's frustration had only escalated. She had just turned down one date, five inappropriate compliments and one offer of personal training. She decided to quit and leave. Fitness was important, but so was sanity and privacy. But as it turned out, or as her bad luck would have it, that wasn't the end of it.

Outside the gym, on a small grassed patch, someone had set up a timber picnic table and benches from the mess. When she emerged from the gym, there were at least ten guys seated around that table drinking and laughing loudly. Most of them had stripped off their work uniform and were wearing tank tops and shorts with no shoes other than a pair of thongs here and there.

'Hey there, it's Madame Engineer,' one of them called out. 'Would you like to join us? We've been waiting for you.'

His friend lifted the lid off the Esky next to the table and waved his hand over the contents, *Sale of the Century* style.

She clutched her towel tighter. 'No thanks.'

'Come on, baby.'

'What's the matter? None of us good-looking enough for you?'

She stopped walking, running her eyes over them in disbelief. It wasn't like they were all young studs in their twenties. There were a couple of fifty-somethings, mixed in with a healthy dose of mid-thirty pot bellies, and leather-skinned forty-year-olds who really should have got out of the sun ten years ago. Half of them were probably married, or divorced, or both, with families back home in Perth. What were they doing chasing after her? And like a bell going off in her head, the answer suddenly came to her.

She was sport.

It wasn't personal. Their flirtation wasn't serious. It was just that she was a distraction – a form of entertainment, a competition of sorts. Somewhere along the line, she had become a game and she didn't like it.

Instinctively, her hands went to her hips and she surveyed them as a teacher might the rottenest year nine students. They must have caught her mood because they all sat up straighter and a couple pulled in their bare feet, so that they were tucked under the bench.

'Have you no shame?' she demanded. 'Can't I have a simple work-out at the gym in peace?'

'Come on, Madame E, it's all in good fun.' One of them spread his hands jovially. 'There's a shortage of pretty girls in this town, so when the skid boys told everyone –'

Lena pounced. '*The skid boys.*'

'Yeah, Fieldmouse and the others said that you went to the gym and they found out from Ethel what time so –'

'The skid boys,' she repeated, belatedly remembering that she might have let her gym visits slip to Fieldmouse while talking to Mike. 'Those roaches!'

She shook her head and started walking, ignoring the protests from behind. Her anger had already left the men on the picnic benches and redirected itself. As her brain sorted through the issues, a new truth revealed itself.

So far, she had dealt with harassment by feigning deafness or giving a polite but firm brush-off. But the behaviour was only getting worse.

She had to do something more.

She had learned the hard way that letting people continue to make false assumptions about you only led to trouble. It was about time the skid boys knew who was boss. Suddenly a grin tickled her lips. What if she . . .? No, she couldn't. The Barnes Inc Human Resources team back in Perth would have simultaneous coronaries if they found out. Bugger that! It was all well and good for a city-slicker HR manager to sue for sexual harassment. But how was that going to give her good engineering experience? How was that going to help her clear her conscience and earn her degree?

Her decision solidified. Lena was going to do this her way.

With new optimism, she looked at her watch. It was six-thirty pm – still a bit early to head over to the mess for dinner. She decided to do some laundry instead. Pulling a pair of baggy tracksuit pants on over her revealing bike shorts, she grabbed a sack of dirty clothes and headed in the direction of the nearest washing machine in donga seven. She was nearly there when she realised it was also a Monday which meant Bulldog would be doing his laundry there too. She spun around, intending to head to a different laundry donga on the other side of the camp site when guilt seized her. Did she really need to be so petty? The man was too arrogant for his own good but so far he was the only person who had decided to give her a second chance without being asked.

Really, if anything, she owed him a thank you for not getting her fired over the whole flag incident. If it weren't for his silence, she'd be sitting on a plane right now, her career in shreds. Squaring her shoulders and tilting her chin up, she turned back to donga number seven.

Somebody had to be the bigger person here and this time it was going to be her.

Chapter 6

She entered donga number seven, a long rectangular box housing ten top-loaders and five dryers, one of which was humming gently. Bulldog was sitting on a bench waiting for his cycle to finish; and her feet slowed.

Was this really such a good idea?

He looked up from the magazine he was reading when she stalled in the doorway. The smell of freshly showered male assailed her. Wet black hair curled attractively over his ears. His shirt was uncollared and casual, setting off his broad shoulders to advantage.

'Er . . . hi,' she said, hoping that she didn't sound too nervous.

'Hi,' he replied. By contrast, his tone sounded somewhere between annoyed and resigned. He certainly didn't smile. Instead, he returned his attention to his magazine, lifting one booted ankle and resting it casually on his knee. It was clear that he had decided to ignore her. Her resolve strangely strengthened by this attitude, she deliberately tried to prolong the small talk.

'Busy day?'

He raised his eyes but not his chin. 'Always.' The twitch of his lips told her he knew what she was doing and was amused by it. It also made him look human. Human and unexpectedly more approachable. Encouraged by this, she chose the washing machine directly next to where he was sitting and opened the lid.

'I'm glad I ran into you actually.' She tried to keep her voice as laidback as possible. 'I wanted to thank you for not saying anything about the flag.'

Silence.

She glanced over at him as she pulled her clothes from her sack and threw them into the machine. He had returned his attention to the magazine but feeling her eyes on him he nodded.

'I mean, you were right. You could have had me fired, which would have been terrible for me. Not to mention humiliating.'

He nodded again without looking up.

'I'm really glad you didn't do that. This job means a lot to me. I'm just starting out, as you've probably guessed, and I want to do well at this. Get some good experience, if you know what I mean.'

He nodded a third time.

She bit her lip. 'What are you reading?'

He closed the magazine. 'Do you always talk this much?'

'You consider this talking a lot? I –' She broke off as something fell from the underside of the bundle she was transferring to the machine. A red number that could hardly be unfamiliar to him now lay draped over the brown boot propped on his knee. They both focused on it for a stunned second as she silently wished to die. 'Er . . . that's my, er . . . that's my . . .'

It's obvious what it is, idiot. Don't say it! Lena shut her gaping mouth.

Her heart rattled against her rib cage as he leaned forwards, inserted his long fingers between the lacy cups and lifted them off his boot.

'So you can be rendered speechless.' His blue eyes seared through hers. 'Good to know.'

She snatched her bra from his proffered hand.

'Thanks.'

He leaned back in his chair again but his attention did not return to his magazine as she now hoped. Hastily, Lena packed the rest of her clothes into the machine, tipped in some powder and closed the lid with a thump.

'I was right about the gym, wasn't I?'

His sudden re-entry into a conversation he had never wanted in the first place startled her. She turned around. 'I beg your pardon?'

His gaze flicked to the clock on the wall. 'It's only six-thirty and you're not there. Get a bit too crowded for you?'

Her lips thinned. 'Something like that.' His smile was just a little too I-told-you-so, so she decided on attack.

'What about you? I haven't seen you at the gym recently.'

One black brow lifted. 'Been looking, have you?'

Okay, so maybe not the most well-thought-out attack in the history of repartee. 'Of course not,' she replied just a little too forcefully and then paused to modulate her voice. 'Just a casual observation.'

He re-opened the magazine, flicking through it efficiently as he searched for something of interest. 'Actually,' he mentioned as an aside, 'I've taken to running. It's nice to get out of the camp sometimes.'

'So what's wrong with taking your R and R then? I hear you're giving it a miss.' The question left her lips before she could stop it. She looked down in mortification. She might as well have just admitted his every move fascinated her. *Damn it.*

Fully expecting to be told it was none of her business or teased once more about following his movements, Lena was surprised by his reply. 'They need me here. They don't need me at home.'

He spoke the last words as if they were forced from him and she immediately knew that she was probing the edge of his 'secret'. The question was, should she ignore it or press him further? She knew how carefully she guarded her own history. But her incurable curiosity won out.

'Are you talking about your family? Why wouldn't they need you?'

'Did I say need?' he mused. 'I should have said want.'

'They don't want you?' She shook her head. 'I'm sure you're over-dramatising.'

'You wouldn't understand.'

'Maybe if you –'

The hostile expression on his face cut her dead. 'Don't try and fix me, *Madame Engineer*. I'm not one of the camp drongos who'll let you play Freud to get in your pants.'

His pointed use of her site nickname worried her. Previously she hadn't minded being given this pompous calling. If she was going to be lumped with something, which was a guarantee, it might as well be that. Better than Sod or Plod which were very pickable given the guys liked to choose things that rhymed with a person's last name. But the way Bulldog said it made it sound so presumptuous, like she was trying to put on airs or something.

Lena frowned. 'I'm not trying to fix you, whatever that means. Why would you say something like that?'

Bulldog didn't respond to her question and then to thwart her further his dryer stopped and beeped. He rolled up his magazine and stood to collect his clothes. Without thinking, she put her hand on his wrist to stop him.

'Wait. You can't just accuse me of something and then take off. Clearly, you have a problem with me and I want to know what it is.'

He looked down at her hand and she quickly detached it as though she'd been burned. He took his shirts from the machine and stuffed them in a laundry bag.

'I asked you a question,' Lena said, desperation squashing her fear.

But when he turned around to confront her, she had to step back from the storm gathering in his eyes.

Talk about making the wrong demand.

'My problem is this,' his voice was soft and deadly, 'you are the least experienced person on this site and you don't seem to know it. You want to be taken seriously but you organise fishing trips, steal flags and parade around in your underwear. You've got no life experience, no prudence and no ability to see beyond your own little bubble. You're naive, stubborn and reckless. And the only reason you've had it so easy so far is because you're so damn good-looking.'

Her eyes widened. 'Gee, don't hold back or anything.'

It was the most thorough insult she'd ever received. But what was it they said about Bulldog? He was a perfectionist. Clearly he applied that to his every pursuit.

His lips hardened. 'You think this is a joke. Don't you? Just like everything else. When are you going to learn that you can't get through life on a smile? It doesn't work that way. Especially not out here. You're going to get hurt and you won't see it coming.'

When he said nothing more, Lena decided it was her turn. Something in her brain was flashing in warning, but she was too appalled by his speech to remember that the client is always right.

'Thank you very much for that illuminating review of my character, but it's not as if you're Mr Perfect. Sure, you've got heaps of experience, but no understanding of people. You want your men to respect you, but instead you've got them looking over their shoulders to make sure you're not on their back. You're domineering and obnoxious and you have no ability to see any point of view but your own. And, just to set the record straight, I have not had it easy!'

He opened his mouth and then shut it.

Lena shook her head. 'If you dislike me so much, why the hell didn't you just tell Carl about the flag? That would have got me off this site and out of your life as quickly as possible.'

'With your *understanding of people*,' his dark eyes smouldered, 'I don't know why you haven't figured that out already.'

And on this cryptic note, he swung his sack over his shoulder and walked out.

Bulldog and his personality assessment from hell played on Lena's mind all evening.

How dare he judge the way she spent her free time? How dare he suggest she got through life on her looks? How dare he put her in a box and label it 'naive'?

He didn't even know her.

At least Kevin, for all his faults, had only ever jumped to one bad conclusion about her. Bulldog had written a book on her shortcomings and was still adding pages.

Safely back in her donga, wearing her pink pyjamas and snuggled under the covers of her still unfamiliar bed, she was able to consider at leisure the pitfalls of being female in her profession.

Did all men really think that just because she was a girl, she'd never fit into the construction industry? Steel was just iron with a dash of carbon, for goodness sake. Lipstick had a more complicated chemical structure. And as for concrete – *please*. Anyone who made mud pies as a kid could figure out what to do with that!

The more she thought about it, the angrier she became. Normally, she pushed Kevin's words out of her head. But now she found herself trying to recall more. Was there a hint she could pick up among them that could show her how to earn her colleagues' respect? She fast-forwarded through the lovely times and her increasing detachment to their final conversation, about six weeks after her final year exams. They'd had dinner and were drinking some of his somehow-very-special brandy back at his place; and Lena was summoning up her courage to tell Kevin how she'd been feeling – or not feeling. Things hadn't been right between them for almost a month.

She was excited about the future and had a lot of plans. Kevin was critical about most of them. He was happy that she was looking for her first job but at the same time was concerned about the companies she'd chosen to apply to. When she'd suggested that maybe she'd take a year off and go backpacking around Europe instead, he hadn't been pleased about that either. They hadn't fought about it or anything, but Lena recognised the vibe she was getting from him. He wanted things to stay the same while she knew it was time for change.

That night, she'd had a speech fully rehearsed. But frustration and nerves made her just blurt it out. 'Kevin, I want to break up.'

He'd whipped off his silver-framed glasses and fixed her with dark brown eyes that were both concerned and wary.

'What did you say?'

She leaned forwards, clutching a sofa cushion for support. 'I'm sorry. It wasn't meant to come out like that.'

He ignored her apology. 'Where is this coming from? It doesn't make sense.'

She searched for a place to start. He took her silence for indecision and stood up, a smile of gentle indulgence curling his mouth. 'Lena, if we have a problem, we can talk about it. Get through it together.'

Kevin put his glasses down, came around to her and placed warm hands on her shoulders. 'We're so close now. In a couple of days, exam results will be out and you'll be a graduate. All these covert meetings will be at an end.'

'I know and –'

'We should be celebrating,' he insisted, anxiety wrinkling his brow. 'We're done hiding now, Lena.'

'It's not that.' She looked away. If she still loved him, she wouldn't care who she had to keep it a secret from. But that was just the thing.

She didn't.

How did you tell someone that you'd fallen out of love with them? Not because they were a bad person or they'd done anything wrong but just because the two of you didn't view the world the same any more. She didn't want to hurt him – he'd been good to her.

She got up too, but stepped out of his reach and walked over to the bookshelves on her right, scanning the titles in search of enlightenment. Finally she found her voice.

'Kevin, when we started going out, keeping our relationship a secret was the best part. It was exciting and dangerous and sexy. And you . . .' she turned back to him, indicating his person with a reverent lift of her hand '. . . are a beautiful man. Generous and confident in a way that none of the guys my own age are. I was attracted to that beyond anything. But now –' She broke off as pain twisted his mouth.

'Are you trying to say you've outgrown me?'

'I still care for you a great deal,' she protested. 'I just don't . . . love you.'

'Well, it makes sense, doesn't it?' His voice was suddenly bitter. 'That you would wait till now to tell me this?'

'I don't know what you mean.'

'You needed me to help you finish your degree. Now that you have, I'm dispensable.'

'You can't honestly believe that, Kevin,' she returned hotly.

He raised his eyebrows with dark scepticism. 'Do you mean to tell me you didn't notice the way you seemed to miraculously pass all the subjects I teach you?'

What the –? She had not expected him to say that. A fever ripped through Lena's body like the lash of a whip. 'What are you talking about?'

He shrugged. 'The benefits of having a boyfriend who marks

,your assignments and exam papers, of course. Face it, Lena. Without my help, you never would have made it through.'

Lena's throat constricted. 'What do you mean, your help?'

His face hardened. 'I marked you *leniently*, of course.'

She felt sick. 'Kevin, I *never* asked you to cheat for me and I never would.'

'But it was implied, Lena, it was always implied!' he threw at her.

'How? When?'

He raised an eyebrow derisively. 'How often did you confess your worries about passing to me? You –'

'For support,' she cried. 'For reassurance!'

'I told you you weren't built for this profession but you wouldn't have it. So I made it work for you. It was what you wanted.'

'Never.' Her voice shook. 'I sat every paper in good faith. You should know that: you helped me study. You were always helping me.'

'Yes, I helped you all right.' His tone was cruel. 'What I didn't know was that you were just using me for it.'

'This can't be right.' Lena's lips trembled as she searched Kevin's face for the right answers. 'Third year exams maybe, but this year I worked damn hard.'

'Obviously not hard enough.' His words were like a physical slap. For a moment she couldn't speak.

'You're a beautiful girl, Lena. I was a fool, an absolute fool.' His eyes burned her. 'The real world won't fall for you as easily as I have.'

She stood taller, fists clenching at her sides, sweat dampening her neck. 'All I ever wanted was for you to believe in me, Kevin. That's all!'

'How can I believe in someone who spent more energy on her wardrobe than on a subject at the heart of her degree?'

Her eyes widened at this vindictive blow and she struck back as best she could. 'One subject, more than a year ago.

You know I'm not that person any more. Our relationship was real to me, Kevin. It wasn't a plot. It's your own twisted mind that's changing the facts.'

'Don't worry.' He turned away. 'I'm not going to tell anyone. Your degree is perfectly intact.'

But that was where he'd been wrong.

Her degree had meant nothing to her after that.

Absolutely nothing.

Chapter 7

A new day brought a new resolution – to keep her mind off all things Kevin and Bulldog. Wallowing was not helping.

She was pleased to finally meet Lance the next morning, by the office printer. He was a funny-looking guy: skinny, with long brown hair that was on its way to dreadlocks and a mouth that was really far too big for his face.

'Great to meet you!' He stuck out a hand as he jumped from foot to foot, a mannerism she noticed didn't leave him for the rest of their conversation.

'Great to meet you too.'

He shook her hand vigorously. 'Madame E, right? The boys told me you don't fish either.'

She couldn't help but smile that he'd already checked out her fishing credentials. 'Afraid not.'

He rubbed his palms together. 'Not to worry. I work best alone anyway.' On these cryptic words he walked off. Shaking her head, she turned back to the printer and the first task she had set for herself that day.

Teaching the skid boys a lesson.

Only minutes before she had opened the photos she'd taken on the skid on her computer and flicked through them until she had located the best one. She'd blown this up to A4 size and added a large caption at the bottom. She now took this full-colour mini poster from the printer and walked out of the office with it.

Lena entered the lunch donga next door. Every day the boys had the option of catching the bus back there for their breaks. It was the only sheltered area available to them that was air-conditioned. On a hot day, it packed out pretty quick. Eight white trestle tables took up most of the space. In the corner by the door was a small kitchen boasting a bar fridge, an urn and a sink. A big noticeboard hung on the wall that was not lined with windows.

As it was neither lunch nor smoko when she walked in, the only person in there was Sharon. She was re-filling the fridge with milk.

'Whatcha got there?' The bus driver smiled in greeting.

'Payback.'

Sharon's eyes brightened with interest. 'Really?'

'I don't suppose you heard what happened at the gym last night?'

She shook her head. 'No.'

'The skid boys told everyone I go there at six o'clock.' Lena walked over to the noticeboard and pinned the photo over the top of a Barnes Inc safety calendar.

Sharon covered her gasp with her hand. 'Oh, that's price-less! How did you –?'

'They were teasing me on the skid yesterday.'

Lena stood back to admire her handiwork. Five skid boys, knees bent, fists clenched and biceps curled as they cast 'come hither' looks at the camera. In black block capitals beneath: 'MAN-O-MAN, MONTH OF MAY.'

'What do you reckon?' Lena asked Sharon. 'Think it'll teach 'em a lesson?'

She choked. 'One they'll never forget.'

Moments later, safely back in the main office, Lena went in search of Carl. Her plan for the new access platform was set to go. She just needed consent from the client, which meant a meeting with Bulldog. She found Carl in Gavin's cubicle.

'What do you mean they're fuckin' warped? Ring the fuckin' shit-kickers and tell 'em to unwarp 'em.'

Gavin ran an agitated hand through his hair. 'They're claiming the girders weren't warped when they left their yard.'

'Fuck! If you believe that, then you're the piece of shit they're kicking around!'

Lena stuck her head over the cubicle wall and Gavin looked up in relief. 'Hey, Lena.'

She threw him a grin and then examined Carl's brooding countenance. It didn't seem like a good time to bother him, but it wasn't like she had choices. The man was never around.

'Er, Carl,' she began, 'I kinda need to see Bulldog. I've got a new concept I want to show him to speed up installation of the headstocks.'

'Fuck.' Carl's expression was keen but his voice was reproachful. 'Don't you think you better run it by me first?'

'Sorry,' Lena said. 'It's just that you're always so busy and –'

'Todd, quit the bullshit and cut to the chase.'

Lena quickly outlined her idea for the new access platform.

'That could fuckin' work,' Carl finally acknowledged. 'Have you got a sketch?'

'Yes.'

Carl looked at his watch. 'Gavin, Fish and I are seeing Bulldog at eleven today. You should join us.'

Lena wrinkled her nose. 'Fish?'

Carl didn't appear to understand her confusion but luckily Gavin intervened. 'That's what the boys have taken to calling Lance. If you ask me it suits him.'

'Oh.' Lena didn't disagree but she was more interested in the upcoming meeting. 'So is Bulldog coming here?'

'Fuck no!' Carl was appalled at the prospect of letting the enemy see their hallowed halls – or disorganised, dust-infused jungle, more like.

'We're going there,' Gavin put in. 'We always do.' He looked around the office. 'Safer.'

'Fine,' Lena agreed, rubbing her hands at the chance to check out enemy territory. Her excitement was silly, really. What was she going to do? Mentally price all their furniture and compare it to Barnes Inc's stuff? Eavesdrop on their telephone conversations to catch them in an act of ignorance? Taste their coffee only to confirm that her company's was better? Lena rubbed her forehead.

I've been spending way too much time with the skid boys. She grinned to herself. If nothing else, Radar was going to be insane with jealousy.

She went back to her computer and spent the next few hours sourcing potential steel suppliers for her new access platform and confirming with Tony that they had the yard space to build it. She wanted to have all the facts at her fingertips before the meeting. Every conversation she'd ever had with Bulldog so far had been an exercise in humiliation. Today, she wanted to impress him.

If that was possible.

Just before eleven o'clock, Fish called. He was still in Karratha seeing a supplier and could not make it back in time for their meeting with Bulldog. Carl was not pleased, but there was nothing for it: they would have to go without him. So as planned, Gavin, Carl and Lena piled into Carl's ute and drove down to the TCN site offices. Lena reflected on what a luxury it was to be going to the top of the wharf in a car rather than having to wait for the bus.

TCN reception consisted of a simple counter manned by a sour-faced female. Lena had seen her and another female TCN employee in the camp. But they were so hostile that she and Sharon did not speak to them.

True to form, the receptionist deliberately ignored them for a while, shuffling papers and arranging her pens neatly in a cup before lifting her eyes to Carl's blackening countenance.

'Can I help you?'

Carl leaned on the counter. 'We're here to see Bu–Dan Hullog.'

Her unfriendly grey eyes registered that his elbow was touching one of her files and she snatched at it, as though the slight contact would be enough to cause contamination. Carl straightened indignantly, taking his arm from her desk and eyeing her with distaste.

'Can you just tell Bulldog we're here?'

'You mean Mr Hullog.'

'Fuck, yes.'

Her eyes hardened. 'Do you have an appointment?'

Carl looked like he was going to explode so Lena hastily intervened. 'Yes we do.'

The receptionist glanced at her phone and they both saw that one number was flashing. 'He's on the phone at the moment.' Her voice was triumphant. 'You'll have to wait.'

Lena knew the two sides didn't like each other, but this was ridiculous.

Remembering that she was partly there on a fact-finding mission, she looked beyond the receptionist to the office behind her. It was open plan with no cubicles, so even though they stood by the front door, they could see everyone's work stations. It was then that Lena noticed how much interest their arrival had generated.

None of it was friendly.

The receptionist must have noticed that her gaze was wandering because she jumped to her feet. 'Would you care to take a seat in our meeting room?' She indicated the closed-off area to their left.

'Why not?' said Carl.

The receptionist closed the door to the meeting room as they seated themselves around the large rectangular table. Lena shuffled her files into a neat pile and leaned on them.

'What's their problem?' she whispered to the others.

Carl grunted. 'Small dicks.'

Lena choked.

Just then Bulldog walked in. For an awful moment, Lena thought he might have heard what Carl had said. But he gave no indication. In fact, he gave no indication of any emotion at all, simply holding out his hand to Carl, who rose peevishly to take it.

'I apologise for the wait.'

In these few seconds when his attention was engaged, Lena allowed herself to examine him. He looked different. Maybe it was because the last two times she'd spoken to him he'd been in casual clothes. His face seemed more set, the glint in his eyes a little harder, his jawline a bit tighter. He also hadn't shaved.

And Bulldog always shaved.

'No problem,' Carl lied gruffly at his apology. Bulldog then extended his hand to Gavin and finally to Lena.

Lena tried not to make too much of the brief contact but found herself analysing every millisecond of it. His fingers were warm and firm. His shake, controlled. But his eyes were cool. Too cool.

I guess he still hasn't forgiven me for the insult I dealt him in the laundry.

Bulldog's mouth twisted into something that could not be described as a smile and Lena felt the sting of him telling her off all over again. She withdrew her hand before he completed the shake and sat down.

Carl and Gavin, who were still standing, each cast her a confused look before following suit. Bulldog sat down also, laying a black diary and a few data sheets on the table. Her indiscretion had not fazed him in the slightest. He was straight down to business; all client; all boss. Though they were both managers, he had a presence that poor Carl could never hope to compete with. They had the same level of power and responsibility, but Bulldog held the room.

'I didn't know Ms Todd would be joining us.' He looked directly at her, his gaze measured and a little accusatory. 'Is there a reason for your presence?'

'I had an idea for the skid that –'

'Yes, Mike told me.'

Lena stopped. 'Mike?'

'Yes.' Bulldog folded his arms. 'He happened to be at the end of the wharf at the same time I was this morning.'

Happened to be? Lena digested this with annoyance. Mike's job was on the skid: he never just *happened* to be at the end of the wharf.

'Well, I don't know what he told you,' she began, 'but this new concept I've come up with could improve our progress speed –'

'Not if you're taking men off the skid.'

'I beg your pardon?'

'Mike told me your idea involves taking men off the skid to fabricate a new platform. That's going to slow us down.'

It was clear. Mike had completely sabotaged her. Bulldog's distrust of the scheme was as plain as the mulish bend of his mouth. Mike had no doubt loaded him with as many negative views about the platform as possible.

She tried to inject a note of calm rationale into her voice. 'Fabrication will slow us down temporarily but in the long term we'll be better for it.'

'*If* the men take to your new system easily. That will take leadership.'

What is he saying? That I can't lead them?

He didn't explain himself further, however, just stared at her as though waiting to be confirmed or denied. Lena licked her lips and pulled her sketch out of her file. 'I understand that. I have a sketch of my design. If you'll –'

'Your design?' Bulldog's long fingers rubbed his stubble, the sound of flicking bristles immediately conjuring images of white sheets, streaming sunshine and hot coffee.

Man! Where did that come from?

With iron effort Lena pulled her mind back to the office as he held out his hand.

'Let me see.'

With relief she passed it to him. Finally, she was making some headway.

'It looks too light.'

Or not.

Lena lifted her chin confidently. 'I designed it to be light. We need something that can be moved with manpower.'

'Yes but are the members strong enough?' He scratched his chin. Again the sound of bristles distracted her. The hairs on the back of her neck rose and she almost missed his next question.

'What grade of steel are you using?'

'Huh? I mean 450MPa.'

He frowned. 'You'll definitely need to specify that more clearly. Will these sizes work for 250 or 350 grade?'

'I'm not sure.'

'Well, then you'll need to find out.' His tone was impatient. He turned to Carl.

'Has anyone checked this?'

'I haven't had time to crunch her numbers,' Carl returned. 'But I am confident that Lena –'

Bulldog interrupted him. 'Lena is a graduate. I want someone chartered to check this.'

Would anyone *ever* believe in her? The helplessness of her case made her snap, a little more viciously than necessary. 'It's just a simple platform, not the Empire State Building.'

His blue orbs stabbed hers. Lena felt their impact like a bolt of lightning. 'Every design on this project is important, especially one that concerns the safe working environment of our men.'

His voice was so intense, it was like he'd reached inside her chest, grabbed her heart in his fist and squeezed.

Carl remained unaffected. 'We don't have a fuckin' chartered design engineer on site. Fuck. If you need someone other than me to check this, we'll have to send it back to the city. It'll be a two-week turnaround at the fuckin' least. Do you really want such a fuckin' fuss over a little platform?'

There was a weighty pause, as Bulldog again looked from Carl to Lena and then back again. Expression had once more withdrawn from his face. Finally he spoke but it wasn't about the project.

'Carl, can you please watch your language?' He looked at Lena again without smiling. 'There are . . .' he paused perceptibly as if the point were up for contention, '*ladies* present.'

Here we go.

He might as well have lit a stick of dynamite. No one criticised Carl's language. It just wasn't done. Everyone just accepted that 'fuck' was a part of his vocabulary and got on with life. He probably couldn't stop saying it if he tried.

Lena glanced at her boss to examine the effect of Bulldog's words. It was almost comical. All he needed was puffs of steam to blow from his ears to round off the image of suppressed rage. Bulldog had just made an enemy for life.

As Carl's expression turned from fury to pain, Lena realised that the only reason he hadn't said anything yet was because of the 'client is always right' policy touted by Barnes Inc top management. She waited with bated breath.

'I apologise, Lena.' The words were squeezed from him.

'Oh, there's no need –' Lena began in haste but Bulldog interrupted her.

'There will be men working on that platform, twelve hours a day, perhaps lugging heavy equipment on and off it. I want to know this platform's limits.'

'I am happy to do up a formal report, detailing safe working loads for different scenarios,' Lena suggested.

Bulldog's enigmatic gaze flicked over her again. His long tanned fingers drummed impatiently on the desk like they were plucking her nerves, one by one. 'Very well,' he conceded. 'But I want Carl's signature on this and a copy of the calcs before fabrication. I'll check it myself.'

'Fine,' Lena said stiffly and Carl nodded. She took her sketch back and put it in her file. So much for impressing him. Why did he always make her feel like she was nothing more than a splinter he couldn't get out?

They heard the rumble of a truck outside as it passed the window. The loud noise did nothing to defuse the tension in the room.

Bulldog drew his hands together on the desktop, as though gathering forces for a new assault. 'I suppose you're all aware as to the real reason why I called this meeting today?'

We are?

Lena was dismayed: Carl hadn't briefed her. She thought *they* had called the meeting. Clearly not.

Carl opened his notebook. 'I'm assuming you wish to discuss the progress of the project.'

'What progress?' Bulldog retorted. 'There is none. In fact, if I didn't know any better, I'd say you were going backwards.'

Lena winced. Bulldog's eyes passed to Gavin, who moved uncomfortably in his seat.

'Piling is fifteen per cent behind the skid.'

'The hammer broke down last week. But we're back on schedule now,' Gavin tried to reassure him.

'Not quite.' Bulldog shook his head. 'Where's your deck engineer? I thought he was coming to this meeting too.'

'He got stuck in town talking to suppliers.'

'Still treading water, I see.' In exasperation, he turned back to Carl, who was pulling at the collar of his shirt. 'What about the trusses?'

'They haven't arrived yet.'

'They should be in the yard by now.'

'And they will be,' Carl sat up confidently, 'by the end of the week at the latest.'

'By the end of the week,' Bulldog's eyes glittered dangerously, 'you'll be twenty per cent behind on that front as well. This is not acceptable.'

Carl's fingers curled into fists against the desk. Lena could tell the effort to stop himself from swearing was a considerable strain. She intervened to buy him time.

'There has been improvement, but catching up will take time. You can't expect it to be instantaneous.'

'Yes, as a matter of fact I can,' Bulldog fired at her.

'And how do you expect us to pull off this f– this miracle?' Carl demanded.

'You can put on a night shift.'

Lena and her colleagues gasped and Carl just couldn't help himself. 'Fuck that!'

Bulldog's eyes narrowed upon him until finally, tight-lipped, Carl turned to Lena. 'I apologise.'

She swallowed under the furious apology and refrained from comment. Carl turned back to Bulldog after visibly taking a breath. 'Putting on a night shift will be an extremely expensive operation. Especially if you don't mean to compensate us for the logistics of setting it all up.'

'It's my right to see this project completed on time,' Bulldog stated firmly. 'And you have a duty to make sure you live up to our contract.' He shrugged. 'The ball is in your court.'

Carl's control slipped a notch. 'Well, I don't appear to have much of a fuckin' choice, do I?' he said and then, without even looking at her, 'Sorry, Lena.'

When Bulldog said nothing to confirm or deny this, Carl's fury only seemed to heighten. 'A night shift isn't going to fuckin' happen over-fuckin'-night with half the fuckin' town already working on this fucked-up job anyway. Sorry, Lena.

Who knows where we're going to get a fuckin' night-shift work-force? Sorry, Lena. This fuckin' idea is going to take up time I can't fuckin' spare! *Sorry*, Lena. And let me tell you, you can't do every-fuckin'-thing in the fuckin' dark! Lighting is going to cost the fuckin' earth. Shit! Even you should fuckin' know that!' He paused to draw breath. Then he turned back to Lena, but she held up a hand, trying to wipe the grin off her face.

'I know,' she nodded, 'you're sorry.'

'More fuckin' sorry than you fuckin' know,' Carl growled at her.

Lena chewed on the inside of her cheek to keep from laughing.

'Well, it's the solution that we're demanding,' Bulldog said. 'Cyclone season is coming and we need to stay on target as much as possible. If you don't consider this request, you will be compensating us for delays.' He stood up. 'If you'll excuse me.'

And then just like that, he left them still reeling from the aftermath of the bomb he'd just dropped.

'I can't believe how badly that meeting just went,' Lena said as she closed her file.

'It wasn't a meeting. We didn't discuss anything. We just got told.' Gavin shook his head.

'Look,' Lena injected some confidence she didn't feel into her voice, 'we can turn this around, we just need a few smart moves.'

'Night shift! Fuck!' said Carl.

Lena could see the receptionist craning her neck with an effort to see what they were still doing in the meeting room. 'Come on,' she said, 'we should go. We can't discuss strategy here, of all places.'

Carl suddenly seemed to remember where he was. 'Fuck no!'

It was about twelve-thirty when Lena, Carl and Gavin got back to the Barnes Inc offices. They were just in time to see some boilermakers and scaffolders exiting the lunch room.

'Hey there, Fabio, can I have your autograph?'

There was a lot of wolf-whistling and jeering going on. Only this time it wasn't directed at Lena or Sharon. Lena watched the commotion with satisfaction. From the centre of the crowd, Biro and Fieldmouse emerged. They made their way towards the bus, trying to avoid their peers as they jumped on their backs and ruffled their hair.

'Show us some skin, baby!'

Fieldmouse gave Lena a pained expression as he scurried past, looking more like a twitchy rodent than ever. He jumped on the bus and raced to the back. Lena chuckled.

'Never thought you'd double-cross us like that, Madame E,' Biro threw at her, pushing a hand away from his butt. The sound of loud slurpy kisses filled the air.

'Fabio's trying it on, Madame E!'

The heckling laughter escalated.

'It was a thank you,' Lena said in a low voice only Biro could hear. 'For telling everyone about the gym.'

He reddened, but immediately tried to shift blame. 'That wasn't my idea. It was –'

'I don't care whose idea it was,' Lena said firmly. 'Don't ever do something like that to me again.'

'All right, all right,' he said and jumped onto the bus, followed by his group of loud admirers. Sharon winked at Lena from the wheel and then shut the bus door so she could drive them back to the wharf.

'You've got the boys fuckin' toeing the line, I see,' Carl shot at Lena. 'Can't you work some of that magic on Bulldog?'

A hot flush rose up her neck but luckily he'd already turned to go and didn't notice. As he made for the office Gavin joined her. 'You know,' he said, scratching the back of his head, 'if some of the boys are giving you a hard time, I don't mind having a word with them for you.'

'I doubt it would make a difference.' Lena shrugged. 'Let me handle it my way.'

'I'm sure you will, Madame E.' Gavin grinned. 'Say, what are you doing on Friday?'

'Friday?' Lena gazed wistfully into the horizon. 'Same as any other day. Working. Missing home. Dreaming about a dust-free environment.'

'Some of my guys were thinking of going to a pub in Point Samson for a drink after work. I thought it was a good idea. Why don't you come with?'

Her first thought was Sharon. It was the scenario they'd been waiting for. Alcohol, a moonlit night, the possible chance that Sharon and Gavin could connect.

'Sure,' Lena said, 'I'll tell Sharon. We'll be there.'

'Sharon?' He stilled. 'Yeah. Sure. 'Course.'

Lena rubbed her hands together as he headed back towards the office.

Brilliant!

Lena's first priority the next day was to give Mike a piece of her mind. At eight am, Sharon dropped her off at the skid and she climbed the ladder to the deck. He was located in his usual position with his hands tucked behind his back, staring out to sea. Lena often wondered what Mike was thinking about in these quiet moments. He seemed like such a lonely man. Not many people on site liked him. He turned suddenly and glared at her. All sympathy evaporated. It was plain that he knew why she was there and wasn't in the least bit sorry for it.

Lena felt her lips tighten. 'I know what you did, Mike.'

'I have no idea what you're talking about.'

'Play dumb if you like, but I just wanted to let you know that your plan backfired.' She walked towards him cheerfully. 'Not only is the platform still going ahead but Carl's giving me some extra men to fabricate it, so we don't slow anything down.'

Mike's expression got even grimmer than usual.

'Thanks to your well-timed comments,' Lena continued, 'Carl's decided to let me employ a subcontractor.' It was true. She'd spoken to Carl about it before going home the night before.

Mike shrugged. 'Thanks to *my* comments, not yours.'

Her jaw dropped. She couldn't believe he was actually trying to take credit for the success of her idea. 'You're kidding me, right?'

He raised an eyebrow. 'You said it yourself.'

If violence wasn't against company policy, Lena would have hit him at that point. While she contemplated what her other non-physical options were, a shout rang out over their heads.

'Roo!!'

Roo? What the –? Whales she could understand. But this was absurd.

Lena stopped glaring at Mike and looked at Fieldmouse, who was jumping up and down and pointing landwards.

As if on cue, the radio on Mike's shoulder started beeping. 'Mike! There's a giant red heading right for ya.'

Mike and Lena raced to join Fieldmouse at the railing and they all looked down the jetty. Sure enough, there it was, bounding towards them at a startling pace. Its long tail flew out a metre or more behind as it ate up the ground. Although it was still at least half a kilometre away, Lena could tell it had to be at least six feet tall – its leaps were almost that high.

'Shit,' said Mike.

'Fuck,' said Fieldmouse.

'Oh crap,' said Lena.

Chapter 8

Lena heard the racket of the boys racing up the ladders to get on the deck of the skid but kept her gaze trained on the kangaroo. As did Mike and Fieldmouse.

Biro was the first to reach them. 'What should we do?'

Radar was not far behind. 'What if it jumps into the conveyor?'

Images of splattering guts and bone flashed across Lena's mind. Suddenly, the steady hum of the conveyor beneath their feet seemed to be a premonition for impending doom.

Her mouth dried up. 'Surely it won't be that stupid.'

'Roos *are* stupid.' Radar's knuckles gripped the railing. 'Should we pull the emergency switch and stop the conveyor?'

'Not yet,' Mike said. 'If we stop the conveyor and it's not necessary, the client will kill us. It takes hours to reset. It'll really knock the ship schedule out of whack.' He picked up his radio receiver and called Gavin's right-hand man at the end of the wharf. 'Charlie, there's a roo heading your way. A big one. Over.'

There was static and then a voice crackled in the receiver. 'What the fuck?'

Mike spoke into the radio again. 'There's a roo on the wharf. It'll be at the end of the jetty in about ten minutes. Over.'

'You've got to be –' The line crackled and then went silent for a moment. 'Okay, we see it.'

The skid crew could see it clearer now too. Lena knew kangaroos, including red ones, were most active at night. She figured this one must have had a scare or something. It looked crazed, which didn't bode well for any of them. Angry roos had been known to kill a man with a single kick of their powerful legs. It wasn't the kind of animal you wanted to be in close proximity to when it was frightened or mad. Lena chewed frantically on her lower lip. There wasn't exactly a lot of space at the end of the wharf. Everything and everyone was in close proximity. 'Can we stop it before it gets to the end of the wharf?' she asked her companions.

'Don't be stupid,' Mike said. 'What are you going to do? Tell it to turn back.'

Lena sucked in a breath, not wanting to concede to him, but knowing that for once he was right. There was nothing they could do but wait and see what it did. As if to echo her thoughts, the first sound of big feet on bitumen reached her ears. The light thumping grew louder. The kangaroo was going to pass the skid frame very soon. Stiff-legged, the guys backed away from the railing. But the movement must have caught its eye because the kangaroo stopped.

'Aw, shit,' Fieldmouse muttered under his breath.

The roo's ears twitched as though he had heard and straightened to full height. He held his paws in front of his broad, heaving chest.

Lena swallowed. *Far out! He's big.* She couldn't have been more thankful to be on the skid and not down there on the road with it.

Large black eyes stared up at them; the nose was raised to the wind to catch their scent. The sound of the conveyor seemed amplified in Lena's ears as the roo's gaze lowered to the lumps of ore passing before him. Her breath caught in her throat. The steady rumble of the machinery seemed to hypnotise it. The roo crouched again and leaned forwards, its legs pulling in momentum like a coiled spring. Lena's tongue cleaved to the top of her mouth. He was going to do it.

Without thinking, Lena whipped off her hard hat and threw it Frisbee style over the road. It flew straight over the kangaroo's head and then dropped into the ocean on the other side. The roo's head snapped up, following the path of the white top. With a sudden jerk, he whirled around and jumped after her hat. In the next second, he was over the edge. This time Lena heard the splash as the big red hit the waves.

She winced. That would have hurt. After all, they were eighteen metres above the water. 'Oh man!'

The sound of the impact seemed to spring the boys into action.

'Bloody oath, Madame E's just drowned the roo.'

'I haven't drowned the roo,' Lena protested but followed them as they hurried down the skid ladder and made their way to the edge of the road to see what had become of the animal. If she was honest with herself, Lena didn't really know what she had intended when she'd thrown the hat over the roo. It had been an impulse move, much like a leg kicking out when a doctor tapped a knee at just the right angle. There had been very little thought attached to it. She certainly hadn't expected the kangaroo to play fetch with her hat.

Radar was right. Roos were stupid.

Mike came up behind her, unable to resist a dig. 'That was the dumbest thing I've ever seen anyone do.'

Lena grimaced self-consciously; she couldn't disagree with him.

'Crikey!' Radar gestured at a patch of ocean. 'He's still alive.'

Lena and the skid crew followed his pointing finger and spotted the poor animal struggling to keep his head above water.

'Yeah but he's got no idea where he's going.' Biro shook his head. 'He's one and a half kilometres out to sea. I don't like his chances. Kangaroos aren't big swimmers.'

Lena cringed. Maybe she had just drowned the roo. Guilt seized her. Despite the fact that she was glad to be safe, she didn't want the mammal's death on her head. She would never intentionally endanger wildlife.

Tell that to the drowning kangaroo bobbing in the waves.

She swallowed. 'I didn't mean to.'

Biro laughed. 'It was him or us. Besides, look, he's already figured out which way is land.'

Sure enough, the kangaroo was paddling, if feebly, towards the shore.

Fieldmouse also looked up from his inspection of the waves. 'Bet you a hundred bucks he makes it.'

'One-fifty,' Biro challenged him.

Fieldmouse stuck out his hand. 'Done.'

The two-way on Mike's shoulder crackled.

'Did that roo just commit suicide? Over.'

Glaring at Lena, Mike picked up his receiver and clicked on. 'It jumped off the wharf. Over.'

There was a deep chuckle across the airways. 'Geez, Mike, heard you had a pretty bad set-up on the skid. Didn't realise it was that fuckin' scary. Over.'

'Give it a rest. Over.'

Again they heard the laughing across the airways. Mike switched off his radio. 'Okay, boys, back to work.' His gaze returned contemptuously to Lena. 'You better hope Bulldog doesn't catch you without your hat.'

A little shaken by the whole scenario, Lena decided to wait on the road rather than join the boys on the skid. They were in a taunting mood, calling her the Kangaroo Hunter among other things. Personally, she was starting to feel just a little sick. After all, she'd just threatened the life of a national icon.

Fifteen minutes later, the bus pulled up, the doors slid open and she looked up with relief into Sharon's friendly face. 'Hey.'

'Hey yourself,' Sharon grinned. 'Everyone's been glued to the airways. What's this about a kangaroo you tried to decapitate with your hard hat?'

Lena said, 'That's definitely not what happened.' She got on the bus and slumped into the seat behind Sharon, trying to ignore the cheers from the men at the back.

'Way to go, Madame E!'

Yeah. Yeah. Whatever.

The bus was facing the end of the wharf, so she'd be taking the round trip back to the office. She sighed. It was the last thing she felt like doing.

'It was awful,' she told Sharon as she filled her in on the real story. By the time they reached Gavin's crew, Sharon was still trying unsuccessfully to console her for having sent the kangaroo to a watery grave.

'Lena!' Gavin hailed her with a wave as she got off the bus with Sharon. 'Well done.'

Lena shook her head with a groan and said the first thing that came to mind. 'I need a drink.'

'Well, Point Samson is coming at a good time then,' he grinned. 'You, me, Sharon and a couple of my mates at the pub tomorrow night is just what you need.' His eyes rested a second longer on Sharon and the slight pause buoyed Lena's drooping spirits. They were connecting.

She looked away to hide her glee. 'Yeah, sounds good.'

It was like the men around them had sonar scanning for the words 'drinks', 'Point Samson' and 'tomorrow night' because a shout went up behind them.

'Drinks at Point Samson tomorrow night!'

Gavin's head snapped up. 'What? No. I meant –'

But the eavesdropper had already passed the message on and it was heading round the end of the wharf like Chinese whispers, before being shouted across to the men on the piling barge.

'Drinks at Point Samson!'

'When?'

'Tomorrow night! Gav's organised it.'

Lena cocked her head to one side and eyed Gavin and Sharon apologetically. 'Looks like it's not going to be that quiet.'

Gavin frowned. 'Bloody hell.'

She nodded in sympathy. If he was going to make the moves on Sharon tomorrow night, he probably didn't want a massive audience. She decided to keep as much attention off the two of them as possible.

As the commotion died down, she saw Bulldog striding across the deck, a clipboard tucked under his arm and a grim expression moulding his lips. He was wearing a light blue shirt with the TCN company logo on it and somehow making the bland garment sexy. Nonetheless, she was still smarting from his last batch of insults and if he was about to tell her off for not wearing her hard hat, she was in no mood for it.

He stopped by their little group, his arrogance and focus seeming to sweep Gavin and Sharon aside. Awareness tickled her spine as their gazes collided.

'Can I talk to you for a minute?'

'If this is about my hard hat,' she began.

'It's not about your hard hat,' he returned tightly, 'it's about the access platform.' He indicated the small office donga sitting on the end of the wharf and headed in that direction, clearly expecting her to follow. It took all her self-control not to stamp her foot and refuse. Sharon shot her a sympathetic look and, with an inward sigh, she gave up the fight and made off after him. After all, she was trying to be professional not childish.

The donga in question was mainly used as a storage facility by Gavin and Fish. It contained all the drawings and codes they needed to keep handy, in addition to a fridge, a sink and a trestle table for the odd tea break.

Bulldog closed the door behind them and turned around.

'I heard what happened on the skid. Are you okay?'

Is he for real?

'I beg your pardon?' She looked for signs of mockery but found none.

'Are you okay?' His gaze was serious rather than cynical. Her senses heightened as the smell of man and aftershave began to curl around her. The problem with dongas was that most of them weren't very well ventilated – whatever you put in them tended to stink them up. Not that Bulldog stank. She breathed in the scent that was only him before realising he was still waiting on her answer.

'Um . . . yeah. Sure. I'm fine. I mean, the kangaroo went over the side before it had a chance to do any damage.'

He nodded, removing his hard hat and laying it on the table. His fingers went straight into his dark hair and she followed their path hungrily. 'You know, you think you're prepared for everything and then something like this happens,' he said.

She looked away from his hair and frowned. 'There's nothing you could have done to prevent it, Dan. Don't worry about it.'

His gaze snapped to hers. *Dan?* Tension stretched between them until he spoke again.

'It's my responsibility to make sure you have a safe work environment.'

'Well, it's over now.' She shrugged. 'And I don't think there's much chance that something like that could happen twice.'

'I just don't understand how that thing managed to get past the boom gates.'

She couldn't help it; her sense of the ridiculous was tickled. 'Yeah,' she nodded. 'I mean, it would have failed the PPE check for sure.'

Almost imperceptibly his lips began to curl, until it became obvious that he was smiling. And not just any smile: a huge grin with teeth and everything. It lit up his whole face and knocked the wind out of her pipes in one unexpected punch.

'Yeah.' He took his hand out of his hair. 'It would have.'

A bitter-faced Bulldog rankled her senses, but a smiling Dan she was just not prepared to deal with. She stared at him like an owl with a torch in its face. But almost as quickly as it had appeared, his smile left him.

'I should have known you would find my concern amusing.' He paused, drumming his fingers on the tabletop. 'I wanted to see you because Carl passed me your reports and calcs this morning. I've decided to give you the go-ahead for the access platform.'

'Thanks.' She hoped the nonchalant tone of her voice adequately disguised the fact that she was dancing on the inside.

'You'll need to keep on top of it, though. I don't want it falling behind like everything else.'

'Of course.'

He made to go, hesitated and then turned back. 'Look, some things were said the other night and . . .' This time it was he who couldn't meet her eyes. Was he actually trying to apologise?

She folded her arms. *This ought to be good.* 'Yes, they were.'

'I just wanted to tell you that the reason I didn't tell Carl about the flag is, despite what you might think, I don't want you to fail. You make me think about my brother. Mark.'

Lena's trademark curiosity was piqued. 'Is he an engineer?'

He paused. 'He was.'

'Okay.' She nodded and waited for something extra but his expression was blank. She guessed that was as close to 'I'm sorry' as she was going to get.

'Well, I think I was a bit harsh with you too,' she offered. 'You're not a totally bad manager.'

'Is that an apology?'

Her jaw dropped at his audacity and she gave him the best 'You wish' expression in her repertoire. 'Nup.'

His lips kicked in one corner as he picked up his hard hat, turning it over in his hands. 'When are you going back to the office?'

'Well, I thought I might check out the piling and decking progress while I wait for the next bus run back,' she told him.

'Well, I brought my ute, so I'm going back now. You should take my hat.' Before waiting for her assent he put it on her head, his hands grazing the sides of her face on their way down. Suddenly, they were standing too close for comfort and she felt her chest tighten in anticipation as she looked up at him.

'Oh,' she said breathlessly. 'That's okay. It's really not necessary.' She lowered her head and put her hand up to catch the front rim. But he intervened with a warm hand under her chin to force her face back up.

'You be careful.'

She didn't know whether to be indignant or touched by his order. While she was still deciding, he left, her chin tingling in his wake.

Outside Lena watched the hammer for a while, until Sharon approached her to let her know the bus was leaving for shore.

The bus driver's eyes flicked up to the TCN emblem on her hat and frowned. 'Something you want to tell me?'

'Not really.'

'Come on, Lena. You're wearing his hat? Not to mention the fact that he's already seen you in your unmentionables.'

'Sssshh!' She followed Sharon back to the bus. Carl and Gavin were chatting in front of it when they got there. Carl's eyes flicked to her hat also.

'I see Bulldog couldn't let you go without a hat for fuckin' five seconds.' He shrugged. 'Just as well, I suppose. We don't need more fuckin' trouble on our hands. I've been looking into the night shift. Fuckin' nightmare.' He sighed and looked at Gavin who was nodding and a thought seemed to suddenly occur to him. 'Hey, aren't you organising some big shindig at Point Samson tomorrow?'

Gavin started. 'No, that's not –' He sighed with resignation. 'Do you want to come?'

Carl looked at Sharon. 'You birds goin'?'

'Sure.' Sharon licked her lips nervously. Lena had already told her about the plan and she was looking forward to it, if somewhat uncertainly.

'Fuck, I need a night on the piss,' Carl sighed and then looked at Lena as another thought brightened his face. 'Fuck, I just thought of something. If everyone's fuckin' going –'

'Not everyone's going,' Gavin made haste to insert. 'At least, they're not supposed to be. I –'

But Carl wasn't listening; he was rubbing his chin thoughtfully. 'The bullshit flying around between us and the client is getting fuckin' worse. I might tell Bulldog to tell his people about it. Fuck, let's invite 'em. Bit of a peace offering, so to speak. Build some better client relations. I'll even set up a bar tab.' He slapped Gavin on the back. 'Well done, mate. Best fuckin' idea anyone's had in a while.'

Gavin choked. 'But –'

Carl was already half walking away. 'I'll leave you to organise it,' he threw over his shoulder.

Friday passed uneventfully. Lena realised that everyone was too keyed up for Gavin's big party to raise any big issues. It was like they were all just pushing through the hours to get to the good stuff.

It was pathetic how excited they were. After all, when she thought about it, it was just a pub. But they were treating it like Elvis was in town for one show only. Personally, she was excited for many different reasons. One of them, trivial or not, was that she was finally going to be able to wear something other than her gym clothes or her site uniform. This was a very special treat, especially considering she had three suitcases of clothes to choose from.

Point Samson was a tiny fishing town about nine kilometres north. It was supposed to be much more touristy than Wickham, with beautiful sandy beaches that offered safe swimming and snorkelling all year round. Its central pub allegedly did the best garlic prawns on the Pilbara. She figured there would be other non-project women at the Point Samson pub – plenty of females to take the attention off her and Sharon. So it should be okay to dress pretty.

In the end, she chose a little red camisole top that tied at the back and really dressed up her dark blue jeans. She wore a red pendant to match and left her hair out and curly.

Carl had offered up his five-seater ute for transport if either she or Sharon drove. He wanted to drink. Lena volunteered her services as skipper because she thought Sharon would need the Dutch courage more than she would, especially if Gavin made his move. At six-thirty, the two friends met Carl in the parking lot next to his vehicle.

Sharon looked fantastic and Lena could see by the surprise on Carl's face that he thought so too. She'd clearly taken a curling wand to her short red bob, which looked great with the black halter-neck top she was wearing.

'You look awesome!' Lena beamed and, when Gavin turned up shortly after, she immediately scanned his face for a reaction. 'Doesn't she look great, Gavin?'

He paused to give Sharon the once-over. 'Yep.'

Sharon blushed. 'Thanks.'

He turned to Lena. 'And so do you.'

Lena waved the compliment aside: he didn't need to worry about her feeling left out. Tonight was their night.

'Fuck, I'm thirsty.' Carl rubbed his hands together. He was wearing a Hawaiian shirt, which he later told Lena was his 'drinking shirt', and a pair of blue shorts. She'd never seen him more set to party. Just as she was about to ask what they were waiting for, Fish turned up, also wearing a Hawaiian 'drinking shirt'. She had been told that he and Carl had a history but up until this point hadn't been able to see what they had in common – Carl wasn't into fishing and Fish didn't seem to be into anything else. She figured it out as they made matey fun of each other during the drive to Point Samson. She learned that they had first met at a pub over more than a few drinks. Apparently, they had quite a number of party stories to share on the way to their next crime scene.

When they finally did arrive, Lena noticed there were other women at the pub but not enough to make a dent in her and Sharon's minority. She realised in dismay that half the project workforce was crammed into that little pub at Point Samson.

Overall, however, it was a great set-up. It had a huge balcony area that overlooked the beach with a long bar servicing the crowd. The majority of people were standing as most of the tables were inside where meals were served. When Lena's party arrived, the festivities were well and truly under way. Some of the guys had not bothered to change out of their site uniforms and had just come straight from work. There was a quiet group of client personnel drinking by themselves in one corner and before she could stop herself she was searching for Dan's face among them.

He was leaning against the wall in a TCN shirt, which probably meant he'd come straight from work that night too. With a beer in hand, he was talking to not one, but *two* women. Lena was momentarily struck. Until then she hadn't credited Dan with any ability to be socially charming. Her eyes narrowed stubbornly. There was still no proof, really. The women could be his administrative staff, being criticised for late typing submissions. The brunette, a rather good-looking one too, threw back her head and laughed at something Dan had said. Lena eyed them both crossly.

As though feeling an arrow of disapproval hit the wall above his head, Dan looked up and met her gaze across the room. Heat crept up her neck and Lena tore her face away. How embarrassing. She needed to steer all her thoughts as far from Dan as possible. Lately, she couldn't seem to trust either her body or her brain whenever he was around. She seemed to lose all aptitude for reasonable behaviour.

Instead, she turned her attention to Carl and Fish, who were anxious to get started. They headed straight for the bar. Apparently pre-dinner drinks were a must. The food would come later. This was fine with her, as she was eager for a chance to scope out the scene. There were a couple of secluded areas on the balcony, where a couple might move away to catch a private moment if they so desired. One of them was a selection of large pot plants on her far left, the other an isolated table on her right. Keeping these two areas in mind, she turned to see where Gavin was and watched him get hailed by one of his men. Before she knew it, he had also been dragged away. She clicked her tongue in frustration, wondering how she was going to get him and Sharon alone. Sharon recalled her attention by shoving a glass of house white into her hand.

'Penny for your thoughts.'

Lena turned a cheeky smile on her. 'It'll cost you way more than that.'

Sharon laughed and clinked her glass to Lena's. 'To good times.'

'To good times.' They drank. As the cool woody flavour hit her tastebuds, she sighed. When it was all said and done, it was just nice to be out, relaxing with friends, totally dust-free.

'You know,' she said to Sharon, 'I don't know what I'd do without you.'

Sharon winked. 'Right back at ya.'

Half a glass and fifteen minutes later, they'd been chatted up by at least five guys.

'Hello, ladies.' Lucky Mr Six wiggled his eyebrows at them as he walked by. 'I'll be back soon.' Sharon shifted uncomfortably beside Lena.

'Don't they ever give up?' she muttered under her breath.

A Barnes Inc welder sitting at the bar seemed to have overheard her comment and turned around. 'Yeah, I'd watch out for Tim.' He pointed after Mr Six. 'He's a real womaniser. But you can trust me.' He held out his hand and Lena and Sharon shook it reluctantly. 'I'm Brad.'

Lena noticed out of the corner of her eye that Gavin was watching. The schemer in her immediately jumped to high alert. Jealousy was a great motivator. She decided to encourage Sharon to add fuel to the fire.

'Can I buy you ladies a drink?' Brad was saying.

Lena polished off the rest of her wine and set her glass on the bar. 'Sure, Brad, why not?'

Sharon's eyes shifted curiously to Lena. She nodded reassuringly, so the bus driver also placed her empty glass on the counter. Delighted, Brad moved down the bar towards a waiter.

Just then Tim returned from wherever he had gone and joined them with a grin. 'Saw you guys talking to Brad and thought I better give you a friendly warning.' He lowered his voice as though confiding a secret. 'He's a bit of a ladies' man.' He rocked back on his heels and stuck out his hand. 'But you can trust me, my name's –'

'Tim,' Lena finished for him. 'We know.'

His brow wrinkled in confusion as Brad returned with the drinks. Lena watched as the two men sized each other up before suddenly coming to an unspoken truce – they would share. One each, Lena supposed, torn between amusement and indignation.

It continued like that for another hour or so. Lena and Sharon collected a couple more glasses of free booze although Lena refrained from drinking hers as she was driving. The men around them continued to get drunker and drunker. Carl, Lena noticed, was leading the crowd.

Soon dinner was forgotten. The men were filling up on alcohol and seemed in no hurry to move inside for a feed.

'Damn it,' Lena told Sharon, 'I think they're all going to skip dinner.'

Sharon nodded hazily. 'Nothing like drinking on an empty stomach to get you plastered real fast.'

'So you want to go inside for a bite then?' a voice whispered in Lena's ear. She spun on her heel.

It was Gavin.

Why is he asking me?

Warning bells started to tingle in her head but she ignored them. Surely not. Gavin and Sharon would make the perfect couple! No other outcome would be permitted.

'You know what, that sounds great. Why don't you two go inside and find us a table?'

'But –'

'I'll be in shortly.' She looked meaningfully at Sharon. 'Okay?'

'You sure?' Sharon's eyes were a little wide, so she touched her arm reassuringly.

'Yep, just save me a seat.'

The two of them headed inside and Lena pretended she was going to the toilet. She was delighted by her own ingenuity. It was the ideal plan. They'd go inside, order their food, get to talking and after a while forget she was even supposed to join them.

She moved towards Carl's group at the bar. The man was definitely in his element, entertaining the guys with his repertoire of lewd jokes. He hadn't seen her yet and was in the process of delivering the punchline of an incredibly filthy number when she cleared her throat. She grinned, as the guys laughed harder, more at Carl noticing her standing there than the end of his joke.

'Come on, Carl, tell us another one.' Fish slapped him on the back. 'I know you've got more.'

To her surprise, he reddened and hid behind his beer. 'No, no. Got fuckin' told off the other day. No fuckin' bullshit with the ladies present. I've already scared one of them off.'

His reference to Dan's comments immediately made Lena's back stiffen.

'If you mean Sharon,' she reassured him, 'she's just gone inside for a bite. Not scared at all.'

But Carl refused to budge, the liquor in him bringing out a stubborn streak. 'No, no,' he slurred. ''Bout time I became a fuckin' gentleman. Been thinking about it since the other day: never been any good with the fuckin' ladies. I'll tell you what, got some clean jokes for ya.'

The men groaned loudly and booed him but Carl was determined. He raised his pint and began yelling at the top of his lungs.

'Why did the leper meet with a car accident? Left his foot on the accelerator. What's long, brown and sticky? A stick. Why do giraffes have such long necks? So their heads can connect to their bodies.'

He didn't stop.

Lena didn't know where he was pulling them all from but they were the worst jokes she'd ever heard in her life. Luckily, the men had enough alcohol in them to find anything funny. The laughter got louder and louder as each consecutive joke got worse and worse until everyone was choking on their beers. The noise was drawing the sober crowd too. So Carl kept going until he had tears in his eyes. In turn, Lena was laughing so hard she couldn't talk and when she thought she couldn't possibly laugh any more Carl shouted: 'Confucius say, man who drop watch in toilet keeps shitty time.'

Clutching a stomach aching with laughter, she didn't resist the arm that came around her shoulders and pulled her aside. Still hiccupping with mirth, she turned to find Gavin there.

'Gavin?' She wiped a tear from the corner of her eye. 'What are you –?'

'Aren't you going to join us?'

She glanced back at Carl and the boys, who were still laughing hysterically. 'Yes, no – I thought I might give dinner a miss.' She patted his arm distractedly. 'You and Sharon go ahead.'

'Lena, I need to tell you something.'

'Huh?' She suddenly realised he'd pulled her over to the pot plants. She looked behind him, wondering where Sharon was. 'What's going on?'

And it was only then when she saw his too-intense brown eyes that she realised what a very terrible mistake she had made. But it was too late. He had already grabbed her face between his palms and lowered his lips to hers.

She froze in shock, until the sound of a glass shattering broke her stupor.

Their lips disconnected and she took a giant step away from him, turning quickly to view the damage. There were a lot of people staring.

A lot.

Her skinned burned hot as she turned from one amused person to another, like a bird in a cage. The bar was almost quiet with the weight of the speculation going on. But all other faces blurred into the background as one person's suddenly came into sharp and painful focus.

It was Sharon, her broken glass at her feet.

Chapter 9

Sharon's face was as red as her hair. She spun on her heel and stumbled into the crowd. Lena's throat closed up.

Oh crap.

'Lena, what's wrong?' A gentle hand on her cheek pulled her attention back to Gavin, who she realised was standing far too close. She swiftly stepped back.

'I really wish you hadn't done that.'

He lowered his hand, his eyes reflecting the concern in his voice. 'Why?'

Her reply was lost in the cheer that rose up around them. The drunk and the drunker raised their beers.

'Way to go, Gav!'

Double crap.

Lena did her best to stem her rising panic as they converged on them, their teasing remarks filling the air.

'We knew there was something going on between you two!'

'Too cosy by half!'

She looked beyond their ranks, trying desperately to spot Sharon. It was useless. Hands stretched out to ruffle Gavin's hair; grubby fingers waggled wickedly in front of her nose.

She pushed them aside, craning her neck to see past them.

'I have to find Sharon,' she said to Gavin. When he didn't seem to hear, she made her announcement louder and to everyone at large. 'I have to find Sharon!'

They blatantly ignored her, too busy congratulating Gavin, clicking their beers together and laughing at some lewd joke, of which she was no doubt the centre. With a frustrated groan, she shoved the guy in front of her out of the way.

'Hey.' His tone was exaggerated hurt but she didn't care.

Finally, she broke free of the crowd. Sucking in a breath of clean air, she crashed face-first into the flat plane of a hard male chest.

'Guess you've never heard of the golden rule.'

Lena fell back and looked up to find Dan's mouth pulled into a taut line. A muscle worked in his lean cheek as he stared down at her, less than impressed. The last thing she needed was a riddle. What was wrong with these people? But like a log caught in a rip, she went along for the ride.

'What rule?'

'Never dip your pen in the company ink.' Each word was pronounced slowly and succinctly, like he was throwing darts at a bullseye one by one. A shot of anger heated her body. The fact that it was the advice she'd been giving herself ever since her break-up with Kevin only served to heighten her resentment. Instead of agreeing with him, her shrill voice jumped right to defensive.

'Excuse me?'

'How long have you and Gavin been seeing each other?'

'How is that any of your business?'

'You're the one keen on a public display.'

She put her hand up. 'I don't have time for this. I have to find Sharon.'

He indicated to her left with his head. 'She went inside. Toilet, I think.'

Lena sighed, relieved he wasn't going to try to rile her further. 'Thanks.'

'Stole her boyfriend, did you?'

What?!

The off-the-cuff remark stopped her in her tracks once more. '*No*. Not that I need to explain myself to you.'

He shrugged. ''Cause if you meant to send her some sort of message,' he sipped his beer, 'you nailed it.'

Before she could reply, he strode away, leaving her steaming. If he was going to be so interested in her business, the least he could do was give her the last word. Of all the inconsiderate, Bulldoggy things to do. She reined in her temper, however. There would be time enough later to put his head on a stick. Right then, she had a friendship to save. She headed for the toilets.

Pushing open the door, she stopped short when she saw Sharon poised over the sink in front of the mirror. She was dabbing beneath her eyes with a tissue, trying to repair damage to her mascara. Damage that had clearly been caused by crying. Their gazes clashed briefly in the mirror before Sharon jerked away, as she threw her tissue in a bin against the wall. Lena waited for her to turn back around but she didn't. Instead, Sharon stood there with her hands on her hips, her gaze locked firmly on the dirty white tiles at her feet.

Lena closed the door quietly behind her and came further into the room. 'Sharon –'

'Don't you dare speak to me,' her friend hissed. 'There's no excuse for what you did.'

Lena tried to inject calm and logic into her tone. 'It was a misunderstanding. Before I knew what was going on, it just happened. He kissed me.'

'I'm not seeing the misunderstanding in that explanation.'

Lena had never heard so much bitterness in Sharon's voice before and it scared her. Sharon still wasn't looking at her either, which wasn't a good sign. Lena wrung her hands, knowing that she needed to do better but wasn't sure where to start.

'It came as a shock to me too,' she tried again. 'I didn't want him to kiss me.'

'It's not like you were pushing him away.' Sharon's voice cracked like cooled glass as she finally spun around. 'How could you encourage him like that? Did you lie to me? Or decide later that you wanted him for yourself?'

'*No*.' Lena was horrified. 'It wasn't like that at all.'

'Like what? Like you knifed me in the back, made me look like a fool?'

'I didn't make you look like a fool.'

'I came onto him, Lena,' Sharon cried. 'When we went off to dinner I practically threw myself at him.' She pushed the words through her teeth bitterly. 'You built up my confidence. Made me think I had a chance, plus the wine . . .' Her voice trailed off.

'Sharon, I'm so sorry –'

'You didn't look very sorry when I found you a minute ago.'

'It wasn't –'

But Sharon would not let her speak. 'I don't understand you, Lena. Why would you do this to me, especially after all that rubbish you sprouted about how great Gavin and I would be together?'

'It wasn't rubbish. I meant every word.' Lena came forwards and laid a hand on her shoulder.

Sharon rolled her shoulder violently, displacing her hand. 'Well, then that just makes you a two-faced bitch, doesn't it?'

Lena reeled back. Her voice was barely a whisper when she finally found it. 'I can't believe you have so little faith in our friendship.'

'What friendship?' Sharon retorted. 'Friends don't betray one another. Friends don't trick each other.'

'Are you suggesting I planned this?' Lena's sympathy was slowly evolving into anger. 'What possible gain could I have for hurting you in this way? You are the best friend I have out here, Sharon. You're the only one I can count on.'

Sharon snorted cruelly. 'Not any more.'

'Sharon –' But there was nowhere else to go. No other way Lena could explain it.

Sharon dashed away fresh tears. 'I was just fine before you came along. Better actually,' she amended. 'Didn't have to deal with an up-herself city girl always knee-deep in trouble.'

A lump the size of an apricot lodged inside Lena's throat. 'That's . . . that's what you think of me?'

Sharon tossed her hair and straightened. 'Come on, Lena, you've been a disaster zone since you got here and somehow I get the impression it's not a new thing.'

Blood receded from Lena's face and her lips went numb. She couldn't respond. Couldn't say anything to a fact she now knew was ingrained into everything she did. Sharon seemed satisfied with the effect of her bullet because she hitched the strap of her shoulder bag with the confidence of one who knew she was leaving and added, 'You and Gavin deserve each other.'

It took a second for Lena to recover and in that time Sharon departed. When Lena finally turned around, the only evidence of her friend's presence was the still-swinging bathroom door.

Tears smarted behind Lena's eyes in the wake of Sharon's parting. She caught her reflection in the mirror. The festive nature of her outfit mocked her. She was in a dirty toilet in a pub full of drunks and her only friend in town had just dumped her.

She felt like Bambi after his mother was shot.

How could this have happened? Was their friendship so fragile that it could be broken by a single mistake – a mistake that wasn't even hers? Tears spilled over and trickled silently down her face. She didn't bother to brush them away. Instead, she reached into her handbag and pulled out a hair elastic. With jerky hands, she arranged her usual dumpy site ponytail. It was mildly comforting, like putting her mask back on. Her stomach twisted as she pushed open the door and went in search of Carl. All she wanted to do now was go home. Back to camp would have to do.

Lena found Carl and Gavin drinking together on the balcony. They had a score of shooters lined up on the bar and were taking it in turns to tip them back. She could see Fish down the opposite end buying jugs and five guys waiting rather impatiently beside him.

'Sharon's taken the car home,' Gavin offered by way of greeting. 'Wasn't feeling well or something and Carl thought it'd be a good idea.'

'The bird looked upset if you ask me.' Carl gave Lena a look that was way too knowing for a man half tanked. 'Everything all right?'

Lena looked away. 'Fine. Fine.'

'Anyway,' Gavin continued, clearly unconcerned about Sharon, the rat that he was, 'Carl, Fish and I were thinking about finding somewhere to stay in Point Samson tonight. Sort out a ride home in the morning.'

Trepidation rolled through Lena. 'Where does that leave me?'

Gavin shrugged slowly. 'Thought you might want to do the same.'

'You've got to be kidding me.'

She'd rather walk back to camp than spend the entire night there with them. Gritting her teeth, she checked the scream that begged to emerge.

Carl toasted her with a shooter. 'Point Samson's got some good hotels on offer. Fuck me if it ain't better than sleeping in a donga.'

Lena couldn't care less. She just wanted to leave. Her party mood had definitely died and weariness was beginning to seep into bones, already weak from an emotional flaying. Flipping over her wrist, she checked her watch. Three hours till the pub closed and the site bus would come to take the men back. Any remaining sympathy she had for Sharon disappeared. If she could do this to her, she wasn't worth feeling sorry for.

'Lena,' Gavin interrupted her brooding, 'is there a problem?'

She pressed her palms over her eyes. 'Not one that you can fix.'

He wiped his hands down the side of his jeans and stood up. 'Look . . . er . . . can we talk?'

She knew he meant privately but she wasn't falling for that again. She shook her head. 'I don't think that's a good idea.'

'Please.' Something in his tone made her hesitate.

Carl rolled his eyes and swiped a shooter off the bar. 'Look, why don't I just fuck off then?' Then he half walked, half staggered away in Fish's direction.

'You've got five seconds,' Lena said as soon as he was out of earshot. She tried not to think about how many people might be watching them, making the gossip worse. The clink of glass and plates around them made her itch with impatience. But Gavin seemed to be taking his time.

'We kissed.' His brows knitted together. 'Don't you think we should talk about it?'

'We didn't kiss: you kissed me and I didn't return the favour. There's nothing to talk about.'

To her annoyance, he stepped closer and lowered his voice. 'I think there is. I mean, I wouldn't kiss you unless it meant something to me. I respect you too much.'

'If you respected me, you would've asked first.'

'I didn't want to ruin the moment.'

She stared at him in disbelief. 'What moment? You hijacked me, that's what you did. I was completely unaware of what was coming next. Otherwise, I would have tried to stop you.'

He coughed, unable to meet her eyes. 'I've never been that good with women. You know, reading the signals and everything. I didn't mean – I just assumed –' He broke off.

She took a firm step back. 'You *assume* a lot, Gavin. I thought you were better than this. Hell, I thought you'd be good for –'

It was his turn to stare. 'Good for what?'

She bit her lip and looked away, inwardly cursing at the slip. 'Nothing. Forget it.'

Luckily he did, apparently deciding to plead his case from a different angle. 'Clearly I jumped the gun. Maybe we could start over? Take it slower.'

Lena sighed. 'Gavin, I don't mind being your friend. But anything more is out of the question.'

'Why?'

If he wanted blunt, he was going to get it. 'Because I'm not attracted to you.'

'Oh.'

At last, he seemed stumped. And as he rubbed his left hand awkwardly across the back of his neck, she almost felt sorry for him.

Almost.

He grimaced sheepishly. 'I guess that's telling me, isn't it?'

Lena shrugged. 'I'd apologise, but I don't think you deserve it.'

He chuckled and held out his hand. 'Friends?'

With a sigh her anger faded to a simmer. 'Friends.' She shook his hand.

'Now if you don't mind,' he grinned boyishly, 'I might go drink myself under the table with Carl.'

She didn't try to stop him, heading back inside the pub on her own instead. This seemed to offer some modicum of privacy as the majority of the project revellers were outside.

To be honest, she didn't quite know what she was going to do next. She was stuck in the middle of nowhere, no car, no ride home and pretty much friendless. She supposed vaguely that she could try to find Leg or Radar. But the odds that they weren't both wasted and unwilling to drive were a hundred to one. The other option was the bus. However, the prospect of waiting till midnight to share a bus packed to the brim with drunk men made her feel ill. She sat down at an empty table and tried to think of an alternative without much success.

Hitchhiking: too dangerous.

Walking: too far.

Cab: unlikely to be available.

She rubbed at her moistening eyes and blinked furiously, drumming her fingers on the tabletop to distract herself.

Damn.

'Trouble in paradise?'

The low male voice gnawed on her frayed senses. Just what she needed – another lecture about company ink and dipping her pen. Why couldn't he just stay out of it?

She looked up and registered Dan's broad shoulders, chiselled cheekbones and dark glinting eyes. 'There's no paradise to speak of.'

His right brow lifted. 'Well, that doesn't surprise me. After all, we're talking about Gavin, aren't we? You could have chosen better.'

Her control broke.

'In case you didn't know, the client doesn't actually get to comment on the dating practices of the contractor. Your opinion is neither warranted nor required. And if I needed a character assessment of Gavin, which I don't, you'd be the last person I'd go to. So just back off.'

She looked away then, staring blankly at the people milling by her table. Cupping her chin in her palm, she pressed her little finger against her mouth to conceal its tell-tale trembling.

Go away. Go away. Go away, she chanted silently, hoping that her secret telepathic powers of persuasion would work.

They didn't.

The shadow he cast across her table didn't move and, as the silence lengthened, she finally looked up.

'For goodness sake, *what do you want*?'

He seemed to hesitate but then sat down across from her, placing the plate he was carrying between them.

'Hungry?'

She was starved but she wasn't going to tell him that. 'No thanks.'

His lips twitched. 'Go on, have one. They're good.'

The plate held succulent prawns covered in creamy garlic sauce; saliva filled her mouth. Her hand moved before she could stop it, picking up one of the many forks laid out on the table and stabbing a prawn. He watched her pop it into her mouth. The tender, buttery flesh burst upon her tastebuds.

'Oh my God,' she groaned, putting a hand to her mouth. 'These are to die for.'

He nodded knowingly as she forked another.

She groaned with pleasure again. 'These are the best garlic prawns I've ever tasted.'

'They're probably also the freshest.' He grinned. 'It's likely they were swimming twenty-four hours ago.'

'Poor little things,' she said and stabbed another.

'That's one thing about the Pilbara. No better place on earth for seafood.' He lifted his fork and took one for himself. She watched it pass his lips, searching his face for clues about what he was thinking. His dark hair was windswept, probably from the breeze on the balcony. Her fingers itched to smooth the wayward tufts or brush his lean cheek.

'You shaved.' The words were out before she could catch them. He looked at her strangely and she wished that she could bite them back. 'When we had that last meeting at your offices you hadn't shaved,' she said by way of explanation.

'Hadn't I?'

If it were possible, she would have kicked herself under the table. 'I don't know,' she tried to go vague. 'I think so.'

He forked another prawn. 'I guess I just didn't have time that day.' His expression darkened as though he were remembering something. Curiosity won out over good manners again.

'Why?'

For a second, it looked like he wasn't going to answer and then he shrugged. 'I had a long phone call from home that morning. Made me late.'

Oh, the girlfriend. She groaned inwardly.

He pushed the plate towards her. 'Last one, you want it?'

She took the prawn and raised it to her mouth, unwittingly giving him the opportunity to change the subject.

'So are you going to tell me why you're sitting here all alone feeling sorry for yourself or not?'

She put her fork down and grabbed a napkin to dab her mouth. So that's what this whole sharing-his-dinner scenario was about. He was softening her up for another interrogation. She raked his face with what she hoped was her best I-got-your-number expression and pulled her lips tightly shut.

He shrugged. 'We can do this the hard way or the easy way. That's up to you.'

The challenge pricked her interest. 'What's the hard way?'

'I could call your boyfriend over and get him to fix his mess.'

'Oh.' She screwed up her face, not liking the sound of that at all. Gavin *was* the mess.

Dan leaned forwards, his eyes glowing in the dim lighting. 'Just *tell me.*'

Something about the way he said it stirred moths in her stomach. She quickly glanced around the room. No one was watching them. Everyone was outside. They were probably the only two sober people from the project in the whole pub.

She returned her gaze to his. 'I'm trying to figure out how I'm going to get home. Sharon's taken the car.'

'And Gavin?'

'He's staying overnight at Point Samson.'

'Nice.' His voice was scornful.

She shrugged. 'He and Carl want to have a big one.'

'At your expense?' He stood up. 'Come on, I'm taking you home.'

'What?' she said, startled. 'Don't you want to stay?'

'No. Let's go.'

'Carl's got a bar tab. You'll be missing out on –'

'On what?' His voice was incredulous. 'Free booze? Come on, Lena, don't be ridiculous.'

'But –'

'Have you got a better plan to get home?'

She passed her tongue over dry lips. 'No.'

He started walking, taking it for granted that she would follow him. And she did, relief washing over her like warm water. The lift was definitely a godsend. Why not just shut up and take it?

The car park was unlit and quiet, in direct contrast to the noisy pub they had left behind. She could hear the sound of their shoes on the gravel as they made their way towards his ute and then both climbed in. He started the engine as she put on her belt. The radio was playing 'With or Without You' softly.

The cabin seemed to shrink in size. Suddenly, the air was just a little too cosy and the night just a little too dark. He backed out of the car bay in silence and she laced her fingers together on her lap, sucking in a deep calming breath.

It was just a ride home, for goodness sake.

Yeah, with Dan Hullog.

Her fingers tightened on themselves.

Why did he always have this effect on her? It wasn't like he was ever flirtatious or anything. Certainly not in the way Kevin had been when she first started getting to know him. Always complimenting her, offering her things. Bulldog was more insulting than he was nice, and more stern than playful.

Of course, it *was* kind of him to have shared his garlic prawns with her. And he was really helping her out with this lift. But what was that laid alongside the criticisms, the reprimands and the threats?

It was a lowering thought, really: not only was she attracted to the one man who stood for the worst decision she'd ever made but he considered her no more than an irritating pest.

Lena sneaked a peek at him through her lashes. His gaze was intent upon the road. There were no streetlights. It only got darker and darker as they left the township. His face was deep in shadow. She could just make out the lack of smile.

What would it be like to kiss Dan Hullog?

She cringed, as though the forbidden words had been spoken out loud. Thank goodness it was too dark for him to make out her expression. She rubbed her wrist, trying to steady her throbbing pulse.

Kissing Dan Hullog would be like slaying a dragon.

Terrifying, rough and . . .

Magical.

She shivered.

'Cold?'

She nearly jumped as he leaned over and turned on the heater. Embarrassment flooded her body as though he had heard everything she'd been thinking. Her voice came out barely a whisper. 'Thanks.'

Warmth swirled around them, raising her already elevated temperature. If anything, she wished he would turn the radio off. The slow melodic beat did nothing to dampen the mood.

Lena cleared her throat, desperate for a distraction. 'So, you worked late tonight.' She indicated his shirt.

'I got stuck on the phone.'

She shook her head. 'I wouldn't have worked late tonight for anyone.'

'It wasn't work-related.'

'Oh.' A faster song started up on the radio, easing some of her tension and making her speak without thinking. 'Geez, that girlfriend of yours is pretty high maintenance.'

'Girlfriend?' His voice was amused. 'What made you think that?'

'Oh, I –' She wiped clammy palms down her thighs. 'You . . . er . . . You just seem to have a lot of personal phone calls back to Perth, that's all.'

Damn my loose lips.

At first she thought he wasn't going to reply and then he surprised her. 'I was talking to a lawyer actually.'

'Oh right.'

Even though curiosity was poking her in the ribs with a stick, Lena just couldn't bring herself to pry further. If Dan was a criminal, she didn't want to know about it. At least not in the middle of the night on a lonely road, miles from anyone who could help her. An awkward silence stretched between them.

'You're not going to ask?'

She heard, rather than saw, the amusement on his face. 'I didn't want to be rude.'

'Oswalds, the company I used to work for, is being sued. I'm a witness.'

'Oh okay.' She nodded. That was a relief – for her, anyway. For him – not so much. 'That must be rough.'

'You have no idea.' His tone was harried, not insulting, so she nodded again with understanding. He had to be so stressed out. She couldn't imagine working twenty-four-seven as well as being caught up in a lengthy court battle. She'd heard terrible stories about people, stuck in litigation for years, suffering depression or even mental breakdowns. She frowned. It was no wonder she hardly ever saw him smile, with this constantly in his thoughts. Before she was aware of what she was doing she had launched into a series of concerned suggestions.

'You know, you should really take your R and R. You need it. Recharge your batteries. Go on a holiday. Get your personal stuff figured out. People will understand. It's not worth pushing yourself so hard.'

He tore his gaze from the road to glance at her briefly. 'Trying to kick me out?'

'No. I just –' Lena broke off. She just what?

Cared?

She swallowed. *Don't go there, Lena.*

She couldn't care about Dan Hullog like this. It was wrong, dangerous and inappropriate on so many levels. It was too late, though: her feelings for Dan were already – more than a colleague – *no, a subordinate* – should have. The hairs on the back of her neck were prickling in warning. *This is not happening again. I refuse to be a party to it. I refuse!*

Dan pulled into the camp parking lot, found a spare bay and killed the engine.

The silence was deafening.

She scrambled for the doorhandle and hopped out. If she didn't mess around she could be in the safety of her donga within minutes. He came around to her side of the car, stalling her escape. His eyes were on her face and she could almost hear his brain ticking over as he studied her, a gentle breeze rustling his black locks.

'There's no need to worry about me, Lena.'

She shuffled on her feet and snorted in what she hoped was a convincing imitation of surprise and dismissal. 'I'm not worried about you.'

He moved a little closer. All her blood went to her head as awareness coiled around her like a boa constrictor preparing its dinner.

'Of course not, my mistake.' His voice was wry. He lifted a hand and tucked a stray strand of hair behind her ear. She felt the brush of each individual finger against her hairline and almost fainted from the shock of it. The mood had suddenly shifted.

His eyes glittered in the moonlight and he wasn't taking his hand away.

Is his face moving closer?

Her heart bounced into her mouth as his breath whispered across her cheek.

Was she going to slay her dragon?

The earth tilted on its axis.

The fingers behind her ear moved down her neck, causing her bones to liquefy. Involuntarily, her eyes fluttered closed and she rocked forwards towards him . . .

'I hope your boyfriend makes it up to you.'

It was amazing she didn't fall. She certainly stumbled, embarrassment flooding her senses.

She straightened quickly, trying to pretend nothing had happened. Because nothing *had*. She rubbed newly wet palms down the front of her jeans, nerves making her babble. 'As to that, Gavin and I are –'

'Goodnight, Lena.'

'Okay, yeah, goodnight,' she responded clumsily to his retreating back. 'Thanks for the, er –'

But he was at least five feet away from her by now. Cold and distant.

A chilly breeze whipped into her hair. She folded her arms protectively across her chest. He didn't look back and she watched him until he disappeared into the darkness.

The next morning, Lena did her best to put Dan Hullog out of her mind and focus on the things in her life she had a better chance at fixing.

Like her relationship with Sharon.

The passing of the night had fizzled her anger and strengthened her remorse. After all, Sharon had feelings for Gavin. Seeing him kiss another woman, especially a friend she thought she could trust, would have been a devastating experience. Lena was resolved to make it up to her.

The first thing she did when she arrived at work was go in search of the bus driver. Unfortunately, she soon found out that Sharon was delivering supplies to the end of the wharf and would be unavailable until seven am when the bus returned. It was a hellish hour. She felt like everyone was watching her. Twice, she caught the secretaries whispering behind their hands.

No doubt everyone knew what had happened at Point Samson and they were all enjoying a good gossip about it at her expense. The only thing that occurred to break up the focus on her was that the yard manager, Tony, had had a haircut. Radar and his band of merry men had been spreading it around for weeks that he wore a toupee. The new cut certainly laid these rumours to rest and various amounts of money had been changing hands all morning as bets were settled. She would have felt sorry for Tony if his hour of fame hadn't coincided nicely with hers.

In the end, Lena didn't catch up with Sharon until nine am due to her own work keeping her in the office. Sharon was unloading boxes of paper from the bus when Lena found her.

'Sharon, could we talk for a minute?'

Sharon slowly put down the box she was carrying and nodded. 'Okay.'

'I just want to apologise again for last night,' Lena began quickly. 'I don't want this whole Gavin thing to ruin our friendship.'

Sharon folded her arms and examined a scuff on her boot. 'I appreciate that and I apologise too for leaving you at the pub last night. I shouldn't have done that.'

Lena's body started to relax. 'Thank you.'

'But can you see why I was so upset?'

'Yes, of course I can,' Lena immediately declared, glad they were already making progress towards a reconciliation. 'I totally understand why you were hurt by me. Who wouldn't be in a situation like that?'

'Well, good,' Sharon nodded, still not looking at her. 'So . . . I guess you can understand then why I might want to keep my distance from you for a while.'

The statement took the wind out of Lena's sails. 'Sorry?'

'I can't be around you while you're with him.' Sharon's hands dropped to her sides. 'Just for the moment anyway; it's too awkward for me.'

Lena's eyes widened. 'But I'm not with Gavin, Sharon. It's all a big misunderstanding – just like I said last night. I don't like him that way.'

Sharon's brow wrinkled as she finally lifted her eyes. 'If you can't be honest with me, Lena, then what's the point of this conversation?'

'I *am* being honest with you.'

'Everyone knows you and Gavin are an item now.' Sharon shook her head. 'It's all over site.'

'It's just gossip.' Lena couldn't believe Sharon was taking their word over hers.

'It's not just gossip,' Sharon said. 'I saw the boys laying into Gavin about it this morning on the bus. They were all laughing about his new girlfriend and he just went red and *smiled*.' Sharon's voice wobbled, but she got herself in hand immediately.

Lena faltered. 'He w-what?'

With a sigh, Sharon picked up the box at her feet again. 'When you're ready to admit the truth, Lena, we might be able to talk properly.'

Outrage with Gavin and frustration with Sharon rendered Lena temporarily speechless. In the end, it didn't matter because her friend had already walked away. Lena would have followed her, if Radar hadn't chosen that moment to stroll by.

'Heard Gavin's on cloud nine this morning. Must have been some night.'

Outrage floored frustration and Lena pounced on him like a woman possessed.

'Hold it right there!'

Radar looked back in surprise. 'Something got your goat, Madame E?'

'Don't give me that,' she growled. 'You're the king of gossip. Tell me what the hell is going on here.'

'With what?'

'These rumours about me and Gavin.'

'Oh ho ho.' He leered at her. 'Calling them rumours, are you? A little too late for that with all the eyewitnesses floating about.'

'Radar, are we friends?' she demanded.

''Course we are.'

'Then be straight with me.'

'I'm *straight* with you all the way, baby.'

Her fingers itched to strangle him. He wasn't her friend. He was just another teasing, hormone-driven male who would never be sincere with her.

'I'm serious.' Her voice broke as she turned away.

She didn't expect her pain to have much effect on him. In fact, she'd been speaking more to herself than to him. But her words seemed to get through because he sobered suddenly and put a hand on her shoulder. A friendly hand.

'No one means any harm by it, Madame E.' His voice was gruff. 'In fact, I think it's great you and Gav got it together. At least nobody thinks you're gay no more.'

'Great. Lucky me.'

He took his hand away. 'Look, er . . . what's the problem?'

'Gavin did kiss me last night, but I had no idea he was going to. I told him to back off,' she explained. 'We're not together; we never were. He should be telling people that.'

Radar shrugged. 'Don't see why he should.'

'But it's the truth.'

'It's an opportunity is what it is,' Radar said wisely. 'Everybody's been watching out for who you'll get with. He probably wants to enjoy the fame a little longer.'

'For Pete's sake, why does anybody care?'

Radar choked and looked away. 'Have you seen yourself?' he mumbled.

'I know exactly how I look,' Lena replied tartly. 'I put a lot of thought and effort into creating this look. Do you think I enjoy the frumpy uniform, the lack of mascara and the hair untouched by product? I haven't filed my nails in days.' Her hysteria increased in intensity as she warmed to her theme. 'The only thing I don't deliberately apply is the dust. Lucky for me I attract the stuff along with every other loser on this job without any effort on my part at all.'

His cough sounded suspiciously like a chuckle. 'All the same, I think he'll risk your anger for a couple of weeks, just to show off.'

'So what you're saying is, this is all male pride and testosterone. Testosterone, at the expense of my professional reputation.' *And my friendship with Sharon*, she added silently.

'Yep.' Radar nodded in a manner which made her think that he considered testosterone a good enough reason.

Her anger reached its peak. 'Yeah, well. Two can play at that game!'

Chapter 10

Five days passed.

Sharon went on R and R, a circumstance that Lena was actually grateful for. Gavin's rumours were still flying free and fast and she hadn't figured out a way to scotch them yet. The man himself was proving to be singularly unhelpful, avoiding her whenever possible. The one time she managed to corner him, they got whistled and heckled at before she could get a word out. He made his escape while she was still glaring at the perpetrators.

Meanwhile, work that needed to be done for the skid team was piling up fast. She knew that instead of focusing on her personal life, she should be concentrating on what she'd come to the Pilbara for. She did her best to clear the colossal list of tasks she had on her plate, but there was not a single move she did not question, what with Kevin sitting on her right shoulder shaking his head and Sharon perched on her left, repeating the words she couldn't seem to get out of her head.

'You've been a disaster zone since you got here.'

It was true on all fronts, including her engineering.

She tapped a pencil on her notepad. What she needed was some firm goals – a road map she could use to avoid the personal traps laid for her by Mike and Gavin . . . and Dan. Something that would prove her worth, not by getting Dan's approval or even Carl's but something tangible that she could hold up and say, 'That's what I did and that's why I'm good.'

Lena knew it would be nice if the guys looked past her inexperience and sex and said, 'She's a great engineer.' But what would be better than all that is if she actually believed it herself.

She flicked through her drawings, ran her finger down the index and shuffled them into a pile again.

They were twenty per cent behind and setting up a night shift. So what if she could catch the skid boys up? What if she could make it so that they didn't need a bloody night shift to keep the skid on track? What if –?

'Todd, you fuckin' daydreamin'?'

Shit. Can I cut a break around here?

She glanced up and saw Carl peering over her shoulder. 'Hey, Carl.'

'I hear your R and R is coming up end of next week.'

It is? She nodded anyway, not wanting to appear ignorant.

'Have one of the girls book a flight for you,' Carl instructed.

'Sure.'

She turned back to her work, shocked that she'd actually forgotten she had a holiday coming up. It was amazing how quickly her five weeks on site had almost disappeared. Despite the welcome knowledge, she suddenly wished she had more time. As it stood, she had just over a week left to make some sort of headway with her new goal: zero per cent behind.

Lena worked solidly for the rest of the day, her new goal adding an extra layer of stress. As if that wasn't bad enough, at about three o'clock Tony from the yard called.

'Hey, Madame E, the first of the trusses have arrived.'

The trusses were her next task. They sat on top of the head-stocks and made up the layer that widened the jetty.

Glad for an opportunity to stretch her legs, she went outside to have a look at them being unloaded off the truck. The trusses were like steel-framed building blocks. They were eighteen metres long, 1.5 metres deep and weighed about eight tonnes each. Once installed, the new conveyor would sit inside them.

All up, Lena knew there were one hundred and seventy trusses to be installed. Of these only five had arrived and the sight of them being placed on the red dirt behind the dongas did nothing to assuage Lena's stress levels. In fact, it only served to increase them. One problem that had been lying quietly in the background of her mind leaped noisily to the forefront.

She hadn't quite figured out *how* to install them . . . exactly.

I mean, how do you get an eight-tonne piece of crap two kilometres out to sea and welded to the side of a jetty?

Her heart sank even further as she reached one that was already resting on the dirt. The paint job was terrible! Nowhere near acceptable. Dan would chuck a fit if she tried to install them in this condition.

With a sigh she returned to the office and hit the phones to the fabricator. She wanted an explanation and also a repaint. They must have known she'd be after them because she had to chase their manager for the next couple of hours. Some idiot in their office kept foiling her attempts to make contact. The first time she called he said, 'I'll get the manager to call you back.' The second time she called he said he'd forgotten to pass on the message and the manager had since gone out. And the third time she called he said the manager was actually home sick for the day.

What the –?

The manager was called Neville Smart, which only infuriated Lena further. After all, if you were going to go around publicly passing yourself off as 'Neville Smart', the least you could do was actually *be* smart, she reasoned. If she had to call him again, he'd have to settle for her calling him Neville Dumb. By knock-off, her mood was acid. There was nothing like going backwards when she'd just made all these plans to go forwards, to really make her jumping mad.

Lena went to dinner early, not looking forward to her meal, given there was no Sharon to sit next to and she was fed up with all men in general. She noticed Harry sitting on his own and decided to join him. Perhaps she could tell him about her zero-per-cent-behind goal and see if he had any more brilliant suggestions.

He jumped as she sat down next to him.

'Whatcha reading?' Her eyes flicked to the pink leaflets scattered on the tables. He had picked up one and was reading it.

He reddened. 'Oh, just some . . . propaganda.' He cleared his throat. 'See for yourself.'

She picked up one of the pamphlets and read the title on the cover. *Prevention of Suicide. Do you know someone who's thinking about it?* 'Geez,' she muttered.

'Yeah.' Harry went silent.

'Do they put these out often?'

'Once a month.' Harry swallowed a mouthful of food. 'The isolation gets some guys down. You know, being away from family and everything.'

She felt goose bumps on the back of her neck. 'There haven't been any suicides on this job, have there?'

'Oh no.' Harry's Adam's apple jiggled in his haste to reassure her. She saw Dan walk in at that moment, looking equally weary. Immediately, the weight of his brooding touched her.

'I guess it's easy to lose touch with your loved ones out here,' she said, watching Dan's progress across the room, remembering the long phone calls he made to his lawyer instead of talking to his family.

She hadn't seen him since their . . . what could she call it? Near miss? She cringed every time she thought about herself standing there with her face up and her eyes closed waiting for his lips to meet hers.

What an absolute idiot!

Maybe it was even a plus that he thought she was with Gavin. At least that indicated that she wasn't, as he might think, pining for *him*. Even now she wriggled uncomfortably in her seat trying to banish the disturbing thought from her mind. Thankfully he had not noticed her, but was also engaged in reading the pink leaflets on the table. She watched his brow darken even further before he screwed up the paper into a tight ball.

'I miss my kids.' Harry's soft murmur broke into her thoughts.

'You have kids?'

'Yeah.'

It made Lena feel bad for not having talked to him more around the office. She didn't like to think of herself as one of those people who ignored their friends when they weren't useful to them. She was embarrassed to remember that she'd only sat down next to him to ask his advice about the trusses.

Very bad form, Lena.

'So how many do you have?'

'T-two.'

'I guess you only get to see them on R and R.'

'No, not really.' He hesitated as though trying to figure out whether he could trust her or not. She kept her features neutral.

He looked away. 'My ex has a new partner. She'd rather I didn't see the children at all any more.'

Lena gasped. 'Harry, you can't let her do that!'

'There's n-nothing I can do about it. She's very g-good at . . . never mind.'

'Of course there is something you can do.' Lena was appalled. 'Take her to court. Get joint custody. You have rights. You're the father.'

'I don't know.'

'Harry, do you care about your kids or not?'

Harry's knife clattered loudly on his plate. ''C-course I care. Love 'em, you know. H-heaps.'

Her heart sank looking at Harry's stricken face. He was the kind of guy who was too sweet to have a backbone, too nice to take a stand – but really the sort of person who should. *He must be a great dad.* Lena chewed on her lower lip. *He helped me out of a jam once, maybe it's time to return the favour.*

Her gaze drifted to Dan, who was sitting quietly on his own, also with a bowl of soup.

'Leave it with me,' she said to Harry. 'I might know someone who can recommend a good lawyer. In the meantime –' She threw down the pink leaflet. 'What are you doing this Sunday? We've got it off, you know?'

Harry looked startled. 'Me?'

Her mood lifted as a plan to annihilate Gavin, his testosterone and any other masculine attribute he may have had sprang fully formed into her mind. 'Of course.' She nodded and then lowered her voice. 'Actually I'm inviting everyone.'

'W-what are we doing?'

'We're going to Millstream.' She flicked the pink leaflet so it blew down the table. 'Hell, I would have done it sooner if I'd known this camp needed cheering up.'

The following day, Lena asked Carl for the bus.

'You and your fuckin' jaunts.'

'I can't sit around camp on my day off, Carl,' she protested. 'No one should have to.'

He gave her a long resigned look. 'I suppose these trips do boost morale. Fuck. Take it.'

Despite her ulterior motives, Lena firmly believed that too. Nothing appealed to her less than a day in her aluminium box and she was sure others must feel the same way. Something to look forward to improved her whole attitude towards the week. Nonetheless, there was no way she was going bloody fishing again. So instead of enlisting the help of Leg and Radar to inspire her with options, she had gone on the internet and googled things to do in the Pilbara. That's when she'd discovered the Millstream–Chichester National Park, a lush oasis of palms and cool lakes. Perfect.

Apparently, it used to be the estate of some rich European settler who had tried to transform the Australian landscape to match the Old Country. The original homestead was still there and the green gardens he had planted had been maintained. Nothing like a piece of history and a barbecue.

Pleased with her own ingenuity, she put together a colour poster with some of the photos from the internet and stuck it in the tea room. Soon word was out that a new adventure was being planned for Sunday and she didn't want for takers. All in all, she was pretty proud of herself.

Carl returned from the yard after lunch and saw her advertisement on the noticeboard. 'Fuck! You'd think you were selling blocks at Millstream or something. No wonder everyone's gone fuckin' mental.'

Lena blushed but luckily he changed the subject. 'How's it going with the trusses?'

'Still no word from Neville Du– *Smart*.'

'Call him again.'

She did. Surprisingly, this time she got through. However, instead of dealing with her issue, Neville asked her to explain it formally to him in an email so he could keep his records straight.

Great. Three hours later, Mr Smart replied, saying that after much thought he had decided that he didn't quite understand what she was talking about and was passing her on to a colleague called Paul Belch, who would be better equipped to deal with the matter. He then included the number to call Paul on. Her fury knew no bounds when dialling it meant hearing the following message:

'The number you have called is not connected. Please check the number before trying again.'

Luckily, when she then called Neville Dumb to get the right number, it was a secretary who picked up his phone. She was able to simply put Lena through to Paul and they set up a meeting on site for the following day.

It was, in her opinion, a fluke win.

Time was running out and she was still putting out fires. At least Mike wasn't playing up. The skid was finally getting faster. Now that the new access platform was up and running, they were putting in four headstocks a day, sometimes five. After a routine stop at the skid, she rode the bus to the sea end of the wharf, enduring the stone-cold silence of Sharon's temporary replacement. Loneliness sharpened her determination. She hated the fact that Sharon had left for R and R still angry with her.

She needed to find Gavin.

Today she would give him one more chance to tell people the truth before she unleashed her punishment on Sunday. When she got off the bus, she scanned the end of the wharf for him. He was standing on some temporary scaffolding erected over freshly driven piles. She joined him there, noticing in disgust that the other guys who had been talking nearby melted away discreetly, grinning at each other as though they were doing her a huge favour.

'Hey, Lena.' He greeted her with unrepentant cheerfulness.

'You know, this has got to stop,' she said through clenched teeth.

His innocent look was clearly feigned. 'What has to stop?'

'You know what I'm talking about. Tell everyone the truth about us.'

'You tell them.'

'I have. They don't believe me. Think I'm protecting myself . . . or something.'

Gavin chuckled, making her even angrier.

'I'm sick of your lying,' she said.

Gavin coughed uncomfortably. 'I haven't lied to anyone. They've jumped to their own conclusions.'

'Same thing.'

He had the grace to redden. 'Just give me some time. Let them lose focus on us. You can't imagine the ribbing I'll get for this when they find out you rejected me.'

'I'm giving you till the weekend.'

He looked away, not dignifying her ultimatum with a response. Her fingers itched to slap him but instead she grabbed the front of his shirt and moved closer so that her whispered threat could be heard.

'If you don't do something about this soon, you'll get more of a ribbing than you bargained for.'

That got his attention. He looked down at her, his eyes narrowing warily.

Neither of them noticed that a third party had joined them until he spoke. 'If Barnes Inc personnel gave half as much attention to the project as they do to their personal lives, maybe they wouldn't be so far behind schedule.'

Lena released Gavin's shirt and jumped back as Dan's harsh reprimand bounced between them. Seeing him again up close and so unexpectedly had its usual effect on her senses. For a moment she was completely unable to respond. He didn't seem to need her to, however, as he stood there eyeing them both contemptuously, his expression as scorching as a blowtorch.

Lena noticed she wasn't the only uncomfortable one. Gavin shuffled from foot to foot and looked over the side as though contemplating diving in.

It was so typical of Dan – turning up at the worst possible moment. The only thing that could have made the situation shoddier was if she was standing there in her red underwear which, given her luck, wasn't that unlikely.

It was Gavin who finally broke the silence. 'Can we help you with something, B– Dan?'

For a moment she had an awful premonition that Dan was

going to hit him. The knuckles on the hand clutching his clip-board had turned white and he seemed to have unnaturally stilled, like a cheetah waiting in the reeds.

But the moment passed.

Dan looked out to sea. As quickly as the tension had filled his body, it seemed to drain away, like he was pouring it into the ocean.

'No.' He shook his head. 'I'd like to set up another progress meeting with the two of you, Lance and Carl. But I'll contact Carl about that later.'

'Not a problem,' Gavin replied. When Dan offered no more he added, 'Well, I'll get back to it then.' He sent Lena a mean-ingful glance, as though telling her to do the same, and then walked away. She watched his back with annoyance as he went to talk to one of his men. The cheek of it. How dare he try to tell her what to do?

'I see you two have patched things up.'

She returned her gaze to Dan's once more expressionless countenance. 'Hardly.' Seagulls squawked overhead as a ship approached in the distance.

'Good job on the skid, by the way.'

She was surprised and instantly happier. 'Thanks.'

'I have definitely noticed improvement in speed since the installation of your new access platform.'

'Y-yes,' she stammered, unused to such praise. 'It's worked out well.'

His expression softened. 'Don't you think I give out credit where it's due?'

'To be honest, no.'

He seemed to accept this as fact and turned to leave.

'Dan, wait –'

There were lots of things she wanted to tell him.

I'm not with Gavin. I didn't want to kiss him. We haven't patched things up. He's a pain in the arse. And . . . I wish you'd kissed me last week.

But, of course, she didn't say any of that.

'I was wondering about that lawyer of yours. Is he any good?'

'She,' he corrected her.

'*She?*'

He was having long evening phone calls about his personal details with a 'she'. Her hackles immediately rose. So much for not having a girlfriend. Then it occurred to her that he hadn't actually denied having one.

'Yes, she. And *she* is exceptional.'

'Oh really, that good?' The fact that she had been hoping his lawyer was good did nothing to keep the resentment out of her voice.

He raised his eyebrows. 'Why do you ask?'

Lena worked hard at an expression of indifference. After all, what did she care? She was asking for Harry. Nothing more. Nothing less.

'Well, I have a friend who's looking for some legal advice; are you able to pass on her number?'

'Sure.' He nodded.

'Okay well, maybe when you get back to the office you could –' She broke off as he was already scribbling some digits on the back of his business card. He knew her number off by heart! How often did he speak to this woman?

He held the card out to her. 'I really recommend her. She's young and enthusiastic. You won't go wrong.'

Young.

Enthusiastic.

Bloody hell.

Lena took the card and pocketed it, her response coming out scratchy. 'Thanks.'

Dan spotted Carl and left her side to go talk to him. She watched their conversation from afar, noticing how Carl's expression got darker and darker as it progressed. It looked like life wasn't getting easier for anyone.

Carl proved it five minutes later when he joined her on the bus.

'Bulldog's fuckin' pissed about the trusses needing a repaint. Tell you what, this job is so fucked. Your trip to fuckin' Millstream is better organised. Fuck!'

Millstream *was* one of the best ideas she'd had since she'd got there. By the time Sunday arrived she had about fifty takers, including Gavin, her actual target. Ethel had the kitchen staff pack them a stack of sausages and buns. It was perfect weather for a barbecue.

Millstream was about two and a half hours' drive from Wickham. Despite not having Sharon by her side, the bus ride was relatively pleasant. The boys seemed to respect Gavin's 'claim' to her. There was virtually no sexual harassment at all and for a moment she actually found herself wondering why she wanted to cut the pretence. Gavin himself was being extra sweet too, helping her load the bus with the food. Ha! Sucking up was not going to deter her. She had her independence to rescue.

They left camp at nine am and stopped at Python Pool along the way, an unforeseen treat. The pool was a beautiful and isolated waterhole right at the bottom of a cliff face in the middle of nowhere.

The water mirrored the jagged red rock of the cliff. Even the occasional green shrub breaking through the cracks was reflected precisely in the still glass surface. She was sad she didn't have her bathers with her, until she remembered the fifty or so spectators on the bus.

Millstream itself was also a sight to behold – not only for the gardens but the history. The homestead was a real education, complete with nineteenth-century kitchen. The oven was a definite classic. She would *not* have wanted to live in those times. The settlers had built the place to be self-sufficient, so the gardens were not only picturesque but also edible. There were fruit trees, foreign flora and palms lining the banks of a running creek that eventually opened out into a huge pool full of pretty English lilies. It was just amazing.

With no shortage of testosterone to operate the barbecues, the project group was soon dining in the picnic area on hot dogs. To her amusement, Gavin brought Lena her food, true boyfriend style.

'Hey,' he said in lowered tones as he passed her the hot dog. 'Still mad at me?'

She leaned back on her rock, drinking in the twinkling sunshine and laughing kookaburras. 'I'm getting over it.'

The birds knew what she was on about. She was gearing up for the moment she'd been waiting for all day.

Crossing Pool.

It was a bigger and much deeper waterhole than Python Pool. Not as pretty, but more appropriate for swimming. People didn't normally swim in it, though, unless it was the peak of summer: the water was absolutely freezing. There was virtually no embankment, so when a swimmer stepped into the water, they were already in the deep end, which was well shaded and quite narrow. It was easy to see why the water stayed cold all year round. Being the end of autumn, Lena imagined that despite the sunny day, it would still be cool enough for teeth chattering.

As the boys lounged around drinking beers, she called Gavin over.

'Can I talk to you for a minute?'

Radar, who must have been watching her face closely, sniggered. 'I wouldn't go with her if I were you.'

She glared at him as other eyes rested on Gavin to see what he would do. Luckily, even though he probably guessed the risk was high, he didn't want to lose face with his mates. He stood up and polished off his beer. 'Sure, why not?'

She led him away from the others so that they were walking along the edge of the pool. She threw a couple of stones in, watching the round ripples they made.

'I said I would give you till the weekend, Gavin.'

His voice was soft when he responded. 'I thought you said you were getting over it.'

'I am and I'll be very over it in just a minute.'

'And I'll tell everyone we're not together as soon as possible.'

'How about right now?' She put her hands on her hips.

'Right now?' He frowned at her. 'You mean like make an announcement?'

'Yeah. Why not?'

He glanced over her shoulder at the guys scattered among the picnic benches, their eyes not so subtly trained on the 'couple' as if they were some sort of free outdoor movie. This time, however, she was counting on their appetite for gossip. He cleared his throat nervously. 'Why spoil the day? How about tomorrow?'

'Tomorrow never comes with you, Gavin.'

'This time it will.'

She shook her head. 'I'd prefer to do it right now. You could say I dumped you. Literally.'

With two palms flat on his chest she gave him one almighty push. The shock that registered on Gavin's face was far too late. His arms flailed madly as he teetered on his heels. And then with one enormous splash, his body entered the water, causing him to squeal like a girl.

'You little bitch!' he squawked, coughing madly and struggling to tread water.

'Thank you very kindly,' she said, making a grand show of dusting her hands.

A laugh erupted among the spectators and Radar raised his beer to the air.

'Guess she's done with that one, boys!'

Chapter 11

'Lena!' Robyn squealed, rising from her chair and throwing both arms around her. 'OMG,' she added as she pulled back. 'You're soooo brown.'

Lena grinned. 'Thanks.'

She felt fantastic. Her hair was dust-free, trimmed and currently sitting on shoulders covered in brown leather – a brand-new purchase from her favourite boutique in Hay Street. She was also wearing make-up. *Blue* eye shadow to match her blue skirt; knee-high boots to match her jacket.

Oh, fashion. How I missed you!

After touching down at Perth Airport two days earlier, it hadn't taken very long to get back into the city swing of things. She'd eaten out every meal since she'd arrived, watched all her favourite shows on television and just marvelled at having so much female company to choose from.

'So how's it all going?' Robyn plopped back in her chair. 'You stopped calling the last few weeks.'

'Sorry. I've been so busy I haven't had time to blink.' Lena pulled her Louis Vuitton handbag off her shoulder and slung it under the table as she sat down opposite Robyn.

'Really?' Her friend's eyes widened. 'So I take it things are looking up.'

Lena winced. 'Kinda.' She was about to elaborate when a waitress paused at their table, pulling out her notepad and pen.

'Can I take your order?'

'Two cappuccinos,' Robyn said and then looked across at her. 'Cake?'

Lena smiled. 'Why not?'

She chose chocolate and then idly glanced around the room as Robyn ummed and ahhed between carrot and very berry. No one was the slightest bit interested in them. Not even the man sitting all by himself by the window reading the paper, or the sports fans streaming past en route to some fixture at the WACA. They were just two girls having a coffee. Lena felt deliciously free and lonely all at the same time.

'So you were saying,' Robyn prompted when the waitress left them.

Lena didn't know where to start. So much had happened since Robyn had told her to rebel. Her last week on site in particular had been hectic. But at least the trusses were getting repainted. She was officially single and straight and the skid was only seven per cent behind instead of ten per cent. It was a start – if not a finish. She was still worried about Sharon though: they hadn't mended fences yet.

'Lena, are you okay? You seem a little spacey.'

Lena blinked, giving her head a shake.

Geez Louise. You can take the girl out of the Pilbara, but not the Pilbara out of the girl. She firmly focused on Robyn. 'I'm fine.'

'What about those job issues you were having?' Robyn folded her arms. 'Are they treating you better, giving you a bit more responsibility?'

Lena sighed. 'Yeah but it's a constant struggle. I mean, I've got these really interesting and challenging tasks, but people are watching so closely. Maybe I should have stuck to data entry after all.'

Robyn frowned. 'Lena, you need to have more faith in yourself. You can do it, I know you can.'

It was both heartening and numbing to hear Robyn's usual pep talk. Her best friend would always be in her camp. If only some other people would join her.

'Lena, have you thought about going to see Kevin?'

This unexpected question jolted her out of her musings. '*What?* Why?'

'Well, for one thing you could smack that SOB across the back of the head,' Robyn snorted. 'And for another, don't you think it would help?'

It was Lena's turn to snort. 'What makes you think I need his help with anything?'

'What that guy did to you is still affecting you now. Maybe confronting him is the only way to get over it. And he can certainly tell you what you need to learn so you really do know as much as any other graduate.'

Lena firmly shook her head. 'Seeing him is not going to make a difference. What would I say? "Oh hi, Kevin, you ruined my life, just thought I'd check in so you can see how that's going"?'

Robyn laughed. 'No, of course not. I just thought –'

'Look, Robyn,' Lena interrupted her, 'I know you're just trying to help, but the last person I want to see is Kevin. My confidence, or lack of it, is something I have to work through on my own.'

Robyn hesitated as though she were going to say something further, and then decided against it. 'Whatever you say, Lena. You're the boss.' Her lips broadened into a smile. 'Hey, there's a sale on at Georgette's on Murray Street. Fifty per cent off everything. Want to check it out?'

Lena grinned. 'Sure.'

***

The next morning Lena woke up at the leisurely hour of ten and took a mug of coffee and a slice of toast out onto her balcony for breakfast. Her apartment was on the fifth level and, even though her view was composed mainly of the shops across the street, the sunshine beat down warmly on her face and she lapped it up. She had four days left of R and R and no idea what to do with herself.

Even as Lena pondered the problem, her mind wandered back to site and what might be going on there. As soon as she realised what she was doing, she groaned. Why did she even miss it? What she needed was a new hobby – something to channel all this unused energy into.

The phone disturbed her meditation. Polishing off her coffee, she got up and staggered back inside to pick up the cordless.

'Hello.'

'Hi, this is Sarah Michaels's assistant. I'm just returning Lena Todd's call.'

Sarah Michaels? Oh, Dan's lawyer.

She'd tried to reach the woman several times since she'd arrived in town, without success. Apparently Sarah was young, enthusiastic – and busy.

'Yes, this is Lena Todd.'

'Oh good. If you'd like to come into our office tomorrow at one pm, Sarah will be available to talk to you about your case.'

'Oh, actually –' She checked her immediate impulse to reject the appointment. It wouldn't hurt to see what Sarah was like. You could always assess someone more accurately when you met them in person rather than over the phone. Lena couldn't just recommend any old lawyer to Harry, could she? No matter how exceptional they might be? Or good-looking for that matter. Looks had no bearing on skill. Generally the most beautiful of people were useless when it came to their brain.

At the thought, her decision solidified. She better just check that Sarah was as ugly as sin. Besides, she had time to kill. Why waste it?

'One pm would be fine,' she said to the secretary and hung up.

Lena chose her outfit carefully the next day. A navy business suit and black heels. Sarah Michaels worked for Lidmans Barristers and Solicitors in the city. They were a top-tier firm so she knew that everyone in the building would be dressed to corporate code and she didn't want to be out of place. She arrived about five minutes before the hour and was ushered into a meeting room by Sarah's secretary. There she was made to wait a good ten minutes before her majesty graced her with her presence.

The second Sarah walked in Lena was glad she had made the effort with her appearance.

For starters, Sarah wasn't that young. She was at least five years older than her, maybe more. And secondly, she was stunning.

Long blonde hair.

Killer legs.

Gorgeous bedroom eyes.

Clearly a bitch.

Sarah held out her hand with a megawatt smile that Lena reasoned had to be fake. 'Hi, I'm Sarah Michaels.'

'Lena Todd.' Lena took the outstretched hand, noticing how Sarah's nails were in much better shape than hers.

Damn.

Sarah sat down opposite her and positioned her notepad. 'Now, I'm not sure if you're aware how this works, but the first appointment is free. I'll give you some preliminary advice which we'll make a note of. If you decide to use the firm, we'll work out a cost agreement next appointment.'

Lena frowned, noting that the lawyer really should work on toning down that bedroom voice of hers. It was so unprofessional. Not to mention intrusive.

'Lena . . . is that all right?'

Lena lifted her chin. 'Perfect.'

'May I ask why you chose Lidmans?'

'A close personal friend recommended you,' Lena lied. 'Dan Hullog.'

She didn't know why she said that. It seemed to trip off her tongue before she could stop it.

Damn.

In any case, Sarah didn't give her time to contemplate the pitfalls of her fib or even what it meant, before coming back with, 'Oh Dan,' with such easy familiarity that Lena immediately forgot all else to eye her suspiciously. Sarah put her palm flat on the table and cocked her head to one side. 'Did you also know his brother?'

'Of course.' After all, what close personal friend wouldn't?

'Then I'm also sorry for your loss.'

My loss?

A cold fist clutched at Lena's heart.

Was Dan's brother dead? Of course she couldn't ask and look like a right fool. Not that Sarah would tell her, given client confidentiality and all that.

But as the fist tightened she knew it made sense. No one got as unapproachable as Dan without experiencing tragedy of some kind. But what was more disturbing was the fact that he'd told her she reminded him of Mark. The name flashed back to her as did their conversation at the end of the wharf. If only she'd known there was so much subtext.

Unfortunately, her silence also gave Sarah Michaels the perfect opportunity to change the subject. *Sly snake.*

'So how can I help you today?'

Lena laced her hands on the table in front of her and tried to look important. 'I'm er . . . I'm actually here on behalf of a friend who is too anxious to approach a lawyer himself.'

Sarah raised her eyebrows. 'Okay, and what sort of matter would your *friend* be looking for advice on?'

The way she said the word 'friend' made her think that Sarah didn't really believe that she was there on behalf of someone else at all, but rather that she'd done something dodgy herself and was trying to work out whether she could get away with it.

Hmmm . . . sly and judgemental.

She sat up straighter. 'It's his kids,' she explained. 'His ex-wife is not letting him see them; can she be taken to court for that?'

'Definitely.' Sarah nodded.

Lena followed this up with a few more token questions including, 'Do you have much experience with that sort of case?'

'I wouldn't take the matter through myself. We have a family law division though – I'd refer your friend to someone there,' Sarah responded.

'Not a problem.' Lena nodded, rising from the table and buttoning her jacket. 'I'll give him your number.'

Or not.

She hadn't quite decided yet.

Three days later Lena was back on the plane to site having not really achieved much of anything else. This time fear and dread didn't grip her. She was actually looking forward to getting back and seeing everyone again. Even Mike, who she thought might be picking her up from the airport. As it turned out, it was Gavin this time.

He had a meeting in Karratha with a supplier, so was charged with the task of picking her up as well on the way back. It was good to touch base with him again after his little dip in Crossing Pool.

'You know I had nuts for earrings for days after that little swim,' he shot at her as they drove back to the camp.

'Really?' She grinned, unable to keep the pleasure out of her voice.

'You're not even sorry?'

Lena wound down her window, breathing in the humid air as the familiar red landscape with short shrubs and snappy gums filled her vision. It didn't look so barren any more, now that she knew about all the snakes and lizards crawling around in the short grass.

'You deserved it and you know it.'

'Hmmm,' he said but she knew he was over the worst of his embarrassment.

After a reasonable silence had passed she changed the subject. 'So how's it all going on site anyway? I feel like I've been missing everything.'

'Oh, you know,' he sighed, 'the usual chaos. The night shift is in full swing but of course there are problems and Bulldog's livid about it. But when doesn't the bastard have a chip on his shoulder?'

This time her reply was not so jovial. 'Well, he must have his reasons.'

Gavin cast her a quick look. 'Taking his side now, are we?'

'No.' She turned away so he couldn't see her blush. 'What kind of problems are we having?'

'Communication problems,' Gavin replied. 'Some things are getting done twice or not at all because day shift isn't telling night shift what they're up to before they knock off. Or night shift specifically needs day shift to make sure supplies are on hand when they come in. And they don't, so half the night is wasted when materials run out.'

'That's easily fixed, isn't it?'

'You'd think.' Gavin grimaced. 'But there are too many big egos out there. They all reckon it's someone else's job and blame-shifting is standing in the way of progress.'

They were silent for a while as the ute ate up the road. There was so much other stuff Lena wanted to know but wasn't sure if she could ask him.

'How's Sharon?'

'Sharon?'

'Yeah.'

'Same as always, I guess. Haven't really spoken much to her. Kind of shy, isn't she?'

'Not always.' She frowned.

'Have you two had a blue or something?'

'Sort of.' She hunched her shoulders miserably. What on earth was she going to do if she and Sharon never made up? She would give talking to her another shot. Sharon had to miss her.

Didn't she?

'What did you mean the other night when you said you thought I would be good for something?'

Crap. Now he's perceptive. She'd forgotten she'd said that in the heat of the moment. She couldn't seem to get anything right. If Sharon knew she'd almost betrayed her confidence as well, she'd never swim out of these deep waters.

'Lena, don't go quiet on me.'

She cleared her throat. 'Didn't mean anything by it, Gav. Let's just drop it.'

'Yes you did.' To her alarm the car seemed to slow down. 'Is this why Sharon and you aren't speaking – because of me?'

Lena looked heavenwards. 'Don't be ridiculous.'

He continued as if she hadn't spoken, excitement in his tone. 'Makes sense. I mean no wonder you went so mental after I kissed you, given she saw it and everything.'

'Concentrate on the road, Gavin,' Lena instructed, desperate to distract him. Much to her relief the car sped up again and he seemed to grip the steering wheel with more focus. Lena relaxed in her seat, feeling like she'd dodged a bullet.

'She likes me, doesn't she?'

And then copped a hand grenade.

'You wish,' she threw at him, glancing at his face only to discover he was grinning like Pooh Bear with his paw in a honey pot.

'I mean, she's not a bad-looking chick, is she? I kind of like the whole red hair thing she's got going on.'

It was clear he just wanted some female attention. Didn't matter who it was. 'With that attitude, you'll get nowhere with her,' Lena said before she could stop herself.

His eyes sparkled with triumph as he briefly took his eyes off the road to look at her. 'So she *does* like me.'

'If she did,' Lena retorted, 'she's definitely wised up since then.'

'Well, maybe I'll ask her out.'

Lena's heart sank but she tried to make out that it made no difference to her. 'Whatever.'

In the end, Gavin's attitude and his upcoming courtship of Sharon were the least of her worries. When she got to the office and tried to contact Mike on his radio, he simply wouldn't pick up. He was definitely out there. She knew he could hear her. He was just deliberately not responding. She figured it must be his new tactic. After all, she'd given him a free week to come up with something different. She really should have expected it.

In any event, she was just getting ready to launch herself into figuring out a way to install the trusses when something unexpected happened.

The men decided to go on strike.

It was money issues of course – the whole 'we're not getting paid enough for working twelve-hour shifts, not seeing our families and living in a box' beef.

Carl's reaction was 'What the fuck?'

Harry, Lena noticed, got the brunt of the yelling. Carl wanted reports from him immediately that would predict how far behind they'd get if the men stayed on strike for three days and then how far behind after a week. And after two weeks. Basically, it was all bad and the management team had to get negotiating with the workers quickly. This was pretty difficult given all any of them could really get out of Carl was 'Fuck. Fuck. Fuck.'

Lena returned to camp that evening feeling gutted. How could she ever get ahead? It was simply useless. Far easier to win a starring role in a Hollywood blockbuster than get the jetty built.

She hadn't seen Sharon all day either and looked out for her at dinner, but her friend wasn't in the mess hall when she arrived. Harry was though. She took a seat beside him and they were able to catch up. She also gave him Sarah Michaels's number.

Harry finished up after twenty minutes and left. Lena was just about to do the same when Sharon walked into the room. Their eyes met briefly and for a second it looked like the redhead was about to come over. But then she turned away and strode towards the buffet. Lena let out a breath. That short contact had given her hope. Sharon looked both sad and weary. Her lively eyes had definitely lost their sparkle. Could it be that she was just as miserable?

Lena watched her put a pitiful portion of shepherd's pie on a plate before going in search of somewhere to sit. In a daring move, she hailed her. Sharon looked up in surprise, mixed with uncertainty. After a slight hesitation she slid into a seat at Lena's otherwise empty table. 'Hi,' she offered tentatively.

'Hi.' Sharon licked her lips. 'So how was your R and R?'

'Fine. How was yours?'

'Good.'

An uncomfortable silence followed; it was about a minute before Lena gathered her courage and spoke. 'Sharon, I hate this. How can we make it right?'

Sharon put her fork down. 'Lena, I feel terrible.' She looked up, her expression an exercise in guilt. 'When I came back from R and R, it was all around camp about you dumping Gavin at Crossing Pool and then Radar told me everyone knew now it was all a scam anyway and you were never together –'

'Sharon –'

'No, I treated you appallingly. When I think about how I left you all alone at Point Samson to get home on your own, I just want to slap myself. Can you ever forgive me?'

'Can *I* forgive *you*?' Lena was incredulous. 'What about me? I was such an idiot! I had no business trying to fix you up with Gavin. I'm the most naive woman on the planet when it comes to men. And I proved it too by totally messing up and hurting you in the process.'

Sharon's bottom lip wobbled. 'No, no, I'm the one who should be apologising.'

'Too late, because I'm sorry first.'

'But it's my fault all this happened,' Sharon protested. 'If I hadn't asked you to help me get to Gavin –'

'No, it was my idea to set you two up in the first place.'

As they both realised what they were doing, twin grins stretched across their faces. And suddenly Sharon laughed. 'Okay.' She picked up her fork again. 'You're right. It's totally your fault.'

'What?!'

Sharon's lips twitched. 'For being such a caring, wonderful person and wanting to help people all the time.'

Lena breathed a sigh of relief. 'I wouldn't go that far. But, Sharon, I really am sorry.'

'So am I.'

'Can we please make a pact?'

'What sort of pact?' Sharon cocked her head to one side.

'Never meddle in each other's love-lives.'

'Done.'

They both reached across the table and shook on it. Their camaraderie thus restored, Sharon immediately launched into a catalogue of her most pressing complaints. There was a scaffolder who was making unwanted overtures, the air-conditioner in her donga kept cutting in and out and the kitchen had served nothing but mince- and potato-based dishes since Lena left. Lena sympathised and threw her own gripe about Mike out there for debate, but already her future was feeling much brighter.

The next day Lena went into work as usual but had to knock off after half a day due to the fact that Barnes Inc had no men on the job. The strike was still in force and it was left up to Carl to do the hard-nosed negotiating.

Lena borrowed a company ute. It was one of the few times they were readily available. She and Sharon took off for the afternoon on their own little adventure. They'd heard good things about the Point Samson yacht club, and so decided to go there for a late lunch and a look-see.

Lena wasn't impressed. Despite the fact that it was called a yacht club there were no boats, no green grass and no landscaping. Rather, it was a tin shed with an old mast erected in the ground beside it.

'This is what the locals have been raving about?' She looked incredulously at Sharon, who was shielding her eyes against the sun to take in the view.

'There's gotta be a catch,' the redhead muttered in response.

And there was.

The food! Lena nearly died when she tasted it. They didn't cook seafood this good in heaven. She feasted on giant prawns, top-shelf fish and bugs. Having never eaten a bug before, she was rather fascinated by the things and also a little afraid of them. They were a cross between a crab and a crayfish but basically looked like giant red cockroaches. After hesitating for half an hour, she eventually tucked in and found the flesh delicious.

'So,' Sharon said as she tore off a piece of her own sea urchin, 'you never said what you got up to on your R and R.'

Lena shrugged. 'Not much, really.' She grimaced. 'To be honest, I spent a lot of my time trying not to think about what was going on back here.'

Sharon grinned. 'You've got the Pilbara under your skin.'

I've got more than the Pilbara under my skin, Lena thought sheepishly as she reflected on her meeting with Dan's lawyer. Out loud she said, 'It's like I want to be here and I don't. I can't seem to make up my mind.' She paused. 'What brought you to the Pilbara, Sharon?'

'Are you kidding me?' Sharon's eyes widened. 'I'm a bus driver. I get paid three times as much being out here than I do in Perth. I don't have a family or a boyfriend. So it's easy. This is the third outback project like this I've worked on. They're almost addictive after a while.'

Lena nodded as she de-shelled a prawn. 'I guess.'

'You guess what?' Sharon looked at her carefully. 'If you're not here for the money, then what are you here for?'

Lena averted her eyes. She wasn't so sure she wanted to confide in Sharon so soon after their reconciliation.

Sharon let loose a low whistle. 'Well, well, well. I don't know how we all missed *that*.' She laughed. 'Radar will be delighted.'

'Delighted about what?'

'Bulldog's not the only one with a secret.'

Lena gasped. 'Sharon, please don't put Radar on my back.'

Her friend's eyes reflected her concern. 'Of course not, I was just teasing. What's the matter? I'm not going to tell anyone.'

She hesitated and Sharon immediately put up a hand for silence. 'Look, don't worry. I shouldn't have pressed you. You don't have to tell me about it if it makes you uncomfortable.'

Surprisingly it was this statement that made Lena want to tell her. 'Well, the thing is . . .' she licked her lips '. . . my engineering degree is kind of illegitimate.'

Sharon choked on her crab. 'It's what?!'

'Not to the university,' Lena made haste to explain. 'They think it's all hunky-dory but in reality . . .'

She explained her affair with Kevin and how her presumptuous ex had thought fit to fix her marks for her.

'So what did he teach you?'

'Two core subjects.'

'Over how many years?'

'Two. It's basically almost half my degree.'

Sharon paused, then asked, 'Did he say by how much he changed your marks?'

Lena shook her head. 'He didn't give me any details and, to be honest, at the time I was too distressed to ask.'

'Well, don't you think you should have at some point?' Sharon frowned. 'For all you know it could have been one subject one time. It's ludicrous to waste all this angst over nothing.'

Lena wrung her hands. 'I don't want to see or speak to him again.'

Sharon sighed. 'Lena, that's not going to solve anything.'

'That's what my friend Robyn thinks but, you know, I *am* doing something about this. I'm out here proving myself and my degree.'

'You're –' Sharon broke off. 'So this,' she waved her fork in a circle, 'being here, taking all the crap that you do, is about proving you can do your job.'

Lena lifted her chin. 'Yes.'

'Not that I don't enjoy having you around,' Sharon said, laughing, 'but personally, I think it would be much easier to report that professor of yours to the university and get him kicked to the kerb.'

'And risk losing my degree? I don't think so.'

Sharon frowned thoughtfully. 'Fair enough: you don't want to do that. Though anybody with half a brain can see that you make a good engineer.'

Lena perked up at her words, her back straightening in her chair. 'You really think so?'

'Of course. You've come up with some great ideas, you know how to handle the boys, and Carl thought enough of you to give you the huge responsibility of widening the jetty.'

Lena's heart sank again. 'Well, I haven't done it yet, have I? There are still heaps of steps to go. God knows what half of them should even be! We're also still so far behind in terms of the schedule.'

'Well, I think you're way too hard on yourself,' Sharon said firmly.

Lena responded with a weak smile. The thing was, she knew Sharon meant well and her support was definitely a help. But like Robyn, she wasn't an engineer. She didn't really know what Lena was supposed to have achieved by now. People like Bulldog were critical of her methods and Carl's attitude to her, as much as she liked him, was mostly impatient. She hadn't proven she deserved her degree yet.

Not by a long shot.

Sharon shrugged. 'Well, even if you don't believe me, I'm here for you.'

'Thank you,' Lena said. 'Actually, I have another confession to make.'

'What's that?' Sharon looked up.

Lena winced. 'I kind of almost told Gavin that I thought you two would be good together that night at Point Samson. He figured it out and now he's got it in his head that you like him. I tried to dissuade him the other day but . . .' She paused. 'Has he said anything to you?'

Sharon coloured up like a tomato but shook her head. 'No.'

'Well, maybe he'll wimp out.'

Sharon bit her lip. 'What should I do?'

'Do you still like him?' Lena held her breath.

'I don't know.'

'Then do nothing,' Lena advised. It was certainly going to be her policy from now on. She knew to suggest anything else could only lead to trouble. 'Wait and see.'

'Okay.'

'In the meantime,' Lena lifted her empty plate, 'let's have seconds.'

Sharon nodded enthusiastically. 'You're on.'

Chapter 12

Monday morning Barnes Inc managed to cut a deal with the unions and the strike ended. Lena launched herself back into work with a vengeance. The skid had slipped back to five per cent behind and starting truss installation was becoming urgent. Therein lay Lena's next problem.

The crane on the skid could only lift five tonnes and the trusses weighed eight tonnes each. Finding a bigger crane was definitely her next task. However, she decided to deal with the communication problem between day shift and night shift first. She figured she could speed things up at least another two per cent if people had their facts straight.

With this in mind she hit the jetty to have a chat to a few site supervisors. Mike was singularly unhelpful which came as no surprise. So she caught the bus to the end of the wharf to see what was going on there. Unexpectedly, Gavin's men were also less than friendly.

'It's their fault not ours,' was the general consensus.

They were full of protests but not much in the way of solutions. Apparently, just the day before, day shift had installed and painted a beam that night shift had NDT-tested and found faulty. So in the end, night shift had to uninstall the beam, strip the paint off (a painful task) and have it sent back to the yard to be repaired. The site supervisor in charge of the whole scenario had been so enraged by the incident he'd gone ballistic and erected the mascot Lena found in front of the wharf office. It was a scarecrow of sorts made out of two brooms. It had a hard hat, dust mask, and safety glasses for a head and face. An orange reflector vest was stuffed full of rags for a body with safety gloves tied to the ends of the broomstick for hands. A large white sign had been erected beside it, on which the supervisor had written in black Texta: *Communications Coordinator, special skills: Deaf, Dumb and Blind.*

While his meltdown was pretty funny, he had hit the nail right on the head – the project needed someone who actually had the role of gathering and transmitting information from one shift to the other. She couldn't believe no one had realised this yet. At the moment, there was no such person or persons and everybody was delegating that job to everybody else.

She got out her clipboard and revisited all the supervisors she had just spoken to, this time telling them that Barnes Inc was thinking about getting communications coordinators. She asked them what sort of information they would need to have relayed. This time they were much more helpful. By the end of an hour, she had at least thirty items on her list without even going back to Mike.

Lena was just about to go wait for the bus when she saw Dan striding across the deck. It was the first time she'd seen him since returning from R and R and, as their eyes met, her feet stalled and her heart rate automatically rose.

He was not so incapacitated and came forwards to join her.

'Welcome back.'

'Thank you.'

'Did you have a nice break?'

She was unused to small talk with Bulldog of all people, but cleared her throat and stated confidently, 'Yes I did.'

A gentle breeze brought his aftershave to her as they stood there sizing each other up. What was on his mind, she had no idea, but there seemed to be something because he wasn't moving on. She had a lot of questions too. Ever since her meeting with Sarah Michaels, she had wanted to know everything. What it was he had witnessed, why he'd chosen Sarah to represent him, why his brother was dead, why had he told his lawyer Mark had died and the most curious of all, why did she remind him of Mark?

'Listen,' he cut into her thoughts, 'I heard about what happened with you and Gavin at Crossing Pool and it got me thinking.'

Of all the things she had expected him to say, this was not one of them.

'About what?'

He paused, his expression serious, pensive even. 'If someone on site seeks to take advantage of you like that, you should report it. If not to me, then to Carl.'

A wry smile curled her lips. 'Are you talking about sexual harassment?' Trust Dan to turn an apology for misjudging her into professional advice.

He nodded.

Involuntarily, she laughed. 'Dan, if I reported every guy who tried to take advantage of me like that, I'd be here till the cows come home.' With a casual shrug, she turned away. 'But thanks for the thought.'

Before she could start walking, he put a hand on her shoulder. 'Wait.'

'What for?' She tried to pull away.

But he steered her towards the office donga. Once inside, he tossed his clipboard and hard hat down on the trestle table and turned to face her.

'Lena,' he put his fist into his palm, 'this is not something to joke about. I'm serious.'

'I know you are,' she responded with a sigh. 'You just need to trust me. Let me handle things my way.'

His mouth twisted sceptically. 'And how's that been working out for you so far?'

'Well, actually.' She lifted her chin.

He shook his head. 'I know you don't want to rock the boat but there is no shame in asking for backup.'

'Dan, I'm fine.'

'For the moment.' His eyes sparkled dangerously as he straightened. His gaze strayed to the window as he sucked in a breath between his teeth. 'But life sometimes has a way of getting out of hand. Don't try and take it all on by yourself. Things can go wrong in an instant and you'll never get the time back.'

He looked down then, as though trying to banish an uncomfortable thought. He wasn't just thinking about her unwelcome advances any more.

'Dan, what is it?'

Silence.

She took a risk. 'Is this about your brother?'

His gaze snapped up to hers, his face white like she'd just slapped him. 'What do you know about my brother?' 'You said I remind you of him.'

'I wouldn't get too pleased about that.' His left hand went into his hair. 'He was reckless, stubborn and completely unreasonable. I could never get through to him.'

'Oh.' She nodded, a little disappointed but not surprised that his reason was critical rather than complimentary. 'You must still miss him, though.'

'I must still . . . what?' He looked up sharply.

Oh crap.

'I just meant . . . I mean . . . you know, since . . .' She trailed off.

'Since he died,' he finished for her, his eyes narrowing like twin lasers. She swallowed hard as he advanced towards her. 'Who told you that?'

'I-I can't remember.'

'Bullshit.'

It was the first time she'd ever heard Dan swear. And unlike Carl's frequent expletives, this single word gave her goose bumps, and not in a good way. He was always so businesslike, so professional. She must have really shaken him up.

'There are rumours flying around site all the time.' She made haste to save the situation. 'Can you blame me if I can't remember who says what?'

'This bloody team has an unnatural obsession with my personal life,' Dan growled bitterly. 'Why can't they leave well alone?'

'Maybe they care.'

'Maybe they just want something to gossip about.' His eyes raked her body in a way that made her feel like he'd just ripped off the top layer of her skin. 'Although, I hardly think chatting about a graduate who died at work would make very good light entertainment.'

She covered her gasp with her hand. 'He – he died at work?'

'Oswalds needed some machinery inspected at a lumber mill and Mark was sent there. Let's just say an accident occurred.' He squeezed out the final sentence between his teeth and she felt the second layer of her skin burn away and sweat break out on her brow, particularly because she thought she finally understood something dreadful.

'Oswalds: wasn't that the company you used to work for?'

'Yes,' he hissed, picking up his hard hat and putting it roughly back on his head. But there wasn't just anger in his voice any more and, as she looked into his face, which suddenly wore the expression of someone who had been to hell and back many times over, she knew exactly what he was going to say next before he said it. 'I was his manager.'

She pressed her hand to her chest to ease the sudden ache behind her sternum. Fragments of conversation came back to her, scene slices from her memory piecing together to make perfect horrible sense.

Mike telling her smugly on the skid, 'You may not be so lucky getting Bulldog to agree to this idea. Is it safe?'

Her asking Dan about his family in the laundry. 'Why wouldn't they need you?'

Sarah Michaels across the desk from her. 'Then I'm also sorry for your loss.'

Dan on the drive home from Point Samson. 'Oswalds, the company I used to work for, is being sued. I'm a witness.'

A witness.

A witness.

Her eyes rose to meet his; she knew they were full of tears, but she didn't care.

His clipboard scraped the table as he scooped it up, his lips pulled back over his teeth in a snarl. 'So now you know it all.'

And then with a slam of the donga door, he left. Lena collapsed into the chair behind her, put her head down on the table and shut her eyes in a futile attempt to block everything she had just learned.

It took her a long time to focus that afternoon. In fact, after Lena got back to the office, Dan's story played on her mind so much that she was desperate to fill in the gaps. She googled his brother's name and ended up finding the whole story on the Worksafe Australia website. The accident was dated almost two years ago.

Mark Hullog, mechanical engineer age 25, died at MacArthur Lumber Mill during an inspection in October this year. Workers had complained that the feeder was constantly jamming and wanted to know how it could be fixed. Oswalds Proprietary Limited was commissioned by MacArthur Lumber to investigate the situation and provide a solution. Mark Hullog, who had been working for Oswalds for 14 months, went with his manager to MacArthur Lumber to inspect the log feeder and crusher unit. Mark Hullog went into the unit

*via a spring-loaded door and became trapped. He was pushed
through the crusher and killed instantly.*

Lena's hand trembled over the mouse as she read the
last line. To say it was a horrible way to die was a gross
understatement. And to think that Dan had been there while
it had happened.

She couldn't imagine it.

She didn't *want* to imagine it.

Being present while someone you loved died violently,
powerless to stop it . . . He must blame himself. He must. She
blinked rapidly to stop the tears: she couldn't cry here. Not
when someone could see her and start asking questions.

No wonder Dan had come up to the Pilbara. If it was her,
she would run too. She would run as far as she could.

Lena got up and went to the kitchen to get herself a much-
needed glass of water. The cool liquid soothed her throat but
did nothing for the ache in her heart. What was worse than all
the rest was that Oswalds wasn't letting Dan heal. They had
him bloody representing their side of the story in the courts.
She shook her head. And then suddenly something occurred
to her.

Who was suing Oswalds for Mark Hullog's death?
It wasn't Dan – he was a witness – so it must be Mark's family.
Was Mark married? Did he have children?

She returned to her desk, her fingers shaking as she googled
key words from the Worksafe article. It wasn't long before
some old newspaper stories came up.

*Lumber mill accident destroys family . . . A brother's alleged
dereliction of duty . . . Parents refuse to acknowledge surviv-
ing son . . . Deceased leaves behind pregnant wife.*

Lena choked and clicked the browser off. That was more
than enough.

She didn't want to find out any more. What she already
knew sat heavily in the pit of her stomach, her insides churning
around it like a broken dishwasher.

Since the moment she'd met Dan she'd always thought of him as fearless and unbreakable. The way he looked at her, she'd thought she'd never get the better of him. Never break through that heavy armour he wore. No one could touch him. Now she knew that he was already broken, already hurting. That hard facade was just the dressing over a deep wound he was still recovering from.

Lena had heard of that feeling called an epiphany. A moment when you realise that everything you knew, never was. All your problems and understandings pale in significance beside a truth that comes startlingly to light. In that quiet afternoon, alone at her desk, a glass of water in her hand . . .

Lena had an epiphany.

Chapter 13

Knowing Dan was probably still cross with her for sticking her nose into his business, Lena decided to keep a low profile for a few days. She concentrated instead on hanging out with Sharon and pushing non-controversial ideas at work – like her communications coordinator scheme.

She was going through it with Gavin when Carl and Sharon walked in from the latest bus run. Sharon was carrying the morning mail and Carl was holding his hard hat and frowning. It was Gavin who called them over.

'Lena's got a new idea.'

'Fuck.' Carl stopped by their side. 'It better be a bloody good one, with the morning I've had.'

Sharon began sorting the mail into piles on a nearby desk as Lena quickly outlined her idea for two communications coordinators – one for day shift and one for night shift. These coordinators could start later so they had a couple of hours in the next shift. Carl was not as impressed with the idea as she'd hoped.

'It's what we need, of course. But fuck, who's going to put their hand up for that?' He shook his head. 'The men have already been on strike because they reckon their pay is shit. Who's going to volunteer for extra work without being compensated for it?'

Lena shrugged. 'Well, maybe we just have to bite the bullet and pay the communications coordinators a little extra.'

Carl sighed. 'You think it's that fuckin' easy?' She opened her mouth to reply but he waved his hand dismissively. 'Do you know how much money we've lost on this job already? *Fuck*. I feel like I'm working with a bucket that has six holes in it. Can't you come up with an idea that increases productivity without actually costing us anything?'

Suddenly his mobile rang and in frustration he fished it out of his pocket and stepped back from them a little to take the call. 'What?! Why the fuck did you let fuckin' Stuart Carn do it? You know he's fuckin' useless. Now we're bloody fucked, aren't we? No, I ain't got no fuckin' solution . . .'

Lena tuned out of his conversation. She noticed that Sharon was quietly smiling to herself as she neatened her envelope piles. 'What's up with you?'

Sharon's lips twitched suspiciously as she tried to turn her face away. 'Oh nothing.'

'Don't give me that,' Lena urged. 'What's so funny?'

'Yeah,' Gavin joined in. 'Tell us.'

'Well.' Sharon shot a quick glance at Carl to make sure he was properly distracted by his phone call. 'I just had an idea that's totally cost-free but will definitely help get things done faster.'

'Really?' Lena saw the mischief in her eyes and was intrigued. 'Do tell.'

'If Carl took the f-word out of his vocabulary, he could speed up delivery of his orders by fifty per cent.'

Sharon had lowered her voice to say this but unluckily Carl chose to abruptly hang up his mobile in anger in time to hear her 'idea'. Gavin sniggered as Lena put her hand over her mouth to cover her grin. Poor Sharon went as red as a chilli pepper under Carl's icy glare. He pocketed his phone wordlessly, his eyes fixed on her as she quickly turned away to fumble with the envelopes on the table. Picking up one pile and shoving two more under her armpits, Sharon made haste to leave. 'I . . . I'll just get these to the right . . . er . . . in-trays.'

Unfortunately, she dropped a couple as she passed Carl and was forced to stop and watch open-mouthed as he bent to pick them up for her. She took them with unsteady hands, eyes downcast and a muffled, 'Er, thanks,' before making a quick exit.

When Sharon finally disappeared through the door, Carl's dirty expression swung to Gavin and Lena in accusation. Lena didn't know about Gavin, but she was still desperately trying to keep a straight face.

'Does that bird have a problem with my swearing?' He jerked a thumb over his shoulder.

Gavin choked and looked away. Carl's frown deepened. 'Never complained about it before,' he said gruffly. 'Though, don't expect I was supposed to hear what she said just now.'

'Don't worry about it, Carl,' Lena tried to reassure him. 'She was just joking around. Didn't mean anything by it.'

He opened his mouth to say something more but seemed unable to formulate the words, so shut it again and stormed off. It was an hour before he reappeared, seemingly recovered from Sharon's joke. He yelled across the room at Lena.

'I've fuckin' thought about it and I've decided. Use the fuckin' communications coordinator idea. It's shit about the money but I can't see another way. We'll wear a ten per cent pay rise. Can you organise it?'

She nodded, turning back to her computer in delight. It didn't take long to put the new proposal in writing. Their resident human resources officer helped her to draft the new job profile so that he could interview candidates and award the position.

With that problem sorted, Lena turned her attention to the trickier dilemma of the trusses. She couldn't install a bigger crane on the skid because the actual skid frame itself couldn't take it. Yet the trusses couldn't be lifted with the small crane currently on the skid.

So what am I supposed to do?

That's when she finally had a decent brainwave. What if she could kill two birds with one stone?

If she had two identical skid frames with two small cranes, she could install headstocks twice as fast and also have the capacity to install a truss. The trusses could be installed using two skid frames sitting side by side. She quickly scribbled down a sketch in her notebook. The two cranes could lift one truss off the back of a truck together.

It would take more money to make another skid and buy another crane. But she was hoping, given she would be increasing the efficiency of headstock installation as well, Carl might go for it. Besides, any way they addressed the problem would cost more money or more time or both. If they were to beef up the current skid for a bigger crane, that would take it off the jetty for a while. They'd get more behind before they could get in front. This way, the current skid could keep going as usual while the new skid was fabricated in the yard.

She spent the rest of the morning ironing out the details and almost missed lunch because she was so deeply absorbed. Luckily, her growling stomach prompted her to take a break. Sharon was lying in wait for her in the smoko donga. The second Lena walked in, she pounced on her, grabbing her by the arm and pulling her into a corner.

'*Please* tell me I'm not fired.'

Sharon's face was so comically distraught Lena had to laugh. 'You're not fired.'

'Thank God.' Sharon dropped her arm and covered her flushed face with her hands. 'I am *so* mortified.'

'Don't be.' Grinning, Lena went over to the fridge and retrieved her sandwich. 'It was hilarious. Well worth the embarrassment.'

'Lord no.' Sharon also got her sandwich from the fridge. 'You may be comfortable being cheeky to Carl but a boss is a boss. I need this job. I'm not taking any chances.'

'Seriously, Sharon, he's already forgotten about it.' Lena gestured to the door. 'Picnic?'

Her friend nodded. 'Sure.'

It was a beautiful day outside – sunny and balmy – typical winter weather for the Pilbara. They sat down on a backless bench near where the bus was parked and started munching. A comfortable silence settled between them as they listened to the gentle rumble of cranes and waves. Sharon managed to break the peace, however, with one blunt sentence.

'Gavin asked me out last night.'

Lena swallowed too quickly. 'And you're only just telling me this now,' she half choked. The news put a block of lead in her stomach but she schooled her expression to one of delight, praying to God her smile wasn't too bright to be unbelievable. She didn't want to be anything less than one hundred per cent supportive this time. Butting in only got her in trouble.

She turned to face Sharon fully, looping one knee up on the bench. '*Go on*, tell me everything.'

Sharon shrugged, her mouth quirking in the corner. 'It was a bit of a non-event, actually.'

Lena plucked an imaginary piece of fluff from her pants as she tried to eliminate the hope from her voice. 'What do you mean?'

'I said no.'

Thank goodness. She couldn't keep the excitement out of her voice. 'Really?'

Sharon punched her shoulder playfully. 'You're relieved, you little faker.'

Lena hung her head. 'I'm sorry but in my opinion he's not good enough for you. He's just sometimes a bit too . . .'

'Shallow?'

Lena grabbed both her hands. 'Yes! Truth is, after he nearly destroyed my friendship with you, I've kinda seen some of his true colours come to light.'

Sharon nodded. 'Me too. I mean, he's not evil or anything.'

'Oh no.' Lena swatted away the suggestion. 'Just . . . a little selfish.'

'And vain.'

'And cowardly.'

'And childish.'

'And desperate.'

'*Okay.*' Sharon laughingly held up her hands. 'I think we've definitely settled the fact that he's not my type.'

'Or mine,' Lena added forcefully. 'Never was.'

'I know,' Sharon sighed softly.

They munched on their sandwiches again in amicable silence until Sharon shoved Lena's shoulder. 'So who is?'

Lena rolled her eyes. 'No one I can put my finger on.'

'Rubbish.' When she didn't take the bait, Sharon prompted her further. 'What about a certain tall, dark client, who saw you in your scarlet unmentionables?'

'Bulldog! No way he –'

'Lena, you're talking to me here,' Sharon interrupted, giving her a pointed look. 'I'm not going to tell anyone. Besides, we've just established that you're not a very good liar.'

She was right. What was the point in denying it any further?

I have feelings for Dan.

Their last meeting had proved that beyond a shadow of a doubt. She was no longer able to trick herself into believing that what she felt for him was nothing more than a crush. The attraction ran deep. Deeper than she had ever suspected.

Damn it.

She looked at Sharon's raised eyebrows and sighed. 'Okay, okay. But it doesn't matter. I'm not going there.'

Eager to have her honesty at last, Sharon sat up straighter. 'Why not?'

'Do I have to spell it out for you?'

'If you're talking about Kevin,' Sharon rolled her eyes, 'this is not the same thing.'

'Of course it is,' Lena protested. 'How can I possibly trust myself in life if I'm constantly getting personally involved with people who are supposed to be evaluating me? I'd be like one of those actors who sleep their way into lead roles.'

'Don't you think you're confusing two different things?' Sharon's tone was exasperated.

Lena hugged her arms. 'No, not really.'

'What about Bulldog? How do you think he feels about you?'

Lena gave a humourless laugh. 'Well, I'm safe there. He hates me.'

'Now *that* is definitely not a possibility.'

'Believe me, if you knew what happened the other day, you wouldn't be saying that.'

A truck laden with rubber pipe rattled by loudly as Sharon pondered her words. 'What's changed?'

Lena looked at her hands, studying the chipped fingernails with an indifference she wouldn't have felt two months earlier. 'I know Dan's secret.'

Sharon let out a long low breath. '*Oh*.'

'Yeah.'

Sharon grabbed her hand and squeezed sympathetically. 'Is it bad?'

Lena groaned. 'Worse than bad.'

'If he let you in, though,' Sharon said thoughtfully, 'he must think pretty highly of you.'

'He didn't let me in,' Lena replied bitterly. 'I forced my way through with the subtlety of a pickaxe.'

Sharon released her hand. 'Ouch.'

'Tell me about it. What's worse is that's exactly what he doesn't need. He needs support not interrogation.'

'So be supportive. Does he know your secret?'

Lena felt her face flush with both guilt and defiance. 'Hell no.' The thought of airing her dirty laundry to Dan filled her with nothing but shame. He thought so little of her already.

'Hey.' Sharon poked her. 'I didn't say it to get you down. Let's talk about something else, okay?'

Lena brightened. 'Yeah! Like how Gavin reacted to you saying no.' She grinned as she pictured his face. 'Must have put his nose out of joint a bit.'

Sharon collected her lunch things. 'That's the worrying thing, it didn't.'

Lena also finished her sandwich and stood up. 'What do you mean?'

'You know, when guys think no means yes.'

'You've got to be kidding me.'

'He kind of went off on this whole tangent about having caught me at a bad time. He said he was happy to give me more time to adjust.'

Lena laughed. 'Dumb arse.'

'I couldn't have put it better myself.' Sharon stood up and was about to take her leave when she remembered something. 'By the way, Ethel's given me a new donga.'

'Why?'

'My air-conditioner finally broke down completely and they can't get a new one installed for weeks – easier to move.'

'Okay.' Lena nodded. 'What number?'

'B15,' Sharon said over her shoulder and then waved goodbye.

Much to Lena's delight, the extra skid and crane idea turned out to be an easy sell. Carl had a meeting with Dan the next day and he wanted new ideas for improving productivity to present to him.

They got approval and mid-week Lena's team started fabricating the new skid. It was now time to go shopping. Up until this point, she had considered herself to be rivalled only by Robyn as a serious consumer. But even her best friend couldn't say she had gone bargain-hunting for a crane, much less bought one and for a good price too.

On Friday, the HR manager awarded the communications coordinator positions. The weekend passed quickly and they started in their new roles on Monday. It seemed to work really well, for which Lena was glad. She had another team meeting with Dan on Wednesday. With the bitter aftertaste of their last encounter still clinging to her, she didn't want to be anything less than impressive when they broke their unspoken code of silence.

On the appointed day, Carl drove Gavin, Fish and herself to the TCN offices in his ute. They were greeted at TCN reception with the usual antics. The receptionist was rude and kept them waiting at least fifteen minutes. When Dan finally walked into the meeting room, a file of drawings under one arm and a notepad in the other, Lena's doodles were almost covering a full page in her notebook. She hastily ripped it out and shoved it at the back of the book. Dan put his things on the table, nodding to each of them in turn.

The sexy stubble was in full effect but this time he had dark rings under his eyes to match. His lips were tight as he looked at her. There would be nothing but professionalism today and probably more than a little criticism. Lena sat up straighter and collected her thoughts.

'Good afternoon,' he said. 'Thank you for coming. I guess we should get right to the point.'

And he wasn't kidding. He flipped open the drawing file and began lecturing them on a number of design changes that had occurred since they last spoke. Gavin and Lena frantically took notes while Carl argued. In the end, compromise was reached and new drawings would be released the following week. That sorted, they moved on to quality issues. The hottest topic, of course, was the trusses due to the initial bad paint job.

But between Lena and Carl, they managed to reassure Dan that it was a problem of the past.

They spoke about progress last, no doubt because it was the touchiest subject. Dan was surprisingly gracious. While he was still unhappy with Barnes Inc's status, he praised their improvements so far. In fact, in Lena's view it was all going dandy until the topic of the communications coordinator was raised by Dan.

'The transition between day and night shift seems to be a lot smoother.'

'Yes.' Lena nodded. 'The communications coordinator scheme seems to be working well.'

'A good idea,' Dan nodded. 'Let's hope Mike has more like that in the future.'

She blinked. His words were so shocking that for a moment she thought she must have heard him wrong. 'Mike?'

Dan looked up impatiently from his file notes. 'Yes, I spoke to him yesterday on the wharf. He said you interviewed all the site supervisors about the problem and he suggested the idea.'

'*He what?*'

'Lena.' Carl shot her a warning look as if to say, 'Do we really need to debate this when there are more important matters?'

She sat there fuming in silence, fisting her hands in her lap till the knuckles turned white as they moved on to another topic. She didn't hear what was said for the rest of the meeting. Her focus was on Mike and whether she'd prefer to hang him over the side of the wharf by the back of his jocks or by the scruff of his neck.

'Okay, so we'll leave Lena here to wait for those.' She caught the tail-end of Carl's parting statement and jumped.

'Sorry?'

Once again, Carl's annoyed expression rested on her and it was all she could do not to hunch her shoulder petulantly.

'Dan is going to answer and sign off a couple of our urgent TQs now. Can you wait for them and bring them back to the office? I'll let Sharon know she has to pick you up on the next bus run.'

She cleared her throat. 'Sure.'

Gavin and Carl got up from the table and left the meeting room. Dan's cool expression swept her face, his mouth twisting with clear dissatisfaction. 'You'd better come with me.'

Lena followed him through the guts of the client workplace to his own private office at the back of the open-plan area. He sat behind the desk and gestured for her to take a seat in the visitor's chair. And then, as though she wasn't even there, he opened one of the files on his desk, withdrew a couple of sheets and began ticking things off. She'd never felt more invisible in her life – which was probably his intention.

After about ten minutes, and with a heavy sigh, he lifted his pen from the page and looked at her. Even this one concession seemed to cost him. 'All done.' He pushed the papers across the desk to her. 'You know your way out of here, don't you?' he asked.

'Yes.' She got up, went to his office door and then shut it. She turned back, to his startled expression.

'What are you doing?'

Lena returned to her seat and sat down. 'We need to talk.'

He shut his eyes and leaned back in his chair as though gathering patience. 'No, we don't.'

'But I need to apologise for –'

His eyes flew open. 'Apology accepted.'

'I also wanted to let you know,' she began slowly, 'that you needn't worry I'm going to tell anyone about what I know.'

His nod was abrupt. 'Thank you.'

'I wouldn't do that to you or your family,' she continued.

His fingers tapped on the desk. 'Good. If that's all?'

She glared at him in frustration. 'No, that's not all.' Couldn't the man just lay down his arms for ten seconds?

He sighed. 'Lena, I don't think we need to talk about this any more than we already have.'

'Fine.' She shrugged, shooting him another glare and standing up. 'But you look terrible.'

'What?'

'You look like death with a hangover.' She let her eyes rove over him pointedly and he reached up, brushing the bristles on his chin with thumb and forefinger.

'Is this about me not shaving again?' A spark finally lit his dulled eyes.

'It's more than that.' She put her hands on her hips. 'Look, I'm sorry that I stumbled on this secret of yours, but if I can help in any way –'

'You can't help me.' He pushed at the desk impatiently and his chair rolled back. He stood up also and went to the window. She could tell that the ocean views did nothing to calm him.

'I know you can't turn to your family,' she said quietly. 'It must be hard.'

'What do you know about my family?' he demanded harshly.

'Only what you've told me,' she made haste to reassure him. 'I remember you telling me a while ago that relations were strained.'

His laugh was bitter. 'Strained is hardly a strong enough word. My sister-in-law holds me personally responsible for her husband's death, my mother, who always favoured Mark, never wants to speak to me again and my father only stays in contact to keep tabs on what might be said in court. The one member of my family who doesn't hold anything against me is my two-year-old niece. But how could she, since I've never been permitted to meet her?'

She opened her mouth to speak and shut it again. What could she say to that? What could she say to someone whose entire family hated them?

Lena licked her lips. 'All the more reason to have a friend in your court. Er . . . pardon the pun.'

He finally turned away from the view to eyeball her. 'You and I aren't friends.'

She tried to smile under his frosty gaze, but couldn't quite manage it. 'There's no reason why we can't be, is there? I mean, I know I've been a bit insensitive in the past but that was only because I didn't know what you were going through –'

'Okay, let me rephrase this so you understand.' He pressed his thumb and forefinger together to enunciate his words. 'I-don't-want-to-be-your-friend.'

Lena's ribcage contracted, killing one heartbeat. 'W-why?'

But he didn't answer the question, instead he went in for the knife twist. 'I don't want to talk to you about my problems. I don't want to be barricaded in my office with you demanding answers. I just want you to stay away from me.'

There was only so much bashing pride could take and as Lena saw her own lying there unconscious before her, she decided it was time to salvage what little was left of it and get out of there. She didn't look at him as she gathered the papers she had waited to collect.

'I'm sorry to have overstepped my bounds. It won't happen again.'

'Lena –'

But as she turned away, she realised he was right. This situation was absolutely none of her business. Besides the fact that trying to be his friend when she knew she secretly had feelings for him was likely to get her hurt. Was she so far gone that she could now ignore what had happened with Kevin?

Get your act together, Lena! You're better than this!

'You're right.' She nodded without meeting his eyes. 'There is nothing more to say about this. Goodbye, Dan.'

And as she shut the door behind her, she shut it on her heart as well. It was high time she put up some boundaries . . . no matter how difficult that was.

* * *

The only thing that kept Lena's head held up for the rest of that day was her vendetta against Mike. Having words with him about his false claim to credit helped in some way to fizzle her frustration concerning Dan. Not that it changed Mike's attitude in the slightest. He was just too smug: he counted this blow as his first win. She had a word to Carl about it later and, although he was actually rather apologetic about what had happened at the meeting, he basically told her to let it go. Without seeming like a petulant child, there was not much else she could do. So Lena put the whole scenario into her Lessons Learned box. She just had to be more careful in future.

With this in mind, she turned her focus to the trusses, writing detailed method statements for their installation. Carl approved them without blinking and life seemed to be moving along much more smoothly. She was more and more certain that Dan's rejection had been 'for the best'.

There was no use in pointless internal diatribes, involving questions like,

Why doesn't he want to be my friend?

What's wrong with me?

Doesn't he trust me?

The obvious truth was she was clearly nothing to Dan – or at least, nothing more than an annoying colleague who knew too much. Her feelings for him were her own problem, not his, and she had to cure herself of them quickly.

Thursday and Friday came and went without incident. Disaster did not strike again, until around five am on Saturday morning, when a really weird nightmare woke Lena early. She was living in England, trying to visit Dan at his mansion in Bath. His rude butler not only wouldn't let her in, he also set the dogs on her. She was about to be mauled by a hungry purebred when her eyes flew open and she sat up with a start.

Whoa.

Her breath came short and sharp and she had to wait a minute for it to steady. When it did, she wiped the sweat from her brow and threw off her covers. It was getting beyond ridiculous. Honestly! Did he have to invade her dreams as well? She groaned and swung her feet onto the floor, shoving them into a pair of thongs as she decided to visit the loo.

Rubbing her eyes, Lena staggered out of her donga and headed down the short weedy path to the toilet block, which wasn't more than a hundred metres away. When she was done, she paused at the sink, cupping her hands under the water and splashing some on her face. The cool sensation freshened her a little and she studied her reflection in the bathroom mirror critically. Her hair was pulled back in a loose ponytail and her colour was pale, making the dark rings around her red eyes all the more prominent. She definitely needed more sleep this week. With a sigh, she left the toilets and headed back to her donga, mentally resolving to go to bed early that night. She put her hand on her doorknob and tried to turn it. It stuck.

Horror shot through her body like a shard of ice. In desperation, she rattled the handle again. It still didn't budge.

Shit.

I've locked myself out.

Chapter 14

Lena let her head rest against the door as she evaluated her situation. She was in her pink cotton pyjamas and thongs. It was chilly and dark and if some roving psycho attacked her now, no one would know about it until it was too late. How could she have been so careless? So stupid! She moved sideways and with trembling fingers tried the window. It was as locked as she expected it to be.

Useless.

Sucking in what was supposed to be a calming breath, she turned around. The darkness of the camp engulfed her, intensifying the sound of chirping crickets and croaking frogs. A lizard scurried across the gravel in front of her, like a little flash of black lightning, almost making her yelp with a start. She wasn't normally afraid of lizards, but at this point nerves had taken over.

The rows of dongas around her were suddenly looming threats. The toilet block was the only brightly lit building in the area. It shone like a haven, beckoning her. She shivered, rubbing her arms.

Idiot! Idiot! Idiot!

If it were possible to kick your own bum, she would have done it. One thing was for sure: she would be wearing the keys to her donga around her neck from now on. Lena glanced down the path at the silent and dark reception building. No hope of help there.

She shut her eyes. She had at least half an hour to kill before she'd be able to access a spare key back into her room. Half an hour before she would be forced to parade in front of the men in her pyjamas when they all woke up for the day. Her eyes flew open with sudden hope.

Sharon!

Maybe her friend would let her wait it out with her.

Lena looked at the maze of dongas before her. She couldn't remember Sharon's new number. And they all looked the same, especially at night. She ground her teeth.

What was it again?

B15 or B16?

Wrapping her arms around herself she hit the weedy path, her feet quickening from fear. It wasn't long before she reached row B. The two dongas she had guessed were directly opposite each other and she stood between them trying to decide which one to take a punt on.

Finally she decided to go evens and chose B16. Just to be safe, though, she picked up a medium-sized rock from the gravel path and held it behind her back. Better to have a weapon in case number B16 was not Sharon but a horny guy who thought she was throwing out lures. Chewing on her bottom lip like it was mutton, she tentatively approached the door and knocked.

There was a moment's silence before she saw the bedside lamp go on and heard the bed creak. It was still impossible to tell whose donga it was.

Then the door opened.

She dropped her rock.

Dan!

Sexy, rumpled, half asleep, and fresh from his bed, leaning heavily against the door edge. He had bare legs, bare forearms and bare feet. When you had to wear long-sleeve shirts and pants to work every day for safety reasons, any extra skin exposure was a revelation. And yes, she revelled in it.

He was silent. The shock had clearly hit him as hard as it had her, but she couldn't tell for sure because most of his face was in shadow. Suddenly he straightened, advancing and filling the frame with his person.

'*Lena.*' Her name hissed from his lips like an accusation.

'Dan.' If he'd taken the time to notice, he would have heard that her hoarse whisper sounded as incredulous as his, but he was already on some other bandwagon.

'I can't believe it.' He looked heavenwards, running a hand through his messy hair. 'Are you crazy? What do you hope to achieve now?'

She gaped at him, her hands going immediately to her hips. It was an effort to keep her voice low. 'You think I did this on purpose?'

'Well, you always did have trouble keeping your nose out of other people's business.' His tone was soft but harsh. 'I'm not one of your pet projects, you know.'

'*What?*'

'Stick with the people who actually want your help.'

'I have no idea what you're talking about.'

He wasn't listening. 'If anyone sees you here . . .' He massaged his temples before he looked at her. 'They'll never let it go.'

'No one's going to –' He put a finger to her lips as a light opposite and two doors down went on. She held her breath, more due to the effect of his touch than the danger of being exposed.

As a neighbour's door began to slowly open, Dan swore under his breath. In the next second, an arm circled her waist and she was scooped into his donga. The door clicked shut, leaving her back flat against the inside of it as he leaned over her, his breath on her cheek. Awareness fizzled down her spine as the confined space of the dimly lit room penetrated her senses.

'Too close,' he whispered, parting the blind beside the door so that he could peer out. It took her a second to realise he wasn't talking about their physical proximity but the near miss of being discovered. It was dark and he smelled like man and soap. She wanted to press her body into his, but of course didn't dare.

'Bloody idiot's going to the toilet.' He stepped back, returning her personal space to her, much to her relief and disappointment. 'You'll have to wait here till he's safely back inside his donga.' His sigh was jagged and once again his hand was in his hair pulling at the locks in agitation.

To distract herself from wayward thoughts, Lena decided to take the opportunity to defend herself. 'You know, you've really got the wrong end of the stick this time.'

He didn't seem to be paying attention – in fact he had begun to pace – so she continued a little more forcefully. 'I've locked myself out. That's why I'm here. I thought this donga was Sharon's and was going to ask her if I could wait with her till the office opens.'

He stopped pacing. 'I see.' She couldn't make out his expression in the dim lighting but his voice sounded sceptical.

'Look, it's not my fault all the dongas look the same. This wasn't planned, despite what you and your overly large ego might think. I'm not *stalking* you.' When he said nothing she added with raised chin, 'I have more pride than to beg friendship from someone who clearly holds me in such contempt, thank you very much.'

He closed the distance between them again, so that they were nose to nose. 'That's what you think? That I believe I'm above you?'

If he had meant to be intimidating, he was way off the mark. Her thoughts immediately returned to jumping him and she sucked in a breath to calm herself.

'Well?'

'Well, yeah,' she squeezed out somewhat hoarsely. 'Why else would you –?'

'Oh, shut up,' he snapped and suddenly she realised his voice was as hoarse as hers. 'The reason I avoid you, the reason I can't ever be your friend, is because I'm *protecting* you.'

Her eyes widened. 'From what?'

'Me, you fool.'

He grabbed her face between his palms and brought his lips to hers in a kiss that was as drugging as it was unexpected. Her heart jumped and she seized handfuls of his T-shirt to steady herself and pull him closer. She had once thought that kissing Dan would be like slaying a dragon. Now she knew that she was the one being slayed.

'Do you know how hard it is for me?'

She couldn't answer because his lips brushed the words against her mouth and didn't lift to let her speak. She assumed it was a rhetorical question though. In any case, she couldn't think, let alone reply at this point.

She arched her body into his, fitting her curves into his hard male planes and delighting in the sensation of feeling like they were two pieces that fitted perfectly together. In the haze that was passion, she heard him struggle to talk again.

'Every time I see you . . . every time you walk into the room . . . every time you look at me with those damned eyes . . .' finally, he lifted his head and his own eyes bored into hers '. . . this is *all* I want to do.'

Her heart beat like a tribal drum, reverberating through her ribcage as he suddenly released her hands to touch her hair, pulling out the black lackey band and dropping it on the floor. Her hair fell out, wisping against her cheek. His fingers threaded through the loose strands, splaying them on her shoulders and down her back with such gentleness she almost choked.

A soft sigh whispered off his lips. 'Tell me to stop.'

She shook her head. She couldn't.

With a groan, he hooked an arm around her waist and took her lips again. Of their own accord her hands moved up his chest, exploring the contours, until they reached his shoulders and tested their broadness. He tore his mouth away, his breathing laboured as he touched his forehead to hers.

'We shouldn't.'

'I know.'

He started at her words. Slowly his free hand feathered down her cheek, under her chin and down her neck. His fingers caught on the collar of her pyjama shirt; he undid the top button and then the next one. Her breath never made it out of her windpipe when he paused on the third. His eyes searched hers for any sign of withdrawal. She knew she could stop him if she wanted to.

She didn't.

After what seemed like an interminable moment his fingers undid the third button and moved down to finish the rest. She couldn't meet his gaze as he parted her shirt and brushed the underside of her bare breasts with the back of his knuckles. 'Lena, look at me.'

There was a need in his voice and she couldn't deny him. She raised her chin to drown in the dark pools that were his eyes and his hands moved upwards to caress her breasts.

The last of her restraint was gone and she plunged her hands under his shirt. His skin was smooth, warm and firm. There was a sprinkling of soft hair in the centre of his chest. His muscles jumped under her fingertips as she brushed over them; she felt the rush of his desire almost as if it were her own.

He picked her up and pulled her legs around him; she threw her arms around his neck as they stumbled towards the bed and fell.

She rolled with him, entwining her legs through his, their lips quite frantic now.

In one swift move, he pulled off his shirt and covered her with his body but not his weight. Their lips didn't break contact as he crushed her breasts against his now naked chest.

And then into the heady silence plunged the sudden and eerie wailing of an alarm.

BEEP! BEEP! BEEP!

At first she didn't know what it signified or where it was coming from until Dan reached over her body and slapped a clock beside the bed so hard it smashed into the back wall. Although his hand returned immediately to her waist and his lips to her neck, the noise had already jolted Lena back to reality.

She was in the client's bed. Pretty much naked. And it was five-thirty am.

Five-thirty am?!

Oh, God!

Not only had she done the one thing she swore she'd never do again, but in minutes the whole camp was going to know about it.

Very soon outside Dan's donga would be a bustling traffic jam of men getting to the showers and the mess hall. When they saw her leaving Dan's room, they would think the worst. And why shouldn't they? It was the truth!

Oh hell, was she really one of those women who just kept making the same mistake over and over again?

With a strangled gasp, she pushed frantically on Dan's chest. 'I can't do this. I can't!'

Dan immediately pulled away from her and sat up. 'Lena, it's okay.' He touched her shoulder. 'You're trembling.'

'Can't you see how wrong this is?' She threw the words at him as she covered her body with his sheets.

The bed creaked as he stood up, his expression cast in shadow.

She glanced frantically at the door. 'I have to go before somebody sees me.'

He nodded. 'Then you better hurry.'

His words kicked her into action. Lena scrabbled off the bed, almost falling over as she snatched up her discarded shirt. Her fingers fumbled a little too roughly on the buttons and one of them popped off, bouncing on his vinyl flooring. She groaned in frustration. Her shirt now gaped open over her breasts. Dan went to his wardrobe. Shadows played across his naked chest and back, making her ache. A flying T-shirt hit her chest. She put her hands up to catch it.

For Pete's sake, focus.

If anyone saw her leaving Bulldog's donga at five-thirty am, in his clothes no less, they'd both be burned at the stake. And that was after World War Three ensued.

Lena pulled the shirt over her head. 'Is the coast clear?'

He went to the window and peered through the blinds. 'Yes.'

Suddenly she got cold feet. She couldn't just leave without saying something about what had just happened – maybe apologising for her behaviour or at least trying to explain it.

'Dan, wait –'

'There's no time.' He turned around to look at her, his voice firm, his eyes blank. 'We'll talk about this later.'

For now, it was clear he had packed his emotions away, so Lena said no more and instead moved towards the door.

He opened it and she stepped out onto the gravel. There were noises coming from the dongas all around them; she could hear alarm clocks and thumps. She could hear shoes on gravel in the next row along. Panic started to set in. It wasn't going to work. They weren't going to get away with this. Lena's heart leaped into her throat as she heard a door creak. But to her greatest relief, the tousled bed-hair emerging was bright red – Sharon. She stepped out of her donga onto the path with a towel and toiletries bag in her hand.

Thank you, God.

Lena felt Dan's presence behind her. 'It's okay,' she threw at him breathlessly. 'It's Sharon; she'll look after me. It's better that way.'

'If you're sure.'

'Yes.'

When Sharon noticed Lena moving towards her, her mouth fell open and her eyes practically popped from their sockets. 'Lena?' She stopped walking and simply stared.

Lena didn't look back at Dan as she reached Sharon's side, but heard him go into his donga and shut the door behind him.

'Sharon.' She clutched her friend's arm. 'I need your help.'

'No shit.'

Sharon was a lifesaver but her help didn't come without a price that was called best-friend privilege.

'You better tell me everything!'

They met for smoko at ten am and took a walk on the coastline, away from the bustle of site. Everything looked so normal. The stark white office boxes sat in solitude on the red dirt while trucks drove by; men hailed their mates; and a smattering of utes ran errands back and forth across the yard. As Lena looked out over the water at the wharf, she could see two big ships moored near the end. The ship loader crane was filling their bellies with iron ore straight from the conveyor and Gavin's crew was driving another pile. It was just an ordinary day. The sea was so calm. So undisturbed.

So *unlike* her.

She had butterflies for blood. She was frantic and cool all at the same time. She didn't know what to do. What to say. What to think. Where to start.

But Sharon did. 'So what are you going to do about this?'

She swallowed. 'What do you mean?'

Sharon folded her arms. 'I mean are you and Bulldog an item now?'

Lena started. 'No! I mean . . . I don't know.' She shook her head in confusion. 'We never spoke about that.'

Sharon was silent for a moment. 'I take it he's not as indifferent to you as you thought.'

Images of their encounter burned their way across Lena's mind, leaving her weak at the knees. 'No.'

'Is that really such a bad thing?' Sharon enquired cautiously.

Lena was silent for a moment, trying to get a handle on her emotions. 'Apart from my questionable history and the promise I made to myself never to let this sort of thing happen to me again, if the men were to find out about it, all hell would break loose.'

Sharon shoved her hands into the pockets of her jeans, worry lines creasing her forehead. 'Well, I can't deny it would be best to keep it a secret. The guys hate those idiots at TCN. Not that I blame them. There's too much bad blood. You don't know half the things they do to each other. Because I'm the bus driver I hear everything, and let me tell you, some of it's pretty malicious. If the Barnes Inc boys discovered you were doing the client –'

'I'm not doing the client!' She hated the way Sharon kept talking about it like it was a done deal.

'Then what are you doing, Lena? 'Cause you're certainly not being very responsible. If I hadn't been there this morning . . .' She broke off.

Lena cringed. She was right. There had only been a lucky ten seconds between Sharon whipping her into her donga and the next guy coming out of his. She would have been seen for sure, in Dan's T-shirt no less. Sharon had given her one of her shirts to put on instead before she left to go to reception to get the spare key. Dan's T-shirt now lay neatly folded under her bed, the only proof her early morning escapade had really happened.

'I know,' she croaked. 'If any of the guys had seen, it would be all over camp in seconds and then the men would take it as a personal betrayal.'

'So don't tell anyone,' Sharon suggested. 'I won't either.'

'Don't you see?' Lena gritted her teeth. 'That's exactly what things were like with Kevin. I am not sneaking around again. The men won't find out because there is nothing to find out.'

'And what does Bulldog think about all this?' Sharon demanded.

'I don't know.'

Sharon said no more, but Lena got the impression that she found this answer highly unsatisfactory. Perhaps she thought Bulldog could persuade her where she couldn't. Sweat broke out on the back of Lena's neck. If Bulldog did have feelings for her, they would be difficult to resist, but she had to stick to her guns. She made up her mind long before she even met Dan that this wasn't going to happen a second time. All the same, an uneasy feeling did prick her conscience. She really had no idea what Dan was thinking at this point.

Did he believe they were destined for a relationship? That maybe this was the beginning of something more? As much as she liked to deny it, she did care about him and hurting him was the last thing she wanted to do. But wasn't it better in this case just to rip the Band-Aid off rather than let wounds fester for days?

Her resolve to see him and sort it all out as soon as possible strengthened. They needed to talk. Only then could she get past this and move on with her life.

When she found a private moment later that morning, she rang his office and asked to be put through to him. His rude secretary said that he was in a phone conference with head office, to be followed by a series of meetings, and would be unavailable for the rest of the day.

'Can you just tell him I called and need to speak with him regarding an urgent matter?' Lena finally said.

There had been no response from Dan by the time she went outside to have lunch with Sharon. She knew she was being lousy company and was glad for the distraction when Carl came storming out of the office minutes later.

'There you are!' His eyes roved over both of them with satisfaction before turning to Sharon and saying, 'Would you mind coming to my office after you've eaten? I have a few documents I need you to deliver to Bulldog's dongas.'

'Sure.'

He cleared his throat. 'I was going to give them to him myself but apparently he's cancelled all his meetings with Barnes Inc personnel today.'

Lena perked up. 'Really? Why?'

'How the fu–' Carl swallowed, threw an uncomfortable glance at Sharon and then continued. 'How should I know? Got this shi– this phone call from his receptionist saying something had come up.'

Lena was momentarily diverted from her concerns about Dan. Was it her imagination or was Carl trying hard not to swear? She decided to ask another question. 'Did she say what it was?'

'No,' Carl spoke slowly. 'Just that it was important. No apology, though; apparently I'm not fu–' His head jerked slightly as he cut off the word and tried again. 'I'm not worth the consideration.'

Lena bit her lip to hide her delight. She had not been imagining things.

'I wouldn't worry about it.' Sharon threw him a grin. 'She's rude to me too.'

Carl went pink.

He actually blushed. And then he did the most alarming thing Lena had ever seen him do . . . or rather *never* seen him do.

He tried to smile.

Carl was good-looking in a rugged kind of way – stocky and broad shouldered with dark, weathered features. But his natural state was cranky – displeased at best. So this new expression sat so unnaturally on his face that she couldn't help but stare at it in shock. It was not a perfect effort by any means, little more than a slight turn of the lips, so that he actually looked more constipated than happy. Sharon, however, didn't appear to notice.

'I'll come by in fifteen minutes.' Sharon raised her sandwiches. 'When I'm done with my lunch.'

Carl's colour was subsiding but he coughed slightly. 'No rush, no need to cut your break short on my account.'

'Thanks,' Sharon said.

He nodded and then, ignoring Lena, walked back into the office donga. Lena choked and then turned wide eyes upon Sharon, who stared at her with complete innocence.

'What?'

As Lena continued to stare at her but said nothing, Sharon's eyebrows drew together. 'Do I have something on my face?' She reached up and touched her cheek.

Lena quickly cleared her throat. If Sharon hadn't noticed, she wasn't going to tell her. Why spoil the fun?

'I just thought that was odd,' she quickly improvised. 'About Dan, I mean. Why do you think he's cancelled all his meetings?'

'Who knows?' Sharon shrugged. 'Try not to overthink things, Lena. It'll do your head in.'

After a few minutes, the bus driver stood up and dusted off her hands. 'Well, I've finished my sandwich now so I might just go get my errands over and done with. You don't mind, do you?'

'No, not at all,' Lena assured her. 'Go ahead.'

She watched Sharon enter the office donga and struggled to keep a laugh from escaping.

Carl and Sharon.

She never would have thought it possible if she hadn't seen it with her own eyes. After all, on *her* first day Carl had told her that if she had a problem with his swearing, she could get stuffed because he changed for no one. Yet here he was tying his tongue in knots in an effort not to offend Sharon.

They were perfect for each other.

Well, sort of.

Later that day, Lena went down to the wharf to check on things, but mostly in the hopes of running into Dan. To her disappointment, she didn't see him anywhere. That night in the mess, she also scanned the room for him. But he was nowhere to be seen.

She tried not to be too frustrated as she grabbed a plate of salad and lasagne and sat down beside Sharon, Harry and Leg. Where was he? You'd think he would have tried to contact her today after what had happened that morning. Although she was sure about her decision to end whatever had started between them, she couldn't help but feel just a little hurt that he didn't care enough to see her as soon as possible.

She tuned in with half an ear as Leg raised amusing gossip about another rigger who'd pissed off one of Bulldog's men by refusing to redo a job. Harry was also in high spirits. He'd just come back from R and R which had included a lovely visit with his kids. Apparently, he hadn't even needed to use Sarah Michaels. The mere threat of getting a lawyer involved had frightened his ex into being cooperative. Lena would have been more happy for him if she hadn't been so distracted.

Suddenly, Radar tumbled in the door looking flushed with success.

'Ho ho ho.' Leg whistled low. 'Looks like someone's got a new story.' Sharon and Lena exchanged amused glances as he eagerly waved Radar over. Radar gave him a naughty wink, shook his head and gestured to the buffet. By the time he finally joined them, Leg was practically jumping in his seat.

'What's your radar picked up this time?'

'How do you know I got anythin'?' Radar teased him.

Leg punched his arm. 'I haven't seen that look on your face since Tony cut his hair. Now spill it.'

'Well, this is way bigger than a haircut, let me tell you.' Radar tapped his twitchy nose. 'Got the lowdown on Bulldog!'

Lena held her breath. What did he know? Had somebody seen something after all? Sharon stilled as well, and then shot her a warning look.

'Hell's frozen over, ladies and gents,' Radar announced proudly. 'Bulldog's gone on R and R.'

'What?!' Luckily the hurt in her voice went undetected as Harry, Sharon and Leg all said the same word at the same time.

'Yeah, well, you know how he's been lookin' all tired and well . . . just crap lately? I think it finally all caught up with him.'

'No.' Leg shook his head. 'That wouldn't be it. He ain't so soft. Somethin's happened. Something to do with you-know-what.'

'You know what?' Sharon repeated quickly. 'And what's that?'

Lena held her breath.

'You know,' Leg nudged Sharon as if she were playing dumb and then when she continued to look at him blankly, he twinkled his fingers, 'his *big* secret.'

Lena's breath whooshed out.

'Actually,' Radar nodded thoughtfully, 'I reckon you might be right about that 'cause from what I heard, he'd left the office by lunchtime. Had a meeting with his boss first and then told his secretary to spread the word that he'd taken off.'

Lena pushed the remaining food on her plate around with her fork. All of a sudden she wasn't hungry any more. In fact, the thought of eating another bite made her feel sick. How utterly naive and indeed arrogant of her to have supposed that Bulldog might be looking for a relationship. *What a joke!*

Sharon picked up her drink and made a big show of polishing it off. 'Well, I'm done for the evening and I've got heaps of laundry to do.' She put a hand on Lena's arm. 'You coming?'

Lena looked up at her gratefully and pushed her own plate away. 'Sure. That's just what I was thinking.'

Chapter 15

Dan had skipped town without so much as a 'see ya, thanks for last night'. It was scumbag behaviour, plain and simple. Lena didn't care that she had fully intended to tell him that nothing else could happen between them. After all, he didn't know that. In fact, he hadn't had any regard for what she might be feeling at all.

If and when he did come back to site, she certainly wouldn't be banging on his door, begging for some sort of recognition or explanation. Hell no. If this was the way he was going to play it, fine. She didn't need a deep and meaningful intimacy debrief. She had a life to get on with – work to do.

Pushing Dan to a secluded corner of her mind, she focused all her energies on the new skid frame, which was now operational. She had two skids going at once and the next day they were going to install their very first truss. That was more than enough to worry about without throwing Dan into the mix. Lena had looked over every part of the procedure at least a dozen times. But with Murphy's law and the 'Mike sabotage factor' possibly at play she didn't want to miss a thing.

By the end of the week she could breathe again. The first truss had gone in without mishap and as a result was followed up by two more uneventful installations. Lena almost wished they had been more of a distraction. Dan was still not back in town and there was no word of when he would return.

Despite her better judgement she was still keeping track of the number of days it had been since he'd disappeared. She didn't realise she was being so obvious about it either until Sharon pulled her aside to tell her off.

'I'm sick of that long face of yours,' her friend complained. 'You need to think about something else. You know, we've got this Sunday off. Why don't you piss off Carl and organise another one of your famous jaunts?'

'Well,' Lena hadn't actually intended to tell her, but the words slipped out, 'it *is* my birthday on Saturday.'

'Why didn't you say something earlier!' Sharon grabbed both her hands. 'Now we *have* to do something.'

Reluctantly, Lena warmed to her enthusiasm. She'd never been one to turn down a fuss before. She loved celebrating and hadn't missed the opportunity for a party since birth.

'Let's go to Karratha, Saturday night,' Sharon suggested excitedly. 'Dine at the best restaurant in town and get totally sloshed.'

Even as she said it, a germ of an idea began growing inside Lena's brain. And like a druggy desperate for a fix, she pounced on it. 'Actually,' Lena said, making it up as she went, 'why don't we invite a few others?'

Sharon blinked. 'Like who?'

'Just our closer friends, like Leg and Radar and Harry and Carl.'

Lena glanced at her face to see her reaction to the last name but there was none. She'd half expected that though and, after what happened with Gavin, didn't want to be pushy this time. She was just about to retract the idea, when Sharon brightened.

'You know what? The more the merrier. I'll help you organise it. After all, you can't be responsible for planning your own birthday party.'

'Birthday party?' Lena repeated, startled. 'Oh, I didn't mean it like that.'

But Sharon wasn't joking. Before Lena knew it, she was having a full-on birthday extravaganza. Carl even offered to rent a mini-van on Barnes Inc to get them all there and back. To excuse the expense, he said that after the event they could keep the van on site to run errands to Karratha. But Lena would have bet money that it was because it was Sharon who asked him for the vehicle, not her.

In any case, Sharon picked up the mini-van, which Leg and Radar nicknamed the 'Bongo Bus', early Saturday morning and brought it into camp. The arrangement was for everyone to meet out the front of the camp at ten past six that evening for their big night out. Sharon had volunteered to drive.

Harry turned up first and handed Lena a big box of chocolates all beautifully wrapped up, with a card.

'This is from me, Leg and Radar.'

'Aw, you didn't have to do that,' Lena said, knowing that he must have been the brains behind the operation. There was no way Leg or Radar would have come up with the idea and then on top of that gone shopping for it and wrapped it so beautifully. That's when Gavin, Fish and Carl arrived, the latter dressed in their matching Hawaiian party shirts. It hadn't been Sharon's original intention to invite Fish or Gavin, but they'd overheard her telling Carl and basically invited themselves. Leg and Radar turned up last; and it was easy to see why they had taken so long to get there. They were carrying an Esky between them.

'What do you think you're doing?' Sharon demanded.

'Come on, mate,' Leg protested. 'We need some for the road.'

Lena moaned inwardly. It was going to be one of *those* nights.

Despite her reservations, however, they took off in the Bongo Bus as planned. The trip to Karratha, which took less than an hour, was pretty uneventful. Too much guzzling in the back seat for talking.

Sharon had booked a restaurant called Orchids. It was situated inside a hotel, Karratha Resort. Lena was pleasantly surprised to find that the bar and restaurant could easily have competed with any of the ritzy hotels in Perth. Beautiful brightly coloured paintings of marine animal and plant life hung on the walls. Smart but comfortable couches and armchairs were grouped around polished wooden coffee tables. Beyond the bar was a row of glass doors through which she could see a gorgeous swimming pool, its still surface glittering under the fairy lights. A spa and sauna area behind this was sheltered by palms. With the weather so perfect, she could just see herself out there, sipping a cocktail under the stars.

Despite the fact that they had already tipped back a few, Leg and Radar still wanted pre-dinner drinks so their first stop was the bar. Carl bought Lena a cocktail as a birthday present and Sharon one because she'd organised such a good party. Everyone else had a beer. Lena was just settling into the beginnings of a great evening when who should walk into the room but Mike Hopkins.

He was accompanied by a woman of similar shape and build to himself, short and plump with greying blonde hair. He stopped just before reaching the bar and Lena could tell he was as unpleasantly shocked to see her as she was to see him. But then his gaping mouth slowly closed and with a scowl of resignation he ushered his date across the room in their direction. To cut him some slack, Lena realised he couldn't exactly snub his boss and it was Carl he walked towards, not her.

Thank goodness.

Carl hadn't noticed him yet, however. And so when he turned around was just tipsy enough to say, 'Fuck, Mike, were you invited?'

Mike went purple.

'No, I'm on R and R. Decided to holiday in Karratha.' He gestured to the woman beside him. 'This is my wife, Patricia; flew up from Perth yesterday.'

Patricia nodded contemptuously at the group and fingered the pearls at her throat.

'Right.' Carl couldn't seem to think of anything else to say.

'And what, may I ask, brings all of you to town?' Mike glanced at everyone except Lena.

'It's Madame E's birthday,' Radar jumped in. 'We're celebrating.'

Mike's accusatory expression zeroed in on Lena immediately and she knew he was laying all the discomfort he was currently feeling firmly at her door.

Geez, this guy seriously needs a new scapegoat.

'Well,' he grunted. 'Patricia and I are booked for dinner, so I think we'll head to our table now.'

Carl raised his glass a little too gratefully. 'No worries, you do that.'

As Mike moved away, Fish immediately leaned forwards. 'Who shoved the great big stick up his arse?'

Leg and Radar rolled delightedly on their feet and Radar's tipsy voice answered, 'Madame E.'

'Hey,' Sharon looked at them sharply, 'Lena didn't do anything to Mike. He's just a sour-faced troublemaker. Always has been.'

'Sour you say.' Fish leaned casually on the bar. 'In that case how's about we send him a drink?'

Only Carl laughed. The rest of them looked a little nervous. Fish raised his pointer finger. Lena and her friends watched in curiosity and then growing amusement as Fish asked the barman for one of his lemons. Grabbing a pen out of his pocket he drew a face with its tongue sticking out on it on one side and, *Best wishes from the Barnes boys* on the other. When he had completed the artwork, he balanced the lemon on top of an empty wineglass and called the barman back over. 'We'd like to send this to the gentleman at the table under the tree outside.'

The barman didn't bat an eyelid and called a waiter over. The waiter placed the wineglass on a large black tray and with much flourish made his way outside. Lena couldn't help it: she watched Mike's reaction with the others. He blanched when the drink was placed in front of him, looking back at them as the waiter pointed in the direction from which the drink had come.

Fish, Radar and Leg all waved at him jovially. He didn't even crack a smile, pushing the wineglass away and turning his attention back to his red-faced wife. The boys roared with laughter and even quiet, non-confrontational Harry couldn't stop the grin from stretching across his face. Lena had to hide her own smile behind the rim of her glass.

'I don't like this,' Sharon whispered at her elbow. 'If Mike hated you before, he'll be out for blood more than ever now.'

Unease rippled through Lena, but she refused to be over-powered by it. This was her night: she couldn't let worry spoil it.

While she was making this decision Gavin, who had been fairly quiet up until now, moved across the circle and stationed himself at Sharon's side. Lena frowned. She wasn't keen on this turn of events at all. It was clear he was going to make a pain of himself by giving his courtship a second shot. The fact that he was halfway to drunk didn't bode well either. She could tell though that Sharon wasn't ignorant of what was going on. So she continued to allow Fish to tease her and a rather bewildered Harry with a rather long and convoluted story of his latest problem. Ethel would not allow him to put a freezer in his donga and the cook in the mess was refusing to store any more of his catches.

'The thing is, not overly fond of the taste of fish, myself,' he said sadly. 'Not sure what to do with the half of it.'

'Why not just throw them back?' Harry asked.

Fish was horrified. 'Discard the proof of my greatness? Not on your life!'

As Lena turned her head to hide her smile, she saw a disturbing scene a few metres away. Gavin had got hold of Sharon's arm and wasn't letting her leave his side, as she clearly wanted to do. Lena took a step towards them, but Carl was there before her.

'Let go of her, you stupid bastard.'

Gavin's head jerked up and he dropped Sharon's arm. 'Carl –'

'I've been watching you behave like a regular prick for the past twenty minutes. Back off. Can't you see the bird don't want you?'

Gavin was extremely flushed but he straightened his spine nonetheless. 'To be honest, Carl, I don't think that's any of your business.'

'If you want me to make it my fuckin' business,' Carl growled, 'I certainly will.' He jerked his head over his shoulder. 'But outside.'

Go, Carl!

Lena watched Sharon follow the exchange, white-faced and shaken. She hurried to her side, slinging an arm across her shoulders. Meanwhile, Gavin had pulled back and was swallowing convulsively. Lena realised it had just dawned on the idiot that he was picking a fight with his boss. Not exactly good for his future employment.

'You know what?' he said slowly. 'I think it might be best if I just go. Cool off a little.'

He looked around at the group. If he was hoping someone would ask him to stay or offer him some company, he was disappointed. He nodded in resignation. 'All right then.'

They watched him walk, somewhat unsteadily, out of the bar.

'You guys shouldn't have had so much to drink on the way here,' Lena said as soon as Gavin was out of earshot.

'And you women shouldn't have had so f–' Carl licked his lips. 'So little.' His gaze roved over Sharon's face and Lena was surprised and gratified to see gentleness in it. 'Can I buy you a drink?' he asked her. 'To help settle your nerves?'

Lena felt Sharon tremble under her arm as she nodded. 'Perhaps some water? I'm driving after all.'

'Forget that,' Lena interrupted quickly. 'You need something stronger and lots of it.'

'But who will drive?'

'I will.' Lena squeezed her shoulders but Sharon immediately pushed away from her.

'Lena, you can't drive. It's your birthday.'

'I don't mind,' Lena said, smiling. 'Honestly. Besides, with Mike here and everything, I'd rather keep my wits about me.'

It was the truth. She really didn't feel like drinking heaps. And she'd rather see Sharon enjoy the evening – maybe even open up a little to Carl.

Sharon eyed her carefully. 'You sure?'

'Positive.' Lena turned mischievously to Carl. 'Buy her something fun, like a Screaming Orgasm.'

Under Sharon's gaping gaze, Lena rejoined the other half of the group.

Half an hour and a few more drinks later, they finally decided to sit down to dinner. It was going to be an interesting meal considering Leg and Radar were smashed. Harry was drinking tentatively but steadily. Fish was seeing stars. Carl and Sharon were the most sober. After her experience of Carl's behaviour at Point Samson, Lena knew he was holding back. Maybe he needed the brain cells for speaking. He was still struggling not to swear in front of Sharon and she wasn't the only person to notice this time.

Fish found the behaviour very peculiar and was too drunk for tact.

'What's got your goat, Carl? You're talking funny and you ain't drinking.'

Lena thought Sharon must have finally got it because she flushed slightly and looked away.

'Nothing's got my fuckin' goat,' Carl blustered. 'Don't know what you're fuckin' on about.'

'Then have another beer.' Fish leaned in. 'And stop being such a wuss. You'd think you were trying to impress some bird or something.' His beady eyes moved between Sharon and Lena. 'You two ain't up to something, are you?'

Lena glared at him as Sharon's flush deepened. 'Don't be ridiculous.'

Fish shrugged. 'I've known Carl for seven years. Never been a ladies' man.' He turned back to his friend. 'Have you, Carl?'

Carl was looking almost as red as Sharon. 'Fuck off.'

Fish frowned. 'You always told me that women placed too many demands on a man and we were better off without them.'

'I'll drink to that,' said Radar, lifting his glass.

'So will I,' Harry agreed.

'You ain't changed your tune, have you, Carl?' Fish wanted to know.

Carl hesitated, grunted and then seemed to square his shoulders as though shaking an imaginary load off his back. 'Not in this lifetime.' He stopped a waiter who was passing. 'Could I order a bottle of wine, please?'

After the waiter departed, Leg sent his slurred compliments across the table. 'Good one, Carl. We could do with another red for the table.'

'It ain't for you, dumb arse,' Carl shot at him. 'I'm drinking the lot.'

Great.

Fish had just shot Lena's beautiful budding romance in the foot. She wanted to kill him. Instead, she had to settle for throwing silent curses like Frisbees in his direction.

Sharon returned to her meal. They'd both ordered the same thing. Marinated barramundi on a bed of sweet potatoes and asparagus. It was delicious but, in typical five-star style, there was very little of it.

When it came time for the bill, Carl shocked Lena by putting a company credit card on the table.

'Carl,' she gasped. 'What are you doing?'

'Paying for everyone.'

'But there's no need.'

'Lena,' Leg nudged her in the ribs, 'if the man wants to be gracious, don't ruin his moment.'

Lena turned and nudged Leg back. 'But this is my birthday party. It shouldn't be a company expense.'

Carl dismissed her remark with a drunken wave of his hand. 'As project manager, I get a certain percentage for entertainment purposes. Haven't had a fuckin' chance living in Wickham. This is just what we need.'

Lena shook her head. 'I think that money is for entertaining the client, not your employees.'

'We are entertaining the client,' Radar piped up. 'He's been sitting over there watching us for the past twenty minutes.'

It was like someone shot Lena in the face with a water pistol. She turned startled eyes on Radar. 'What did you say?'

He jerked his head over his shoulder. 'Over at the bar. Looks like Bulldog's taken R and R in Karratha like Mike.'

In slow motion, though in reality it must have taken a second, Lena turned her head and looked across the room.

And there he was.

Just like that.

Sitting on a bar stool, right arm on the counter with what looked like a shot of whisky next to his hand. He was just sitting there, his enigmatic gaze trained on hers as hers was on him.

Lena heard a vague movement to her right as Carl shuffled in his chair. 'You've got to be shitting me. Now I've got to fuckin' go over.'

'Can't you snub him?' someone asked.

'Fuck no. Bad for PR.'

Lena focused on the tablecloth. He'd left without a word and he'd been here that whole bloody time. It wasn't like he couldn't have picked up the phone and spoken to her.

Anger bubbled up her throat.

If he didn't want to talk to her, she sure as hell wasn't going to look like she was at all interested in talking to him.

Leg, who was sitting next to Lena, leaned across the table to plead with Carl. 'You're not going to invite him to join us, are you? We'll never be able to relax with bloody Bulldog at our table.'

For once Leg and Lena were in absolute agreement. 'He's right, Carl,' she added her two cents. 'Besides, you're all far too drunk to behave decently. It would be bad PR, not good PR.'

Fish lifted his glass. 'Spot on, Lena.'

Carl nodded slowly as the notion registered with him. 'Fuck if I don't think you're onto something.' Just as she relaxed he added, 'Lena, *you* should go over.'

'*What?!*'

'You're the only one of us who ain't pissed.' Carl shrugged.

'Carl, I –'

'In fact,' he went on, ignoring the gathering panic in her voice, 'as the project manager I officially appoint you our PR rep for tonight.' He gave her a thumbs up and a wink. 'Go and do us proud.'

Lena glanced at Sharon, who returned her gaze sympathetically.

It looked like she was well and truly done. Done like a Christmas turkey.

She stood and made her way across the room to the bar, descending into the sunken lounge on slightly unsteady legs. She hoped Dan couldn't read how nervous she was, or how much this simple task affected her.

Back: straight. Voice: professional. Expression: distant. She sucked all her emotion into her heart and then encased it in lead. 'Hi,' she said blandly when she reached his side. 'Carl wanted me to say hello. I'm afraid he's had a little too much to drink to greet you himself.'

Dark brooding eyes captured hers. The shadows were still prominent under them. But this time he was clean-shaven. He was dressed in a short-sleeved collared shirt, coupled with a pair of casual trousers. His hair was tousled as though he'd just come out of the wind – but her guess was that he'd been pulling on it again. She wanted to smooth it straight and gave herself a mental slap for even going there.

Lena leaned against the bar, looked at his left shoulder and began to speak in her best Channel Seven News voice. 'The project's been running pretty smoothly since you left for R and R. No major hiccups. We're installing trusses now, piling is nearly on schedule and Lance has put his fifth deck module on.'

'Lena, what are you doing?' His voice was low and gravelly and her body resonated at the first sound of it.

But she kept her voice even. 'PR.'

His lips twitched before he polished off the last of his liquor and set the empty glass on the counter. 'So I guess you're going to ignore the giant elephant in the room, then.'

'Oh.' She feigned surprise and finally focused her gaze squarely on his. 'You mean the one that you've been avoiding for the past seven days?'

'You've been counting.' His mouth turned up briefly.

She glared at him. 'You wish.'

'I'm sorry I didn't contact you after . . . after what happened. I –'

'No need to explain, Dan.' She broke eye contact again, knowing that if she didn't she would give too much away. Her gaze sought the pool outside instead and she added with a careless laugh, 'It was nothing. I'm over it.'

'I see.'

A short silence followed in which time she decided her visit with the devil had gone on long enough. She looked back at him. 'Look, we're about to leave soon so –'

'Why are you here anyway?' He frowned.

'It's my birthday.'

'Happy birthday.'

'Thanks.' She straightened. 'Shall I give Carl your regards?'

'Lena, wait.'

She stopped mid-turn and looked back at him, eyebrows raised in question.

He hesitated. 'Can I buy you a drink?'

'No.'

'I know you don't want to hear it but I need to apologise.'

She turned back, unable to keep the sarcasm out of her response. 'Really? For what?'

Lena thought she saw a brief flash of pain cross his face but couldn't be sure. 'I'm sorry that I didn't catch up with you immediately. But, to be honest, I thought I'd done enough damage and it would be better to see you when you'd cooled off a little bit.'

'Cooled off?' She wrinkled her nose.

'The look on your face when you pushed me off is burned into my memory,' he returned hoarsely. 'I have been unable to think about anything else for the last week.'

Lena said nothing as she tried to put puzzle pieces together. What expression?

When she'd pushed Dan away that day, she'd been thinking about Kevin and everything that had gone wrong since him and because of him. No doubt horror, fear and shame had been painted on her face. But why would Dan . . . ? The pieces clicked into place. 'Dan, I –'

But he wasn't listening. 'Here I was, telling you to watch out for men who might try to take advantage of you and then

I did exactly what I warned you about. When I think about it, I feel sick.' He spat the word like it left a foul taste in his mouth. 'I abused my position and your plight. It was unforgivable.'

'Dan, you didn't do anything I didn't want you to.' Lena made haste to reassure him. 'I could have stopped you at any point. Perhaps I should have done so earlier.'

'You don't need to lie to me to make me feel better.' He denied her offering without hesitation. 'I know what I did was wrong. You said it yourself that day.'

I did?

As she scrambled to remember her own words, he continued to speak. His voice, however, had lowered slightly and lost some of its earlier passion. It was more matter-of-fact; he sounded more like the Dan she was used to.

'I am fully aware, not only of the inappropriateness of my own behaviour but the disastrous repercussions that could have occurred if we had been discovered.' He shut his eyes briefly and then opened them again. 'One of the biggest problems on site is the fighting and ill-will between our people. If there had been even a hint of something going on between you and me, it would have been like spiking their guns. Morale would have gone through the floor. You would have lost the respect of your peers and I that of my subordinates.' He eyeballed her. 'I can only assure you, if you are scared about me ever doing something like that again, don't be.'

Lena returned his gaze. 'I'm not afraid of you, Dan. Never was.'

His chest rose sharply as he sucked in a breath. For a moment, just a moment, his expression lightened and he opened his mouth to say something but then shut it just as abruptly. Darkness once more settled upon his countenance, this time heavier than before.

'Look around you,' he ordered. 'Your colleagues are watching us like hawks. Even if I were to reach over now and just touch your hand, it would be all over site within hours. If I were you, I *would* be afraid.'

She didn't look at the table behind her; she knew he was speaking the truth. A relationship between them was impossible. So instead she looked down at the countertop, where their fingers were mere inches apart. Electricity raced up her arm as she wished he would touch her hand. His voice seemed to envelop her even though it was no more than a whisper.

'I wish you the very best, Lena.' The hand on the bar next to hers curled into a fist. He stood up, shoving it into the pocket of his pants.

It was like being tossed out of bed onto cold hard tiles. All she could do was shiver and blink as he walked away.

Chapter 16

It was silly to wish that things could be different. He had a responsibility to the company and she had a responsibility to herself. The path they had almost stumbled down could only lead to her getting fired or hurt – or both. She should be grateful that he was sensible enough to realise it. Instead, she felt absolutely gutted. It took a couple of deep breaths before she was able to return to her birthday party with a fairly neutral expression on her face. The only person who was not fooled by her cheerful countenance and jovial comment that Bulldog was as painful on holiday as he was in the office was Sharon. Her friend grabbed her hand under the table and squeezed it. It took all her strength not to burst into tears at the gesture.

Lena's mask was firmly in place when their party retired once more to the bar, which was now empty of Bulldog. In truth, it was the very last thing she wanted to do. But she gave them an hour before she announced that the party was over. Sharon was the only one who was pleased – Lena realised she was pretty tired too.

Under a barrage of protests from the rest of them, Lena managed to get everyone into the back of the Bongo Bus before stationing herself in the driver's seat. Gavin had still not returned to the bar or the restaurant. To her relief, no one could be bothered looking for him; even Carl agreed that Gavin's fate was his own. So Lena started the engine, put the van into gear and made for Wickham. The first ten minutes of the trip were without incident unless she counted the ear-splitting singing that was going on in the back seat.

But then she saw it.

The kangaroo.

Looming by the side of the road in the peripheral dimness of her headlights, straightened to full height. Instinctively, she knew it was going to do something stupid. Since that red jumped off the jetty, she'd been pretty sure roos were capable of just about anything.

Her foot moved from the accelerator to the brake in readiness and the vehicle started to slow down. The words of the safety officer from that dreadful induction she'd never thought would come in handy came back to her: 'It is more dangerous to swerve at high speed than to hit an animal.'

In the last second before Bongo was due to pass it, the kangaroo jumped into the middle of the road. Lena wasn't going fast, but she was going fast enough. She pushed down hard on the brakes and forced herself to keep the wheel steady. But it was too late: the van hit the roo square on.

Sharon, who was sitting in the front seat next to her, screamed; and Lena heard bodies rolling about in the back. Nobody, apparently, was wearing their seatbelts. 'Sorry! Sorry! Sorry!' she cried out to the unfortunate animal, tears stinging her eyes. She dragged it for a few metres before, in a crunch of bone and guts, it slipped under the tyre and they left it for dead. She shivered in the aftermath, unclenching teeth she hadn't realised she'd unconsciously locked.

That poor creature.

She didn't even want to think about what she'd left on the tar.

My first roadkill.

When her nerves had untwisted somewhat, she called out over her shoulder, 'Everyone all right?'

Fish sat forwards, resting his forearms on the back of the front seat, sipping casually from a tinny. It was apparent they were still in the process of emptying the Esky.

'Fine, mate. You done good.'

'Should I stop?' she asked, thinking about the roo she'd left on the road.

'You don't think it's still alive after that, do you?' He burped. 'That poor bastard's puree by now.'

Lena would have covered her ears if she hadn't been holding the wheel. She couldn't believe she had yet another marsupial death on her hands. For goodness sake, she was still getting over the drowning on the wharf. At this rate she was turning into some sort of kangaroo hit man.

'Urgh!' Sharon said. 'How can you be so insensitive? Can't you see she's upset?'

Fish's wicked laugh turned into a hiccup.

'What about the car?' Lena hurriedly changed the subject. 'Perhaps we should stop to check that? There's no roo bar – there could be some damage.' She glanced at Carl in the rear-view mirror. 'What should I do?'

He raised his tinny and was about to answer her questions when he was roughly pushed aside by Leg, who called out the order: 'Turn up the music! Let's get this Bongo crankin'!'

In response Fish reached over the seats and turned up the volume himself. There was an encouraging cheer from the back and a wry smile curled Lena's lips. The bus could be on fire and the boys wouldn't know till their alcohol was set alight. She glanced in the rear-view mirror again. Fish and Carl were singing Katy Perry's latest number to each other. They were out of tune, terribly loud and as they pumped up their imaginary breasts in time, she had to laugh. Carl didn't look like he could run two metres, let alone the construction of a giant iron ore wharf off the coast of Cape Lambert.

'Lena?' Sharon's voice was urgent. 'I think you better stop. The engine is overheating. Look at the dial. It's off the scale.'

'What?' But Lena slowed down and pulled over to the side of the road.

As she stepped out of the car she near gagged at the smell. 'Pong!' She put her hand over her nose and mouth.

Sharon hopped out of the van too. 'What is that *smell*?' She walked towards Lena's side of the van and they met in front of the headlights.

'I don't know,' Lena choked. 'Burning rubber, melted plastic, medium rare kangaroo flesh?' She was still unable to remove her hand from her face.

'Well, the engine is certainly cooked.' Sharon also covered her nose and mouth and gestured to the steaming bonnet with her spare hand.

The door to the eight-seater van slid open and the boys stumbled out. Harry was holding Leg up because the man was swaying like a ship.

'Fuck!' Carl reeled and screwed up his nose. Lena was surprised he could smell anything at all.

Harry and Leg fell over. Radar stuck out an unsteady hand to help Leg up but got pulled down beside him instead. They rolled on the dirt in a roar of giggles. When their laughter subsided, neither of them made any attempt to get up. Harry also simply lay down and looked at the stars.

Lena folded her arms. 'Okay, guys, focus: we need a plan.'

Carl and Fish looked at each other and then at her. Fish cleared his throat in an attempt to hide the slur. It didn't work. 'Ground looks cosy enough.' He cast an eye at his peers. 'Let's just camp here for the night.'

'No way.' Lena held up both her hands. 'I'm not sleeping on dirt and breathing in this stench all night long.'

'Me neither,' Sharon agreed. 'I think we should try and get the van back to Karratha since it's closer than Wickham. Why don't we just wait for the engine to cool a little and then try and start it up again?'

As no one had a better plan, they did just this. Lena and Sharon sat on the back doorstep of the van while the boys finished their tinnies. Lena thanked heaven that was the last of them.

After ten minutes that seemed to last a century Lena roused the troops. 'Come on, we better try that engine again. Everyone back in the van.'

It was like rounding up a classroom of children. They dawdled, they ran away, they giggled and swatted her hands until Lena was ready to just leave them behind. She told them as much and wished she'd made the threat sooner because they finally boarded the vehicle.

Lena hopped into the driver's seat again and Sharon into the front passenger seat. With a little prayer, she turned the key. The engine made an awful gagging noise before dying.

'Try again,' Sharon urged. Her voice was desperate, not that Lena needed much encouragement.

She turned the key a second time. This time the engine didn't even gag. There was just stone-cold silence.

'Are you turning it?' Sharon demanded.

'*Yes*,' Lena replied impatiently. 'Nothing's happening.'

'Okay, nobody panic,' Fish slurred as he fell out of the van onto the dirt again. Lena jumped out of the driver's seat and slammed the door behind her.

'What's left to do?'

'There's no need to get cranky.' He gave her a reproving glance and then burped. 'All this needs is a little male intervention. Since Carl and I are the senior members of staff on this road trip, we'll fix the engine.'

'What?' she said at the same time as Carl said, 'Huh?' He too exited the van, practically falling on top of Leg as he did so.

Sharon put a hand to her forehead. 'God save us.'

In his drunken haze, Carl appeared to notice her doubt and, much to Lena's annoyance, it seemed to give him an incentive.

Please! Now you want to impress her?

Carl lifted his chin and with new determination drained his can before pitching it into the back of the mini-van.

'Ow!' The can had hit Harry in the head.

Carl laced his fingers together, flexed them and gestured imperiously for Fish to follow his lead. Seeing the seriousness the operation required, Fish also drained his can and pitched it into the back of the van.

'Hey, watch it!'

'If we do this right,' Carl said to Fish in lowered tones that she suspected were supposed to be highly knowledgeable, 'this will be a fuckin' piece of cake, mate. Fuckin' piece of cake.'

Fish nodded.

Lena bit her lip, wishing she hadn't been so hasty in showing them her frustration. 'Are you sure this is a good idea?'

'Damn straight it's a good idea,' Carl promised and then took five minutes just to figure out how to open the bonnet.

With a bang, the bonnet flew up and Lena and Sharon stumbled back as they were assailed by a much stronger stench of dead and still-cooking kangaroo.

Completely undeterred, Carl and Fish peered into the engine. Lena didn't know how they managed to see anything because the van headlights pointed outwards and they didn't have a torch. But what really had her worried was that even though she was standing a few feet away she could feel the heat radiating off the engine. Scenes from various action movies involving exploding cars began to flicker through her mind.

'Er . . . maybe you two shouldn't do that,' she cautioned. 'What if you burn yourselves?'

'Relax.'

'What if the van explodes?'

'It's not going to fuckin' explode.'

'This is why.' Fish clamped a grease-stained hand on Carl's shoulder. 'Men like us: we don't tie ourselves down. Women will always try to hold you back from who you can be.'

With a frown, Carl shrugged off Fish's grip and returned to his task. Lena noticed with satisfaction that there was a perfect black imprint of Fish's hand now stamped upon his shoulder. When she glanced at Sharon, her friend's eyes were dancing.

Their attention was pulled back to the men, however, when Carl advised Fish to look in the corner because he thought he might have found the cause of the problem. It was then that they started pulling out all sorts of bits and pieces from the engine. Bits of fanbelt, rubber and other metal pieces flew over their shoulders.

'Don't need this.'

'Don't need that.'

'Hey!' Lena cried as a piece of rubber just missed her shoulder. 'Be careful.'

She could barely see their faces now as both heads were practically buried under the bonnet. They were chatting excitedly to each other like a pair of monkeys but she couldn't make out what they were saying.

'They're ruining the van more, not fixing it,' Sharon observed as another piece of something flew over their heads. 'This is a complete waste of time.'

Fish emerged holding a thing that looked a bit like a fan with a wire attached to it. 'Hey, Carl,' he enquired, 'do you know what this does?'

Carl straightened, looked at it, scratched his head and replied, 'Well, it's not doing it any more, is it?'

Fish nodded. 'Yeah, you're right.' And he chucked that on the side of the road as well.

'Okay, that's it,' Lena called out. 'You better stop. This is crazy. There is no way you guys are helping that car.' She rubbed her arms. 'And the mozzies are starting to bite.'

'We can't stop now,' Carl said, with one hand still inside the engine. 'Not when we're so fuckin' close.'

'Close to what?' she demanded. 'Getting hurt?'

Fish waggled his pointer finger at her. 'You know, your lack of faith is really not helping matters at all.'

'Fuck yes,' said Carl. 'Why do you keep thinking something is going to go wrong? Don't you –'

Suddenly he began to shake violently. The hand resting inside the car seemingly stuck there as he tried to get it free. His eyes rolled back into his head and gurgling noises erupted from his slack mouth.

'Carl! Carl!' Sharon and Lena screamed and ran towards him. Abruptly, he let go of the engine, laughing so hard he was fit to burst. As he stumbled backwards, clutching his belly, he tripped over a tree log and fell on his bum. The abrupt impact, however, did nothing to steady his amusement. He rolled and continued to laugh harder. Fish shamelessly joined in till they were both holding their sides from the pain of snorting.

Lena's blood boiled. 'That was not funny!'

'You scared us half to death,' Sharon cried. 'We thought you were dying!' The distress in her voice seemed to sober Carl. He choked back the last laugh and sat up.

'Sorry, love. Just couldn't resist.'

The endearment distracted Lena for a moment because it was so out of character. But in a second the moment was gone. Carl was up on his feet again, dragging Fish by the scruff of the neck back to the engine. After a bit more rummaging, he announced that he was going under and laid down on the side of the road beneath the car. When he finally emerged again, his shirt was covered in oil.

'Er, think I've worked out what the problem is. The fuckin' roo stuck its head in our radiator. Looks like we can't fix it.'

Lena looked heavenwards. 'You don't say.'

Carl ignored her sarcasm, stood up and whipped a mobile phone from his pocket. 'Better ring Mike; he might be able to come pick us up.'

Lena was so angry she saw spots. 'You had that thing this whole time and you didn't tell us!'

He blinked at her. 'We didn't need the mobile before. Fish and I were fixing the engine.'

A number of rude responses hovered on the tip of her tongue; only the fact that he was her boss held them there. As she calmed down, Carl got busy on his mobile.

She never thought that one day she'd be grateful to Mike or that she'd ever value his intelligence above Carl's. But it looked like she was going to be wrong on both counts. She listened hopefully to Carl's end of the conversation and was pleased to note that Mike was agreeing to come get them. In fact, the conversation seemed to be going quite smoothly until Carl went and ruined it.

'Oh and just one more thing, Mike. Can you bring a carton? The boys have drunk all the piss and the Esky –' He broke off and pulled the phone from his ear to look at it. 'He fuckin' hung up.'

'He better still be coming, Carl,' Lena warned. ''Cause if he's not . . .'

'He's fired, that's what he is,' Carl finished for her, putting his phone back in his pocket. 'Fancy hanging up on your boss, little prick.'

Lena sent up another prayer that Mike would come but without the carton. After that, there was nothing they could do but wait and hope it wasn't in vain. They lapsed into a companionable silence that was broken once or twice by Fish trying to crack a funny joke or two to keep them amused.

Eventually, Lena heard the faint sound of a car approaching. She stood up and went to the roadside. There were headlights in the distance. Someone was definitely coming. Regardless of whether it was Mike or not, she had already decided to flag them down.

Radar and Leg remained in the van but the rest of the group stood on the side of the road, jumping up and down and waving their arms. The ute didn't hesitate in pulling over beside them. It was Mike after all.

When he exited the vehicle, however, his expression was thunderous. A second later Lena found out why. The front passenger door opened. Blind drunk and waving a glass of bourbon in one hand, Gavin staggered out. She slapped a palm to her head.

'You've got to be kidding me. Gav?'

'I was in the bar when Carl called and he was there.' Mike glared at Lena. 'The dropkick insisted on coming. Short of knocking him out, couldn't leave without him.'

'You needed me,' Gavin slurred. He stretched his arms wide, sloshing a bit of his whisky on the dirt. 'They all need me.'

Oh brother.

'Did you bring the carton?' Carl demanded.

'No.' Gavin stumbled, almost dropping his glass. 'Didn't know you wanted one. But it doesn't matter. I'm going to do you one better than that.' He looked at Sharon and flicked his chin as though to say, 'You'll wish you hadn't rejected me when you see this.' He swung his arm at the mini-van, sweeping the entire vehicle with this unsteady but all-encompassing gesture. 'I'm going to fix that engine for you.'

Sharon and Lena immediately barred his path. 'No way!'

As it turned out, Mike had to do about three trips with his ute to get them all back to Karratha Resort. He also called a tow truck to get what was left of the van back there too. Lena thought he was about as furious as she had been half an hour earlier by the end of it. The difference was his rage wasn't directed at the group but at only one person.

Her.

How the ruination of his entire evening was completely her fault was beyond her. Like she could have predicted they'd hit a kangaroo and get stranded on the side of the road. Hell, if she had been able to do that, she would have cancelled the whole event before it even started.

By the time they got back to the hotel, it was two-thirty am and they were exhausted. The reward was well worth the pain though. Sharon and Lena were both looking forward to spending a night, company paid, in the most luxurious hotel in town. The modern decor, the shiny bathrooms, the scented towels. As soon as they entered their room, Lena breathed it all in with a shiver of delight.

'Now this is more like it.'

The two of them fell into bed twenty minutes later and slept without interruption until the shrill sound of their telephone erupted in the silence.

Sharon groaned, pulling her covers over her head as Lena groped for the receiver.

'Hello,' she croaked into the mouthpiece.

'Lena.' The low baritone was unmistakable. 'Are you okay?'

Lena's eyes, which seconds ago had felt glued shut, flew open. 'Dan?'

Like a meerkat suspecting danger, Sharon's head popped out from behind her covers again.

'Yeah, it's me. I saw Carl in the lobby this morning trying to organise some cars for you guys and he told me what happened.'

'Oh.' Lena licked her lips.

'It looks like you'll be at the hotel for most of the day. There aren't any cars until three this afternoon.'

Lena looked at her watch. It was only just past ten. Five more hours in this resort? Who was she to complain? 'Sounds great.'

'Just wondering if there's anything I can do.' Dan paused. 'I mean, I do have a car here, so if you two want to get back to Wickham earlier . . .'

Lena glanced wryly at Sharon. 'Somehow I think we'll manage at the resort a little longer.'

'Okay.'

There was an awkward silence and Lena clutched the phone like it was a lifeline – willing Dan to speak.

'I guess I'll leave you to it then,' he finished finally.

'Dan, wait,' she rushed out, unable to bear it any longer. 'I need to talk to you.'

'About what?'

'I don't like the way we left things last night. You didn't let me explain.'

There was a ragged sigh. 'There's nothing for you to explain.'

Lena glanced at Sharon, who was watching her with some concern. As much as she trusted her friend, she didn't really want to have this conversation in front of her.

'Can I see you this morning? How about breakfast?'

'That'll be difficult considering I just left Carl and your other two colleagues in the restaurant. You know what will happen if we're seen together.'

Lena chewed thoughtfully on her lower lip. 'Okay, what about the gym?'

'Mike's wife has a work-out there every morning. I know, because usually so do I.'

'Down by the pool then?'

She could hear the frustration in Dan's response. 'It's in complete view of the restaurant. Listen, Lena, I really don't think –'

'The spa isn't.' She interrupted him, holding her breath at the boldness of this move.

'What?'

'The spa is almost completely hidden by a ring of palms. No one will see us talking in there.'

Dan's voice was gruff. 'Now that's *really* not a good idea.'

'I only want a minute of your time.' She glanced at the clock beside the phone. 'I can be there in thirty minutes. What about you?'

'Lena, there is nothing more to say.'

'I think there is. Please be there.' She hung up the phone before he could deny her again.

'Lena.' Sharon's tone was distinctly disapproving. 'What are you doing?'

I don't know, I don't know, Lena cried nervously in her head, though she made no reply.

'Lena,' Sharon repeated urgently, 'talk to me.'

Lena threw off her covers and swung her legs out of bed. 'I'm going for a swim.'

'You're going to meet Dan: that's what you're doing.'

'Last night,' Lena tried to explain, 'we spoke about what happened but he did most of the talking. I never got to say much. I feel like it was unfinished.'

Sharon's eyes widened. 'Are you thinking about having a relationship with him?'

'No!'

'Then don't you think maybe what you need is distance?' Sharon also threw off her covers.

'What I need,' Lena stood up and walked into their bathroom, 'is closure.'

'But you don't have any bathers,' Sharon protested.

Lena grabbed one of the hotel toothbrushes above the sink. 'I'll buy some from the gift shop.'

Unfortunately, the hotel gift shop did not sell bathers but they directed her to a surf shop across the road that did. She bought a one piece and headed back to Karratha Resort.

Only a few people populated the pool area and they were all sunbaking rather than swimming. She headed for the palm trees and stepped into the shaded alcove nestled in their centre. The spa was big, deep and steaming. It was also empty.

Perfect.

Without further ado, she walked down the three steps into bubbling ecstasy. Warmth seeped into her bones as she sank up to her neck. The frothing jets gently massaged her body, easing some of her nerves.

Fifteen minutes later, however, Dan still had not showed up and she was beginning to suspect that he wasn't coming. She shut her eyes. Should she really be that surprised? He had said he didn't want to meet her.

Even as the thought pushed through her brain, she heard a slight splash and looked up.

It was Dan, but he didn't look happy.

'I wasn't going to come,' he said. 'But I didn't want you to think I didn't care.'

'Oh,' she faltered, still trying to get over the first sight of him, naked to the waist, muscles shifting as he waded swiftly across the pool to sit opposite her.

'Is this really worth the risk?' he demanded as he turned and sat down. 'Does your career mean so little to you?'

The question snapped back her attention like a mouse trap. 'You'd be surprised how much my career means to me.' She lifted her chin. 'I know you've never had much faith in my ability but you can't fault my willingness to give it a go.'

He looked startled. 'I have never doubted your ability, Lena. Just your common sense.'

'Well, gee, that makes all the difference.' She glared at him. This meeting was definitely not going the way she'd envisaged.

'I didn't mean it like that,' he groaned. 'You're just too impulsive sometimes. I worry about you.'

She didn't know what was more enticing. The fact that he worried about her or the way the steam made his hair curl. In three steps, she could lay her head on his heart. Ironically what held her back was common sense, had he but known it.

'I know I don't always do things the way people think I should,' Lena said softly. 'But I get results, don't I? And if I stuff up, I try again.' Her voice shook. 'If the men lack faith in me, then –'

'But you're wrong, Lena.' Dan shook his head. 'They don't. Maybe they did at first but they have a lot of respect for you now. More than you know.'

'Leg and Radar –'

'I'm not talking about Leg and Radar,' he said impatiently. 'I'm talking about the skid team. I'm talking about Carl – the men in the yard. Some of those guys would go to hell and back for you if you asked them to.'

She looked at him derisively. 'But not you.'

He muttered a curse under his breath, lifted his other hand out of the bubbles and rubbed his temple.

'Damn it, Lena. You can't go to a place you haven't left.'

The jets must have been on a timer or something because quite suddenly they turned off and the water went still. The little pool seemed incredibly quiet now that the noise of the bubbles was gone and her body was no longer hidden by the froth. She shifted uncomfortably under his all-seeing gaze, shivering despite the temperature of the spa. With a determined breath, Dan lifted his eyes, his expression grim.

'You better tell me what you wanted to say before someone catches us in here together.'

She leaned into the centre of the pool, feeling weird to be talking about something so personal from a couple of metres away. Even though just being this much closer to him was already playing havoc with her heartbeat. 'That morning, in your donga: it doesn't sit well with me that you think you somehow took advantage of my situation, because that wasn't the case at all.' She paused, allowing him time to take in her words. 'Trust me, Dan. I was right there in the moment with you and I wouldn't take any of it back.'

His eyes burned into hers. She was sure he could see her pulse leaping at the base of her neck, but he didn't say anything so she continued.

'The last relationship I was in taught me a few hard lessons. I guess that morning with you just brought it all to the forefront again. The long and the short of it is: I said what I did because I was thinking about my ex, not you.'

'Wow.' His voice was deadpan. 'That's telling me, isn't it?'

Her eyes and nose screwed up as she waved her other hand in an erasing gesture. 'No, no, that came out wrong. What I meant was for some reason I started to think about mistakes of the past. My defence mechanisms kicked in and I spoke without thinking.'

He nodded. 'I'm sorry you had to go through that at all.'

She could tell by his tone that her words had made very little impact on him. He still fully blamed himself.

'Dan,' she said crossly. 'I'm not some naive little schoolgirl who needs protecting all the time. I make my own decisions and take the consequences for them as well.'

The jets started up again and mist coiled around them like an invisible force pulling them together.

'Yes, but I'm the one who should have known better.' He refused to be persuaded. Her brows lifted in disbelief. Was there nothing she could say to get him off his martyr's stake? Her resolve tightened.

'So tell me then,' she demanded, 'whose fault is this?' And in a move that was fuelled more by frustration than desire, she slid both arms around his neck and kissed him.

He didn't respond immediately, but when she allowed her body to float into his lap, he shuddered. His arms came around her, drawing her to him. Her point had been made and she should have pulled away in that instant but somehow the threads of her plan unravelled when one of his hands came up out of the water to cradle her face. She felt like the most precious thing in the world. Safe and warm in his arms.

Maybe there was something to be said for his over-protective nature because after that she let him take over, not daring to question the moment. She just wanted to be there in it, because in a minute it would all be over.

In fact, it was far less than that as a rough and wholly unwelcome voice forced them to break apart.

'What the –?!'

Dan's arms stayed protectively around her as they both turned their heads to see Mike's stunned countenance. Her arch nemesis stood on the threshold of their little paradise, slowly but surely sucking the joy from its sphere. His beady little eyes narrowed and his gaping mouth closed and turned up in the corners, as his expression slowly changed from shock to smug enjoyment of things to come.

Lena's heart dropped.

Mike had finally found the ammunition he'd been looking for.

Chapter 17

Mike told everybody.

Or at least, everybody seemed to know. Lena figured that gossip as hot as that could probably move through the ether under its own steam. To say that the air cooled around her was an understatement. If she thought her welcome had been frosty when she'd first arrived, it was nothing compared to this.

It was like being the town leper. None of the men came within a few feet of her, for fear that someone else might think they'd taken her side. The sexual harassment she'd derailed with her calendar picture and through her good work and management was back – and taking a spiteful turn; not the too-enthusiastic wave, the whistle or the offer of a good time, but the head-to-foot appraisal and the behind-the-hand remark just loud enough for her to hear.

'I wonder what Bulldog's getting tonight.'

'She must love a whipping in bed, that one.'

It was degrading and just a little scary, to say the least. Even Leg and Radar weren't impressed.

'Why him, Madame E? Of all people why'd you have to choose him? Isn't anyone on our team good enough for you?'

They didn't wait for her excuses or answers to their questions before leaving her side. Not that she had any. *What do you say to that?*

By rights she shouldn't have to say anything at all. It wasn't the Dark Ages and she wasn't the property of some nasty feudal clan. But living on a remote site didn't help men find their inner twenty-first-century enlightenment. The work was too gruelling, the isolation too unhealthy and the camaraderie too hard won. She knew that the rivalry with TCN was part of how these men got through their weeks away from home. She had been naive to think they'd put it aside for her.

If it hadn't been for Sharon, she didn't know what she would have done. Her friend was a tiny window of light in a dank cellar.

Not that Sharon approved. The expression on her face when she told her that Mike had seen them in the spa had said it all. It was the look a long-suffering teacher might give a wayward student.

'I knew you shouldn't have gone!'

Dan wasn't faring much better. Maybe even worse. Sharon told Lena that the Barnes crews yelled things at him across the wharf. Nothing he could get them for: just embarrassing double entendre. 'Hey, Bulldog, we hear you got some of our engineers doing overtime!'

His own people were far angrier. Sharon had seen some guy come storming out of Dan's office yelling, 'Because of you they think we owe them something!' Fighting between the two companies increased. Dan's men grew pickier. They said that Barnes Inc wasn't going to be cut any slack just because one of their engineers was sleeping with the boss. Of course, this accusation incensed the boys; there were even a few fist fights.

The fact that absolutely no one was sleeping with anyone didn't seem to matter. Lena and Dan had decided to stay away from each other. As soon as Mike had slinked smugly out of their little alcove, Lena had known there was no other way.

When she'd met Dan's gaze, the water still bubbling around them, this time reminding her more of a pot boiling over than a secluded thermal pool, it was the first time she'd actually been able to read his mind. He was thinking exactly what she was.

It was over.

His hands dropped from her waist and with a ragged sigh he brushed a strand of wet hair behind her ear.

'We're in for a rough month.'

'Dan, I'm sorry. I didn't mean to –'

'No,' he interrupted her. The hand at her ear curled into a fist and fell. 'It's the same as in my donga. I think it's clear we –' he broke off, but swallowed and went on, 'we want the same thing. I wanted to kiss you . . . touch you . . .'

She pressed a palm to his chest, seeing building heat smoothing over the regret in his eyes. She wanted to capture this moment in the spa and hold it for a little longer. Maybe he knew what she was doing because he shook his head and said, 'You know what we have to do.' He caught her hand. 'I don't know how to protect you from what's to come, Lena.'

'Are we back to protection again?' she muttered wryly.

'If the men see us together, it'll only provoke them further,' he said softly.

'I know.' She pulled her hand away and put some distance between them. 'I get it. It's finished. We're done.'

He frowned at her as she sank into the bubbles on the other side of the spa. It was almost a goodbye, though without the relief of actual separation. As the silence lengthened, Lena tried to smile at him – lighten the mood.

'It's okay, Dan, really. Besides, I actually only have one week left on site. Then I'm on R and R again.'

'Really?' he frowned. 'What day are you flying out?'

'Next Sunday.' Her brows lifted. 'You don't seem relieved about that.'

'I'm flying out to Perth the same day.' He groaned. 'The men are going to think we planned this – that we're getting away together or something.'

She bit her lip. He was probably right. 'I thought you said there was nothing for you in Perth. What's happened?'

His frown deepened. 'My summons date has come round. I have to be in court Monday.'

'*Oh*.'

No wonder he looked fed up. The demons he'd been running from had finally caught up with him and now on top of that he'd have Mike's malicious mouth to deal with.

'Dan, I'm sorry.'

He shook his head. 'There's nothing we can do about it now. We'll just have to wear it.'

And they did. When it was discovered that she and Dan were not only flying out the same day but on the same plane, the wrong conclusion was reached in very short order. It seemed like the proof the men had been waiting for.

As the days rolled up to their departure, the teasing intensified. Lena was dying to call Dan and ask him how he was holding up. The reports Sharon gave her were sketchy at best. Bulldog had never been one to show emotion and that didn't look like changing soon.

So she stuck to the only thing that made sense.

Work.

The truss installation was actually going really well: Mike hadn't managed to stuff it up for her yet. The system of the two skid frames working side by side was proving to be a good method. The only problem was it was time-consuming. While the two skid frames were installing a truss, they weren't available to continue the headstock installation – and there was still a heap of them to go. And the added delays due to the drop in workplace morale had put Carl into a terrible mood.

'What the fuck are you doing to me, Lena?'

'Carl, I –'

'And don't pretend you don't know what I'm fuckin' talkin' about.'

She lifted her chin. 'I wouldn't insult your intelligence.'

'Well, at least we can cut through the bullshit,' he grunted. 'Break up with him.'

Lena gaped at him, too shocked to deny any involvement. Could he do that? He was her boss, but not of her personal life. He must have seen some of her feelings in her face because he sat forwards, a mulish look about his mouth.

'I'm not telling you as your boss. I'm telling you as a friend; it's for your own good.'

'Even as my friend, Carl,' she told him indignantly, 'you don't have that right.'

He sighed, lacing his fingers on the desk. 'Look, I ain't saying Bulldog's a bad guy. The man's a fuckin' perfectionist but he hasn't got a mean streak. This thing you've got going with him though has really fucked the men in the head and I don't want to guess at what they might do to teach you, but more likely Bulldog, a lesson for this. I would be fuckin' shocked if Bulldog doesn't get a few more unwelcome surprises this week.'

He wasn't wrong about that.

Lena heard through the grapevine that the petrol in Dan's ute mysteriously evaporated the next day just before he had to go to Karratha for a meeting. That same evening, someone hung a pair of lacy knickers on the doorknob of his donga. The matching bra was attached to the radio aerial of his ute the next morning, which luckily this time still had its petrol. No one knew whether the culprits were from Barnes Inc or TCN, but either way the pranks provided a bit of common ground between them. On Wednesday there wasn't that much trouble in the yard.

The project schedule still had big problems though. Harry was really worried. They were falling behind again. Carl called a brainstorming meeting between Lena, Harry, Fish and Gavin first thing Thursday morning. Fish tumbled in ten minutes late in a hopelessly crinkled Barnes Inc shirt that smelled strangely of sausage rolls.

'Sorry I'm late,' he said jovially. 'My shirt needed a few more minutes in the microwave.'

Lena blinked. 'Microwave? As in the kitchen microwave?'

'Forgot to put my washing in the dryer last night,' he said by way of clarification. 'So had to wear a wet shirt to work this morning.'

'He was out late fishing,' Gavin added as if that made the world of difference to his explanation.

'You see.' Carl stabbed the tabletop with his forefinger. 'This is the kind of shit that's putting us behind. Not being organised; waiting for equipment; being tied up with one task and letting other areas go.' He looked at Lena and she knew he was talking about her headstocks. 'We need to cut that out.'

'But how?' Gavin complained, his voice typically whiny. 'How can we do two things at once? And yeah, sometimes we're waiting on our equipment to finish up somewhere so we can move it on to the next place, but more times than not, the men are still painting or welding or waiting for the guys in the yard to float another pile out to us. The equipment, like the barge crane for instance, is just sitting there idle waiting for them.'

'That's true for me too,' Lena piped up. 'The guys who operate the cradles are always scratching around for something to do while the skids are moving. Typically, that's half a day.'

The cradles were like baskets that sat inside the conveyor when it wasn't moving. They held stuff like paint and welding gear and moved along behind the skids. After a truss was installed, it needed to be welded to the one behind and the join area touched up with paint. This was when this equipment came into play.

'Well, our problem is the bloody ships,' Fish spoke up. 'Every time one of those docks, we can't use the shiploader.'

The five-storey-high shiploader crane was always out of action as soon as a ship rocked up: its normal job was to load iron ore into the bellies of the ships, not help them extend the wharf. Barnes Inc used it to pick up and slot in their big deck pieces. This was the support system for the road that went on top of Gavin's freshly driven piles – Fish's job.

'Okay, so what are we fuckin' doing about it?' Carl wanted to know.

Gavin shrugged and then flicked his chin at Lena. 'Get Lena to talk to Bulldog about it. She might be able to swing us an extension.' And then he grinned. 'Pardon the pun.'

Lena gasped. That was mean, even for Gavin. Hurt and anger fought for dominance, the tug of war momentarily rendering her speechless.

'Pull yer fuckin' head in, Gavin,' Carl growled. 'Apologise to Lena.'

'I didn't mean it offensively,' Gavin protested in his usual pig-ignorant fashion. 'Just thought, if she's got some sort of influence over the bastard, I say we use it. What have we got to lose?'

Lena writhed in fury. The guy was practically saying he was happy to prostitute her out for the sake of the project! White-hot rage pushed her hurt feelings aside. Her chair scraped loudly on the vinyl floor as she rose sharply to her feet. 'How *dare* you?'

'Lena, fuckin' sit down,' Carl said. 'And, Gavin, apologise now. I'm sick of your fuckin' antics around the women on this job. Consider this your last warning.'

But she didn't sit down and Gavin didn't apologise.

'Not that it's any of your business,' she swept them all with a wave of her hand, 'but there is currently nothing going on between Bulldog and me.' She eyeballed each one of them individually. 'Nothing. And I have no more influence over him when it comes to this job than any of you do. Never had.'

'Gavin,' Carl prompted again warningly.

'Fine.' Gavin looked down sulkily. 'I apologise. But it's not like anyone's got a better idea.'

Lena lifted her chin. 'As a matter of fact I do. A perfectly ethical, logical one. Unlike you, Gavin, I know how to use my brain.'

No one took offence to this except Gavin. The other three looked up at her hopefully, especially Carl. 'Well, don't just keep us in fuckin' suspense. What the fuck is it?'

Lena had actually been half bluffing to prove a point. She didn't have a whole idea, maybe just half of one. She really needed to think it through properly before it'd be ready for discussion. Heat infused her cheeks as they all continued to stare at her expectantly. When Gavin's expression turned into a smirk, she decided to explain her thought process, hoping a complete plan would flow through by the time she finished talking.

'I've kinda been thinking about this for a while. This job is like a board game. Forwards two places, back four places, skip a turn. All of us are playing with one playing piece. What if we had access to everybody else's as well?'

'What are you talking about?' Gavin shook his head impatiently.

'Well,' she said slowly. 'When the barge is idle, why can't it help me out with the trusses? There's nothing stopping it floating down my end of the jetty and the boys using your huge crane to install trusses while the skids are moving or installing headstocks.'

Fish's eyes lit up. 'The barge crane is as good as the ship-loader. It'd work for me too.'

'Yeah well,' Gavin snorted. 'It seems like you guys get a good deal, but it's not like the skids can drive piles. And what about the guys in the yard? There's no advantage for them and they're always waiting in between tasks.'

'Perhaps the boys fuckin' around in the yard can install trusses instead.' Carl rubbed his chin. 'The yard crane's got a boom long enough to install some trusses from the land.'

'Also, if we're busy installing, we won't need our painters. You can have those, Gavin,' Lena suggested.

He didn't look pleased. 'I still get the worst bargain.'

'But you're running the least behind,' Harry spoke up. 'Piling is only five per cent behind schedule, whereas everything else is back to ten per cent or more.'

Carl rubbed a weary hand across his forehead. 'This is going to be a bastard to organise. The kinda bullshit you don't want is for someone to end up waiting on equipment they've lent out to someone else to stop them fuckin' waiting.'

Lena nodded. 'Like I said, it's a board game. But we need to remove the dice. We need a detailed plan not a play-as-you-go attitude.'

'Well, let's fuckin' get one asap.' Carl stood up, shuffling his files. 'Everyone meet back here tomorrow with their targets; we're going to play this board game to the end on paper.'

Just for fun, Harry and Lena got together later that day and actually made a mock-up board game of the whole project. They stuck together the pages of a month-by-month calendar to make a long playing board, where each day was a move. Then Lena made a little model of each piece of equipment out of bits of cardboard and sticky tape. They also made up a few giant maps of the jetty so at any point during the day, they could put all their playing pieces on and see who was doing what, where.

These visual props turned out to be a real aid at their meeting on Friday. Even Gavin had to concede that the plan might work. It eased Lena's sadness about Dan and the crap they were getting from the men. In any case, the next day was her last day on the Pilbara before a one-week holiday in Perth. She didn't know whether to be relieved or anxious given Dan was going to be at the airport. She asked Sharon to drop her off on Sunday morning as she seemed like the safest bet. Anyone else would have made remarks laced with innuendo the whole way there.

The terminal wasn't very busy so she noticed Dan straight away after she walked through the entrance. He looked tired and handsome at the same time and her heart beat faster. With one hand in his pocket and a backpack slung over his shoulder, he was scanning the floor for someone. The happiness that had been growing since the success of her board game was pumped up even further by the idea that it might be her.

Just then their eyes met and he raised a hand in greeting. Her step quickened and he came forwards, the crisp scent of his aftershave surrounding her as they connected. He put his hand over the handle of her suitcase, their skin touching briefly as he gently pulled it out of her grasp.

'Here, I'll help you with that.'

The suitcase wheels clicked with his faster pace and she doubled hers to keep up.

'Are you sure you should be doing that?' she hissed, feeling like some heroine out of a period romance who'd organised a secret rendezvous with her beau.

'I've already been punished for being on the same flight as you.' He grimaced. 'I might as well enjoy it.'

Enjoy it.

She savoured the words. They were going to Perth together. Excitement and trepidation gripped her. There were no spectators there. No gossips. They were free to be whoever they wanted to be.

As if on cue, her conscience reared its head. *What about Kevin? What about your promise? Are you that weak-willed that you no longer care?*

But as she looked up at Dan there wasn't even a flicker of the gallant beau in his eyes. He wasn't here to be with her: he was here because he had to go to court. Given the forbidding expression marring his attractive features, that's what he was thinking about, not a holiday fling or a forbidden romance. And who could blame him for that?

He paused uncertainly as they got into the short line to check in. 'I . . . er . . . thought we could get a seat together and catch up on what's been going on.'

The vulnerability in his voice touched her. His hard facade was starting to slip whenever they spoke and she liked that. She nodded. 'Sure.'

He looked down at her giant red suitcase with a glimmer of a smile. 'You don't travel light, do you?'

Lena sniffed. 'This is very light for me. You should have seen me three months ago.'

After securing a window seat together they didn't have long to wait before boarding. She was looking forward to being able to relax after all the craziness. But most of all, she was looking forward to sitting next to Dan without anyone watching or judging.

'So did the men get stuck into you too?' Dan asked when they were seated.

'From what Sharon tells me, you've definitely had the worst of it.'

He pulled an in-flight magazine from the seat pocket in front of him. 'I'm just sorry you've had to go through it at all.'

She looked at his face. The lines of concern cut deep. His blue eyes searched hers as though looking for hints of wear and tear.

'Stop that.' She laughed. 'I'm fine.'

His eyes lifted and he nodded. She was sad she hadn't seen them sparkle since that time in the laundry when he'd given her red bra back.

They'd been flirting. She hadn't realised it at the time, or noticed the blooming of forbidden feelings. But in hindsight, she wished for that confusing time again. At least it didn't rub as raw as all this clarity.

'I heard about some of the pranks they played on you,' she began and he shot her a wry smile.

'I'll give them points for imagination, that's for sure. Though, I'll admit, at times I found it difficult not to lose my temper.' He paused. 'It's unfortunate I can't avoid the court summons – I hate adding fuel to the fire.'

'Have you known for a while that you'd be in court this month?' she asked tentatively.

The hand on the armrest next to her clenched involuntarily. And she realised then how much Dan was hiding from her. The tight-lipped disapproval he generally displayed was in fact a Band-Aid for a much deeper emotional wound. This trip was costing him more than he was letting on. 'Yes.'

Their difficulties with the men on site paled in significance to what he was about to go through when he got to Perth.

She licked her lips. 'Is there anything I can do?'

He looked at her sharply, his customary facade back in place – or at least a softer version of it. 'No. Thank you.'

She wanted to tell him that he didn't have to pretend. A person couldn't be strong all the time. But she knew it would be like throwing darts at a whiteboard, so instead she asked another question. 'How long will the hearing take?'

'I've been told three days, maybe four, depending on how long it takes to examine all the witnesses.'

He was silent, staring ahead at moving images she couldn't see.

'Will your family be there?' she asked softly.

'I assume so. I haven't seen them in a long time.'

'How long?'

He let out a ragged breath. 'Just over three years.'

Her eyes widened. That was almost as long ago as the accident. So the first time he was going to see them again was in open court. It was too much.

'Dan –'

'Lena.' He cut her off and once again the hand on the armrest clenched. 'I don't want to drag you into this. This is my battle, which I need to fight alone.'

'Why?' she demanded. His expression hardened but he said nothing. She understood, though. He blamed himself for his brother's death.

'What happened to Mark wasn't your fault,' she said quietly.

'Punishing yourself doesn't help anyone. All it does is encourage your family to behave badly.'

'You wouldn't know, Lena.' She could see him mentally slamming the doors and boarding up the windows of his heart. 'You weren't there.'

'Then tell me what happened.'

'You already know more than I ever wanted you to find out.' He shook his head.

She was fighting phantoms. She wanted to stamp her foot at his stubbornness, until she realised that she, too, could be stubborn. 'Dan, I want to go to court with you.' There was no way she was going to let him face the family he hadn't seen in three years by himself, with not a single friendly face in the room.

His gaze swung to hers, hope and denial clashing in his eyes. She knew his heart craved support, but that damned male ego of his wouldn't allow it. One fierce word whooshed out of his lungs. '*No.*'

'You need me.' She made her face stern. 'I know you don't want to admit it, so this time I'm letting you off the hook. But I'm coming whether you like it or not.'

'Stay away.' He grabbed her wrist, his fingers crushing her leaping pulse. 'Promise me you'll stay away.'

His expression was desperate, urgent, tortured. They both knew he couldn't stop her. Anyone could watch an open court case in session if they had the inclination.

When she said nothing, he dropped her wrist and looked away. 'You've never listened to me before. I don't know why I expected it to be different this time.' His jaw jerked and she knew he was grinding his teeth. His eyes flashed as he looked back at her. 'Don't say I didn't warn you.'

Chapter 18

The Supreme Court of Western Australia was located in the heart of the city of Perth. Ironically, the court was surrounded by a stunning and immaculately kept garden – a bid to take the bite out of a conviction. However, the beauty of the surrounds gave Lena little comfort as she made her way up the shaded paths. She took a seat in the second row of the public gallery, wanting Dan to be able to see her when he went on the witness stand.

In fact, the only reason she hadn't taken a seat in the front row was because there was someone already there and she didn't want to crowd them. The blonde woman seated there was in her early thirties and far too skinny. Her bones were large and protruded sharply on her face and limbs, like she'd once been rather well built but in recent years had been having problems eating. She didn't look at Lena: her attention was focused solely on the bailiff, the two waiting lawyers and the empty judge's seat. The hands in her lap wrung without pause and Lena was willing to bet she was closely involved. Perhaps she was even Dan's sister-in-law.

When an elderly couple entered the gallery and sat down beside the woman, the older woman taking the blonde's hand

and squeezing it, Lena knew she was right. This was Dan's family. They looked harmless and worn and dreadfully sad. Could they really be so heartless?

The bailiff, a middle-aged man dressed smartly in black and white with gold crowns on his lapels, addressed the court. 'All rise.'

As she stood, Lena heard a knock at the door to the right of the judge's desk and then it was opening. Two men, the judge and his associate, entered the courtroom. The judge's expression was indifferent as he sat down under the Queen's coat of arms. There was no jury – as this was a civil case, the judge would decide the verdict. Lena didn't know whether to be glad or worried about that and had no time to contemplate it.

Two lawyers stood robed at the bar table facing the judge's bench: Sarah Michaels and an older man. When the opening formalities were over, the judge said, 'Mr Carter?'

'Your honour,' the man next to Sarah began, 'this suit brought by the plaintiff, Angela Hullog, seeks damages arising out of her husband's death caused by the negligence of the defendant, Oswalds Proprietary Limited. It is alleged that her husband, Mark Hullog, died on a site inspection due to the inadequate supervision and training by Oswalds Proprietary Limited. As your honour is aware, the claim is fully particu-larised in the Papers for the Judge. I trust your honour has perused the papers?'

The judge grimaced. 'I have, Mr Carter.'

'Then in the circumstances,' the lawyer nodded, 'I will reserve further comment on the plaintiff's cause of action for submissions and call the plaintiff's first witness.'

'Proceed,' said the judge.

'The plaintiff calls Daniel James Hullog.'

Lena's breathing quickened as a door to her right opened and the bailiff escorted Dan into the room. His back was straight, his shoulders rigid. He'd put on his armour like a knight before battle. There would be plenty of arrows today.

She swallowed nervously as he was led to the witness stand. She didn't know why she was so nervous but she was – tremblingly nervous – even though it was him standing behind the box swearing on the Bible to tell the truth. Her tongue darted over her parched lips as he looked up and their eyes met for the first time.

Like a wave, his disapproval and gratitude hit her, engulfing her body with their intensity. She got it all in that one long powerful moment, which he broke abruptly as though cutting her out of his head with a flick of his eyelids. Meanwhile, his voice to the bailiff was low and bland, at vast odds with the intensity of his stare. The lawyer's first questions were boring and in Lena's opinion inconsequential. But she knew Mr Carter was just trying to set the scene.

'Mr Hullog,' Mr Carter finally got down to business, 'what was your professional relationship with the deceased?'

'I was his manager at Oswalds Proprietary Limited. He assisted me with all my projects.'

'And for how long did he assist you?'

'About a year.'

'And prior to that?'

'He was at university.'

'So this was, in fact, his first job since graduating.'

'Yes.'

'So would you say Mark Hullog was inexperienced?'

'He had less than one year's experience, so yes, I would.'

'Objection.' Ms Michaels rose hastily from her chair. 'Opinion, your honour. Mr Hullog is not a recognised training expert: he cannot provide an opinion on whether the deceased was experienced; and he certainly can't conclude whether the deceased was experienced or not.'

The judge nodded sagely. 'Sustained.'

Mr Carter, unperturbed, changed tack. 'Were you with Mark Hullog when he died?'

'Yes.'

'Where were the two of you?'

'We were at MacArthur Lumber Mill attending a meeting with the lead foreman there.'

Mr Carter leaned forwards predatorily. 'What occurred during the meeting?'

Dan swallowed. 'When we arrived we watched a ten-minute safety presentation on video. We then met with the lead foreman, Andrew Carrington, inside the lumber mill. He showed us the faulty feeder we were there to inspect. Mark had brought a camera with him to take photos. He went inside the feeder while I was talking to Andrew Carrington . . .' Dan swallowed again and there was a definite gruffness to his voice. 'He became trapped in there, the feeder became active and . . . and it killed him.'

Lena shut her eyes, sending a silent message to the lawyer to give Dan a moment. He didn't, moving straight along to the next callous question.

'How did the machine kill him?'

For crying out loud.

Dan looked like he was about to throw up and there was a prolonged pause before he managed to reply.

'It tore . . . and . . . crushed him to death.'

'Objection!' Sarah Michaels stood up angrily. And so she should. Lena glared at Mr Carter.

'Sustained,' the judge agreed. 'Please refrain from theatrics in my court, counsel.'

Mr Carter said, 'Your honour, it is crucial to the plaintiff's case that your honour has before you evidence from witnesses on *precisely* how it was that the deceased died.'

The judge gestured for Mr Carter to continue. 'So long as you keep it to evidence, Mr Carter.'

Mr Carter turned to Dan. 'Was the deceased within your line of sight?'

'Sometimes.'

'What obstructed your view? Parts of the feeder?'

'Yes, the machine . . . the lumber feeder blocked my view at times.'

'So when the machine became active, you could see the deceased for part of the time as he was, to use your words, "torn and crushed" to death?'

For Pete's sake.

Lena sent silent death threats to Mr Carter.

Dan, eyes reddening, choked out, 'Yes.'

'Objection!'

'Overruled, Ms Michaels,' the judge interjected blandly without looking up.

Mr Carter smiled faintly at his notes before addressing Dan again. 'Did you tell the deceased not to go into the feeder?'

'No.'

'Then you told him to go into the feeder?'

'No.' Dan frowned. 'We never discussed photographing inside the feeder. In fact, I don't know why he went in. It's obviously a dangerous machine: there were signs and stickers about how dangerous it was all over it.'

'But *you* never discussed it with him and you *do not know* why he went in.' Mr Carter repeated the words with slow succinctness. 'As his supervisor, Mr Hullog, don't you think you should have discussed the job in detail before you left for the lumber mill, including the dangers?'

Dan hesitated. 'I did brief Mark before the meeting. I wasn't aware of any gaps in his knowledge.'

'I see. And how many inspections of this type had Mark Hullog been on previously, before this one killed him?'

Dan looked at him uncertainly as though trying to work out his angle. 'I can't remember for certain, but I think this was his first inspection.'

'You think or you know?'

Dan sat back in his chair. 'I can't be certain.'

'So again, you do not know. Well, if it was his first inspection, or even one of his first, could you not reasonably infer that there would be gaps in his knowledge?'

Dan sighed, looked down at his hands before glancing up again. 'We have a safety induction program at Oswalds specifically for graduates, so they are prepared for dangers inherent in site visits. It's a three-day course about how to be safe on construction sites, in factories, power stations and other types of plant. I assumed that Mark had attended the program.'

'But you didn't know for sure that he had, did you?'

'No.'

'When did you find out that Mark Hullog had not attended the induction program?'

Dan pursed his lips. 'After the accident.'

'You mean, after his death?'

Dan struggled. 'Yes.'

'Did it occur to you to check his attendance records prior to taking him to MacArthur Lumber Mill?'

A muscle flexed convulsively above Dan's jawline. 'No.'

'Why not?'

'No reason, it just never entered my mind.'

'Because the job was more important?'

Dan's eyes narrowed on him. 'No, because I assumed HR was tracking that and I would be notified if Mark wasn't fit for site.'

'So, as Mark Hullog's manager, you took him on a site visit for which he needed to be cleared by your human resources department – a visit to a plant whose machinery had clear potential to compromise his safety. And you didn't use your own initiative to confirm with HR that Mark was ready for a site visit? Is that your evidence?'

'The feeder was obviously dangerous –'

'Did you check with HR that Mark Hullog had been approved by Oswalds to go on dangerous site visits?'

'No.'

'If you had known at the time that the deceased had not undertaken the induction training, would you have taken him to the MacArthur Lumber Mill on the morning of his death?'

Dan hesitated. 'No, I wouldn't have.'

A thoughtful smile played around the corners of Mr Carter's mouth. 'So, if you had managed the deceased and not assumed facts about him, Mark Hullog would be alive today, wouldn't he?'

Sarah stood up before Dan could answer.

'Objection: conclusion.'

The judge nodded as he scribbled a note for himself. 'Sustained.'

Mr Carter paused as he consulted his notes. 'Let's return to the safety video you watched when you arrived at MacArthur Lumber Mill, Mr Hullog.' He looked up. 'Did the video warn visitors about the machinery, in particular the dangers inherent in a feeder machine?'

'Yes.' Dan nodded. 'Although it didn't go into specifics, it warned us to keep away from live machinery unless accompanied by an experienced user.'

'And you and the deceased both watched this video?'

'Yes.'

'Were you accompanied by an experienced operator when you went to see the feeder?'

'Yes, both the foreman and one of his hands accompanied us.'

'Did either of these men tell Mark Hullog to go inside the feeder?'

'Not as far as I know.'

'So neither you, nor any of these men, were in communication with Mark just before the accident? You could even say that he wandered off alone?'

'He wasn't very far away from us and I wouldn't say he was alone.'

'Just inadequately supervised then, Mr Hullog?'

Sarah Michaels rose abruptly. 'Objection.'

The judge nodded. 'Please refrain from leading the witness, Mr Carter.' He tapped his pen impatiently on the paper in front of him. 'Do you have anything further?'

'No, your honour.' Mr Carter shook his head and sat down.

Lena let out a breath that until now had been locked in her chest as the judge turned to Sarah Michaels.

'Ms Michaels, do you wish to cross-examine the witness?'

'I do, your honour.' She stood up, arranging her black robes neatly in front of her skirt suit. Even as her eyes met Dan's, Lena felt the tension in the room heighten. She was sending him a warning. He was straightening his shoulders again, metaphorically raising his shield for the first blow.

Lena didn't like it. Something was up.

'Mr Hullog, did you have a personal relationship with the victim?'

Dan's body was impossibly rigid, his voice a rasp that came all the way from the back of his throat.

'Yes.'

'And what is that relationship?'

Dan looked down at his hands. Whatever colour that was left in his face drained away slowly but surely. 'He was my . . . is my brother.'

Lena couldn't understand it. What had changed? Why was Dan suddenly so anxious?

She wriggled impatiently in her seat as Sarah Michaels continued. 'Was he suffering from any kind of medical condition at the time of the accident?'

'Yes. Clinical depression.'

'When was Mark Hullog diagnosed with this condition?'

'About three months before the accident.' Dan raised red-rimmed eyes that came to rest on Sarah; he was bracing himself for the final knife throw.

'And what was the catalyst of this diagnosis?'

'He attempted suicide.'

Chapter 19

Oh shit.

Lena felt like one of Fish's catches just after he'd gutted it. Time seemed to stand still in the courtroom. Pieces were starting to click into place, filling her heart with dread. Hadn't Dan suffered enough without adding this revelation to the mix?

She glanced quickly at Mark's wife.

The widow had a wild-eyed look, torn between outrage and defiance. Her mouth kept moving, forming silent words. Dan's parents were tight-lipped and still. They were eyeing their son in a way she hoped her parents would never look at her. It wasn't hatred or disappointment. It was something in between and all the more potent for it. But what did they expect him to do? Lie?

It had to be killing Dan to be siding with an employer over his family, but even after only a few months, Lena knew that he was an inveterately honest man. Lena clenched both hands. The action helped her get her bearings. Why were Dan's family so angry? If Mark had been treated, his episodes and diagnosis would be a matter of record. Dan *couldn't* lie about it. This was the stuff nightmares were made of. Even so, she wanted to hear the rest.

Once more her gaze was drawn to Dan's. His face was pale and his lips tight. He'd already relived this experience too many times. She wished she could hug him and threw the thought across the room. He didn't turn away when he caught it. But the message he threw back was obvious and not what she wanted to hear.

I told you not to come.

Lena broke the connection, unable to bear his accusing look and focused instead on Sarah who now, having the benefit of the room's full and undivided attention, was about to continue with her next question.

'How did your brother attempt to commit suicide?'

Mr Carter stood. 'Objection, relevance. This has no bearing on the case at hand.'

The judge studied Mr Carter thoughtfully for a moment and then said to Sarah, 'Unless it has some relevance to the point you are trying to make, counsel, I don't think we need specifics.'

'Very well, your honour.' Sarah nodded. She turned back to Dan. 'Do you think it is possible, Mr Hullog, that on the day of the incident, your brother may have been suicidal?'

Again, Mr Carter stood. 'Objection: leading the witness.'

'Overruled.' The judge smugly looked down at Mr Carter. 'You can't have it both ways, Mr Carter. Proceed, Ms Michaels.'

With a sigh Sarah once again addressed Dan. 'Mr Hullog, on the day of the incident, did your brother give you any indication at all that he was thinking of killing himself?'

Dan lifted his chin. 'No.'

'Was he seeing a therapist or on any medication around the time of his death?'

Dan joined his hands on the desk, but his expression did not change. 'I believe so, on both counts.'

Sarah cleared her throat. 'So then, he had by no means recovered from his mental illness?'

'Not one hundred per cent, though I would have to check with his doctor.'

Sarah nodded, consulted her notes and began speaking again. 'Mr Hullog, did you discuss any possible safety issues with your brother prior to the site visit?'

'Not in great detail. I told him we'd be watching a video and that the usual protocol would apply.'

'Did you tell him that the feeder could be dangerous?'

'No.'

'Why not?'

'Well,' Dan licked his lips, 'there was absolutely no need for him to touch it or enter it. It had already been established that the feeder was jamming because its footings were out of whack. One side of the machine had settled more than the other. Our concern was the foundations, not the mechanics of the machine. He had a camera so he could take pictures of the feeder supports, not inside the machine or even of the machine itself.'

'Did Mark know this?'

'Yes, I briefed him fully before the meeting.'

'Thank you, Mr Hullog.' Sarah's lips curled momentarily as she turned to the judge. 'I have nothing further, your honour.'

As she sat down, the judge spoke to Mr Carter.

'Mr Carter, do you have any questions for Mr Hullog regarding Ms Michaels's cross-examination?'

'Two questions, your honour.' Mr Carter laced his fingers in front of him as he stood up. He paused for a long time, much to Lena's frustration.

'Was Oswalds Proprietary Limited aware of the victim's medical condition and recovery program?'

Dan said, 'Yes, certain critical members of the team and upper management were aware.'

'You mentioned the deceased was being treated for his

illness. Did Oswalds consider the deceased unfit for work or otherwise impaired with respect to particular duties while the deceased was undergoing treatment for his mental illness?'

'No, he was not considered unfit for work.'

Mr Carter inclined his head. 'Thank you. Nothing further, your honour.'

So Dan was finally allowed off the stand and the court was told to break for lunch. Lena's lungs contracted at the anti-climax, leaving her panting. Her legs were wobbly, as though she'd just run a marathon. Her heart rate was up and adrenaline was pumping heavily through her veins. She needed to get outside and walk it off.

By comparison, Dan's relatives sat in angry stupor, unable to tear their eyes from the empty witness box. She could *feel* their rage. It was so heavy. If feelings were toxic, she probably would have passed out. But really, what did they think that Dan could have said differently? It was a pointless and ungrounded fury.

Standing up, she slung her handbag over one shoulder. The movement must have caught Angela Hullog's eye because she turned around and for the first time registered her presence. She looked as though she was trying to work out who Lena was and maybe even considering asking.

There was no way Lena was telling her.

She was there for Dan and her reasons were nobody's business but his. She looked away from Mark's widow, concentrating her attention on exiting as quickly as possible. She wanted to catch Dan in the street. When she left the building she saw him walking up the road and caught up.

'Mind if I join you?'

'I told you not to come.'

'And you knew I wasn't going to listen.' She smiled brightly and daringly tucked her hand into his. His arm went rigid but she felt it relax slightly as she put her other hand on his bicep.

He sighed raggedly. 'Do you ever give up?'

'No.'

'Do you ever go away?'

'No.'

'Do you ever do as you're told?'

'Not if I can help it.'

'Thank God.' His fingers tightened deliciously around hers and she felt the warmth of his gaze as much as the sunshine as he finally looked down at her. She raised her eyebrows in return.

'So you *are* glad I came.'

'Yes and no.' It was a small smile, but definitely a smile. 'It meant a lot to have your support and your face to focus on in the gallery. Lord knows, I couldn't look at anyone else.'

'But?'

'But you know too much about me now. I can't hide anything from you any more.'

Lena grinned delightedly. 'How marvellous.'

He untangled her hand and rested his arm across her shoulders instead. 'You are impossible, you know that?' He squeezed her tight into his side.

Bubbles of contentment popped in her head, making her dizzy. She snuggled in closer, enjoying the freedom to do so. The heat from his body warmed hers. She breathed in the scent of him, enjoying the gentle rhythm of their synchronised movement. They wouldn't be able to have this simple intimacy on site. She wanted to savour the feeling – this closeness – which wasn't really casual at all.

She scanned the cafes and restaurants they were passing. 'What do you feel like?'

He shuddered as his body relaxed further. 'A tropical beach, a deckchair and a cocktail far, far away from here.'

'I meant to eat.'

'Did I mention you were there too?'

Her voice trembled on the way out. 'How about a sandwich? We've only got an hour.'

'Okay.'

They turned into the next cafe. The smell of food and coffee filled her nostrils and her stomach growled in response. They ordered and took a seat by the window. She would have felt as though they were on their very first date if the weight of what she'd just witnessed hadn't been sitting so heavily on her chest. For his sake as much as hers, she tried to shrug it off.

'Beautiful day,' she murmured as a crisp breeze made its way through the big front window of the cafe.

A slight smile curled his lips. 'You don't have to try so hard, Lena. I'm not glass.'

'It couldn't have been easy for you in there.'

His hands shook and he quickly put them under the table. 'What's hard is knowing that my parents think my testimony is some kind of betrayal.'

'All you did was tell the truth,' she quickly reassured him. 'They can't expect you to lie in court. And Mark . . . well,' she took a deep breath, 'Dan. It's over for Mark now. He's not in pain any more. And lying about him isn't really going to help with anyone else's pain, whatever they think.'

He gritted his teeth. 'No, it isn't. At least my part is over now. I admit, it's a relief to finally hand this over to the judge.'

'Perhaps you should go home then,' she suggested. 'Try to put this behind you.'

He shook his head. 'No way. I've got to see everything. I lost my brother and my dad. I've wasted more than three years of my life worrying about what the verdict would turn out to be. I want to see what it is and how they get there.'

Lena knew what he meant, what neither of them could say out loud because it cut too close to the bone. Mark Hullog's death was caused by one of two things.

Dan's negligence, or his little brother's decision to commit suicide.

A judge would decide.

The problem was, she didn't know which team to cheer for, because either way Dan lost.

After lunch, she accompanied Dan back to the Supreme Court. This time he joined her in the gallery. Now that he was no longer a witness under examination, he was free to watch the case proceedings.

Lena wondered if his family had even left to eat. They were huddled together as she had left them. Nonetheless, they raised their eyes when they walked in. Her fingers tightened involuntarily around Dan's hand as Angela's features contorted.

'You fucking bastard!' she hissed. 'How dare you show your face back here? Haven't you done enough damage?'

Her words were so sudden and so scathing that for a moment Lena could only stare at her in shock. Dan went white.

His mother stood up, the heavy lines on her face deepened by her frown.

'Please be on your way, Daniel. Don't you think we've suffered enough?'

Frustration burned its way through Lena's body like the wick of a candle. She was desperate to defend Dan but knew she had no right to interfere. Who was she to judge people who'd experienced what they had? Luckily, Dan spoke up instead.

'We've all suffered.'

His father snorted and said without turning to face them, 'If it's guilt you're feeling, I'm not surprised. I hope you're plagued by it day and night.'

Lena didn't understand. Sure, the Hullogs loved Mark, but Dan was their son too. Her fingers itched to shake his mother. Instead of losing one child they had lost both.

Idiots!

Dan tugged on her hand, leading her to the back row. 'Mark was always the favourite,' he said, seeming to sense that she needed some explanation.

Lena sat down. 'But you're their son too. It's not right.'

He shook his head. 'I was always a third wheel. And now, I'm worse than that.'

Angela Hullog looked as though she wanted to force them out with her bare hands but the bailiff called order. The lawyers were already in place.

After the judge walked in and was settled, Mr Carter called his second witness to the stand. It was the HR manager from Oswalds Proprietary Limited. Mr Carter's questioning centred mainly on the safety course and why Mark hadn't attended. The HR manager was indifferent and vague, leaving Lena itching to thump her. The woman came across like a disorganised person with a complete disregard for paperwork.

The case for Oswalds' negligence was certainly building. Sarah's cross-examination revealed nothing further. And then that was it for the day.

As Lena and Dan made their way out of the building, Mark's widow waylaid them in the lobby.

Lena held back, knowing that Dan didn't want her to get involved.

'You knew Mark wasn't suicidal. He was fine! Why didn't you say that in your testimony instead of trying to cover your own arse, you bastard!'

Lena wanted to slap her, even though she knew Angela was probably only able to get out of bed every morning because of the momentum she got from her fiery hatred of Oswalds – and Dan.

'I need to talk to her,' Dan said softly, and then to his sister-in-law, 'Angela –'

'Don't you "Angela" me! I wish you'd never been born.'

'Dan –' Lena began.

But he shook his head. 'My family, my fight. Go home, Lena. You've done enough and I appreciate it. But now you're out of your depth.'

The look he gave her was so fierce that she knew that this time he would physically remove her if he had to.

She squared her chin. 'Fine. I'll see you tomorrow.'

'If that's what you want.' His voice was distant now and he was already turning away.

Court resumed at ten the next morning and Lena was there as promised. Dan joined her shortly before the hour with heavy-lidded eyes. It had been a rough night for him as well. She wasn't surprised. If she'd had difficulty sleeping, she imagined he'd had no rest at all. He sat down beside her and took her hand, whether for support or in greeting, she didn't care. As long as their closeness was important to him. That's all that mattered to her.

Mr Carter's next witness was Andrew Carrington, the manager of the MacArthur Lumber Mill, a thick-bearded man with red hair. He confirmed Dan's testimony about what had taken place on the day of the accident, including the fact that there had been no need for Mark to enter the machine. New information was revealed when Sarah Michaels got up to cross-examine him about the operation of the feeder, but none of it was very useful. Lena sighed with relief when Andrew Carrington finally left the stand.

That was it for Mr Carter's witness list. It was now Sarah Michaels's turn to call her first witness.

Angela Hullog. As she was not only a witness but the plain-tiff, she had been allowed to sit in the gallery and view the entire proceedings. Now, she sat on the stand, eyes downcast, skin splotchy with a cross between paleness and a flush staining her skin, and took her oath. Not that her word meant anything to Lena. She had practically asked Dan to lie for her, for goodness sake. Was she really about to tell the truth, the whole truth and nothing but the truth?

'Ms Hullog, was your husband suffering from clinical depression at the time of the accident?'

Angela replied after a slight pause. 'Yes.'

'Is it true that prior to his death he had tried to commit suicide?'

Again she paused. 'Yes.'

'Since this attempt, how would you rate his recovery?'

Angela Hullog cleared her throat. 'I would say very good, if not excellent.' She fixed a contemptuous gaze on Dan rather than looking at the lawyer. 'He was improving every day. I know, because his illness had been causing some problems in our marriage. But we were really starting to overcome them – really starting to build some bridges, make plans for the future and all that.'

'Did you fight with Mark at all on the morning of the lumber mill accident?'

Angela lifted her chin. 'Definitely not.'

'What about the day before that?'

'No.'

'Did anything at all occur before the incident that would affect Mark's stress levels?'

Angela Hullog frowned. 'The only thing that stressed him out was work. His manager and brother, Dan Hullog, put Mark under a lot of pressure to get things done. Mark really looked up to Dan and didn't want to let him down.' Again she fixed that glare on Dan. 'Despite my protests, Mark was always working late. By the time he got home he'd be so tired. And he was anxious too. I really think that the company and its managers have a lot to answer for when it comes to my husband's mental state.'

'Ms Hullog,' Sarah managed to draw Angela's attention back to her, 'I believe you were pregnant at the time of your husband's death. Is that true?'

'Yes,' Angela spat, the subject change clearly angering her. 'My daughter will never know her father thanks to Oswalds.'

Sarah waited before asking her next question. Lena realised she was giving Angela a second to calm down. 'Ms Hullog, how far along were you at the time?'

Angela swallowed and squinted up at the ceiling. 'I would say . . . ten weeks. We were both really happy about it even though the pregnancy wasn't planned. I love children and so did Mark. We were going to turn his study into a nursery. We –'

'Ms Hullog,' Sarah interrupted. 'Did you say the pregnancy was unplanned?'

Angela hesitated, confusion clouding her eyes. 'Yes.'

'When did you find out you were pregnant?'

'At about . . . er . . . nine weeks. I went to the doctor to have it confirmed. But I was suspicious for ages,' she added as an afterthought.

'When did you tell Mark about it?'

Angela turned pink. 'I can't remember exactly.'

'But you did tell him.'

'Yes, of course,' Angela blustered.

'How did Mark take the news that you were expecting an unplanned baby?'

'Oh,' Angela spread her hands dramatically, as if it were a foregone conclusion, 'he was ecstatic, of course. Surprised and ecstatic.'

Sarah Michaels turned her attention back to the judge. 'I have no further questions, your honour.'

Mr Carter stood up to cross-examine, leaning back into his hip as he eyed Sarah Michaels's witness thoughtfully.

'My colleague here is determined to link this case to Mark Hullog's attempted suicide, so let's discuss it, Ms Hullog. When and where was it?'

'In the evening, at home,' Angela replied quickly.

'Can you describe Mark's mood that day?'

'Distracted, preoccupied.' A spasm of pain creased her face; Lena saw a tiny bit of what the woman had gone through. 'I knew there was something wrong. Not *how* wrong, of course.'

'Did he prepare a note?'

'Yes, there was one next to him when I . . . found him. It was very brief – he said sorry. Nothing more.'

'So then, Ms Hullog,' Mr Carter continued in that thoughtful manner he had begun with, 'if we could just contrast this to what happened at the lumber mill. Was Mark preoccupied or moody that day?'

'No, he was happy.'

'And did he leave you a note concerning his death?'

'No. It wasn't a suicide.'

'Thank you.' Satisfied, Mr Carter sat down.

Sarah Michaels's next witness was Mark's doctor, a white-haired, balding man who looked like he'd been practising a long time. Lena hoped he had. Perhaps he could give everyone some direction – some information that wasn't so uncertain. She looked at Dan but he grimly shook his head.

Great.

After briefly establishing the nature of Mark Hullog's mental illness, Sarah moved into the guts of her questioning.

'Dr Hendricks, in your professional opinion, do you think the incident at the lumber mill that killed Mark Hullog could have been suicide?'

'In my professional opinion, no.'

Sarah Michaels nodded, a gentle smile curving her mouth. 'Dr Hendricks, has your professional opinion ever been wrong?'

The doctor raised his bushy white eyebrows, unfazed by her question.

'Well, it's an opinion, counsel. It's not a fact. Interpret that whichever way you like it.'

Sarah regrouped. 'Very well, Dr Hendricks, have you or any of your peers ever thought someone was recovering and they weren't?'

'Patients can relapse very quickly,' Dr Hendricks returned impatiently. 'Sometimes there is little warning.'

'What causes relapses?'

Dr Hendricks shrugged. 'Anything and nothing. As we are talking about a person's mind here, it's their perception of the world around them that is the problem, not reality. If they think something has changed to increase their stress levels, then it has.'

'Surely finding out that your wife is unexpectedly pregnant would increase the stress levels of any human being, especially someone who has recently emerged from a suicidal state?'

'Yes,' Dr Hendricks reluctantly conceded.

'Just out of curiosity, Dr Hendricks, did you have therapy sessions with Mark Hullog the week before he died?'

'Yes, I did.'

'And during those sessions, did he mention that his wife was pregnant?'

Dr Hendricks reddened. 'No.'

'But wouldn't a patient disclose something as significant as that to his doctor?'

'I am not a member of his family. But I suppose I do encourage my patients to let me in on any drastic changes in their lives.'

Sarah Michaels nodded. 'And just to confirm, Dr Hendricks, Mark Hullog was still on his medication at the time of the incident?'

'Yes.'

'Did you have any intention of taking him off it?'

'No immediate intentions.'

'What about the therapy sessions? Were you going to stop those?'

'Eventually.'

'So what you're saying is, Mark Hullog was still quite seriously depressed, but was recovering over time?'

Dr Hendricks seemed annoyed. 'He had a condition that was less serious than it had been three months previously.'

Sarah Michaels nodded. 'Thank you.' She looked at the judge. 'That's all, your honour.'

Sarah didn't have any more witnesses. Lena didn't know whether to be relieved or disappointed because as far as she was concerned the judge could swing either way. The evidence was all a list of maybes. True, they still had the closing statements by each of the lawyers to go the next morning, but she doubted they would provide more clarity. Dan looked exhausted. She too was feeling the effects of trying to concentrate on every word that was uttered in that room, not wanting to miss a single clue. Her muscles ached from clenching and unclenching. Her limbs were brittle from being held still for so long. Her skin was dry and sweaty from the air-conditioning that often blew too cold.

She was craving the finish line.

And yet at the same time she was scared of the verdict. She couldn't even begin to imagine what Dan was feeling. They walked out of the court quickly, this time managing to avoid his family.

'Dinner?' she asked when they turned out into the street.

'I'm not really hungry.' He ran tired fingers through his dark hair. 'But if you'd like to go somewhere, I'll take you.'

Like she was going to make him treat her to dinner in his condition. 'No, no,' she said quickly. Besides, she wasn't really hungry either, and a noisy restaurant was the last place she wanted to go.

What she did want though was to prolong this togetherness. She didn't want him to spend the night alone, thinking, wondering, what tomorrow would bring. 'Would you like to come back to my place for a while?'

His chin jerked down sharply as his eyes swung to hers. The air crackled with the silence.

He put out a hand and ran rough fingertips down her cheek. 'Lena,' he said, 'as much as I want to –'

She grabbed his hand and laced her fingers through it. 'Just for soup and company. You shouldn't be alone tonight.'

He hesitated.

'Okay.'

Chapter 20

Lena's first thought upon opening the door of her apartment was, *Damn, I wish I'd tidied up a little this morning.*

There was stuff everywhere – she was still in the process of unpacking her suitcase. Shirts and pants were strewn on the couch. Her usual junk – magazines, mail, make-up, shopping bags – was also scattered haphazardly on any other available surfaces.

'It's just tinned soup, I'm afraid,' she said as she walked past the couch, grabbing and piling clothes over her arm at the same time. 'I'm not a very good cook and I don't generally keep fresh food in the apartment.'

Dan stood on the threshold, hands in his pockets, looking around with interest. 'This is exactly what I thought it would look like.'

'A mess?' she grimaced. 'Thanks a lot.'

He chuckled and shrugged. 'No. Just you. Feminine, colourful and all over the place.'

She raised an eyebrow. 'Isn't that still just a nice way of saying I'm untidy?'

He raised his hands in mock defence. 'Believe me, I can't talk.'

'Hmmm.' She threw the clothes into the laundry and shut the door as he approached her, leaning her back against the door, hand still on the knob.

'There is so much you haven't told me about yourself,' he mused. 'And yet, sometimes I feel like I've always known you. Does that make sense?'

She nodded. 'Absolutely.'

He followed her into the kitchen and when she turned around to face him, the space felt crowded. Her brain did a double-take. *The client is in my kitchen.*

Dan Hullog – tired, vulnerable and completely at my mercy.

His black hair was curling just above the rim of his collar in that endearing way that made her fingers itch. He looked impossibly tall as he stood beside her dining table, watching her, watching him. The stove wasn't on yet, but it sure felt like it.

Lena realised she was staring and turned around to busy herself with finding a pot and a tin. The pot was easy. She pulled it from the drawer under the sink and set it on the stove. Then she moved to the pantry, aware that his eyes were on her the whole time. She pulled two tins from the middle shelf and turned around.

'Pumpkin or tomato?'

'Definitely pumpkin.' He came forwards, taking the chosen flavour from her grasp, their fingertips briefly touching in the exchange. 'Let me do it,' he murmured. 'I feel like I've tres-passed on your time enough for one day.'

'Don't be silly,' she protested.

'I insist.' He took the can to the counter, rummaged in a drawer and produced a tin opener. She sat down at the dining table and watched his shirt pull taut over his bicep as he took the top off the can and poured its contents into the pot. His hand trailed across the edge of the counter as he returned to the drawer to find a spoon and she suppressed the need to shudder. He fumbled through the choices and the cutlery clinked against each other. Finally, he pulled a long wooden spoon, which she never used, from the hidden depths of the cavity and turned around.

'So is this your usual dinner routine?'

She shrugged. 'I don't know . . . sometimes. I eat out a lot when I live in Perth.'

'I hadn't realised how much I'd missed the city till we came back.' He sighed as he placed the spoon in the steaming pot and rotated it in slow circles.

'Perth is really pretty.'

'I was thinking more . . . homey. It's a cosy town. That's what I love about it.'

'Do you still have a place here?'

He shook his head without looking up from the stirring. 'I'm staying in a hotel at the moment. All my stuff is in storage – has been for over a year. I plan to keep it that way till I get sick of big projects in the outback.'

'The outback, hmmm?' She got up in disgust, snatched the spoon from him and shoved him gently over with her hip. 'No family, no home to call your own, a friendless workaholic, wandering the face of the earth, hoping to get lost in his own anonymity. Sounds just peachy.'

His eyes widened in surprise and he leaned against the neighbouring benchtop. 'Well, it doesn't sound great when you put it that way.'

'It doesn't sound great no matter how you put it. What are you trying to do? Bury yourself?'

He ran his fingers through his hair with a heavy sigh. 'I guess I never thought of it like that.'

'Tell me,' she turned around and said lightly, 'did you have any pets when you lived in Perth? Perhaps you gave them away, or worse, had them put down? Because clearly death was preferable to a life with you.'

He laughed. Real humour glinted in those rich, catch-your-breath eyes.

She stopped to drink in the lovely moment. He took advantage of her distraction and snatched the spoon back, shoving her over. 'Now you're just being cheeky.'

He carefully spooned out a mouthful, cupping a hand under it and blowing on it gently. He turned, closing the distance between them till their legs brushed, and raised the spoon to her mouth.

'Is this hot enough for you?'

Hello!

The air was hot.

The room was hot.

The hairs up her bloody nose were hot.

The very question threatened to turn her body into liquid lava. Who cared about the stupid soup?

His eyes twinkled at her. 'Go on, taste it.'

She parted her lips and he slid the spoon between them. That thick buttery pumpkin taste, creamy and wholesome, slipped over her tongue and down her throat. She licked her lips. It was the perfect temperature. It was the apartment that was the problem.

'I think it's done,' she said and took a cautious step back.

Am I getting in over my head again?

He put his mouth where hers had been and took the remaining half sip. 'I think you're right.'

He turned off the stove and served up the soup.

They took their dinner to eat on the couch; and she caught Dan looking at the photo frames sitting on the cabinet by her television. There were three pictures in all. One of her and her parents, a Christmas photo that included them again with some of her other relatives and one of Lena and Robyn in Sydney on a trip they'd taken a couple of years earlier. The light-hearted expression he'd been wearing in the kitchen gradually faded under this unsubtle reminder of what he didn't have. She swore under her breath but he heard and looked at her.

'What?'

'You were right.' She sipped her soup. 'You can't hide anything from me any more.'

'I'm sorry,' he sighed. 'It's not your fault you had the perfect childhood.'

She snorted. 'I wouldn't say perfect. But it wasn't unhappy.' She didn't like the whiteness around his mouth. 'Dare I ask about yours?'

'Don't worry, I wasn't abused or anything.' He put his soup on the table and ran his palms down his knees. 'Wasn't loved either, but you must have guessed that by now.'

She thought back to his parents' behaviour. 'I wasn't going to say anything, but it did strike me as odd that these people who nurtured you as a child could turn on you like they have. Especially when they appear to love Mark so much.'

'Mark is their real child.' Dan drew a weary hand across his forehead. 'My mum was Dad's first wife. She died.'

'So,' she said slowly, also putting her soup on the coffee table, 'that woman in the courtroom is your stepmother.'

'Since I was two. Really, she's the only mother I've ever known. She tried. But I always knew she considered me an unfortunate remnant of my father's past. I guess when Mark died she used it as ammunition to tip my father completely over to her point of view.'

'Dan, that's terrible.'

He shrugged. 'It's life.'

'What did Mark think about all this?'

'I don't know; I never asked him. I hoped he didn't notice. I loved Mark, maybe as much as the two of them did. He was the glue that kept us all together.'

She couldn't help but wonder whether his family's reliance on Mark had been the pressure that had crushed his spirit. She didn't say it though – she didn't want to layer any more theories on top of his possible suicide. Especially not one that in effect blamed Dan yet again.

His quiet voice, rough with tiredness and grief, interrupted her thoughts. 'It's okay. I've thought of that too.'

'I'm sorry, I should be trying to take your mind off your family not encouraging you to dwell on it. Let's talk about something else.'

He nodded, swinging his body round so one knee was bent up under him. He rested his elbow on the top of the couch and his head on his palm. 'Let's talk about you.'

Warmth infused her face. 'What about me?'

'Well, you know all about my family, tell me about yours.'

She chuckled. 'Not much to tell. I'm one of two children. My parents are still together. They live on the outskirts of the city and are growing happily into their eccentric habits. Love 'em to bits.' She shrugged. 'My sister, Elle, is a bit of a free spirit. She lives in Melbourne. We've never been that close.'

'That happens. I'm glad your parents are good to you though. Next question: how does a girl like you become an engineer anyway?'

She grabbed the pillow behind her back and threw it at him. 'What do you mean a girl like me?'

He stuffed the pillow behind his back. 'You know what I mean.'

She raised an eyebrow at him. 'No, actually. I don't.'

And then, in an unexpected move, he leaned forwards and pulled one of her feet out from under her. He pressed his thumbs deeply into her arch and she didn't know whether to squeal or moan as delicious pain sent a shaft of relaxation straight up her leg. 'Maybe it's just because you're young.'

'I won't always be,' she said, struggling to keep her wits about her. 'And stop avoiding the question.'

'A girl like you. Hmmm. What did I mean?' She thought he was teasing her, but also trying to figure it out. 'Maybe I was thrown by your looks – no, wait: I'm not saying that's fair,' he protested, as she started to interrupt him. 'I was wrong. Okay? Satisfied? But you must admit that you don't have the same attitude as other engineers, male or female.'

She frowned. 'I work *very* hard –'

'Not that kind of attitude. I mean, you use your heart as much as your brain on the job. You organise social events, you take on board everybody's opinions and I do mean everybody's, and you let people see your . . . I don't know . . . your *enthusiasm*. You're like a really amazing preschool teacher – or a publicist or something. Engineers don't talk like you do. I misjudged you because of that.'

'Yes. You made it perfectly clear that you didn't think I belonged on site.'

'Well, you proved me wrong,' he murmured, his gentle caressing moving up her leg.

She choked and lifted her chin. 'I proved a lot of people wrong.'

'Yes you did – and with such style too.'

This time she blushed, not quite knowing what to say. Had she really proven herself?

'You're not done yet, are you?' he asked seriously.

His words made her think of her promise and of Kevin, and all the reasons why sitting there with him, her foot in his hand, was utterly ridiculous. 'No,' she swallowed hard. 'Not yet.'

She pulled her foot back and tucked it away, putting her hand out imperiously for her cushion. 'Give me my pillow back.'

'Why?'

She rubbed behind her back and glared at him. 'Because I need it.'

He pulled the spare pillow from behind him instead. Leaning forwards again, he passed the pillow over her head with both hands so that it came down behind her and she was cradled in the loop of his arms. They were nose to nose, so close she could register the individual eyelashes framing his deep cobalt eyes. Her heart rattled so loudly in her chest she was sure he must be able to hear it banging against her ribcage.

'What's wrong, Lena?'

She bit her lip, trying to quieten the train roaring through her head. 'You don't know me, Dan. I'm not who you think I am.'

'You keep saying that,' he whispered and closed the minute gap between them with the gentlest of kisses. His mouth sipped from hers and nudged insistently to deepen the kiss.

But his efforts were useless against the voices in her head.

You're a fraud.

An engineer impersonator.

When he finds out the truth, he'll never look at you the same way again.

With a sharp intake of breath she pulled away and he dropped his forehead to hers. 'I'm sorry, I said I'd never do that again, didn't I?'

'It's okay.' She tried to keep her voice light but couldn't meet his eyes.

With a heavy sigh, he put both feet on the ground, so that he was sitting normally. With a soft expletive, he ran a hand through his hair. 'I know you're afraid, Lena. But so am I. These last few days with you . . . I just . . . It's got me thinking.'

Her eyes widened. 'About what?'

He turned his head to look at her again. 'I don't want to keep running any more. I don't want to live like this.'

She let out a breath she hadn't realised she'd been holding. 'Dan, I –'

'No listen,' he urged her. 'I need to fly back right after the case is finished because I took too much R and R in Karratha and –'

She cut him off. 'But what if the verdict . . . What if you need some time out?'

He put a hand out to caress her cheek. 'Don't worry. I process misery best through work.'

She grimaced. 'Guess I should have figured that out by now.'

'When I get back to Cape Lambert, I'm going to hire a third party to host an arbitration for our project.'

'A what?'

'An arbitration. It's when both sides get together to discuss their differences and settle on what each side can do to alleviate the problem.'

She blinked. 'You mean like peace talks.'

His lips curled wryly. 'In a manner of speaking. Workplace morale has dropped so low and is so unmanageable this time, especially by me, given I'm half the cause of it. I think we need this.'

'I see.'

'Maybe there's a way to sort the boys out professionally. And perhaps then we could start seeing each other openly.'

If he had put his hand inside her chest and pulled out her heart, he couldn't have affected her more deeply.

'Dan, I can't.'

A veil fell across his eyes. 'Have I read you so wrong?'

'Yes . . . no. You wouldn't understand.' She looked down in shame.

'Then tell me.' His hand covered hers.

Indecision gripped her. Should she throw caution to the wind? Put herself, Barnes Inc and indeed the whole project at risk with a frank admission to the client of all people? Should she abandon her promise for a feeling more real than anything she'd ever had with Kevin? Risk her heart and her career in one fatal confession? She wrung her hands instinctively, knowing that she was going to make the emotional decision rather than the rational one. Gulping in air, she looked up.

'Dan, can you give me some time? I want to tell you – I do. But there's just one thing I need to sort out first.' She could feel her eyes filling with tears as she asked her next question. 'Will you wait for me? Not too much longer, I promise.'

There was no hesitation in his steady gaze. 'Of course.' And he pulled her firmly into his arms, holding her tight. Nuzzling her face into his neck, she had never felt so happy or so anxious all at the same time before. It was like sitting on the fence between heaven and hell, one foot dangling in each realm.

She knew what she had to do. If she was going to make a full confession then she would do so with all the facts. Besides, it would be too brutal of her to lay all her problems on him now, when his brother's trial verdict was just hours away.

They held each other for what seemed like hours and, before she knew what was happening, she was falling asleep. The warmth and safety of Dan's arms and the exhausting nature of their day had finally caught up with her.

It was nearly morning when she woke up. She felt his body leave hers and a rug from the couch opposite sweep her limbs before he tucked it under her chin.

He was leaving.

She didn't open her eyes, not wanting to make his parting awkward when it shouldn't be. A rough chin and soft lips gently touched her forehead as a finger brushed her fringe away. His voice was barely a whisper. She almost didn't hear the breathy flyaway line that was so quiet it was like a thought.

'I love you . . . Madame Engineer.'

She lay there buzzing with adrenaline until the click of the front door closing finally allowed her to move.

Tossing off the covers she sat bolt upright and wrapped her arms around herself. Her heart faltered, fluttering against her ribcage. Chewing on her lower lip, she tossed her own thought out futilely, knowing he would never hear, just as she was never meant to hear his. *I love you too . . . Bulldog.*

The following morning saw Lena back at court – back in the reality of Dan's situation. When she walked into the gallery and saw him sitting there, her chest tightened. His slight smile did nothing to reassure her, nor did his pale complexion. As she sat down next to him, she found it difficult not to fidget with suppressed emotions fighting for release.

I have to concentrate on the case not what was said last night.

What mattered now was Dan and how the verdict of this case would affect him. There was no room for anything else.

The closing statements given by each of the lawyers didn't improve her mood. Both arguments were so strong. She couldn't pick who the judge was going to side with. When Mr Carter got up to speak, his confidence seemed to shine in every word. He was sure of his stance.

He reminded everyone how inexperienced Mark had been and how reliant on the company he was for knowledge and supervision. He said the attendance of the graduate safety induction program should have been policed better and that Oswalds had serious communication problems. Lena watched Dan's family in the front row, nodding along with every bullseye he made.

When Mr Carter finally addressed the question of suicide his tone was very dismissive. 'There is no evidence to substantiate the claim. According to his doctor he had made a vast improvement over months of treatment and was not suicidal at all. His previously strained relationship with his wife was on the mend and he was ecstatic about the new baby. Hardly grounds for suicide.'

Lena had to admit his self-assurance made him hard to refute.

'Your honour, statistically the most popular methods of taking one's life are medication overdose, hanging and firearms. Yet here we have the hypothesis that Mark Hullog chose to kill himself in a log feeder of all things. Surely it would have been one of the most excruciatingly painful ways to die. I do not think that if Mark Hullog had in fact been suicidal, as my learned friend would suggest, he would have chosen this way to die.'

The judge acknowledged the end of Mr Carter's speech, jotted down some notes and then lifted his eyes to the gallery.

Lena searched for something in his expression – anything to tell her where his allegiance lay – but there was nothing there. She cast a glance at Dan, who very slightly shook his head. He didn't have a clue either. The judge cleared his throat and addressed Sarah.

'Ms Michaels, would you like to close?'

'Yes, your honour.'

Sarah stood up, shuffling her papers as she rose. Her hands linked themselves behind her back and the hairs on Lena's arms prickled with the suspense of waiting for her to speak. It seemed weird now that she'd ever been jealous of this woman. Sarah was more of a soldier in Dan's army than a femme fatale. Her fears had been groundless. Foolish even.

Sarah finally spoke. 'Your honour, perhaps the staff of Oswalds need to improve their communication lines as Mr Carter indicated. However, in this case it was not their lack of talking that killed Mark Hullog.'

She went on to describe Mark's depression in detail, the drugs he was on, the therapy sessions he was committed to. She told the court how many times, statistically, doctors get it wrong and how stressful the prospect of unplanned parenthood could be. Lena thought her argument was just as strong as Mr Carter's. She looked at Dan, but he didn't return her gaze. His attention was riveted on Sarah; he was intent upon her every word.

'Daniel Hullog testified that Mark Hullog had a camera with him to take photographs of the foot of the machine and its foundation. There was absolutely no engineering motivation for him to go into the machine at all. He must have had a personal agenda. Couldn't Mark Hullog, after seeing the danger signs and stickers on the machine and having been told in a safety video how dangerous it was, slipped away from his manager for what by all accounts was no more than five minutes to end his life? Quick and simple. No need for a note. No need for planning, or risk of failure. It wouldn't even look like suicide. Perhaps he thought that his death in an accident would mean his wife and child would be financially secure. He could end it all there and then and this time no one could stop him. A tragic decision and yes, a dreadful loss – but no one's fault but Mark Hullog's own.'

'Thank you, Ms Michaels.' The judge inclined his head when Sarah resumed her seat. He arranged his notes into a pile and muttered something to his associate, who also nodded. When he faced the gallery again his voice was mild.

'This court is adjourned until four o'clock this afternoon.'

Lena flicked her wrist over and looked at her watch. It was nearly lunchtime.

Dan saw the action and tugged her to her feet. 'Let's get out of here before my family decides to notice us.'

Lena didn't blame him for his haste. Angela Hullog turned around to stare at them just at that moment. Dan's parents on the other hand pretended they didn't exist in a manner so obvious that it was just as insulting. Lena followed Dan out.

'If I were you,' she muttered when they were safely outside, 'I wouldn't worry about trying to reconcile with them. They're not worth the pain.'

His mouth kicked up at the corners. 'Well, I'm not pining for a friendship with Angela, if that's what you're worried about. But I do hope someday to reconcile things with my father. He is my dad after all.'

'And your niece?' she asked tentatively.

He grimaced. 'I haven't got high hopes on that score.'

'Well, you know what?' she said brightly. 'Kids grow up. One day she's going to start asking questions about her father and when her mother doesn't give her all the answers she's going to come looking for you.'

'I never thought of that.' He looked at Lena, obviously impressed by her insight. 'It does sound rather daunting though – dealing with a teenager's search for self.'

'Well,' she suggested optimistically, 'you have years to come up with something wise and profound to say. I wouldn't start worrying about it yet.'

He grabbed her hand, lacing his fingers through hers with delicious presumption. 'You've managed to find the silver lining again.'

'It's what I do.'

'I know.' His pace quickened. 'Let's have lunch on the beach . . . unless you already have plans. I mean I don't expect you to –'

'Dan, relax.' She squeezed his hand. 'I'm here for you today. I'm not going anywhere.'

They went to Cottesloe, one of Perth's most popular beaches. Here the coast was lined with popular cafes ranging in mood from swanky to casual. They decided on the latter but instead of eating in, they bought fish and chips and took the rug from the back of Dan's car down to the waterfront. It was another beautiful day, perfect for a picnic. The ocean provided both view and music for their idyllic little date. Lena pushed her toes into the sand and wished it was under different circumstances. Waves crashed and foamed before her much like the rush and ebb of her own uncertainty.

Sharon was right. So was Robyn. She had to see Kevin and find out exactly which subjects she needed to do over to complete her degree. Maybe she could approach the uni about just sitting in on the classes. She could say she wanted a refresher now that she knew what skills were needed in the field. It was purely for her own benefit, after all. She would make Kevin tell her everything: if she was ever to put that chapter of her life to bed, she needed the whole truth. All the details – and a plan to fix things. Only then would she be ready to tell Dan.

'What's the matter?' Dan queried her sudden silence as he polished off the last piece of fish.

'Just thinking.'

'Don't,' he said. 'I'm desperate not to.'

She shook off her demons and smiled. 'You're right. What shall we talk about?'

They chatted about everything and nothing. It was the first time she got to learn mundane things about Dan. Things that weren't groundbreaking or really all that important but made her feel all the more closer to him for knowing them. Like the fact that Dan hated chicken pies but loved pasta. Or when he lived in Perth he was a keen surfer but hadn't been on his board in almost a year. And when he was little, he was in the Boy Scouts. She could just picture him in his little uniform, already honing his professional image. He and Mark had all the badges.

They talked about her too. She couldn't remember what she told him, just his face and the intentness of his gaze. His attention was completely and utterly undivided. The knowledge was an aphrodisiac like no other.

But there was that line they'd drawn between them the day before. Neither of them dared cross it – each for their own preservation as much as the other's. Lena tiptoed around it. Unable to pretend it wasn't there. Conscious of its existence as every precious minute passed.

Just before it was time to go Dan said, 'I have a flight to Karratha booked for tonight.'

'Already?'

'My assistant sorted it out yesterday. It's crisis stations up there at the moment.'

'It's crisis stations down here too,' she reminded him.

He looked away. 'After the verdict, it might be just what I need. A *safe* distraction.'

She smiled sadly. At least she *was* a distraction, if a danger-ous one. They returned to Perth. Dan's family were already seated in their usual spots looking too anxious to be side-tracked by them this time. If fear had a smell, the air around them would have reeked of it.

The bailiff asked everyone to rise as the judge walked in. When he was seated, the lawyers and spectators sank nervously into their chairs.

Lena clutched Dan's hand, giving and taking support in equal measure. The judge arranged the sleeves of his robes as he sat down with a languid insensitivity that made Lena want to throw her shoe at his head and yell, 'Just get on with it.'

And then miraculously, he did.

Chapter 21

'In the matter of Angela Hullog and Oswalds Proprietary Limited, I will deliver an *ex temporae* judgement. I find the plaintiff's case unfounded. I don't believe their evidence makes out their cause of action of negligence against the defendant. Although the defendant had a clear duty of care to the deceased, it is not reasonably foreseeable that the deceased would have ignored the briefing provided to him by his manager and brother, Daniel Hullog, the safety video, the warning of the foreman of MacArthur Lumber Mill *and* the signs on the machine. These four evidentiary factors make any breach of the defendant's duty of care too remote in the circumstances. The evidence that the deceased had a mental illness goes some way to explain his actions. However, in the first instance I find that the plaintiff cannot establish negligence on the part of the defendant whatever the reason Mr Hullog stepped into that machine. It was a risk that he assumed of his own accord. I will publish my full reasons for these findings in due course and they shall be delivered at a court date to be set approximately three months hence. I find in favour of the defendant. The costs of this action follow the event. The plaintiff, Angela

Hullog, will bear them and they will be taxed if they cannot be agreed between the parties.'

There was a collective gasp from the front row of the gallery which the judge ignored.

He lifted his wooden hammer and tapped it on the desk. 'Case closed.'

Lena was confused. *That's it? It's over?*

While she gaped in shock, the judge exited. As soon as the door closed behind him, pandemonium broke out in the court-room. Dan's mother started crying and ranting hysterically. Angela Hullog stood up and turned around as though she were about to yell abuse at Dan but then her eyes rolled back into her head and she fainted. Dan's father, who spared a second to shoot a murderous look at Dan before acting, couldn't seem to calm his wife or shake his daughter-in-law awake.

'Call an ambulance!' he told the bailiff at the same time Dan's stepmother yelled, 'You get that judge back in here right now!'

The bailiff called security instead and Dan and Lena thought this was a good time to leave. They exited the courtroom and arrived in the street breathless. Neither of them had spoken one word to the other about the verdict yet. Lena didn't know about Dan but she was still trying to digest the fact that the law believed his brother had committed suicide.

'Dan –'

'Lena, don't say anything. What's left to say? It's finished.' His face was white, his lips a little blue around the edges. 'I've come to realise that I've been expecting this verdict to answer all my questions but really . . .' He looked at Lena sadly. 'Nothing's changed. I'll always feel partially responsible for my brother's death whether it was suicide or not. It's just something I need to live with.'

Lena wanted to grab hold of him and offer to share his burden – to take part of it on her own shoulders – but he was retreating inside himself again. She could see it in his eyes. Feel it in the slackened grip he had on her hand.

'Dan, you can't fly back tonight.'

'It's for the best.'

She knew that tone. It was the curse of their relationship – the roadblock that got her every time. He was going back to Karratha and there was nothing she could do to stop him.

Dan lowered his head to kiss her softly on the cheek: a feather-touch she barely felt. 'Try to forget about this. Enjoy the rest of your R and R and I'll see you . . . when I can. When you get back to Cape Lambert. Maybe then we can talk about something more . . . cheerful.'

She knew what he was asking her and agreed.

'Yes, definitely.'

In a moment or two he was gone and she was left standing in the street wondering if she'd dreamed it all.

In a way it was a blessing that Dan returned to the Pilbara because Lena would not have been able to spend the next day with him. It was now imperative that she see Kevin and sort out her past so she could start concentrating on her future. She told no one of her intentions, not even Robyn. She didn't want her best friend's opinion yet in case it made her nervous or uncertain. Instead, she rose early the next morning, showered and dressed. She rang the university and asked about Kevin's schedule. After managing to extract his timetable from a receptionist, she worked out that he was most likely to be in his office between two and four. With several hours to kill, she spent the morning cleaning her apartment and trying not to think too deeply. In the early afternoon she left for UWA.

Her intention was to surprise Kevin – and she did. He opened the door to her knock and started at the sight of her.

'*Lena?*'

'Hi, Kevin. Can I come in?'

'Of course.' He stepped back to give her room. While he closed the door behind them she examined his face. It had been just under a year since she'd last seen him, so nothing much of his physical appearance had changed. But in his stagnation, she could see how much she had.

The smart cut of his coat, she knew, hid droopy rather than strong shoulders. His age, a factor that used to make him seem so wise and sophisticated, had lost its appeal. She realised that while he still had seventeen years on her, he was younger than some of the men she managed on site. And when she thought about it carefully, his worldly wisdom probably didn't extend much beyond that one over-talked trip to Europe and a love of SBS. His face was still handsome; the silver-framed brown eyes had a certain attraction. But she couldn't help but contrast it to Dan's kind selflessness and undoubtedly masculine allure.

Kevin walked around to the other side of his desk and said, 'You're the last person I thought I'd see today. Any day, really.'

'Am I interrupting something important?'

'No.' His smile was nonchalant. 'I'm just marking a few assignments.'

'Funny, that's exactly what I came to talk to you about.'

'Oh?' His eyes dilated slightly before he cleared his throat and indicated the chair in front of him. 'Please sit down.'

She did as he asked, trying not to think about the times she'd sat in this chair with a glass of wine and some Chinese takeaway.

'It's been a long time,' he said, putting a voice to her nostalgia. 'How have you been?'

She decided not to waste any more of her life and cut straight to the chase. 'Unsettled, actually.'

He also sat down, locking his fingers together on the desk in front of him. 'I assume this has to do with me.'

She licked her lips. 'I need to know how much you helped me pass the two subjects you taught me.'

'What do you mean?'

'Was it my assignments? Did you give me a few extra marks there? Or was it my exams?' She sat forwards. 'Perhaps you just added twenty per cent to the whole grade at the end of the semester?' Unable to sit any longer, she got up out of her chair, hands wringing in front of her as she began to pace. 'Was it both subjects or just one? It had to be Structural Analysis, right? I was always hopeless at matrices.' She spun around to face him, dropping her hands resolutely to her side as she waited for his response.

He said nothing.

'Kevin, I need to know. Not knowing has been driving me insane this past year. I'm constantly second-guessing myself and my work. Can't you see how important this is to me?'

'Lena, I'm sorry –'

Panic struck her between the eyes and she resorted to threats. 'Kevin,' she pinched her thumb and forefinger, 'I am this close to going to the dean and owning up. If you don't let me see the work you tampered with, I will. Do you really want to lose your job over this?'

'No, of course not.' He paused. 'Thing is,' he licked his lips, his gaze centring on his laced fingers rather than her face, 'I lied to you.'

Lena stared at him. 'I don't understand.'

'It wasn't true.' His voice was soft with shame. 'You passed both subjects fair and square. I didn't do anything to your marks.'

She grabbed hold of the back of her chair to steady herself, pushing words through her teeth. 'So why did you tell me you did?'

He shut his eyes, still not lifting his chin. She stared at him, unable to believe she had been attracted to such a vindictive person.

'It was a knee-jerk reaction to the situation. I was hurting and I wanted to hurt you back just as much. I'm not proud of what I did. But at the time, I just lost control.'

He finally opened his eyes and Lena sank heavily into the chair in front of him as he continued. 'For you, I was an experiment – an adventure to spice up your uni life. But for me . . . I really fell for you, Lena. I loved you. I'd be lying if I didn't admit that I still have some feelings for you –'

'If you cared about me at all, you would have told me sooner that you'd lied,' she accused.

He winced. 'I didn't think it would affect you like this. The day after you dumped me I never saw you again. How was I supposed to know that our final meeting was any more than a blip on your radar? After all, you'd just finished telling me you'd outgrown me.'

'Kevin,' she tried to muster some patience, 'I'm sorry if I made you feel that way. But you were never a blip on my radar: our relationship definitely meant something to me. You were *not* an experiment. But I knew when it was over; and I was just trying to be honest with you. It's no excuse for what you did.'

'I know.'

His helpless, almost shameful, admission made her rage sizzle out, leaving her with a sense of deflation. 'What's done is done,' she said on a sigh and then stood up.

He stood up too. 'Where are you going? Can I buy you a coffee? Perhaps we can go downstairs and talk about this in a more civilised environment.'

She studied his countenance, which radiated both concern and eagerness, and realised for perhaps the first time that maybe she could have been more sensitive to what he might be feeling. She had been so focused on sorting herself out at the time that she hadn't paused to consider the possible intensity of his reaction in any great detail.

Her shoulders relaxed. 'Thank you, Kevin. But I think it would be best if we just left it there.'

'Are you seeing anyone?' he asked tentatively.

Her smile froze as she held out her hand and he took it in

318

both of his. Clearing her throat she admitted unsteadily, 'Yes, actually. I am.'

'I see.'

'Goodbye, Kevin.'

He dropped her hand. 'Goodbye, Lena. Good luck.'

Despite her uncertainty about the reception she would receive, Lena was desperate to hop on a plane back to Karratha. Her meeting with Kevin had totally unburdened her. She felt like a hot air balloon that had just offloaded six sandbags and was about to float away. Robyn was ecstatic when she heard the news and Lena couldn't wait to tell Sharon about it.

Harry picked her up from the airport, all smiles and bursting with news. She was pleased to see him but couldn't help wondering where Sharon was. Didn't she care that she'd arrived?

'The board game has taken off big-time,' Harry announced. 'It's making our job really easy.'

'Really?' She focused on Harry's enthusiastic smile.

'You better believe it. It's been great! The only person who's running behind is Fish and by one per cent. One per cent!'

'We're running on time?'

He nodded vigorously.

She shook her head in awe. 'Unbelievable.'

'And it's all thanks to you.'

'Hardly.' Her head snapped around to study his profile. 'It was a group effort.'

'Your idea, Lena. Your idea.'

'It wasn't really an idea. More like a sort of managing concept.'

'That's an idea. A really good one. Everybody thinks so.'

'Everybody?' she whispered. 'Who's everybody?'

Harry shrugged. 'Just . . . everybody.'

Lena raised her eyebrows. 'But I thought I was in the doghouse because of you know . . . the whole Bulldog thing.'

'Oh.' Harry cocked his head to one side. 'That's old news. I mean, it wasn't even true. You know Mike. Had it in for you from the start, and –'

'What, so everyone's just forgiven and forgotten?'

Lena stared out the windscreen, unable to take in the scenery with his words flashing incredulously across her brain.

'Well, Bulldog brought in this arbitrator. And the supervisors and the managers all went on this, like, debate evening. We hashed out a lot of stuff. Not just about you and Bulldog but other stuff, stuff that's been painful for ages.'

'What do you mean, about me and Bulldog?'

'Well, Bulldog explained that it was a complete misunderstanding founded on rumours. Mike even got up and said he'd made a mistake.'

Her throat constricted. 'Mike said that?'

'Yeah.' Harry nodded merrily, seemingly unaware of her inner turmoil. 'Looks like he must have finally got a case of the guilts and admitted the truth.'

Or Bulldog got stuck into him, blackmailed him or worse.

Lena choked as she tried to imagine what Dan had done to get Mike to publicly confess he was wrong. It had to have been drastic to achieve such a feat.

'Anyway,' Harry was still speaking, 'we didn't just talk about that of course. Most of the arbitration was more business-based, involving a lot of negotiation and just debating about site protocol and processes.'

'Right.'

'Kind of exhausting, really. TCN put on drinks at Point Samson afterwards for the management staff. Radar was real pissed not to be invited – missed the best gossip in town.'

'Oh yeah,' Lena responded absentmindedly, her mind still on Mike's sudden about-face.

'Yeah, you'd never believe it. Dan picked up some local chick at the bar.'

Like someone flicking the channel on a radio over, Lena was suddenly listening. 'He *what*?'

'Funniest thing.' Harry nodded innocently. 'He got talking to this blonde for over an hour at the pub and then took her phone number before she left. Saw that part myself. Pretty girl too.' He took his eyes from the road to send Lena another reassuring look. 'So you really needn't worry about those rumours about you and him. They are definitely dead.'

Dead was exactly how Lena felt inside. What was going on? Dan had said he would wait for her. Had there been a five-minute time limit on that she wasn't aware of?

She licked her lips and addressed Harry again. 'Are you sure?'

'Certain.' Harry nodded, oblivious. 'In fact, morale is so completely restored that everyone really wants to do their best. I think that's why the board game has been so success-ful – everyone has pitched in and stuck to the plan no matter what.'

Lena barely heard his words. She was too busy running through probabilities in her head. If Leg or Radar had told her Dan had picked up some girl, she would have written it off immediately. They were famous for their embellishment. But this was Harry she was talking to. He would never make up tales.

'Lena.' Harry recalled her to the present once more. She was shocked to hear something close to The Tone in his voice. 'I thought you'd be a bit more excited about being the project hero!'

Lena shook her head. 'You're exaggerating.'

Harry glanced at her briefly. It was the first look Lena had ever seen on him that was even vaguely patronising. 'Lena, you complain when no one gives you any credit and now when they do, you don't want it.'

Thankfully, Lena wasn't required to respond because the ute turned into the site, kicking up a cloud of red dust as they left the main road. She was glad. There was too much whirling around in her head for her to deal with more small talk.

Like the fact that she couldn't believe Dan would deny their relationship point blank and then start dating someone else to prove it. A lump formed in her throat.

That's because he's not seeing another woman as some sort of elaborate cover. It was too ridiculous a plan to believe. So what was she supposed to conclude? That he'd changed his mind about her?

Sharon would know the truth.

She got out of the ute, scanning the yard for her friend. Sharon was nowhere in sight but the bus was parked in its usual spot. This, at least, meant that Sharon wasn't on the wharf: she was somewhere around.

Excellent!

The other thing she noticed was that men were striding around with a little more purpose in their faces. There weren't the usual packs of idlers waiting around for the next shipment of goods. Everyone was doing something. So maybe the board game *had* worked its magic.

'Thanks for the lift,' she said to Harry before walking off towards the main office donga.

Running up the office steps, she entered the dust-ridden cabin and took in the messy decks, the coughing air-conditioner and the smiles of greeting from various cubicles.

'Hi!'

Impatiently, she did the rounds, greeting everyone and fielding the usual 'How was your break?' questions. There was no hint of the animosity she had left. Perhaps even a few sheepish looks lingered on the faces of her peers as they addressed her.

Gavin gave her his usual cocky grin, totally shame-free. 'So you're back, are you?'

No, Gavin, what you're seeing is a hologram.

She was too distracted to stop and tease, however, so she merely nodded and asked, 'Have you seen Sharon?'

'Nope. Have you seen Carl?'

'Not yet.'

Carl could wait. On this thought, she made her way back out to the bus. Sharon wasn't sitting in it or cleaning it, so she jumped out and decided to try the smoko donga. Perhaps Sharon was stacking the fridge or the storeroom.

The smoko kitchen was empty but she saw Sharon's handbag on one of the tables – which was odd – so she headed to the back of the donga where the storeroom was.

Grabbing the handle, she swung open the door. 'Sharon, are you –?'

Lena stopped, open-mouthed on the threshold, completely forgetting the reason she was there. Sharon was in the store-room all right. But so was Carl. He had her back up against some shelving and there wasn't a single part of their bodies that wasn't connected. Lips to lips, chest to chest, thigh to thigh. He had his hands on her waist . . . no, her bum. And Sharon's hands were in his hair, pulling at tufts with such force that Lena couldn't resist tilting her head to one side to see if Carl was starting to get any bald patches.

They gasped for air as their lips pulled apart. Sharon's fingers slipped from Carl's hair to his neck and they turned, cheek to cheek, to look at her.

'Lena!' said Sharon.

'Fuck!' said Carl.

Both their lips were red and puffy and Carl's hair was standing at least an inch off his head in all directions.

Struggling to hide a smug grin, Lena began to back out of the room. 'Oh, don't mind me. I'll just get out of your way.'

'Lena.' Sharon broke away from Carl as she turned to go. 'This –'

'*This*,' Lena said as she turned back, 'is exactly as it should be.'

'It is?' Sharon touched her hair self-consciously.

'I'd be more worried about his.' Lena pointed at Carl's mop.

Sharon turned around to examine her sweetheart. 'Oh shit.'

Carl put his hands up to feel his coiffure. 'Fuck!' he said again.

They both started patting him down, which was the funniest thing Lena had ever seen and also the most endearing. They looked great together. They fit. Even while they were engaged in this silly task, you could see the love in their eyes.

She let an indulgent smile tickle her lips. 'I'm happy for you guys: seriously.'

Carl glanced uncertainly at her, his ears a little red around the rims. When they were done patting down his hair, he came forwards. 'Look, Lena, I know after the way I took you to task over Bulldog you're going to think I'm a fuckin' hypocrite, but no one knows about this and –'

The mention of Dan brought Lena's reason for being there back to her. But as she studied Carl's anxious countenance, she couldn't bring herself to drag Sharon away at that moment. It would be hard but she could wait a little longer.

'Relax, Carl. I'm not going to tell anyone.'

His shoulders slumped in relief and Sharon squeezed one fondly. Lena backed towards the door, grabbing the handle as she passed it. 'I want details, Sharon,' she warned with a grin. 'I'll talk to you later.' She pulled the door shut and dusted her hands with satisfaction as she strode off.

Carl and Sharon. Who would have thought?

Lena spent the rest of the morning catching up on her email backlog, though Dan was never far from her thoughts. It was an effort to sit there when all she wanted to do was rush down to the client's offices and ask him if he'd moved on. Pride restrained her.

Instead, it was Leg and Radar who made a special trip to visit her just before lunch. They came in carrying a pink box about the size of a hard hat and put it on Lena's desk, looking as pleased as two rabbits with a bunch of carrots.

'Hey, Madame E. Bought you a gift.'

Lena studied the poorly constructed box – it was held together with duct tape rather than ribbon – and then back at them.

'Is this a prank?'

Leg wrung his hands, his eyebrows drawing together. 'Now really, Madame E, have we ever given you any reason not to trust us?'

'Yes.'

Radar grimaced, swatting the back of his hand on Leg's chest. 'Shut up, you knob. You're making things worse.' He turned back to Lena, apology singing soulfully from his eyes.

She leaned back in her chair and folded her arms. *This ought to be good.*

'Well, we felt really bad about, you know.' Radar rolled his eyes. 'Accusing you of being with Bulldog when it turned out you weren't.'

'And we didn't mean to have a go at you,' Leg added. 'Especially after you've been so good for the project and protecting us from Mike and everything. I mean . . . we should've stuck up for you whether you were with him or not.'

'Told the other guys to piss off.' Radar nodded seriously. 'It's not anyone's business who you date and we should have told 'em so like real friends.'

Lena's heart warmed. 'That's very big of you.' It was the first time the guys had suggested that they considered her as more of a friend than a boss. It was nice to have the confirmation.

'Damn straight.' Radar beamed in pleasure. 'Now you have to open our gift.'

'Oh.' She glanced back at their peace offering. 'I guess.' She pulled off some of the duct tape and opened the lid of the box. Hmmm. Synthetic brown fur. Dubiously, she tugged the item out. It was a stuffed kangaroo. A cute little skippy – except for one thing. Someone had taken a scratched, dented Mitsubishi emblem and stapled it to the kangaroo's chest.

An unwelcome suspicion assailed her. She touched the emblem with her finger. 'Where did you guys get this?'

'Didn't you hear?' Leg asked brightly. 'Bongo was a total write-off. Radar pulled the emblem off the bonnet as a souvenir.'

'Especially for you,' Radar added.

'You've got to be kidding me.' She put the kangaroo down. 'Why on earth would I want a souvenir of the day I killed a roo?'

'It was a fun night,' Leg began and then when he saw her face quickly added, 'Oh, except for that part.'

'Besides, kangaroos are your thing,' Radar tried to explain from a different perspective. She raised her eyebrows, daring him to continue. But he was completely unperturbed. 'You know. First there was that one that jumped off the jetty and now there's the Bongo-bashed one. We wanted to give you a personal gift.'

'Oh, it's personal all right.'

'You don't like it.'

She sighed. 'No it's fine. A little macabre, but fine.' She put the stuffed kangaroo on top of her computer and glanced back at them. 'There. Happy?'

They were. In that weird way men are when they think they've done something sentimental when really they've only stuck their foot in it.

The final hours of the day passed without mishap and at last Sharon and Lena were lounging on the front step of Lena's donga. It was beer o'clock but instead the two of them were drinking cola.

'You seem pretty tense,' Sharon commented. 'You better start at the beginning.'

Lena didn't need any further encouragement. Although she didn't think it her place to give Sharon the details of Dan's court case or his private family woes, she did spend a lot of time recapping having Dan over for soup and sleep. She told Sharon about the momentous 'I love you', the promises exchanged and how confused she now was to hear rumours he was seeing someone else.

'Is it true, Sharon?' Lena demanded anxiously. 'Have you heard them?'

By the look on her friend's face, she knew she wasn't going to get the answer she was hoping for.

'I wish I could tell you a different story,' Sharon frowned, 'but Harry's pretty much spot on. Carl told me about it afterwards too. Said Bulldog was taken with some hot blonde he met at the bar. Apparently, at the end of the night, he gave her his phone and she typed her number into it.'

Icicles seemed to form on Lena's heart. 'I don't get it. He said he would wait for me.'

Sharon squeezed her hand. 'Well, I wouldn't say Carl or Harry's story is concrete evidence. After all, there could be any number of reasons one stranger might give another one their phone number.'

Lena perked up a little bit. 'Of course there is.' But when she tried to come up with one, nothing sprang to mind.

Seeing her struggling, Sharon jumped in to the rescue. 'For example, she could be his sister, freshly moved to town, just passing on her new contact details.'

Lena bit her lip. 'Dan hasn't got a sister. He told me all about his family.'

'All right then, how about a cousin or even a friend?' Sharon suggested optimistically.

'In a crowded bar, on a balmy night in Point Samson?' Lena's voice sounded sarcastic even to her own ears. 'I don't think so.' She paused with difficulty. 'Maybe he got back to site and realised how foolhardy us as an item really is. I mean, morale before the arbitration was so low. Why go back there and put the project in jeopardy?'

'I think you're over-thinking this.' Sharon shook her head. 'You won't know the truth until you ask Dan yourself.'

'Should I call him?'

'I think it would be better if you did it in person.'

'When? How?' Lena cried. 'Everybody's watching all the time.'

Sharon was thoughtful for a moment. 'I'll convince Carl to lend you his ute at knock-off tomorrow. You can drive up to the client dongas and catch Dan at his office. He always stays late.'

It seemed like a good plan so Lena agreed. After all, what other options did she have? After that, she firmly shook off her demons to focus on Sharon. 'Enough about me. What's the deal with you and Carl?'

Sharon blushed. 'It all happened so fast. Carl was giving me a lift back to camp one night when . . .' Her lips curled shyly. 'One minute he was taking me back to my donga and the next we changed direction and were heading somewhere else for dinner.'

Lena squealed. 'He hijacked you!'

'Oh, I wanted to be hijacked.' Sharon grinned. 'And I made that perfectly plain. But you know what, Lena? He's a great guy.'

'I don't doubt it.'

'I mean, I'll never have to worry about him lying to me or playing games. He's brutally honest.'

'I can see how that would be the case.'

'He's protective too. Like every night you've been away he's invited me back to his place so I don't feel lonely at camp.'

'I'll bet.' Lena grinned wickedly.

Sharon swat her arm. 'We talk too,' she replied defensively and leaned back against the wall of the donga. 'Sometimes for hours.'

'Hours?' This had Lena flabbergasted. 'Seriously? What on earth about?'

'Just stuff.' Sharon's reply had her even more flabbergasted. 'I'm telling you, Lena, there's a side to Carl you haven't seen. He's so cute when he's out of his element too. Under that big tough manager hat of his, he's really not that cluey when it comes to women and he's so desperate to do the right thing.' She laughed fondly. 'I mean, I don't think he's really had a long-term relationship before.'

Lena pounced on this. 'So it's serious then?'

Sharon reddened. 'I think it's heading in that direction.' She paused. 'I really like him, Lena. I mean, *really* like him.'

Lena hugged her. 'Good for you. Hell, good for him. Good for both of you.'

'Thanks.'

'You know,' Lena began tentatively, 'I don't think it would matter if the guys knew about you and Carl. Fish's nose is going to be put out of joint but everyone else would be fine with it.'

'Well, it's early days,' Sharon explained. 'Carl doesn't want us to have spectators and gossip to deal with until we're ready and sure.'

Lena smiled, but was soon worrying over her own situation again. Sharon was right: she needed to see Dan. And come the next evening, that was exactly what she was going to do.

Chapter 22

Lena rocked up to work the next morning and felt like she'd never left. Fish was in the kitchen microwaving his shirt again. He came over to her cubicle afterwards to welcome her back and also borrow her stapler. When she assented, he began to staple the front of his shirt together. It looked as though constant microwaving had ruined the buttons. That wasn't the weird part, though.

'Fish, why are you wearing boardies with your shirt instead of pants?' Lena pointed at his rainbow-coloured surf shorts.

'Forgot to dry my pants last night too.'

She laughed. 'So why not just microwave them as well?'

'Metal zipper,' he said seriously. 'Everybody knows you don't put metal in the microwave.'

'You're kidding me, right? That rule you get.'

'Well, aren't we all high and mighty this morning?' He turned up his nose at her. 'It's not like you can talk with that roo sitting on your computer.'

She stuck out her tongue at him.

Shortly after lunch, she decided to make her routine inspection of progress on the skids. The boys stopped work and came up on deck to chat with her. No teasing, just good old-fashioned talking with undivided attention and respect. Maybe there was something in being project hero after all. She savoured the moment and the view. As she gazed out over the ocean at whales and dolphins frolicking in the waves, she couldn't imagine how she'd ever considered the Pilbara barren.

The only circumstance that had Lena a little freaked out was Mike's behaviour. At first he hung back, a sour expression on his face. But then he joined the group, to listen, but not to comment. He kept looking at Lena as though he had something to say but it never quite came out. The boys simply ignored him.

After half an hour she decided to take him aside. 'Look,' she got swiftly to the point, 'I heard what happened at the arbitration and I just wanted to thank you for squashing the rumours – for whatever reason.' She cleared her throat. 'In fact, I hope we can have a better working relationship from now on.'

He met her eyes briefly and just nodded.

That was it.

No smart remarks, no goading about how she'd got everything she deserved.

'Do you have anything you want to say to me, Mike?' she prodded him.

He looked at her and his sour expression seemed to deepen. 'I have not enjoyed working with you on this job.'

Lena snorted. *Here we go.* 'I haven't enjoyed working with you *either*, Mike.'

'Yes, but despite that, despite everything I –' He changed tack, saying in a firmer voice, 'You got things done. Better than done sometimes.' With a sigh, he looked out at the ocean again. The whales seemed to calm him. The creases on his forehead flattened, his tight mouth relaxed and his narrowed eyes opened languidly. Both their hands were resting on the handrailing and, while she watched him in confusion, he reached out and briefly patted one of hers. 'It'll be better from now on.'

Her voice gurgled in her throat as she struggled to reply. 'Er, thanks, Mike.' She followed his gaze out to sea, marvelling that it had actually come to this. Mike was apologising. Well, that was as close to an apology as he'd ever come and to have him of all people manage it . . . Well, quite frankly, it had her worried. What on earth had Dan said to him?

After five minutes, the bus rolled up and she climbed down from the skids back onto the road.

'You look philosophical,' Sharon mused as she completed her jump on board.

She shook her head. 'Too many questions and no answers.'

That afternoon passed extremely slowly as Lena counted down the minutes to knock-off. Around three o'clock her phone buzzed and she pounced on it like a hungry cat.

'Hello?' Her voice was breathless.

'Hi, Lena! How are you?'

At first she didn't recognise the voice, only registering that it wasn't Dan's.

'I hope I haven't caught you at a bad time.'

Finally it clicked. 'Ivan?' It had been mere months since she'd last spoken to her city boss but it felt like years.

'Yes, it's me. Just ringing to touch base. I've been hearing a lot of promising feedback about you from Cape Lambert. How are you enjoying it?'

A quiet smile curved her lips. 'Very well, thank you.'

'Good to know. Good to know.'

There was no hint of sarcasm or condescension in his voice at all and Lena had to wonder if The Tone had finally vacated the premises for good. She could only bite her lower lip with hope.

'Anyway,' he continued, unaware of her silent question, 'you've been on the Pilbara for twelve weeks, which is pretty much as long as we'd planned to spare you.'

Lena's chest seized as she realised for the first time that she didn't want to go back. She had too much to do here. How could she leave halfway through truss installation? She wanted to see the new jetty when it was finished.

Not to mention the fact that she still had unresolved business with Dan.

But Ivan was still talking. 'As you know, we like to rotate our graduates through different experiences and projects in their first three years with us so that they can work out where they fit. I have someone on standby here waiting to take your place and we have a couple of great options for you too depending on where you'd like to try next.'

I don't want to try anything else. I want to finish what I started.

But the man wouldn't let her get a word in. 'The new St James Hospital Project we won is assembling a team of design engineers. It'll be city based, of course. Or if you've got a taste for the outback, the Dampier job is in full swing. That's another great project. Different from Cape Lambert. Bigger, I'm told.'

'Ivan,' Lena rubbed her temple. 'This is happening rather fast. I –'

'Yes, you'll probably want some time to think about which project to join next. There's heaps of info on our site if you want to read up about them.' He paused. 'Just so you know, Lena, you're the only graduate we're giving a project choice to. You've really earned your stripes on the Pilbara: well done.'

It didn't sound like much of a choice to her. She heard muffled conversation coming through the phone as she tried to recover from the grenade he'd just dropped in her lap before Ivan said, 'Look, I'm needed in a meeting right now. Take some time, think about it. I'll call you in a few days.'

And then the dial tone sounded in her ears like the knock of that Supreme Court judge's hammer. She listened to the sound for what was probably an unnecessary amount of time before carefully replacing the receiver.

'Wow, you look like you've seen a ghost,' Gavin said cheerfully as he walked past her desk. 'Anything the matter?'

'Nope.' She immediately dropped her head, focusing on the page in front of her but not the words. She needed some time to digest the news before she told anyone about it.

The final two hours of her afternoon were extremely unproductive. Her mind kept bouncing between Dan and her impending departure from the Pilbara. She didn't know which to be more upset about.

At five o'clock, Sharon discreetly dropped a pair of keys in her lap and she finally made off to the yard to take Carl's ute. The drive up to Dan's office was accomplished in two short minutes. As she was hopping out of her vehicle another pulled up beside her. It wasn't a TCN ute but a blue Nissan with floral seat coverings and a couple of stuffed toys peering out the rear window. Lena watched in horror as a tall, leggy blonde in a black singlet and denim skirt alighted from the driver's seat.

The woman threw a friendly wave in Lena's direction before walking off towards the TCN office donga. Lena watched, gobsmacked, as the blonde entered the offices. Now she had all the answers she needed. Dan had a date after work and she had almost interrupted it. With stiff limbs she scrambled back into Carl's ute and drove out of the car park as fast as the speed limit permitted. Tears welled but she blinked them back with iron determination. He didn't deserve her grief. Thank goodness no one else had seen her.

She headed straight to camp as the arrangement was for Carl to collect his car from there. Sharon was meeting her in the mess later so they could exchange the keys. In the meantime she made for the showers, hoping to clean the day from both her mind and body. Unfortunately, it was easier said than done.

She had put so much faith in her own judgement – not quite trusting the rumour until she'd seen evidence with her own eyes. Now it seemed impossible to believe anything else. Her chest tightened. How could she have been so wrong about Dan's commitment to her?

She lay down on her bed in her donga for an hour, staring at the plasterboard ceiling, trying to make sense of it all. But couldn't. Eventually the dinner hour ticked around and she decided to go to the mess. Better to keep busy than dwell on how gullible and naive she was.

The mess was full and rowdy and Sharon hailed her immediately from across the room. She headed to the buffet first, however, and filled a plate with spaghetti. On her way back, she recognised Dan sitting unaccompanied at a table closer to her. Involuntarily, her feet slowed. What was he doing here? Wasn't he supposed to be on a date?

Her ribcage swelled. Maybe it *was* all just a big misunderstanding. Without thinking about the consequences of her actions, she went over to him and sat down.

He looked up when her plate suddenly appeared next to his. A faint stubble lingered on his chin giving him a predatory edge that immediately pulsed the blood in her veins. The intensity of his gaze had not abated one iota.

'Hi,' she said, trying to keep her voice low and casual. Her ears picked up the murmur that rippled through the mess. There was a lot of nudging going on.

'Are you sure this is wise?' Dan's eyes flicked sideways as he dabbed his mouth with a napkin. 'You're creating a stir.'

She picked up her fork. 'Is it bothering you?'

'Not yet.' He returned his attention to his meal, and his indifference unsettled her.

'What do you mean not yet?'

He didn't look at her as he spoke. His voice was dull, bored even. 'I took a lot of trouble to make sure you came through this whole site scandal unscathed. I wouldn't want to see my efforts overturned for nothing.'

'Yeah, I heard about your *efforts*.' She couldn't keep the derision out of her voice and his eyes narrowed on her.

'Have I done something wrong, Lena?'

'Wrong?' she said. 'No, of course not. After all, we never said anything about not seeing other people while you were waiting for me to sort myself out, did we?'

He stopped eating. 'What on earth are you talking about?'

Lena dropped the cool facade. 'I don't know. How about the hot blonde you picked up at Point Samson while I finished my R and R?'

The confusion on his face abruptly cleared and a slight smile curved his mouth. 'I assume you're talking about Wendy, Mike's niece from Karratha. I gave her a job in exchange for his testimony.'

'You . . . you did what?' Lena faltered.

'I gave her a job,' he repeated matter-of-factly. 'Wendy is in occupational health and safety but has been unemployed for the last two years. I said I'd give her a job if Mike denied what he saw in the spa.'

'But I saw her today at your offices after work today, dressed to party,' Lena blurted and Dan's smile broadened.

'Been spying on me, have you?'

'No.' She dropped her gaze to her pasta and became immersed in twirling it around her fork. 'I just happened to be in the area.'

'Really?'

'Look,' she continued, trying to ignore the feel of her face going red, 'it doesn't matter where I was. I'm just trying to make sense of what is going on here.'

His eyes were sparkling with mirth but he let it go. 'Well, it's really quite simple. Mike introduced Wendy to me at the pub and, after a short interview on the spot, I said I would hire her. I took her contact details before she left the bar. As for this evening, she came around to pick up her TCN uniform. She starts work tomorrow.'

Relief washed through Lena. Her instincts had been correct. He hadn't moved on with someone else. She put her head in her hands. 'I should have known,' she groaned. 'Especially when Mike all but apologised to me today.'

'He did that?' Dan's eyebrows raised in surprise. 'Maybe I was too hard on him about his behaviour. But I couldn't resist suggesting that he should imagine Wendy being treated in the same way you were.'

'You definitely pricked a nerve.' She nodded and was silent for a moment, unsure how to go on. Embarrassment kept her focused on her dinner. It was hard not to be ashamed of the fact that while she was busy jumping to conclusions, he was doing nothing but protecting her again. 'You didn't honestly think I could get over you that quickly, did you?' Dan enquired softly.

Her breath caught in her throat as she raised shy eyes to his. Words tumbled out. 'I got back yesterday morning and you didn't come find me and it's been almost two days and I couldn't help but feel that things might have . . . well . . . *changed* since we last spoke in Perth.'

A muscle twitched above his jawline. 'Why would they?'

'Well, I thought you might have realised that it's better for the project if we don't have anything to do with one another. Morale is so good right now. At the moment you've got everyone thinking I'm the project hero. They are singing my praises from one end of the wharf to the other.'

'That wasn't me, Lena; that was you.'

'Are you sure? Because news has reached as far as Perth and –' Her voice trembled ever so slightly. 'They're recalling me.'

This gave him pause. 'Why?'

'It's the graduate program,' she groaned. 'I'm up for rotation but I don't want to go.'

'Then don't.'

'I don't think I have a choice.'

'Of course you have a choice.' He lay down his cutlery. 'Lena, think about who you are. How far you've come. Do you honestly think Carl and the rest of the team are going to let their project hero go without a fight? Do they know about this?'

'Well no, not yet.'

'Exactly.' Dan nodded as if this revelation confirmed everything. 'Trust me when I say the city office was trying to persuade you first before it had to deal with them. Lena,' he shook his head, 'speaking as a manager, I can honestly say these sorts of programs are flexible. Just hold your ground.' His voice softened. 'We both know you're good at that.'

She began to feel substantially lighter until he rose from the table with the clear intention of taking his leave. Again, a murmur rippled through the mess. But Lena didn't care. She too rose to her feet.

'Dan, wait –'

'I *am* waiting.' He turned to eyeball her, his blue orbs searing right through her with the same power as his voice. 'You *know* that, Lena. Don't doubt it again.'

It was probably a comfortable twenty-five degrees inside but her skin suddenly broke out in goose bumps.

'There's so much I need to explain,' she stammered, thinking of Kevin and all her past insecurities, which now seemed as important as dust.

'I've got time.' He nodded. 'But is here the right place to do it?'

She shifted uncomfortably on her feet again, the doubt he had mentioned before trickling down her spine again. 'Dan, you totally annihilated those rumours about us. Is it going to be a problem if they resurface?'

'Why would they?'

She swallowed and decided to just take the plunge. 'Dan, when I'm in a relationship, I don't put work first. This,' she flicked her pointer finger between them, 'is the most important thing to me and other people's opinion be damned. There's no joy in having a secret relationship, trust me.'

His face seemed to take on a certain kind of strain as though he were holding something in check. 'What do you mean exactly?'

She found herself getting frustrated with his lack of comprehension. He'd just said he didn't want to talk about it and now he wanted the full story. With a sigh, she embarked upon it anyway. 'My ex Kevin was my university professor and for a long time I thought our relationship had screwed up my degree. Turns out I was wrong, but the misunderstanding messed with my head all year. That's what I had to sort out, why I couldn't move forwards with you, why I –'

'Lena.' He reached out and grasped one of her hands in a firm grip to make her stop talking. 'That's not what I'm asking. I want to know: are you ready to move forwards with me now?'

'Oh.' Her eyes widened in surprise because she thought she'd made that clear. 'Yes of course. I –'

The rest of her sentence was not destined to be uttered as he tugged on the hand he was holding. Her body jerked and collided with his, breasts crushing against chest. His head swooped down, so that his lips might capture her open mouth in a kiss so intense she felt her soul unravel.

A gasp followed by stamping feet ricocheted off the walls around them as their audience witnessed the climax of the show. The noise was building to a crescendo but they didn't let go of each other, clutching on for dear life.

Okay, so maybe he doesn't care what people think.

It was Lena's last coherent thought before her feet left the floor and he lifted her body straight up, so that they were shoulder to shoulder. Finally, she tore her mouth from his. 'Are you nuts?' she demanded.

'Nuts, crazy, mad.' His voice was husky. 'The whole nine yards.'

Her ribcage felt too tight; joy was bursting between the bones.

He put her down and they looked around at the room, which had degenerated into chaos. Men were banging their cutlery on the tabletops, booing and cheering at the same time, making rude snorting noises, wolf-whistling and yelling dirty jokes across the room.

Radar cried gleefully over the din: 'Get a room!'

'Oh no,' Lena muttered, snuggling into the crook of Dan's arm. 'What have we done?'

'Created a zoo, clearly,' Dan murmured wryly.

'Carl is so going to kill me for this.' Lena grinned unrepentantly.

Suddenly to her amazement she saw Leg and Radar pushing plates aside before jumping up on top of their table and waving their arms for everyone's attention. It didn't, however, seem to be working. Lena looked at Sharon in question but her friend just shook her head with a secret smile. Finally Leg cupped his hands around his mouth and yelled out, 'SHUT THE FUCK UP!'

The roar of voices evaporated and all heads turned to the rigger in expectation.

'Gentlemen,' Radar clasped his hands with a conciliatory bow before extending one of them in Lena and Dan's direction, 'I present to you, Mr and Mrs Cape Fuckin' Lambert.'

As laughter and cheering erupted from all tables, relief washed through Lena's bones.

Everything was going to be okay.

'Come on,' Dan tugged on her hand, 'I think that's our cue to leave.'

With as much dignity as possible they hurried from the room, dodging suggestions thrown at them for what they might do as soon as they found a private and soft surface.

Dan stopped and spun her into his arms when they had reached a safe distance. 'I love you.'

Lena grinned back. 'I love you more.'

'Not possible.' With a bark of laughter, he was pulling her off again. She followed him without a shred of resistance.

Nothing could touch Lena in the days that followed. She was the happiest girl in Western Australia. To say that all obstacles had been pushed from her path was a gross understatement. But instead of looking at them with dread, she revelled in the challenge they offered. Life stretched out before her, a writhing mass of possibilities and opportunities. All she had to do was pick one and she definitely knew which one she was going to tackle first.

First thing Monday she rang Ivan's direct line. He picked up after the third ring and said pleasantly enough when he heard her voice, 'Oh hello there, Lena, I was just about to call you.'

Lena smiled confidently with the knowledge that Carl and the rest of the project engineers on the job were behind her one hundred per cent.

'Hi, Ivan, I'm calling because I've thought about your proposal.'

'And you have a preference?' he prompted smoothly.

'Definitely.' Her response was firm and positive. Then with a deep breath she uttered the words that six months ago she thought she'd never say. 'I'd like to stay on in the Pilbara.'

Author's Note

The majority of this story is set at Cape Lambert Port Facilities, the home of one of the tallest, longest and deepest jetties or open-sea wharves in the world. It is owned by Rio Tinto and is operated by Pilbara Iron. The nearby town of Wickham was built specifically for the purpose of supporting the wharf and other functions of the port, such as train-dumping, primary and secondary crushing and screening, stockpiling and blending of iron ore.

This ore wharf, which is approximately three kilometres long and thirty metres tall, has two cranes or shiploaders that are able to load three ships at the same time. The wharf currently exports 55 to 57 million tonnes of iron ore every year to steel mills in Japan, China, Korea, Taiwan and Europe.

My heroine is sent to Cape Lambert to work as part of a team to lengthen and widen this wharf, which was originally completed in 1972. Over the course of its existence the Cape Lambert wharf has undergone many upgrades of this nature to increase its life and capacity. I was fortunate early in my career as an engineer to witness and participate in one of these upgrades in 2001 – which experience forms the basis of the background of this story.

The project is real, the hardship is real and the conditions are real. However, to reduce the number of characters and engineering jargon in this story, I have condensed some of the professional roles played by my characters. For example, Carl is the project manager, but in my novel he also performs the duties of a construction manager. In real life, his job would have been done by two people. I have also ignored a lot of the other functions of the port and the shipping schedule, which complicated the project far more than shown here. It has been my aim to show the culture and flavour of the people in this environment. Nonetheless, it is important to note that all characters and companies shown here are entirely fictional. Any resemblances to any real persons or entities are purely coincidental.

This is the book of my heart and in little ways mirrors some of the journeys I have taken in my own life, both on and off the Pilbara. The engineering profession is not glamorous or well understood by some people. The challenges and dangers men and women face on jobs such as this, both intellectually and emotionally, are not usually discussed in any public forums. But this book is not just about that. I wanted to capture the beauty of Australia, the colourful characters who live here and why it is so important to never take your friends and family for granted.

Acknowledgements

There are so many people who have given me their time and support to make this book come together. It simply wouldn't be right not to spend a few words giving them my appreciation and gratitude.

My sincere thanks to the girls from WINK for their critical eyes on the first draft.

To my amazing critique partner and fellow writer, Nicole E. Sheridan, who ploughed patiently through an entire rewrite. Your encouragement has meant a lot to me.

To my sister, Marlena, who has been there from the beginning with both complaints and enthusiasm for my heroine, Lena. Thank you for all your help and belief in this story.

To my mother-in-law, Shirley, who proofread the final draft at very short notice and has always had absolute faith in this book.

And of course, this novel simply wouldn't be where it is now without the hard work of my fabulous agent, Clare Forster, and my wonderful publisher, Beverley Cousins.

Thanks also to the rest of the team at Random House for their contribution, particularly Virginia Grant and my publicist, Jessica Malpass.

My family and friends have always been so supportive of my writing over the years. I must mention my parents, Ivan and Juanita, and my other two sisters, Jacenta and Angela, for their enduring confidence in me. Mum, thank you for saving all my emails from the Pilbara and giving them back to me. You were the first person to see a story there.

Finally my love to my husband, Todd, who is my rock and my champion. And to our three beautiful children, Luke, James and Beth. You guys are my inspiration.

If you loved *The Girl in Steel-Capped Boots*
read on for a taster of Loretta's new novel

The Girl in the Hard Hat

What do you do when you are the most hated person in town?

Wendy Hopkins knew her Uncle Mike had got her the job
as Safety Officer at the Barnes Inc. site on the Pilbara. What
she didn't know – until her first day on the job – was that he
achieved it through blackmail . . .

It's not the greatest of starts – and it's about to get worse.

Her new boss doesn't want her there.

The 350 men on site don't want her there.

Even her uncle doesn't want her there now . . .

In fact the only man who does is an outrageous flirt whose
interest is certainly not professional. And yet, he may be the
only person who can help her find the truth she seeks . . .

Available early 2013

Chapter One

Wendy knew something was wrong the moment she stepped into TCN's open plan office.

Perhaps it was the frosty looks she got from the staff as they peered at her over their short cubicle walls. Or the fact that the receptionist wouldn't let her past the hat hooks by the front door but directed her instead to a room set apart from the main office space.

'You'll have to sit in the meeting room until Mr Hullog is ready to deal with you.'

Deal with me? The woman made it sound like she was toddler with a dirty nappy.

This was supposed to be her first day of work. She had dressed carefully in the TCN uniform that Dan Hullog had given her just yesterday. Her shirt was ironed, her khaki pants neat. Her blonde hair tied modestly at the nape of her neck with black elastic.

So if it wasn't her appearance they disapproved of then what had happened between yesterday and today that she didn't know about?

She walked into the meeting room. It was furnished in the usual sparse style of a construction site donga office. A white trestle table and eight uncomfortable plastic chairs filled the space. The vinyl floor was marked red with boot prints and the white board on one wall held a list of milestone dates. She knew the chairs were uncomfortable even before she sat down and after twenty minutes she had to get up and walk around to stave off a numb bum.

Where is he?

She looked out the window, anticipation momentarily overcoming her concern. The Cape Lambert iron ore wharf stretched out before her – a majestic masterpiece almost like a painting framed by the dingy office window. Standing nearly five stories above the water, the jetty wove out more than three kilometres across the sea. The end of it was imperceptible as it faded into the horizon. Every day, ships from around the world docked there, picking up tonnes and tonnes of the precious red dirt that fuelled Australia's economy.

A shiver of both excitement and trepidation flitted through her body.

I can't believe I'm going to be a part of something like this . . . again.

She heard the snap of a door closing and spun around. A tall, dark-haired man with the most intense blue eyes she'd ever seen advanced into the room. 'I'm sorry to have kept you waiting, Wendy.'

'Er . . . that's okay, Mr Hullog.'

'Call me Dan.' He indicated the chair she had been sitting in before and took the one opposite it. 'Have a seat.' He laced his hands together on the white chipboard, somehow lifting the table's image from backyard picnic to boardroom meeting. 'I have to ask. Do you know how you got this job?'

Her eyes narrowed. 'My uncle said you owed him a favour.'

Dan grimaced, 'That's putting blackmail politely.'

Red-hot heat infused her neck, and kept working its way up. She knew she shouldn't have trusted Uncle Mike. She barely knew him and he seemed as inclined to want to get rid of her as to help her, but she had been at her wits' end. Out of money and out of luck. When she'd stumbled across him in Karratha, she had thought it was the hand of providence not the bite of corruption.

What had her mother told her? *Nobody does anything for nothing.*

She swallowed hard before casting an apology at the man before her. 'I had no idea. Honestly. I haven't seen Uncle Mike in years. I should have questioned his motives more closely.'

You should have listened to your conscience.

She had known Mike was the black sheep of the family. No one talked about him unless they absolutely had to and even then their comments were never complimentary. But then she wasn't exactly number one with the family at the moment either. When she'd met Uncle Mike unexpectedly, it had almost been like meeting a kindred spirit.

How wrong you were.

She waited on Dan's response, breath held.

'I had a feeling from our conversation yesterday that you had no idea what the full story was. The truth is,' he sighed, 'there is no real position for you here. I have a safety officer already and he does a very good job.'

Her heart sank. It was all a farce. He wasn't going to take her on, which was a great pity given he had been her last hope at job in the area.

'Also,' he lifted an unsmiling face, 'I no longer care what your uncle says or doesn't say. The person I was protecting . . .' He changed track. 'Let's just say, his silence is no longer of any value to me.'

Pride stiffened her back, causing her to stand. 'Well, I'll just get out of your hair then, shall I? There's no need to drag out this conversation any longer.'

'Wendy, whatever beef I have with your uncle is nothing to do with you or your ability. And I am deeply mortified that you have been used as a pawn in this very tasteless game.'

Used. Yep that's me.

However Dan was still talking. 'I want to honour the agreement, not for his sake but for yours.'

'But you said there was no job.'

'Not here. But somewhere else.' His tone softened. 'Please sit down and let me tell you what I have arranged. TCN is the EPCM for this project. Do you know what that means?'

'You run the show, don't you?'

'Sort of,' Dan smiled. 'The wharf owners make the rules, so we don't have a choice about that. But essentially we govern the place for them. As in, we make sure everyone else such as our principal contractor Barnes Inc, follows the guidelines set by the wharf owners.'

She didn't say anything but sank slowly back into her chair.

'Unfortunately Barnes Inc have not been meeting the safety standard for some time now. They have a safety officer over there but he doesn't seem to be able to keep up with the workload. On behalf of the wharf owners I have rung Barnes Inc and told them that they need to take on another safety person in addition to the one they already have. I've suggested you as a likely candidate.' He paused. 'The project manager at Barnes Inc, Carl Curtis, said he is willing to interview you this morning.'

A job was a job.

This office. That office down the road.

What did it matter as long as she got paid?

She licked her lips. 'When?'

'Now.'

Relief swept through her. All was not lost. 'Well, that's not a problem.'

'I assume you bought your vehicle with you.'

She nodded. She'd passed the Barnes Inc office dongas on the way to TCN so she knew how to get there too.

Okay, let's do this.

She stood up more firmly this time, holding out her hand. 'Thank you for this opportunity . . . er . . . Dan.'

'I'm very sorry that I didn't have a job for you.' His tone at least was genuine. 'I really think we could have worked well together.'

'Thanks.' She had an inkling that Dan Hullog was an honourable man unlike her slimy excuse for an uncle. What the hell was Mike's game anyway?

She gritted her teeth as she made her way out. Was there no end to the lies she had been fed by her family her whole life? Out here in the outback as far away from Perth as you could get without actually leaving the country she thought she was beyond all that. But no, the one uncle she thought might understand her was keen to offer her for sale instead.

Enough is enough.

She couldn't wait to give him a piece of her mind later. Right now though she had a job to score *on her own merit*. After all, she was the only person she could really count on these days.

TCN had three office dongas lined up in a row, framed by red rock on one side and a car park on the other. Her car stood out easily amongst the dirty white utes – a blue Nissan with floral seat covers and a collection of stuffed animals peering out the rear window. It looked completely out of place against the backdrop of iron ore stock piles, cranes and conveyors belts.

She made her way down the well-trodden path towards it, the only asset she had taken with her on her trek across the country in the last six months. For a while, it had been her sole companion in this search that never seemed to end. And those toys had brought her luck. Even in their sun-damaged state, she'd never throw them out.

She got in the car. It was only a five-minute drive down a gravel track that ran alongside the red beach and through the port facilities. Like TCN, there were three Barnes Inc office dongas. An odd looking flag with an extra thick circular pole had been pushed into the ground in front of one of them. The flying emblem of the company was bolted rather than strung on the pole and a group of guys were having smoko underneath it on a couple of sad looking park benches. Two more were sitting in the back of a ute, chowing down on Mrs Mac's pies still half in their plastic microwaveable wrappers. When they saw her car, they immediately all stood up and waved. She parked and they cheered as though she had stopped for them.

Oh brother! Clearly they hadn't seen a new female face in a while.

She alighted cautiously from her vehicle, mentally noting that maybe at some stage (sooner rather than later) she should move those stuffed animals into her boot.

'Hey, love, where you going? Wanna stop for a bite?' One of the guys grabbed his friend's pastry as it was on its way to his mouth and held it up in the air like a trophy. 'We've got a spare one!'

She chuckled at the pie owner's expression of outrage and watched him snatch it back before pushing the thief away. Maybe it was the thief's lack of attention or the roughness of the shove but the man fell out of the side of the ute and landed starry-eyed in the dirt.

The others lost interest in her and roared with laughter. She took the opportunity to slip past and enter the Barnes Inc main office donga.

Compared to the TCN equivalent, it was an absolute mess. All the desks seemed to be covered in a film of dust and papers, with the occasional computer bursting through the chaos. There was no official reception desk. The two guys seated closest to the door both eyed her up and down before one said, 'And who might you be, blondie?' The guy who addressed her had his eye on her shirt pocket, the TCN logo seeming to repulse him. She wished she'd had a change of clothes in the car. The last thing she wanted to do was give anyone any false impressions.

'I'm Wendy Hopkins. I'm here to see Carl.'

The man raised his eyebrows. 'Do you have an appointment?'

'No . . . I–'

'Just pulling your leg.' He grinned. 'I don't think Carl makes appointments. He's never around for them. He must be expecting you though because he's in his office.'

Not quite knowing what to say to this, she merely nodded. 'And which way is that?'

'Only office in this donga, darlin'.' He jerked his thumb over his shoulder. 'Down the end next to the kitchen.'

'Thanks.'

She knew his eyes were on her rear as she walked off in the direction he had pointed. Her skin prickled in annoyance but decided it was a fight for another time. The door to Carl's office was wide open so she heard the man inside before she saw him.

'What the fuck do you mean there's no fuckin' bolts with it? . . . How the fuck should I know? . . . Didn't a pallet arrive last week? . . . Why the fuck would I cancel it? If it's not there then it must be somewhere else . . . Have you looked up your own fuckin' arse before you've shoved your head in mine? *Fuck!*'

SLAM!

Carl reconnected his phone with its receiver before he looked up at her standing there, her hand frozen in the 'about to knock' position.

'Who the fuck are you?'

Wendy licked her lips. 'I'm Wendy Hopkins. Dan Hullog said–'

'Oh shit! You were fuckin' quick! Come in, come in.' He waved his hand at her in resignation. 'And shut the door behind you.'

He was a heavy-set man in his late forties with dark brown hair and skin that tanned easily. In fact, he'd probably be quite a good looking man, if he didn't radiate stress like a wild bird in a cage.

'So you're in OH and S, are you?'

'Yes,' she nodded.

'What's your experience like?'

'I've done about seven years in the field. My last job was at the Parker Point Wharf in Dampier two years ago. So I actually do have some jetty experience in my-'

'You've been out of work two years. Why?'

It was a perfectly reasonable question – one that a future employer was definitely entitled to ask. Her reasons, however, were many, personal and complicated. So she decided to tell half the truth.

'I wanted a holiday.'

'Pretty long fuckin' holiday.'

As she began to bristle defensively, he put his hand up to stop her responding. 'The reason I ask is if I hire you, I want you to stay for the duration of this project. So if you feel like you might need to take off again, like *on holiday*, you need to tell me now.'

He said the words 'on holiday' as if he didn't entirely believe them. Not that she blamed him but at least she could reassure him on one point.

'I will definitely be staying to the end. If you're worried I won't take this job seriously, don't be. I'm not going to let anything happen to Barnes Inc's people. I have a debt to pay to myself and there's no better motivation than that.'

'A debt, eh?'

She buttoned her lip, not really wanting to elaborate any further. She'd already said too much. If he was a gentleman, he wouldn't press her.

'You don't want to fuckin' tell me, do you?' His smile was unsympathetic. 'That's going to cause problems for you, missy.'

He wasn't a gentleman. Her body quivered.

Maybe this was a bad idea. Maybe I shouldn't have come back to this industry.

I could have got a job in a bar or a kitchen.

Yeah right! You would have been bored after five minutes.

Carl eyed her knowingly. 'No point in pretending you don't know what the fuck I'm talking about because we both know that ain't true. It's not that I don't respect your privacy but, believe me, in this fuckin' place no one else will.'

She swallowed.

He sat back in his chair and it creaked loudly in protest. 'There aren't any secrets here. There's only one commodity traded more often on this wharf than fuckin' ore. It's called gossip.'

When she said nothing, he shrugged. 'I'm just trying to fuckin' warn you. You'll be gossiped about from one end of the fuckin' wharf to the other so just be prepared to deal with it. If you have any major problems, like harassment, please don't fuckin' wait on it. Come see me.'

She looked up hopefully. 'Does that mean I've got the job?'

'When Bulldog barks Bulldog gets.' He looked mildly put out by his own analogy.

'Bulldog?'

'That's Dan Hullog's name on this side of the fence.' He sighed. 'The thing is our current safety guy, Neil Cooper, can't keep up with his workload. With fuckin' cyclone season coming things are only going to get worse. I gotta make some fuckin' improvements around here or we'll all be up shit creek faster than this morning's turd. I think Neil will be fuckin' glad of an assistant.'

An assistant. Her body stilled. *Great! Maybe you were better off in a bar.*

She cleared her throat. 'Well, I've got a lot of experience working on sites like this one. I'm really looking forward to the challenge.' She hoped these words indicated that she wanted to be more than just an assistant.

He didn't rise to the bait. 'It'll be a fuckin' challenge, alright. Pushing safety around here is like serving Brussel sprouts to children. Nobody wants a fuckin' bar of it.'

Well, she was used to that. When people had work to do, they just wanted to get on with the job, take precautions later.

They wouldn't want to listen to what she had to say.

But construction on water took danger to the next level, especially if the weather got bad. She would have to stay on top of things.

'There's just one other thing.' She took a breath. 'I'd like to live in the camp.'

His eyebrows jumped. 'Fuck! If you've already got accommodation, I'd keep it.'

'I think the camp will be a bit more convenient,' she tried to explain. 'Travelling from Karratha every day will be really painful.'

Besides, I'm done with Karratha. Didn't find anything there but my selfish uncle.

'Well fuck me, if you don't get a big welcome.' He paused. 'But it's no hotel. And there are only five women in the camp.'

'How many men?'

'Three-fifty.'

She swallowed. 'Right.'

He seemed unperturbed by her alarm, rising from his chair and opening his door. 'I suppose you'll want to be meeting fuckin' Neil. Come with me.'

They walked back through the open plan office and she felt all eyes around her drilling holes in her back.

Carl led her across a short courtyard to another donga. This donga was just as untidy as the first but much smaller and much more claustrophobic. It was also colder. The air conditioner was running so high, it was rattling in its socket on the wall. Wendy rubbed her arms as a chill went through her both literally and metaphorically.

A sweaty looking man was standing by a sink and a bar fridge that passed for a kitchen, dipping a tea-bag in some hot water. He was dark and swarthy and obviously didn't deal well with the tropical weather. His glasses, which were slightly foggy, sat right on the tip of his wet nose. A large packet of Marlboros bulged from the top pocket of his shirt.

He jumped. 'Carl!'

'I got a fuckin' present for ya, Neil.'

'You . . . er . . . do?'

'I've got you some help. This is Wendy Hopkins. She's got seven years experience in the field and I've employed her.'

'She's from TCN.' Neil protested, his eyes on her uniform.

'Huh?' Carl glanced at Wendy, belatedly realising what she was wearing. 'Fuck! Forgot about that. Not an issue, Neil. It's all bullshit. She's not working there any more. Are you?' he prompted her.

'No.' Wendy shook her head. 'Definitely not.'

'There you go.' Carl smiled. 'All right and tight. Put her to work. I want to see some fuckin' improvements around here.'

On this note he left, leaving her standing there awkwardly with her new colleague who was yet to give her a friendly welcome.

'You got a lot of nerve, coming here in a bloody TCN uniform,' were the first words out of his mouth.

'It wasn't intentional.' She tried to reassure him but it was like she hadn't spoken.

'And who said I needed help? I don't need any help. I just hope to God you don't make things worse by getting in the way.'

Although profanities had slipped off Carl's tongue like butter on a hot pan she'd found him less offensive in the half an hour she'd spent with him than she did with this guy after only five seconds.

'Well, Carl seemed to think that you were under the pump–'

'What would Carl know?' He snapped at her. 'He's never around. Never comes into this donga. Keeping safety up to scratch is something I do on my own. He should have asked me first.'

Frankly, Wendy thought Neil was little full of himself. Carl was the project manager, it was his right to hire and fire as he saw fit. She said nothing however, not wanting to rock the boat further. After all, she was going to have to work with this guy. Better to shut up and make peace as quickly as possible.

'Well, I want you to know,' she said slowly, 'that I'm only here to make your life easier. Whatever I can do, just say the word.'

His greasy mouth lifted into something she couldn't quite call a smile. 'I need some milk for my tea and our fridge is all out.' He pointed at the door. 'The smoko donga is down that way.'

Her mouth dropped open in disbelief as he turned and walked away from her. She opened her mouth to yell at him when a man stepped conspicuously in front of her.

'I wouldn't. Wait till you've calmed down a bit.'

The word conspicuously was actually an understatement. The man was, in a word, massive. Both tall and wide, with a butt and stomach so generous that Wendy would be surprised if he didn't have to turn sideways to get through the door. Brown-haired and in his late fifties, he gave her a sympathetic smile.

'I'm Bill Walden, by the way. But everyone around here calls me Chub.' He leaned in, patting his belly affectionately. 'Yes, that's short for chubby. But just between you and me, most of it's muscle.'

'Right,' she blinked.

'I'm the HR manager. So I think you better come with me for the moment. I can get you a new shirt. That one is currently causing a few problems around here, if you know what I mean.'

'Why is everyone so against TCN?'

He tut-tutted. 'That's like asking why everyone smoked in the sixties. It's just fact, love, and if you want to fit in you better learn the rules of the fraternity. Rule number one, all TCN are scum.'

'What's rule number two?'

'Under no circumstance should you forget rule number one. Okay?' He rubbed his pudgy hands together. 'Let's get you a Barnes Inc wardrobe. Now when I turn around to lead you off to our storage container, don't look at my arse. It makes me uncomfortable.'

She choked back a gasp.

He shrugged. 'I've been told it's a real chick magnet. But I wouldn't know. Never seen it myself.' He indicated his thick neck with his pointer finger. 'Can't get my head around that far.'

He was absolutely shocking, yet the first person in this town that she actually found herself liking without hesitation.

She returned his grin with one of her own. 'No problem.'

'Cheers.' He gave her the thumbs-up before turning around. 'Okay, let's go.'

He led her to an old shipping container outside the donga which appeared to act as a store room. There was also a lot of PPE, Personal Protective Equipment, in there as well which was good to know.

'Try not to let Neil get to you.' Chub offered as they trotted out. 'He doesn't eat much and I think he must suffer a lot from hunger pains.'

She giggled.

'He may warm up to you yet,' Chub added optimistically.

If Neil generated any warmth at all over the next six hours he certainly didn't share it with her. After dumping a five-hundred-page safety manual about permits and tagging on her desk and telling her to study it, he pretty much left her to her own devices.

The room itself just seemed to get colder and colder as the day progressed. Neil and Chub kept the air conditioner up so high going outside was actually a relief from the icebox that was now her office. She wondered why the other occupants of the donga didn't complain until she realised that most of them didn't spend much of their time there, not in the way she, Neil and Chub did. They'd grab their hard hats off the wall and be out most of the day.

As she shivered through the afternoon, it became clear that Neil was under pressure. He was on the phone practically the whole time and most of the calls sounded like complaints. He had a mountain of memos on his desk, almost half a metre tall. And there were small piles of foolscap files sitting on the floor behind his desk rather than on the empty bookshelves against the wall. She couldn't work out what his system was but was anxious to get in and lighten his load.

The other thing was, he didn't look well – what with the sweating and the occasional hand tremors. The guy clearly had a problem but refused to ask her for help. When she tentatively suggested she might take a couple of files off him he bit her head off. In resignation, she retreated back to her desk.

By 6 pm she didn't know whether her brain was numb from the cold or the dryness of the material she was reading. In any event, she was very thankful to be getting out of there. The next day she was coming in late so that she could sort out her accommodation and have her safety induction in Wickham at ten o'clock. Once that formality was out of the way perhaps she'd start getting out of the office too and into the real action. She said goodbye to her colleagues. Neil ignored her, Chub gave her a jovial wave and she stepped out into the warm, balmy air.

The red sun, halved by the horizon, made the blue sky pink and the ocean violet. Clouds struggled to keep their own colour too, streaking across the sky, lit from behind.

She decided to take this beautiful sight as an omen.

Everything was going to be okay.

Her search for her father was going to come to an end.

Here.

She got in her car and started her engine. It was a forty-five-minute drive back to her hotel in Karratha. Not that she minded. She was feeling a little philosophical and wiled away the time reminiscing about past fly in, fly out roles she'd taken. It was good to be back doing the work she loved.

After the incident at Parker Point she hadn't been able to face working there any more. Nobody knew what she had done. But she did. So she'd fired herself. Being out of work for a couple of weeks hadn't really helped, so that's when she'd decided to take the extended sabbatical for a year.

Backpacking around Europe had seemed like a good way to get her mojo back.

And the time had given her perspective. She'd realised she couldn't give up a job she loved because of one stupid mistake. After spending over a year overseas, she'd been ready to start again and prove to the world exactly what she was made of.

She went job hunting and soon had one lined up in Port Hedland. She'd been all set and ready to go . . .

Then along came that awful moment that she'd remember for the rest of her life. The revelation that had tipped her world on its side.